# White Monkey Chronicles

## Collector's Edition

*Isabella Ides*
*2018*

# White Monkey Chronicles

## The Complete Trilogy

# Isabella Ides

Lowell Street Press

FIRST LOWELL STREET EDITION

Copyright © 2017 by Isabella Ides
Published in the United States
by Lowell Street Press.

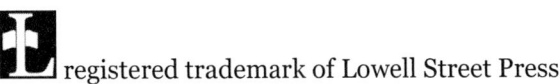 registered trademark of Lowell Street Press.

The Library of Congress PCN: 2017952655
Collector's Edition
**Hardback ISBN: 978-0-9916133-2-8**
Trade Paperback ISBN: 978-0-9916133-6-6
Ebook editions:
WMC Bk I: Humboldt County 978-0-9916133-3-5
WMC Bk II: Planet Grace 978-0-9916133-4-2
WMC Bk III: Her Light Materials 978-0-9916133-5-9

www.WhiteMonkeyChronicles.com
Printed in the United States of America
10   9   8   7   6   5   4   3   2   **1**

FOR ROD,

THE ORIGINAL STARFRIEND

# CONTENTS

PAGE-EATER, THE MUSES' BITTEREST FOE, LURKING DESTROYER ... O WHY, BLACK BOOKWORM DOST THOU LIE CONCEALED AMONG THE SACRED UTTERANCES ...?

EVENUS OF PAROS,
5TH CENTURY BCE

# BOOK ONE
# HUMBOLDT COUNTY

# PRELUDE

ONCE UPON A COLD WINTER'S *night an infant deity was orphaned by his feckless parents. The father was a famous bachelor Jew, and the mother was married to an A-list Hindu. Both parents were reincarnation junkies.*

*The Papa God, never noted for the quality of his parenting skills, scampered before it became evident that his beloved was with child.*

*When her offspring came out a bright, telltale blue—a sign of divine Hindu lineage—the Mama God was desperate to hide the evidence of her illicit liaison with the Semite deity. Alas, the newborn had to go, for the baby's sake as well as for her own.*

*Hence the misbegotten was never registered in the crowded Hindu pantheon, nor mentioned in any neo-biblical testament, nor listed in the catalogues of begats. He might have passed into the annals of oblivion but for a lucky chance.*

*In those days, at the dawn of the twenty-first century, there was a certain rogue order of nuns in a faraway land, a Sisterhood noted for a willingness to take in strays.*

*So it came to pass that the infant was carried across the seas to the Americas. As the baby made his passage in the white furry arms of a powerful protector, it appeared as if a wandering star were crossing the heavens.*

O, HOLY NIGHT.

# THE MONKEY BLINKED

SISTER MARY SUBORDINARY polished the canted bay window until the glass disappeared. Then, dust rag in hand, she stepped back and watched the blizzard white out the woods. After sixty years of practice, Sister was on the brink of achieving Immaculate Mind.

She pictured herself inside a snow globe, everything cool and clean and absolved in the mesmerizing swirl. A black plastic figurine at peace with the muted world, she waited for the last tiny flake to settle at her feet. The little straggler never completed its journey. A leap of snow outside on the lawn split her attention.

The meditation crashed.

The snow globe tipped over.

Sister almost said *damn it*. Instead, she shook her dust rag at the unruly world. *Snow does not leap*, she mildly reproved. Then she brushed off the tingle of a premonition and straightened her sleeves.

Let the others believe in extraordinary events. She preferred to keep her thoughts tidy, her whisk broom at the ready. So she simply whisked. And with that executive whisk, she decided she had not seen a clump of snow spring suddenly upwards. Then she tucked the unwanted image in a drawer labeled illusions.

The phrase *snow blindness* drifted in her mind and banked there. The chill lent a satisfying numbness to a part of her conscience that had been bothering her since yesterday's visit from agents of the Magistere Magisterium, the dreaded inquisitional arm of The Great Church.

Staring into the infinite white had stopped time, blotted out yesterday's sheave of grievances—the red delegation of Cardinals, their strange gifts, the bruise of their boot prints on the pristine crust of snow. All of that, so beautifully obliterated in the silent night, all of that so carefully occluded from the snow globe meditation. Bliss is a brief address.

"There it goes again."

This time she spoke out loud. This time the clump launched fifteen feet upwards and landed on the branch of a neighboring tree.

"Stop misbehaving," she admonished the strange snow, aware she could no more boss the weather than she could boss her own thoughts. The snowfall itself was an anomaly. It never snowed in Humboldt County.

A stray notion shuttled by: *perfect weather for godfall.*

"No, it is perfectly not!" She stopped herself, surprised by her vehemence and embarrassed that there was no one on the other side of the conversation. She lowered her voice to a prayerful whisper, "I must not lose my mind."

As soon as the prophetic words were spoken, there it went— her beautiful mind skittered backwards, tumbled into yesterday and got lost. A bevy of red-robed Cardinals crowded her memory. Like angry red birds they circled and perched uninvited on the backside of her remarkable cerebral cortex; then they set to chattering until the interior red noise completely swarmed her view of the snowy scene outside.

A practiced contemplative, Sister Mary Subordinary resisted the urge to shake loose the clutch of invasive images. Now that she was caught in a recurrence loop, there was nothing for it but to take a clear-eyed look. She had an uncanny ability to replay a memory and note what was missed the first time around.

*Go gentle, Sister*, her inner guide cautioned.

Taking caution as her watchword she rewound time, prepared to let the virtual scene unfold as if she were standing outside the memory.

Once more she heard the insistent knocking, saw her hand on the latch. She braced herself for the onslaught. Then she opened the convent door on yesterday.

There they stood, blood red against the snowy backdrop, three Cardinals—Delacroix, Bunbury and Oolumbo—bearing gifts: gold, frankincense, and a music box. A music box?

Too stunned to invite them in, she remembered staring into a pair of kohl-darkened eyes. All the Cardinals wore make-up, their eyes circled in thick kohl, their lips plum-colored, their pointed fingernails buffed with yellow resin. The visitors were dressed in red sateen robes and tri-cornered red birettas, with the traditional yellow appliquéd beak protruding mid-forehead.

The brood of Cardinals brushed past her. The recollection so exquisitely detailed, she heard the swish of their robes on the marble floor, caught the scent of frankincense that assaulted the room.

The memory spooled out.

She watched herself whirl around and catch the eye of Mother Mary Extraordinary, who stood implacable at the top of the staircase, towering over the unfolding tableau. This time Sister noted the gleam in Extraordinary's eye when Cardinal Bunbury cleared his throat and began to speak.

"We have come at the behest of His Holiness, the Munificentissimus Divine Mallard of All Mysteries, Hierophant of The Great Church." Cardinal Bunbury's eyes slid sideways. His tell was obvious on replay. Sister Subordinary caught the lie, pinned it for later perusal.

"These gifts are for the boy," Cardinal Delacroix stated flatly, not bothering with the courtesy of a salutation. The ferret on Delacroix's shoulder hissed.

Sister Merry Berry hiccoughed.

Sister Subordinary almost said, "What boy?" but hesitated just long enough for Mother Mary Extraordinary to have the first word.

The two Sisters gave no hint of their dismay when the ancient prioress simply said, "Thank you."

Extraordinary's *thank you* hung in the incensed air. Time compressed into a ball of dark matter. The vacuum created by the absence of a boy sucked all the energy out of the room. Then, in one swift movement, the towering Mother Mary Extraordinary descended the staircase.

No. That's not the way it was.

Sister Subordinary corrected the memory. Mary Extraordinary never descended the stairs. One minute the prioress was on the second-floor landing and the next instant she was backing the Cardinals into the foyer. In their billowing robes, the visitors might have been captives of a Titian study in vermilion when they stopped breathing and stood under the Gothic archway, eyes glazed, Magi frozen in time. Bunbury held the bag of gold. Oolumbo, the frankincense. Delacroix, the music box.

"Accept the gifts," Mother Mary Extraordinary instructed her consoeurs.

Sister Mary Subordinary and Sister Merry Berry moved with alacrity and relieved the mystified Cardinals of their offerings, so easily plucked from their cold but pliant fingers.

Extraordinary's powers were subtle and effective. The strange Magi were reanimated and dismissed before the visitation became another holy card in need of redaction. Later, the Cardinals would not be able to explain what had happened—how they came to leave the gifts with not so much as a glimpse of an infant, or why they stood speechless in the convent's foyer, malign blessings stuck in their throats.

At the very last, out of the corner of her eye, Sister Subordinary witnessed a further trespass. When the red-robed delegation swept back out of the drafty receiving room, one of the befuddled Cardinals instinctively reached out and nicked a copy of Mother Mary Extraordinary's book of prayer-poems, then quickly dropped it into his deep pocket. That clip of time was momentarily stuck on replay in Mary Subordinary's mind.

Hand on the book. Hand on the book. Hand on the book.

Cardinal Bunbury was a pack-rat by habit and an inquisitor by nature. He was sure to uncover a trove of deviant leaps of the imagination when he scoured the pages of Mother Mary's eclectic book of prayers. It's a wonder the incendiary book hadn't set his robes on fire. The picture of Bunbury patting out the flames and burning his chubby fingers on Mother Mary's prayers had made Sister Mary Subordinary laugh.

Privately, of course.

———

THAT WAS YESTERDAY.

This morning Sister Subordinary regretted the chuckle, felt the transgression.

There it was: the quibble in her conscience. Why had she dismissed the theft and not told the others? Another question crowded in. Who had sent these gift-bearing emissaries, if not the Hierophant?

She balked at the answer. Whisk.

The old enemy had not been seen since the historic persecution of the Sisterhoods.

Not since the night of the burning cross.

Not since the Sisters of the Joyous Mystery had gone rogue. (Gone gladly rogue, if she were to be perfectly honest.)

Not since The Great Church cast out its rebel brides.

Not since the ecclesiastical axe of severance came winging down had a single birdman set foot on the sacred grounds.

Now this violation. These Cardinals. Possibly factotums of the old enemy.

She knew only one thing. She must dig in and regroup forces. For clearly her ability to slip into a conjured snow globe was no longer proof against the power of the birdmen to unsettle her.

The recollected knocking and the red flashback shut Sister Subordinary so completely out of the day, she forgot all about the mystery unfolding on the other side of the perfectly polished glass where the world resembled nothing so much as a glittering holiday greeting card.

*Reach out, Sister. Open the card.*

A disconsolate Mary Subordinary was about to turn away from the window when another movement caught her eye. This time the curious white clump tumbled out of a tree and scampered across the snow-covered lawn. And didn't it just move as swift as you please as soon as it hit the ground? So much for tidy minds. She had better investigate this anomalous and unruly snow. Her job was to put things to rights.

Sister walked briskly to the double wooden doors and shoved them open on a white-sheathed world.

A moment of grace: the view was empty of Cardinals.

A gust of snow flurries blew back her black veil. She let the delicious cold wet her cheeks. Or was she crying? She'd be the first to deny it; and yet the relief of letting the tears spill unseen was oddly uplifting.

She never knew what made her look down.

An ordinary cardboard box sat on the marble floor of the porte cochere, almost touching the polished toes of her black boots. She barely had time to register the curious fact that the cardboard was dry, when she was startled by a soft mewling sound coming from inside the box.

Unconsciously, she reached for her prayer beads. An Ave hesitated on her lips as she bent for a closer look. That first glimpse of the blue baby knocked the soul right out of her. She had to grab her run-away soul from the very air and press it firmly back into her chest.

This baby's skin was not the bruised cyanotic blue of death. This baby was sky blue, lit from within like a computer screen— this baby was all effulgence.

My Sweet Lord, what in the world? There was a white monkey in the box with the baby. A stuffed monkey, she assured herself, its furry arms wrapped around the luminescent infant.

A scampering clump of snow raced across Sister Subordinary's memory and jumped into the box. Was that possible?

In her entire sublunary existence, this was the most baffling collusion of images that had ever slipped over the threshold of her exceptional mind. With so many impossibilities occurring simultaneously, the sensory data refused to resolve. And so she cannot be blamed for not reaching out immediately and scooping up the babe into her rescuing arms. The narrative part of her brain was stuck on pause. For a moment, the story simply would not move forward.

It was when the monkey caught her eye and blinked that Sister Subordinary came back to herself, as if called home from a distant moon. She reached for the infant and the monkey let go.

Smiling, she lifted what proved to be a naked boy. The fat blue baby had a tag tied to his ankle, an ordinary cardstock tag with a white cotton string knotted through one of the silver links in his anklet of charms. The boy kicked and laughed, and the air was charged with the tinkling of silver bells. Sister Subordinary held him high and watched the universe dance on the baby's tongue.

Time dissolved, and a great translucent drool, suspended from the boy's chin considered whether or not to fall.

Right then and there, the baby spoke. Either out loud or in Sister Subordinary's mind, she could never be certain, but the words themselves were clear and certain.

"Earth is the best place for love."

Then a great silence followed.

Not another word until the boy was seven years old.

———

AS TIME PASSED, Sister Subordinary would give the boy's first words an occasional once over with her feather duster. The best place for love compared to what other place? She flicked a dust mote from the word *love*. Or, did the infant mean the best place to invent love? She ran her duster over the word *Earth*. Or, had he come in search of love?

She stood back and inspected the tidied-up sentence at a distance.

*Earth is the best place for love.*

Perhaps she was making too much of it. Maybe the infant had merely echoed a stray phrase picked up from an itinerant angel who had witnessed a fat blue infant tumble from his mother's arms and fall through the heavens. The angel might have whispered in the babe's ear and with a gentle shove, changed the trajectory of his fall.

There was no telling. So the phrase earned a place in Sister's museum of spiritual mysteries.

Although Sister Subordinary kept the memory of the infant's message spic-and-span, she did dismiss the monkey's blink. Or seemed to. At least she never mentioned the blink to the others. Why occasion disbelief?

She alone had seen how the monkey's soft arms wrapped around the newborn's shoulders, how the monkey's long tail encircled the blue moon of the baby's belly and tickled his omphalos with brisk little flicks, making the baby gurgle with pleasure. She alone had registered the monkey's gaze.

It was an unforgettable jolt—that split-second glimpse into the animal's fathomless wisdom. Then more astonishing still, the wild creature returned the favor.

One blink and the monkey's ancient eyes had penetrated the very rock of her reason. In no time flat, he scrambled through every chamber of her heart, every niche in her mind, every turn of her soul. Only when the examination was complete did the exemplary guardian surrender the baby. As much as memory would later rearrange the picture, so much was clear in those first moments when she lifted the radiant infant from the downy white arms of the monkey.

And yet.

And yet, after the boy and the monkey and the box were brought inside, there was no possible way to argue with the sandpaper crackles of the Velcro tabs when Sister Subordinary separated the monkey's paws. Nor was she even remotely inclined to argue with this newly remade, diminished reality. This nun was infinitely skilled at taking reality on its own terms when it suited her, even at times when those terms were being rapidly renegotiated.

It is a fine testament to the strength of Sister Subordinary's mind that she held herself steady through the remarkable day. More than steady. She was suffused with joy. Her step was light upon the stair. She pulled out one of her dresser drawers and created a snug little nest for the unexpected guest. Then she pillowed the boy nicely among her underthings.

When Sister Merry Berry popped in moments later, Sister Subordinary took the opportunity to dash down to the kitchen. She set water to boil and improvised a baby formula of watered-down evaporated milk, sweetened with a bit of maple syrup.

She sterilized a dozen bottles left over from the days when foundlings were a common occurrence.

Left on her own, Merry Berry picked up the stuffed toy monkey and placed it in the drawer with the sleeping infant. Instinctively, the baby reached out and pulled the monkey close. The darkening room whispered hush, and a soft blue light filled the dresser drawer.

A baby in the house.

———

ONE GLANCE AT THE SLEEPING blue infant and the ancient Mother Mary Extraordinary experienced a painful insurrection of hope. That unwelcome surge of longing had to be arrested before it hijacked her heart.

Mother Mary Extraordinary was a tall woman, topping off at six feet, and she was exceedingly thin despite her extraordinary appetite. It was said that some dark secret was eating her up from the inside and made her appear somewhat like a broom in a modified burka as she swept down the halls. Well into her second century, the white hair hidden beneath her veil reached all the way to her ankles.

Her hair had not turned white; it had always been white. Her eyes were a pale but piercing blue—anywhere from ice blue to diamond blue, depending upon her mood. The angrier she became, the whiter her irises, so that at her angriest there were only little black dots on the opaque white orbs. That extreme of temper will only manifest once, and to startling effect, in the course of this narrative. Frightening off a Cardinal was a trifle compared to what she was capable of in high dudgeon.

Ensconced in her private study, the ancient prioress makes an unprecedented refusal. She sets her will against providence and quickly catalogues an arsenal of arguments for putting the baby up for adoption, her black boot tapping out a Morse code of irritability to cover her mounting affliction.

At the other end of the west wing, Mary Subordinary keeps a prayerful vigil. She dangles questions and listens for Mary Extraordinary's footfall. There is a happy silence in the hall.

Holding the inevitable contretemps in abeyance, Sister Mary Subordinary steals the moment, seals it against time; it is a morning glory moment—the gleaming bottle of formula on the nightstand, the fat drop of condensation rolling down the glass, Sister Merry Berry bending over the swaddled newborn, then lifting him towards the light. There is the smack of a bright kiss that Merry Berry plants on the boy's forehead. Then the holy card resolves—like a classic Madonna with babe in arms, Sister Merry Berry gazes heavenward to make a quick prayer before she places the holy infant back in his nesting drawer.

Mary Extraordinary pauses in the open doorway. She sees how the Sisters are besotted and means to end the insurrection before it begins.

"We have no business raising a child in this, our season of woe," Extraordinary's deep voice throttles to a halt on woe.

Woe hangs in the air, damp and musty.

Sister Merry Berry wants to blast the fog of woe out of the room. Her fantasy entails a certain red plastic ray-gun she'd spotted the last time she'd snuck out to the local 7-Eleven.

"By some chance or mischief, this boy has been endowed by The Great Church. His windfall wealth gives us options. We could send him to a lamasery in Tibet. He does look rather like a fat blue Buddha," Mother Mary Extraordinary smiled.

"Tibet?" Sister Merry Berry pouted, "Why, that's awfully far. I think we should keep him." She poked her head up, blinking against the light much like a prairie dog who's been hiding in the dark safety of her burrow, keeping her thoughts carefully cached.

In the box of holiday chocolates, Merry Berry was the cinnamon-dusted espresso truffle that everyone reaches for first. She was short, round, athletic. She had bounce. Her springy aubergine curls made constant mischief with her veil. An intriguing dimple in the center of her chin suggested that at any moment she might bubble over with laughter. From childhood on, she was always the girl with at least three best friends in tow. Sadly, her last set of besties were currently buried in the makeshift convent cemetery, victims of the prayer eaters.

"At the Chodrak orphanage," Mary Extraordinary ignored Merry Berry, "he would be surrounded by other children."

"What about me?" Merry Berry offered herself, palms up. "I could be his best friend." Merry Berry looked to Mary Subordinary for support.

"I believe," Subordinary entered with caution, "that when a foundling is left on the doorstep, certain obligations are entailed." Subordinary paused to give Extraordinary room to reflect, aware that the elderly nun had been knocking on heaven's door and might not wish to entail new obligations.

For the first time in her very long life, Mary Extraordinary was refusing a call. The celestial phone kept ringing and she kept hanging up.

"We've never raised a boy," she side-stepped. "He would have no father figure of any kind. Well, perhaps that is not altogether a negative. Ouch!"

Sometimes when her conscience pricked her, Mary Extraordinary experienced it as an actual physical sensation. Her eyes rolled up and her head tilted slightly to the right. The two Sisters waited while Mother paused a moment to address her conscience.

Her silent prayer went like this: *Mea Culpa. Mea Culpa. Now leave me alone. I'm busy. I did not mean to anathematize the entire male sex, much less insult our little blue guest. Mea Maxima Culpa. Satisfied?*

Then her voice boomed, "If I do have an incipient prejudice against men, blame it on the Cardinals!"

She realized she had spoken this last out loud and simply continued with a rueful smile, "So blessed be the boys, for Lord's sake."

Having settled spiritual accounts, she returned to the matter at hand.

"We must consider the fact that he would have to be kept in the strictest secrecy. The Cardinals know something. We can't be sentimental. An orphaned boy might prove a temptation too much for The Great Church. Kidnapping is not unheard of, dear Sisters. Remember Edgardo Mortara."

They did not remember. Mother Mary's memories extended to the archaic, if not arcane. Once upon a true but antiquated history, the six-year-old Edgardo had been snatched from his Jewish parents by officers of the Inquisition and secreted away in Rome.

The Sisters took her point. The boy would be in constant danger from The Great Church. True, it was a reformed church, and this was Humboldt County after all. Nonetheless certain vestigial mindsets persisted through the oceans of time.

Now that the baby was safely nestled in the dresser drawer, the Sisters appreciated what a close call it had been. Yesterday's visit from the officers of the Magistere could not have been a coincidence.

"There is only one eminence at the Sanctum Avesticum Quoborium who has the divinatory skill to predict the coming of a deity."

Sister Mary Subordinary bowed her head in silent acknowledgement.

Mother Extraordinary continued, "I am exceedingly surprised that he was off by one day."

―――――

THE EXCELLENT HOLY HIGH MAGUS of The Great Church, His Eminence Cardinal Cassowary, Magistrate of the Magistere Magisterium and Court Astrologer, did not believe for a Schrödinger's second that he had been off by one day. Reading the stars one evening, he had noticed certain anomalous movements. Stylus in hand, he calculated the coming of the holy infant with peerless mathematical precision. He knew when, and he knew where, but he was a little shaky on who. The stars were maddeningly silent on the matter of the infant's patents of divinity.

The child's mother had been exceptionally wily in disguising her pregnancy—a secret locked in her heart's most guarded chamber, a sweet bump veiled in yards of fair white silk. Neither her sacred consort nor her illicit lover knew of the boy's existence. Only the Monkey God had been present at the birth.

Carried across the oceans from the farthest steppes of India, the holy infant arrived in the Americas cradled in the furry arms of a peerless guardian. The white langur monkey was drawn fast by the honeyed scent of prayers, the enticement of metaphysical cookies left cooling on a windowsill in the stonework wall of a secluded convent in Humboldt County.

On first arrival, the monkey hid himself and the boy high in the leafy canopy of the woods that bordered the convent, so he could surveil the scene undetected. He watched the party of three Cardinals come and go from his perch in the tall trees, watched their footprints fill with fresh snow. He watched Sister Subordinary polish the window, appreciated her singularity of purpose, admired the transparent sphere of downy flakes that she balanced in her mind. With a caution born of ancient wisdoms and warfare, the monkey waited a judicious twenty-four hours after the last Cardinal went out the western gate before he kicked over Sister's snow globe and delivered the boy.

———

THE MAGUS WAS CORRECT. The boy had arrived in the Northern Hemisphere on Wednesday, January Fourteenth, 40.8019° north longitude, 124.1636° west latitude, 7:00 am, Pacific Standard Time.

An undocumented deity in the Americas was an unheard-of breach in the protocols of theophany. The thought of some precocious hippie coming of age during his reign, some unsorted barefoot guru gadding about his neighborhood serving fish and fishing his men, nearly scorched the over-amped brain of the Magus.

The Excellent Holy High Magus, His Eminence Cardinal Cassowary, was an impeccable agent of his own ambitions. Currently the second most powerful eminence in The Great Church, his eye was on the Hierophancy. Operation Magi had been his ingenious brainchild.

The unannounced visit to the convent was meant to be a preemptive political strike artfully disguised as a peace-making overture. The historical precedent of gift-bearing royals suggested obeisance. The elegant reenactment was designed to pave the way back into the good graces of the Sisters and thereby gain access to the child.

His Eminence Cardinal Cassowary had much to amend in his relationship to the Joyous Mystery Sisters. The Inquisition of the Order of Immaculate Conceptions had been initiated at his command.

Strange to tell, His Eminence had no particular interest in credos or doctrinal purity. His religious bent was flexible, spongy even. His was an absorbent mind, attracted to the experimental and the unlikely.

Power was his elixir.

And the Sisterhood had dared drink from his cup, the cup of wands: the cup of divine powers. As Magistrate of the collective Magistere Magisterium, he was the Inquisitor of Record, the mastermind who oversaw the eradication of female priests during the historic persecution of the Sisterhoods. He knew better than to show up on Mary Extraordinary's doorstep.

In any case, the art of conciliation was not in his skill set. Nor was his appearance an asset in animating trust. He was ostentatious and terrifying, attractive and repellent in equal measure. The Excellent Magus was literally breath-taking. Women were known to faint at the sight of him.

All the Cardinals were vanity queens and applied theatrical effects to look as much as possible like their totemic avian namesakes. Cardinal Cassowary went them one better. An adept at self-modification, he had recessed his cheek bones, carved out sockets and embedded two gorgeous cassowary eyes. Not satisfied with the merely decorative, the Magus had managed to make the eyes of the raptor operative as well.

His four eyes burning holes in Mother Mary's imperious posturings would have hardly furthered his cause. To avoid provocation, he had enticed the ambitious Cardinals Delacroix and Oolumbo to act as his proxies in Operation Magi. The clever Bunbury stepped up without priming.

At the initial clandestine meeting that saw the birth of Operation Magi, all parties had agreed that the gifts would need to be impressive if the overture were to be successful. But the Magus had argued rancorously with Delacroix and Oolumbo over the sum of gold that was necessary to demonstrate that they were in earnest. The Magus wanted to give away what amounted to a king's ransom.

Gold that could be borrowed from the church treasury, Bunbury reminded everyone present. And paid back with interest, he felt no need to mention. Before promotion to Cardinal, Bunbury had been a dedicated Goldfinch and sat on the board of the One Avesticum Bank and Trust. He still held a major interest in the One.

Bunbury's nose twitched involuntarily at the scent of money.

Delacroix and Oolumbo dug in their heels and closed their pocketbooks.

"Begging everyone's pardon," the obsequious Bunbury had uncharacteristically pushed himself forward and taken the floor at the fateful meeting. "You will forgive me, if I herewith toss in my vote with His Eminence Cardinal Cassowary. Regrettably, we are now two against two. An unfortunate stalemate."

Bunbury was built like a snowman, round in the middle, with sticklike arms, and mittens of plump pink fingers that he interminably rubbed with his thumbs as if he detected something sticky in the air. "All things considered, as it were," he wetted his lips, "I must say that Cardinal Cassowary's is the better argument. Largess is the ticket. So, dear Oolumbo and dear Delacroix, I am afraid we are at an impasse. I stand with Cardinal Cassowary. Alas."

The Magus chuckled and repeated Bunbury's, "Alas."

Then as if a silent alarm went off, all affability vanished. The room went chill, and the mercurial Cassowary turned on the two holdouts. "If there is going to be a new deity darting about the Americas," his voice began to drill, "that deity had damn well better be domed under The Great Church!"

Cardinal Cassowary's face went blood red. His right hand tingled and twitched—the skin began to contract, and the blackened nails were growing.

"Dammit," Cassowary hissed under his breath and placed his left hand over the unsightly right.

The Magus dared not look down lest he draw attention to the hand that was slowly mutating into a raptor claw. He smiled gratuitously at the wondering Cardinals. It was a disarming smile, a distracting smile. And by design, the smile changed the chemical balance in the Magus' brain—a stratagem that halted the anger-driven reconfiguration. Then he slowed his heart rate and lowered his voice to a throaty whisper. "Gold buys access," the smile broadened, "and access means influence."

Calm as you please, the Magus closed his human eyes, but his cassowary eyes remained open.

Bobble heads nodding, Cardinals Oolumbo and Delacroix conceded the argument. Simultaneously, the two Cardinals reached for the jewel-encrusted amulets suspended from gold chains around their necks. They unscrewed the tiny caps, lifted the amulets to their noses, and took long, gratifying sniffs.

The veneer of gentleman's club ambience was restored, although the room remained decidedly icy.

No one, excepting Delacroix's ferret, had noticed the near mishap. The sight of Cardinal Cassowary's nascent claw had sent Felix scampering deep inside Cardinal Delacroix's red sleeve. Now the unhappy ferret tentatively peeked out, sniffing for traces of predator. Detecting no sign or scent of the raptor claw, Felix scampered back to his accustomed perch on Delacroix's shoulder.

"Let me refill your amulets," the Magus offered, flexing the fingers of his restored human hand. Free refills of Prayer Juice were uncommon. Delacroix and Oolumbo were temporarily mollified by the offer.

Bunbury was that rare Cardinal who refrained from inhalants. He claimed allergies and kept his suspicions about the sanctioned drugs to himself.

"What will you have, Bunbury? A shot of distilled spirits?"

His Eminence Cardinal Cassowary now acted the part of genial host. That it was an unconvincing performance no longer mattered. He had succeeding in creating pliable agents—Magi made to order. Besides, he preferred operating in the wings, his fantoccini performing in the spotlight.

"Let the Sisters think you come at the behest of the Divine Duck," the Magus instructed the three subdued emissaries.

"Oh, has His Holiness been put in the picture? Do we have the blessing of the Munificentissimus Mallard?" Cardinal Oolumbo belatedly thought to ask.

"Yes," the Magus reassured, thinking to himself how the Hierophant habitually and indiscriminately blessed everyone and everything.

Assurances notwithstanding, the Munificentissimus Divine Mallard of All Mysteries, His Holiness, Hierophant of The Great Church, remained blissfully unaware of Cardinal Cassowary's machinations. By the time the Divine Mallard woke up from his long winter's nap, the Sanctum Avesticum Quoborium would be in crisis.

———

ON THE DAY OF THE VISITATION, still confident in the divinatory skills of the Magus, the three sateen-robed paragons of orthodoxy had set about their mission with self-important resolve. Gifts in hand, they were mortified to find themselves stomping their boots on the porte cochere of the convent for a good twenty minutes, noses reddened by the cold, knuckles bruised from repeated knocking.

When Cardinal Delacroix examined his bruised knuckles the next morning, his jealousy of the church Magus purpled into disdain. His only consolation was that Cardinal Cassowary and his vainglorious claim that he could read the future was henceforth soundly discredited.

There was no boy.

Operation Magi had proved a mockery. Word of the debacle echoed in chirps and tweets up and down the art-bedecked grand halls of Sanctum Avesticum Quoborium. The power players among the birdmen were jostling for position, hoping to knock the Magus off his perch and take his lackeys down a few pegs for good measure. The winds of contention were blowing high and mighty.

In the east quadrangle of the Avesticum, outside the private apartments of the Hierophant, a delegation of ruffled Cardinals waited impatiently, petitions in hand. The Munificentissimus Divine Mallard of All Mysteries had been asleep for five long days while the crisis roiled.

Avesticum couriers stationed in the hallway were prepared to run through the palace ringing bells to announce the awakening of His Munificentissimus or, should it prove necessary, to run to the campanile and toll the death-knell.

The courier-priests belonged to the Excellent Order of Geococcyx Californianus. These runners sported gold and brown diamond-patterned tights, crested caps, and gold prosthetic beaks. A blue stripe painted across their eyes finished the runway look.

All the birdmen were aware that one of these fine days, in the not-too-distant future, the Mallard's sleep would become permanent. Numerous wagers rode on the daily outcome: to wake or not to wake, perchance to dream on in the sweet hereafter. The Excellent Order of Geococcyx kept dutiful book on the Hierophant's life expectancy.

Cardinal Delacroix passed by a huddle of Geos and gave up a silent prayer. His money was on an even-numbered day. A red day. As Delacroix continued his jaunt through the halls of virtue, he became increasingly aware that heads were turning his way. Conversation stopped at his appearance and resumed at his back.

The Avesticum avians were all aflutter, twittering away in paroxysms of hearsay. Gossip was their daily bread, and on this occasion, they were well-fed birds.

Delacroix straightened his back when three Hooded Crows emerged from an alcove and assaulted him with jests.

"How's tricks in the Magi business, Your Eminence?"

"Would Your Eminence care to see a man about a camel?"

Delacroix increased his brisk pace and pretended not to hear. It was unendurable to be the square toes of every passing joke.

Today, the affronted Cardinal had ditched his dress reds and wore a dark-purple elastane workout unitard. A sweatband tied around his head gave him the appearance of a latter-day ninja. Only a tiny red bird perched on the silver-cross logo stitched on his sweatband evidenced his brand.

Delacroix reached inside his athletic bag for his ferret—the unhappy Felix—who promptly sunk four pointed canines into the Cardinal's hand. The pain was a trusty anodyne. His determination reinvigorated, he ducked down a stairwell and made his way to the ball courts.

———

CARDINALS DELACROIX AND COLUMBO had been giving one blue racquet ball a sound thrashing for the past half hour, a blessed respite from the taunts of their peers.

Unfortunately for Delacroix, self-castigation took up where the chattering Avesticum aviary left off. At one point, Cardinal Delacroix swore he could hear Mother Mary Extraordinary gloating and counting gold coin. The inner critical cawing continued unabated in Delacroix's beleaguered brain until, without warning, he slammed his racquet against the wall.

"You dropped your racquet," Cardinal Oolumbo coolly observed.

"Take a point," Delacroix shot back.

"I'm done," Oolumbo conceded the game. "You win."

"I win nothing!" Delacroix roared. "That preening pretender, predictor of marvels and messiahs, that Holy High Maggot!" Delacroix picked up his racquet and served the ball.

Oolumbo did not engage. Both men watched the ball lose momentum and roll to a stop.

"I, for one, plan on surviving your bruised ego," Cardinal Oolumbo snarked. "The Magus was charged with malfeasance. Give it a rest, Delacroix."

"Those birdbrains who mock me will quiver in their red booties when they discover I was the one who gave the order to have Cardinal Cassowary shut up in the tower."

"The question remains: will the Hierophant honor the charges you brought against his beloved Magus? The Divine Duck takes his beatitudes seriously."

"The question remains: will the Hierophant wake up any time this century? And another thing, where was Bunbury when we wanted a third signature on the warrant? Damn sycophant!"

The bickering Cardinals went silent when Delacroix's envoy, the bear-like Brother Umbruco, opened the door to the ball court. Umbruco was a member of the recondite Hooded Crows, some of whom occasionally hired themselves out to ranking Cardinals for special services.

Without preamble the monk announced, "There's been a double murder."

"Give me more," Delacroix ordered.

"The Magus killed two of the three guards who came to arrest him. Eviscerated them, he did."

The hair on the back of Delacroix's neck bristled. "Did Cassowary get away?"

"No." Umbruco knew Delacroix was not going to like what came next so the monk drew the moment out. "The Magus stepped over the dead bodies and finished the arrest himself. He's in the tower." Umbruco waited.

"You mean *locked* in the tower." Delacroix was clearly shaken.

"There's more. Something happened to his hand. It's not human anymore." Umbruco was enjoying this but hid it well. "Sheer speculation, Eminence, but my guess is that the Magus himself is in possession of the key. In any case, the prison door is wide open."

"Landica!" Oolumbo swore.

After a brief stint as a child soldier in Sierra Leone, Oolumbo was raised in one of the many orphanages where The Great Church incubates its baby priests. Swearing in Latin was mother's milk to the ill-used Cardinal.

"Deodamnatus. This is on you, Delacroix. Arrest the Magus? Futue te ipsum!" Oolumbo picked up his balls and left the court, changed his mind, turned around, and hurled one ball at the back of Delacroix's head.

———

31

"CLOWNS," THE MAGUS RESPONDED when Bunbury shared the gossip.

"As per usual," Bunbury took up his thread, "the Divine Mallard's head was tucked under his metaphorical wing when the order to arrest Your Eminence was stamped, sealed and set into motion by those turncoats, Delacroix and Oolumbo." Expert at keeping his podgy buns covered, Bunbury had scurried into his hidey-hole on the morning of the arrest. Now he was all gracious availability.

"Your Eminence, is there anything, anything at all I can do to make your stay more comfortable?"

"My stay? My stay at the Comfort Prison Suites? Surely, you jest."

"Surely, it will not be an extended stay, Eminence. Besides you hold the keys."

"Be honest, Bunbury. What do you really think of this prison tower?"

Bunbury squirmed. Candor was not his métier. "It's lofty," he ventured.

The Magus actually laughed—a deep sonorous laugh.

The Excellent Holy High Magus, His Eminence Cardinal Cassowary, Magistrate of the Magistere Magisterium and Court Astrologer, was currently awaiting court review. Most likely, there would have been no pending review had it not been for the gold squandered on a nonexistent deity. Allegedly nonexistent, the Magus amended as he reviewed the warrant.

To be sure, the matter of the murdered guards merited censure, but there were rituals that absolved crimes of passion.

Still, the Magus acknowledged privately, he would have to address the murder charges at some point.

*Damned claw.*

It was, however, the missing money that rankled most in certain halls of the Sanctum Avesticum Quoborium. Operation Magi had been a costly, embarrassing error. The violation seemed personal, almost sexual. The much-reviled Mary Extraordinary had grabbed the exclusively-male Avesticum by the purse strings.

The Association of Goldfinch was—not unreasonably—demanding that the Magus reimburse the treasury. They sent him unsigned, urgent notes, delivered by genetically modified carrier pigeons.

Gold was not the only consideration. Now that their prized chemist was ensconced in the Sanctum's prison tower, the aficionados of spritz and sniff were understandably nervous. Surely the Magus would not cut them off.

A flash mob of worried supplicants headed for the cathedral. The basilica under the Golden Duomo began to fill with a steady thrum of desperate Pater Nosters, setting off the intricate and tumultuous choreography of an Avesticum prayer rally. The flock of ardent petitioners shared one desire—that the Divine Mallard of All Mysteries intervene on their behalf and keep the font of Prayer Juice freely flowing.

The momentum shifted when a counter valence of clamorous Aves was launched by a charm of Goldfinch who rushed down the center aisle without ceremony. These dedicated accountants of the One Avesticum Bank and Trust made an unwelcome, but striking appearance in flowing yellow robes trimmed in black velvet. They wore black masks and matching black beanies, studded with neat rings of pointy orange beaks. The Frères Finch were fierce practitioners and meant to outpray the aficionados of spritz and sniff.

The prayer-off was overwhelmed when a funeral march of beautifully groomed Loyal Red Kites entered in military formation with eight pallbearers and a quartet of snare-drummers. Their customary duties more ceremonial than belligerent, the Kites dressed in uniforms made for parade. They wore furry red top hats and feather-tipped red tailcoats with an excess of brass buttons. The high-hatted Kite at the lead carried a gold mace that he tossed high in the basilica and caught with breathtaking precision. He was followed by the Kite Ecclesiarch who swung an incense-burning thurible suspended from gold chains.

One Cardinal stood at the back of the sanctuary, just outside the melee of competitive prayer. As blame for the Magi-debacle accelerated with the drumbeats, the politically ambitious Cardinal Delacroix saw how the botched arrest and the deaths of the two Red Kites might prove providential.

Although assassinations were commonplace on Mount Quoborium, the politically astute hired them out. Cassowary had made a rare blunder. A thrill coursed down Delacroix's spine.

*Bang the drum slowly*, Delacroix whispered, *this is Cardinal Cassowary's funeral.*

The Cardinal with the claw was no longer a contender for the Hierophancy, not with two murders on his account. Were an election held today, with the bloody eviscerations fresh on every birdman's mind, Delacroix was convinced that the Hierophancy would be his. If only the Mallard of all Mysteries would take this blessed opportunity to pass into the sweet hereafter.

Cardinal Delacroix reached for his ferret, but the unreliable Felix was not in a biting mood. The lively creature ran up Delacroix's arm and perched on his head. The Cardinal ignored his fuzzy headgear. The urge was upon him. He went down on one knee and prayed with unaccustomed, but steadfast fervor that the Hierophant—may it please God—not wake up.

Subtly aware of the cacophony of prayer, the Mallard rolled over in his sleep. The titular head of The Great Church, His Holiness, the Munificentissimus Divine Mallard of All Mysteries, was not at all averse to dying, but that finality had so far eluded him. Dozing off was his next best benediction. His Holiness was renowned for his ability to sleep through anything. He happily suffered from a debilitating case of SNS, sudden nap syndrome. Moreover, this well-rested Hierophant was even-handed to a fault, slow to judge and quick to mercy.

Down on his knee, Cardinal Delacroix was forced to consider the possibility that the whimsical Hierophant might do the unthinkable and pardon the murders, might even go so far as to hold Delacroix responsible. In a rare consoling gesture, the ever-alert Felix began industriously licking the Cardinal's ear. Despite the quick action of the ferret's sluicy pink tongue, the Cardinal refused to be consoled. He slapped at the ferret, who finally obliged the Cardinal with a scream-inducing bite.

Two courier Geos ran past ringing hand-held bells.

The Hierophant was awake.

———

THE SECRETARY OF SACRED WRIT sat, pen in hand. An impeccably groomed birdman, Sagittarius Milton wore translucent white face paint with powdery orange shadows around his eyes. His tight thin lips were heavily silvered. This striking look was fashioned after the elegant secretary bird (Sagittarius Serpentarius). The ensemble included black knee breeches, a grey tailcoat, and a smart quill-embellished cap. A model of decorum, the secretary waited—he'd been waiting for nearly a week—while an opinion slowly wound its way through the intricate maze of the Hierophant's lofty mind. At some point the opinion had simply exhausted its will to find a way out.

"I have no opinion." The Hierophant, still in his dressing gown, stood and stretched his creaky bones.

"If you will not meet with the Cardinals, you must at least generate a document, a declaration, some sort of official proclamation." Sagittarius Milton lifted his pen.

The Hierophant took his cue. "In that case, proclaim this— 'His Holiness met with His Eminence Cardinal Cassowary in the historic Sanctum prison tower.' There's a fine opener." Satisfied that he had got off to a good start, the Hierophant wandered over to a well-laid breakfast table, poured himself a cup of tea and took a nibble from a chocolate chip cookie.

"You know, Cassowary has done marvels with his prison quarters," His Holiness spooned sugar in his tea. "You should see it. The view from the tower balcony? Breathtaking. The Golden Duomo is simply stunning at sunset. To observe that architectural landmark from that balcony at that hour was a rare blessing—the Duomo backlit, rosy-fingered, Homeric.

Well, I shan't be climbing those tower stairs again, not I, not on these wobbly stems. Pick up your pen, man."

"His Holiness has not given his—." The secretary was at pains not to use the word opinion. He changed tack. "What did the Excellent Holy High Magus have to say for himself?"

"Cardinal Cassowary claimed the deaths were accidental. As it turns out, he is not entirely in control of his claw. It's newish. He apologized profusely and assured me that he is diligently working on a fail-safe."

"And therefore?"

"Must I write the entire proclamation myself?" The Hierophant was being uncharacteristically snappish.

The secretary put down his pen and gave His Holiness a long look.

"Don't get your quills in a ruff, Milton." The Hierophant blinked several times. "I feel as if I am—I am about to sneeze. It must be an opinion coming on. Dear me. Write this: 'The Divine Mallard of all Mysteries found himself moved by the plight of the Magus.' Now that's poetic. 'And His Holiness, mindful of the beatitudes, offered to bless the claw.' There, you have it."

"Did you?" The rarely startled secretary lifted a brow.

"I did, yes. What? The poor man had blood on his claw. We can't have him Lady Macbething about the sacred halls. Out, out damn spot and all that dramatic queening that goes with a guilty conscience. Don't write that."

"As if," the secretary glanced up, then continued composing the proclamation. After several thoughtful additions and a few formal flourishes, the Secretary of Sacred Writ handed the improved document to His Holiness for perusal, certain that there would be no revisions. The Mallard was not much inclined towards second thoughts, much less first opinions.

Before the proclamation could be read to the assembled Cardinals, rumor got out that His Holiness meant to call Hierophant's Prerogative and effect the immediate release of Cardinal Cassowary. Objection, in the form of Avesticum law, came quick on the heels of rumor. Forgiveness, in this instance, required the assent of the five Cardinals of the Signatura Tribunale.

At the behest of Cardinal Delacroix, the Sanctum Legal Eagles advised the Mallard that Hierophant's Prerogative could not be invoked in the case of homicide, accidental or otherwise. So, despite the Hierophant's saintly intentions, the second most powerful member of The Great Church was left cooling his heels and his claw in the praetorian pokey.

For reasons Delacroix could never fathom, the highly adaptive Magus chose to honor Avesticum protocols and stay put. No guards were posted. No one bothered to lock the tower. No one believed that the Excellent Holy High Magus was much inconvenienced by his change of residence.

———

IN THE SECLUSION of his prison suite, the Magus contemplated the exquisite composition of the claw. He saw that it was a thing of incomparable beauty. The artistry was sublime. The visceral sensation was orgasmic. And the disappointment was crushing.

The Holy High Magus of The Great Church, His Eminence Cardinal Cassowary, wanted nothing so much as to be in control of his splendid claw. Although he was loath to admit it, there was a flaw in its morphological design and, by implication, a flaw in the designer. That irksome paradox dogged him at every turn. How does a flawed creator amend his creation?

It was the perennial question that haunted his every incarnation.

Be that as it may, the primal power of the claw had overtaken Cardinal Cassowary's big brain when it disemboweled the two unfortunate Red Kites. To make matters worse, the Magus was unable to reconfigure his human hand after the blood bath. Now he was stuck with a permanent claw.

Bunbury cleared his throat. The Magus looked up.

"The perils of self-modification," Cassowary sighed, examining the nine-inch sickle-shaped nail on his middle finger.

Bunbury supplied a dutiful chuckle.

"I have not forgotten about the boy." The Magus turned his full attention on Cardinal Bunbury, searching for any sign of doubt.

"Nor have I," Cardinal Bunbury answered too quickly.

The Magus tilted his head. The ovoid center of his cassowary eyes pinned the punctilious Cardinal, searching for the lie.

An understandably anxious Bunbury hunted for a consoling bromide. Any palliative would do, so long as it did not call into question the divinatory skills of the Magus.

"Really," Bunbury settled, "a boy is not of much account until he reaches the age of seven or so."

"Point taken. Seven years. I like it. Tell His Holiness that a seven-year sentence will be acceptable."

Cardinal Cassowary abruptly turned to other matters. "I will need the drafting table brought up from my study. And my case of drawing tools. I want to rebuild my lab here in the tower. I'll need a state-of-the-art refrigerated centrifuge and an electron microscope—those are the pricey items. Here's a list of chemicals, graduated beakers, pipettes and various et ceteras."

Then the Magus took out a pen, inked his distinctive signature and handed his acolyte a sizable check. "Keep the change."

Bunbury made some quick calculations, nodded his appreciation, and left the Magus to his many endeavors. The generous gratuity would swell Cardinal Bunbury's secret off-shore account—brisk business as usual in The Great Church.

Though initially outraged by the effrontery of the arrest, the Magus would come to relish his lengthy seclusion. He was not given to the society of churchmen. He was, prima facie, a maker—a necromancer, a tinker, an engineer, a scientist, a designer. He was crafty.

When the Holy High Magus finally emerged from his prison tower seven years hence, he would be more powerful by leagues. And a good deal wealthier. He had a thriving business of the sort that imprisonment does not impede.

Ensconced in his prison suite, the engine of his ambitions humming nicely, his mind a machine like no other, it would be months before Cardinal Cassowary noticed the spectacular view from the tower balcony that had so charmed the Hierophant.

Now the Magus flexed the muscle of his new monasticism and pleasured in the power of his infrangible will. It would not be breached again, he promised himself. There was a quickening in his bones. His human eyes agleam, he scanned the future. "The next generation of prayer-laced inhalants promises to be my apotheosis," he addressed the bright tomorrows lining up before him.

Then he began browsing Mary Extraordinary's prayer book, *What the Goat Girl Dreamed at the Holiday Inn.* The mysteriously titled book that Cardinal Bunbury had passed along held the key ingredients for the next generation of designer inhalants and atomized Prayer Juice. Merely reading Extraordinary's poems created an intoxicating chemical cocktail in his brain. The distilled essence of her ungoverned prayers promised untold illuminations. He looked forward to drawing under the influence.

"DWI, drawing while intoxicated," the Magus intoned and closed the book.

As one black sickle-shaped nail traced the gold embossed lettering on the pink leather cover, Mary Extraordinary felt the graze of a raptor claw on the backside of her mind.

———

THE SISTERS WERE at an impasse. No decision had been made about the baby. Each night was one more night to be savored, and each morning they hesitated on the brink of giving the boy up.

One day more to find a reason to stall one more day.

At a critical pause in the ongoing debate, Sister Merry Berry made the mistake of admiring the Magi's gifts. She was particularly enchanted by the gold-encrusted ormolu music box. Wary of enchantments, Mary Extraordinary determined how Sister Merry Berry must consign the three gifts.

"Go on, then," Extraordinary directed. "Now is as good a time as any."

"Whatever you say," Merry Berry soothed, while silently promising herself that she would decide whether or not to obey the letter of Extraordinary's law. She missed the more equable Mother Mary Extraordinary of the convent's heyday. More to the point, Merry Berry was partial to presents. She was certain that this was one time when Mary Extraordinary ought to mind her own mysteries.

*Almost* as Mother ordered, Sister Merry Berry went about dealing with the gifts of the Magistere cum Magi. She locked the gold in the vault behind the tabernacle exactly as proscribed, and unceremoniously dumped the incense in the trash pile as ordered.

Incense made the air dirty, Mother Mary Extraordinary had opined. It was bad for the lungs. Breath was sacred and so on.

Merry Berry allowed herself the critical observation that Mary Extraordinary had far too many opinions these days. As for the ormolu music box, with its delightful nursery tune, there was no good reason on the good green Earth to stuff it away in a dark musty vault. Why should Sister Merry Berry deprive herself of such an enchanting object? Still, she did not wish to openly defy Mother Extraordinary, so that is why Merry Berry placed the music box on a shelf in the underground wine cellar where she had frequent occasion to visit.

Lucky thing.

Unbeknownst to Merry Berry, a voice-activated listening device had been cleverly hidden inside the music box. Its maker had envisioned the gift sitting on a shelf in the nursery, monitoring the boy—his cries and whispers, his first words. Had the box been placed nearby the infant, the Magus would have been a well-rewarded and rapturous listener this very night.

As it was, only certain celestials were privy to the Sister's ongoing debate. The baby's fate hung in a delicate balance, a cradle blowing in the rock-a-bye of indecision.

Newly refreshed from a tipple of cabernet and her small act of rebellion, Merry Berry rejoined her consoeurs. As Mother rambled on, turning over the question of what to do about the boy, Merry Berry's attention drifted back to the music box tucked away in the wine cellar. It might be just the thing to amuse a blue baby one day.

"Care to join us, Sister Merry Berry?"

"What? Of course. I was just thinking—"

"Please don't."

"I wouldn't dream—"

"As I was saying, I do not want a plague of social workers to descend upon the cloisters with advice, and forms to fill out, and inspections, and interrogations, and whatnot. The baby would have to be our very closely guarded secret," Mother Mary bent over the infant who slept on in happy oblivion in the dresser drawer.

It seemed to Sister Subordinary that there was a decisive shift, but that was not the case. The ecclesiastically tall and lean Mother Extraordinary was merely listing to prevailing winds in the recondite precincts of her mind.

"If we could manage to somehow keep the baby off the books and undiscovered," she listed one way.

"On the other hand, it is not a healthy prospect for a child to be raised on the QT," she listed the other.

The catalogue of objections had merit. The convent was not safe. Long stretches of silence hinted at hidden sorrows and darker matters. A powerful current held them back. The decision grew impatient.

Just when it seemed they must let the boy go, Sister Subordinary, recalling her singular exchange with the monkey, introduced the deciding factor.

The baby was blue.

"Wouldn't his color attract a veritable circus of all the wrong sorts of attention, if we gave up the infant to the secular world?"

Sister Mary Subordinary allowed herself a moment of self-congratulation, certain that she had at last taken charge of the conversation. Then the monkey entered her mind, and all certainty vanished. In an instant, she was suffused with the warmth of the langur's approval, haloed in yellow light as if his personal sun were rising above her crown chakra.

*Surya namaskar*, the monkey chanted.

*In the name of the sun*, Sister easily translated. A linguistic adept, she quickly surmised the identity of the white monkey.

"Sister, you are positively glowing," Merry Berry exclaimed.

Somehow Sister Subordinary stumbled forward despite the alarming intimacy with the monkey and the novelty of being lit up like a holiday tree-topper.

"Blue," she repeated. "Dear Sisters, even in far off Tibet, word of a blue getsül would surely get out. The boy would become a curiosity."

This consideration of the infant's color cleared the community conscience. Heads bowed, they gave out a collective sigh. What a relief to discover that the best course of action was the one the three nuns most ardently desired.

They had fallen in love with the babe, each nun in her own way. Each harbored an unspoken hope, almost too sensitive for private meditation, much less public airing. Each was taken aback when her hope lifted sail and left safe harbor.

They were in the deeps now.

# Foundlings

WHILE IT WAS TRUE that the Sisters had taken care of infants in the past, they had never kept one longer than a week or two. It had been years since anyone had rung the foundling bell. Perhaps that was because the untended convent grounds were disenchanting, the tangle-wood forbidding. Or it could have been that rumors of the contagion had gotten abroad and frightened off the young unwed mothers. Likely enough, the foundling door itself had been reduced to a foggy rumor, as easily dismissed as an old wives' tale.

The door was still there, cut in the wall of the chapel—an ornate carved oak panel, not altogether unlike a cat door that swung on creaky hinges. When the panel was lifted up by its brass knob, a swaddled babe could be slipped through the opening.

A pair of stone angels flanked the foundling door, their hands covering their eyes to protect the mother's identity. The abandoning party would ring the foundling bell, then hurry off into the woods. The Sisters would ring out an answering bell to let the mother know her child was safe. Sometimes the poor girl would linger at the edge of the woods. The Sisters would find notes pinned to the trees, or school-girl pictures. Sometimes a pair of booties or a knitted cap dangled from a branch, and once a silver rattle was left tied to the brass knob on the foundling door.

Each of Sisters was currently given over to private ruminations about her own journey through that very foundling door. The infant girls were always named Mary. The boys were given any variety of names. Francis was a favorite. The old Roman saint was universally admired.

In bygone days, some of the adopted Marys would return to the convent—young women who had tried the world and found it wanting. These joyfully celebrated Marys professed their vocations with happy tears and were then invited to enter the novitiate. And while all young women with callings were welcomed with open arms, the postulant Marys were secretly revered and held themselves not above, but apart.

Those who had once entered through the foundling door had powers that the others did not. These powers were often discovered at chapel, in long stretches of deep, soul-searching meditations. It was a private matter between the Mary and her own unfolding nature. No Mary ever spoke of her personal mystery to another. They adhered to a variation of the ancient Socratic dictum of justice—each one minding her own mystery.

In the history of the order, there was only one case where an infant was kept and raised to adulthood in the convent; that girl was Mary Extraordinary. She too was an effulgent baby, positively glowing with an extraterrestrial light. Both beautiful and somewhat alarming to behold—she was covered with the softest white down, a dandelion of a girl.

The Sisters would blow on her tummy and make wishes. As she grew into her maturity and shed her down, it was clear that her gifts were both extraordinary and wildly variable, almost like weather. She also had the singular distinction of never once having left the convent grounds.

Mary Subordinary and Merry Berry were returnees, part of the circle of sacred Marys. Merry Berry had whimsically changed the spelling of her name, an innovation that was applauded, as were most innovations. All the Marys, orphaned as they were at birth, spent their days binding themselves to their makeshift family by continuous prayer. And thus bound in love, their love for the infant was boundless.

————

A QUICK CHECK of their supplies told the Sisters that the expiration date on the baby formula stored in the pantry had long since passed. Here was a conundrum. Sister Mary Josephus, the only nun licensed to drive the old Ford Fairlane, was buried at the far end of the garden. At some point Sister Merry Berry had driven the Fairlane over the grave to serve as a marker and makeshift chapel in the field.

Over time, the Fairlane became Sister Subordinary's sometime refuge and Sister Merry Berry's sometime tavern on the green. In the glove compartment Sister Merry Berry kept remembrances of her departed consoeurs—a carved Dao Mau, that once belonged to the Vietnamese conjoined twins, the Sisters Mary Tuee; a set of fountain pens that belonged to the scribe and librarian, Sister Mary Rose; and the driver's license with its small photo of Sister Mary Josephus. The Fairlane Chapel had long since settled into its spot, the tires long since gone flat.

The practical matter of fetching baby supplies for the infant began to work a matrix of changes in the cloister.

Mother Mary had few connections in the secular world, and the Marys did not as a rule leave the convent grounds. It seemed risky, just now, to enlist the help of a stranger. Who could be trusted in these dangerous times?

One of the Marys—a defector—tapped insistently on memory's window. Despite Mary Extraordinary's several attempts to close the blinds, there was the apostate forever peeking through the slats of Extraordinary's mind. Mary Mirabelle. She would have to be nearly one hundred years old. Extraordinary herself was approaching one hundred and fifty.

Mary Mirabelle had once been a favorite. She took her vows the same year Mary Extraordinary became prioress. But Mirabelle slipped out of those vows as easily as she took them on. The slip occurred the very second she set eyes on the well-digger's son. And it was true: Dagoberto Rosario Emilio Marquez did look like a sun-burnished Apollo seated on top of that yellow backhoe. The two lovers conceived and married, in that short order.

Mary Extraordinary was Godmother to Mary Mirabelle's daughter Grace, but through the years the two Marys lost touch. The bond between them remained tightly laced, although neither the spiritual mother nor her wayward spiritual daughter entirely approved of the way the other wore the traceries of this incarnation.

What no one realized was that Mirabelle had not lost her Mary power when she left the convent. She was something of an oracle. Her gift was to see deeply into the future. It was only when her love-struck gaze met Dagoberto's answering glance that she discovered how very far that sight extended. She knew that one day the phone would ring and much more besides.

Mother Mary Extraordinary took a deep breath and prepared herself to call Mary Mirabelle. The Sisters followed the prioress to the library. A telephone call was a great occasion. It turned out that Mirabelle's expiration date had passed some years back, and so Mother Mary found herself talking to Mirabelle's daughter Grace who had to run, for Lord's sake, and passed the phone to her daughter Alyssa Rosaria. So the course of this history was radically altered because Grace had to run.

It was a holy card moment, an annunciation worthy of the painter Raphael. Alyssa's hand on the telephone; her long hair flows over her shoulders, a soft yellow light pours through an open window. The painter dips his brush, adds a pair of cherubini leaning in at the windowsill. Alyssa is the first, outside the convent walls, to hear of the arrival of the infant. Mother Mary Extraordinary is her announcing angel.

Numerologically auspicious, Alyssa Rosaria, granddaughter of the backhoe driver Dagoberto Rosario Emilio Marquez, is the seventh first born of seven first-borns. There is an interesting deviation in her DNA strand. Oh, glorious mutant genes.

"Hello. Hello. Yes, Alyssa, very nice to meet *you*, on the wire, as it were. You've heard a lot about *me*? Oh, your grandmother. Yes, Mirabelle. Well. I've no time for chit chat. Yes, yes, very sad indeed, her passing. What? She stays in touch? Heavens."

Alyssa Rosaria had a lot to say. She was recently married to Rios Dante on a beach. The wedding party wore flip-flops. The final blessing was given by a rogue wave, drenching the bride and groom. Hadn't Mary Extraordinary received the invitation? It was the best wedding ever! Alyssa was studying molecular genetics and was onto herself, genetically speaking. Just two more years interning and she'd be a Doctor of Medicine. Real medicine, she added unnecessarily Extraordinary thought.

The young woman's voluble enthusiasm was causing a crick in Mother's neck. Next Alyssa was filling in the details of Mirabelle's death.

"She had a vision at the very end, of an oracle who lived on the moon and—."

"An oracle on the moon? Holy saints in heaven! May I please interrupt? There's an emergency *here*. On Earth. We need supplies for an infant."

"What does she say?" Merry Berry was beside herself, bouncing on the balls of her feet. She had never used the telephone and didn't like to be left out of this important conversation. Too bad Extraordinary's patience wore thin just as Alyssa Rosaria came to a thrilling turn. An oracle on the moon?

Mother Mary held her hand over the mouthpiece and addressed the irrepressible Merry Berry. "Mirabelle's granddaughter, Alyssa Rosaria, among other anecdotes and oddities, says that absolutely everything we need can be found in a 7-Eleven—whatever in the world those numbers might signify. Or, we can order on line."

The infamous scowl was dragging at the corners Extraordinary's mouth. With an arch of her brow, she returned to Alyssa.

"I *am* on the line, dear. Would you care to take my order? What? A computer? For baby formula? Nonsense."

The phone call ended shortly thereafter.

Sister Merry Berry was burning with shame. There was nothing for it; she would have to admit that she knew the location of a 7-Eleven. Six miles, if you went through the woods. A twelve-mile round trip. Longer, if you took the road. She had discovered it on a meandering walk one morning.

She never could say why she bought that first Hostess Twinkie.

Almost immediately, her cheery nature intervened, and Merry Berry saw the upside. Since she would be making regular formula runs to the 7-Eleven, her stash of Hostess Twinkies might be maintained indefinitely. An eternity of Twinkies danced in her brain, much like visions of sugar plums are said to dance in the heads of children who dream of Santa.

Sister Merry Berry had been meaning to repair one of the bicycles in the garage and give herself the freedom of a wider neighborhood. Ever since the loss of her friends, convent life had begun to feel restrictive. Now she felt prosperous, expectant—the map of her future threaded with bicycle rides. Best of all, a baby to love. She would repair two bicycles. Oh, sweet nirvana. How the future brightened with the arrival of the miracle boy.

Sister Mary Subordinary recounted how the infant had spoken on his foundling day, and for those first few weeks they each waited for him to speak again. It would be seven years before Merry Berry and Mary Extraordinary would hear his voice. It was a worrisome wait, and as the years passed, the Sisters began to think something wasn't quite right with their bright blue boy.

At some point, Mother Mary Extraordinary and Sister Merry Berry concluded that the baby had never spoken in the first place. Sister Subordinary did not press her personal conviction on her confederates, although she could call up that crystalline baby voice and replay it at will. She wore an entrancing little smile whenever she listened to that memory.

The toddler was clever in so many other ways. Crayon in hand, his drawings were remarkable. They soon covered the surface of the refrigerator, overflowed onto the cupboards, and eventually the walls of his nursery. Portraits were his specialty.

Still, his doting caretakers didn't like to admit that their holy infant was possibly just a little bit slow in the speech department. They'd rather have it that speech itself were an aberration than concede a flaw in the child. Nonetheless, the unmentioned reservation marked a considerable downgrade for the precocious deity, and just as well. He needed a particular unqualified spaciousness to adapt to this incarnation, and lowered expectations provided the happiness of unexpected freedoms.

The body is a tricky vehicle, especially for first-timers.

It would have been a hindrance to have the Sisters hovering over him, expecting daily miracles and wisdoms and weather forecasts. He was spared being treated like a live-in almanac. Furthermore, the good Sisters had no earthly idea how lucky they were that the boy was unable to pray out loud. When he finally uttered his first prayer, it hit the air waves with such a celestial thwang that three adolescent angels tumbled right out of the sky.

———

LATER THAT FIRST WEEK, when the joyous éclat of baby tending quieted, Sister Subordinary set out on a midnight walk to catch up with herself. Wrapped in a great cape of deep purple Tibetan wool, she made her way across the snowy field by the light of a handheld gas lantern. She pictured herself—a dominie walking on fields of cloud, the Ford Fairlane parked just up ahead, waiting to taxi her to the starry side of another midnight.

She climbed in and was braced by the chill solitude.

Certain celestials marveled at the sight of the Fairlane Chapel haloed in lamplight. Encapsulated in the holy night, under the watchword angels, Sister Subordinary unlocked her heart and examined its secret contents. She took out the image of the monkey—that particular clip of time when he turned his head and locked his eyes on hers. Examining the moment closely, she picked up something that hadn't registered before.

When the monkey had scrambled through every niche of her being with his mischievous chalk stick, she'd been graffitied—end to end! Heart, mind, soul—all were covered with his imprint, his name, his logo, his footprints. What a game of tag!

"O great and glorious monkey," she nearly laughed out loud.

Yes. The monkey had blinked. She did not doubt it. But she took that blink and locked it away in her safe place, determined to forget about it. Sister Subordinary was a master at safeguarding precious contraband, including her own heterodox sanity.

The monkey with its Velcro paws was a fact. She herself had placed the unmistakably stuffed monkey on the dresser top in her room where the baby slept on that very first night. Now Sister Mary Subordinary silently thanked Sister Merry Berry for restoring the monkey to his rightful place beside the infant. Subordinary resolved to give reality its due without compromising the ineffable—the blink, the blue glow, the baby's first words.

"Blessed be," she gave praise. What a gift had been given! A reprieve from mourning had been granted the convent. Now it was imperative to mount an answering effort, nourish hope, conquer doubt, and shake off every last residual grievance.

———

LIFE AT THE CONVENT had existed in a holding pattern of grief ever since the plague year ravaged the order. No conceptions had occurred, material, spiritual, immaculate or otherwise. All was elegy since the mysterious contagion leapt from one bed to the next.

The terror often struck at vespers, in the silence before evening prayer. The Sisters would kneel, open their prayer books and wait. It was a subliminal wait—the heartbeat under the heartbeat, the sudden arrhythmia, the tell-tale gasp that signaled the discovery that yet another prayer book had gone blank. Then came the furtive glances, looking about in rising panic to ascertain who among their beloved consoeurs was holding the desecrated book.

No one survived white pages.

Once the prayers were expunged, the Sister who composed those prayers would be erased as well. It began with a bone-rattling chill. Later that night, the Sister's temperature would soar. By morning she would be gone.

Mother Extraordinary ordered a surcease. All prayer books were locked in the aumbry.

No matter. The Sisters continued to fall ill. Afterwards, the departed Sisters' books were brought out and the worst was confirmed. Licked clean by the prayer eaters.

"There is no such thing as prayer eaters!" Mother Mary Extraordinary had declared. "We must not fall into medieval superstitions!"

"Someone is licking off the plates of our souls," the steely Sister Mary Josephus talked past the prioress. "There is an observable correlation between a Sister's death and her book. That is not superstition. That is science," Mary Josephus had argued. "We are dealing with spooky action at a distance—an analogue of quantum physics."

"What is more," Sister Mary Rose gentled into the discussion, "each Sister created her prayers from the very marrow of her most evolved, most cherished spiritual beliefs." Sister Mary Rose brushed away a tear. "I have a strong premonition I shall go next."

"When I go," Sister Mary Josephus enjoined, "someone had better bury me under my Ford Fairlane."

Both Sister Mary Rose and Sister Mary Josephus went the next night. They were found wrapped in each other's arms.

The order lost nine ordained Sisters, twenty-six consecrated Sisters, fourteen postulants and one novice. The garden, where they once held Holy Mass under arbors and angels, had inexorably become bordered by a cemetery.

How had things gone so terribly wrong?

For decades the Sisters' various unorthodoxies had been tolerated by The Great Church, if not altogether approved. Then one egregious canonical trespass so enraged their spiritual fathers that all tolerance ended. One unpardonable anathema brought the Inquisition to the convent's doorstep—the elevation of consecrated Sisters to the priesthood.

"The gangrene-infected limb must be severed to preserve the Holy Body of the Church," the Magus declared on his authority as Magistrate of the Magistere Magisterium. And the dark wing of the Magistere threw its shade over the convent.

When spies in the employ of the Magisterium initially reported that forbidden female priests were conducting Holy Mass, the Machiavellian Magus knew he had struck political pay dirt. With astute deliberation, he set about aggravating the latent fears of the second sex that had always vexed the Church Fathers.

Ordination, Holy Orders, was the longstanding privilege of the male priesthood. The very notion of a priestess caste evoked disturbing pagan atavisms—sex, fertility, motherhood. Besides, The One True God had no mother. That was axiomatic.

Envoys of the Magistere Magisterium, dressed in deep purple robes appliquéd with gold crosses, came seven abreast carrying flaming staffs in the dark of night. A hooded agent nailed a Document of Excommunication and a Decree of Divorcement to the front door of the convent. Gathered on the other side of the door, the Sisters listened to the slam of the hammer: once, twice, thrice.

Mother Mary Extraordinary opened the door and ripped off the document, her eyes locked on the Excellent Holy High Magus, Magistrate of the Magistere Magisterium. At a discreet signal from the Magus, a cross of condemnation was set afire on the lawn.

Mary Extraordinary stepped aside and the Sisters flowed out into the volatile night. Sister Mary Subordinary broke from the ranks, ran towards the conflagration and gave the burning cross a good solid kick. The cross tumbled.

All at once the Sisters raised their voices in a thrilling chorus and pushed back the black ululations of the mob of angry priests. The Sisters advanced. The priests retreated.

The morning after, the prioress addressed her gathered consoeurs in the chapel. "Sisters, we have been given a great gift," Mother Mary Extraordinary held up the scrolled document.

Then with the help of two altar maids, she ceremoniously tore the screed into pieces, filling a golden chalice with scraps of text. When the ritual shredding was complete, the congregation of Sisters knelt at the communion rail.

The Sisters Tuee rang the offertory bell.

Sister Mary Rose stood and ceremoniously removed Mary Extraordinary's black veil. There was a collective gasp. How beautiful their prioress appeared with her white hair falling in waves all the way to her ankles.

"Open your prayer palms and form a cup," Mother Mary instructed.

One handful at a time, two altar maids, dropped wafers of excommunication into the waiting palms of their kneeling consoeurs.

Again the Sisters Tuee rang the offertory bell.

"Prepare to receive glad tidings," Mary Extraordinary intoned, leading the Sisters into the heart of a mystery. "In your own hands you now hold the entitlement to your soul, as it ever was, and will be forevermore. We are free, dear ones. Let us confetti the chapel."

The Sisters Tuee rang the offertory bells with a renewed vigor and the collective rose up as one and tossed the wafers of excommunication and divorcement into the air.

Later that day, Sister Mary Subordinary dragged the burnt wooden cross to the edge of the woods. She made it her solemn practice to visit that site every day, rain or shine, and give that cross a good solid kick.

Cast outside the aegis of The Great Church, the order did not founder. Against all expectation, the Sisters of the Joyous Mystery flourished. For nearly ten golden years, they reveled in newfound freedoms. Like many before them, the transgressors discovered that the taste of the forbidden was delicious. Their songs and prayers and celebrations practically reinvented themselves overnight. A renaissance of poetry and liturgical innovation filled their daily journals.

Their transformation from orthodox nuns was so rapid and radical that when they looked back, they could barely recognize the outlines of their originating beliefs.

Their great discovery was that religion is an artform, an act of the imagination. And among holy acts, the greatest by far was to imagine a new God. Theogony was their apple pie, their chocolate soufflé, their lemon tart. They were constant bakers. That is, until the white terror of the plague year. It struck where it hurt most, in the heart of the art, the soul of the makers, the communion of bakers.

By the time the blue boy arrived, the Sisters had taken off their pink habits and flower diadems and resumed the traditional black of orthodoxy. At first, they had donned the black only on the occasion of funerals. But there were so many funerals in such a short space of time that the joy was sucked out of the mystery. Barely begun, the decade-long renaissance ended. They became Sisters of the Sorrowful Mystery. A black shroud was thrown over the sign at the entrance to the convent.

Spread over the dome of midnight, the wheeling cosmos watched Sister Subordinary pray for the strength to throw off the shroud of grief:

"For the sake of the foundling, O teeming heavens, hear my prayer. We are only three, but the Sisters of the Sorrowful Mystery must be reconceived, reanointed, refreshed. Dear stars, I implore you, light a pathway back to the Joyous Mystery."

The notion that the three nuns could once again put on their pink habits and flower diadems seemed an absurdity. But surely, their habits of mind could be changed. That much was possible.

Sister Subordinary did not like to litter the heavens with supplications. But for tonight, she made an exception. After addressing the stars, she silently petitioned her particular Goddess to intervene for the Sisters on the boy's behalf.

Then the freshly prayed and graffitied nun stepped out of the Fairlane Chapel full of doubt and heightened resolve. As she marched with resolute steps into the indigo night, her boots punched blue holes in the snow's crust and her meditations mingled with the songs of the local spheres.

She came to the place where the blackened cross slept in the uneasy woods. Sister gave the cross the blessing of her boot, one last kick. After the snow melt, she would plant wild roses on the spot.

That settled, she marched to the front of the mansion that housed the convent. Reaching up for the rope, she pulled the black drape from the sign that graced the entryway. Tears blurred her vision.

An enchanting hand-painted sign read: The Convent of Immaculate Conceptions—the letters nearly one-foot high. It was her finest creation. There was a sliver of moon and a folksy, but brightly painted Virgin Mary mounted between the points of the cutout crescent. The Virgin, as conceived by Mary Subordinary, was a whirligig affair; a puff of wind from passing putti would set the statue spinning between the horns of an eternal dilemma: Who am I? Who am I? Who am I?

All the woodcut letters but one were painted with cloud-inflected cerulean blues. The final letter s on the word conception was painted silver and enhanced with gold good-conduct stars. The s had acquired a jaunty tilt since last she'd seen the sign.

Sister Subordinary reached out to straighten the disorderly s, but thought better of it. She would keep it at a tilt to please the Monkey God and as a welcome to the creative chaos that was sure to come with the advent of the boy.

Back in the days of spiritual renaissance, it was Sister Subordinary who had added the s to the name of the order. One conception would never suffice. To this day, she remained proud of that innovation.

Standing beneath the sign, Subordinary allowed herself a private little bake, gave herself one brief romp with the mind of her particular deity—the Goddess of Plurality.

Orthodoxy only allowed for the singular: The One—the one and only this, the one and only that. Mary Subordinary tripped back in silent reverie to the moment when she first saw the letter s move across her mind and affix itself to the word conception. Her cup had brimmed full and spilled over in a chorus of sibilance. The letter s became her personal savior— Subordinary, sanctuary, syllabary, sign, sweep, sublunary, sundry, safety, superluminary, soufflé, salutary, salve, soap, savior, soul, sum. Like all saints, her genius lay hidden in the subtle play of her private meditations.

Well, not altogether private.

Earlier, when Sister examined the monkey's blink, one of the seven Wheels that turn the universe, the one that had recently gone into retrograde, swiftly readjusted its wobble by an infinitesimal fraction. One blink carefully observed was all it took.

Now with the scent of Sister's lemony prayer soufflé filling the heavens, The Goddess of Plurality struck the celestial bell. It was time to reset the game—really more of a refresh than a reset. A high-risk cosmic gamble was already in play.

The great dice were rolling.

———

SOMEONE ONCE SAID that God did not play dice with the universe. However, that particular halo-haired scientist was not aware that there were amateur deities abroad, apprentices and suchlike.

He was also unaware that the oft-overlooked Godma was herself an unrepentant gambler. Nor had the scientist ever entertained the possibility that deities were limited by the imaginations of their creations.

The much scoffed at Tinkerbell Paradox states that the relation between creator and her creations is at the very least a two-way street. But there are also multi-laned broad highways traversed by intricate multi-leveled mix-masters, not to mention the dimly lit one-way alleys, or the bright cosmic thoroughfares on the alternate switchbacks of the etherworld.

Countless vehicles passengered with tricksters, hitchhikers, traffickers, and roadway angels are constantly hauling mind-blowing spiritual cargos of every weight and variety—mythos, credos, logos, metaphysical quanta, and holy mathematical theorems. And perhaps the most mind-altering of the many under-examined metaphysical axioms on the etheric shuttle is the proposition that Earth is the hope of heaven.

Stop. Repeat. Earth is the hope of heaven.

Somehow the religious-minded among the sentients on that blue planet had got it exactly backwards. And whose fault was that?

Masters of sublime indifference, the great cosmic Wheels turn in their infinite wisdom, charging their beautiful minds, sounding out one phoneme at a time in the ever-expanding lexicon of holy logos.

What a song. What a sound. What bliss.

What unhelpful nonsense.

If the blue jewel and its riotous life blew out, it would be only that. A beautiful blow out. The Wheels would continue their revolutions speeding along the cosmic thoroughfare, blissfully unaware of anything but their own harmonic convergence. From the eternal point of view, there is always a next time and a time after that.

"*This time. This time. This time,*" whispered one particular Wheel, as it ground its gears and began a great unwind.

It was an inelegant wobble, a retrograde motion, a rogue movement of mind, a reminding of matter. The matter of Earth and its sentient beings. She would take it on *this time.*

*This time* occurred some two-hundred Earth years ago, when Wheel Number Seven, seat of the Godma, made the decision to redeem the jewel in the crown of heaven. No easy matter penetrating that blue diamond.

Her plan was constantly evolving in the creative play of her luminous mind. It was a great show, a showing up, a showing off. Her much revised and unrehearsed production opened simultaneously in multiple theaters, material and Supernal. It was a wide release, premiering before the desired happy ending was scripted and before the hoped-for supporting cast was assembled. Ready to redeem, the headliner double cast herself in two starring roles.

First the Godma bound one aspect of herself to an abandoned pair of wings that she had lovingly preserved in the arc of her sacred covenant. When the Godma stretched the wings from horizon to horizon, rapture consumed her and set her ablaze.

As She cooled, She began incubating baby angels. She created the planet Grace and placed it close to Earth, an etheric playground for her new celestials. She called them her light attractions. First the searchlights, then the show.

*This time.*

*This time.*

*This time.*

She balanced the frothy blue planet Earth on her finger and contemplated its lovely tilt and spin. All at once She experienced a quickening desire to know the Earth intimately, its joys and sorrows. A flock of angels and a mere appearance would not answer. Only one uncertain gateway could give her access to the heart and soul of humankind—incarnation.

Many a deity before her had stumbled on that path. Many a deity forgot their celestial origins and originating purpose when mired in the limitations of embodied life.

Incarnation looked easy when contemplated from afar. Up close and personal, incarnation often proved disastrous—lost nerve and abrupt departures were commonplace. Mother Mary Extraordinary had been teetering on the verge of the commonplace for some time.

———

JUST NOW STANDING WATCH over the sleeping infant, Mary Extraordinary experiences a disconcerting epiphany. Flooded with a succession of startling, albeit strangely familiar images, she sees herself falling through a void illuminated by trillions of stars. She watches herself reach for a wet blue ball, all sparkle and spin—Earth, the crowning jewel of creation.

There is so much longing in that remembered reach, she almost passes out then and there. Placing an unsteady hand on Sister Subordinary's dresser, she props herself up. The ancient prioress is staggered by the realization that her unusual incarnation may not have been a failure after all.

She reaches for the blue baby in the drawer.

———

CERTAIN CELESTIAL WATCHERS take notice that Mary Extraordinary has become a mere wafer when what is needed is a yeasty risen loaf.

"Omnipresence is taxing," the much divided Godma reminds her critics, "Mary Extraordinary will gather to a greatness when the moment is upon her. Be still, spirits."

The Godma is, by self-admission, a profligate showrunner— so many channels, pilots, casting calls, episodes, specials. So many cancellations. So many re-stagings of impossible hope. Her infinite amplifications, her angel experimentations, not to mention her occasional command appearances as this or that Goddess in this or that part of the globe, as well as various minor manifestations on lampshades, sea shells, grottos, clay pots, taco shells, circus tents, tenement walls and the like—with such a tumult of activity, She herself is understandably taxed.

Against the great roar of cosmic ongoingness, what is the sound of one iffy incarnation in Humboldt County? In the vast remove of the Cosmic Wheelhouse, the Seventh Supernal Wheel, seat of the Godma, remains intermittently aware that one of her descents is at risk. But in the realms of bliss, Extraordinary's difficulties are mere pings—pings that have already been answered with a blink.

"A significant blink," the Godma reminds her critics.

It was all to the good that Sister Mary Subordinary secreted away that blink, therewith protecting it from Mother Mary Extraordinary's disbelief. A day will come when the ancient prioress will appreciate the furry white gift that arrived in the box with the baby God.

Oh, blessed and mischievous monkey!

The monkey bangs the celestial drum, jumps on the counterpane, scatters plates and planets alike.

"If you want to shake things up, toss a monkey in the mix," the Godma teases her attending angels.

Despite how theological aestheticians like to privilege monotheism, solemnity, and white beards, the meta-realms are raucous, diverse and riddled with paradox.

And color!

Think of the progression of crayons from the original standard pack of eight to the tiered box of sixty-four, and then onward to the fluorescents, metallics, silver swirls, changeables, pearl-brites and gem-tones. The litany of colors is long.

So is the litany of infants.

———

IT WAS TIME TO ADD one more child to that illustrious roster.

Sister Merry Berry dressed the amenable blue infant in an antique-silk cap and a flowing gown with eighteen green satin-covered buttons and lace cuffs tied with pale green ribbons.

Sister Subordinary took on the office of deaconess of books and hours in the absence of the much-missed Sister Mary Rose. The substitute Sister ardently wished that she could devise a special verse for the initiate, as Mary Rose had always done.

In happier days, all the Sisters would gather in chapel in the event of the arrival of a foundling. Once convened, they would read the foundling's litany from The Book of Holy Infants. Tonight, Sister Subordinary opened the tabernacle, only to remember she had locked the books in the aumbry, a discrete cabinet camouflaged in the wall behind the altar, a caution against the prayer eaters.

She flashed back on the moment, mere days ago, when Cardinal Bunbury had lifted that copy of Mother Mary's book of prayers. The Cardinals had always been beyond suspicion; but why should they be?

It was supposed that the birdmen would have no taste for the Sisters' heterodox prayers. The Inquisitors were all about book burning and censorship. Was it possible that they were the prayer eaters as well?

What a horrific thought.

She set the thought aside to examine later. She was in the chapel after all and must let her mind fill with light. They were initiating a new foundling and inaugurating a new era. Or so they prayed.

After setting out three copies of The Book of Holy Infants, Sister Mary Subordinary rang the chapel bell. She was joined by Mother Mary Extraordinary and Sister Merry Berry, who held the babe in arms.

This is how they prayed:

> The infants come
>> on fresh beds of hay
>> on sterile hospital sheets
>> down dark Calcutta streets
>> on the back seats of taxi-cabs
>> on the beds of Mack trucks
> they come
>> in woodshed and chateau
>> in barn and bordello
>> on the snow belt
>> and bible belt
>> on the green veldt
>> and parched plains of Africa
> they huddle
>> in refugee camps
>> in quarantined villages
> they set sail in Moses-baskets
>> afloat on the Nile
>> launched
>> from Bodrum
>> from the shores of Vietnam
>> from the banks of the Rio Grande

"Sister Merry Berry, you are making quite a racket in that busy brain of yours," Mother Mary Extraordinary expostulated. "Take a deep breath and make an effort to keep pace with us."

The threesome resumed their prayer:

> they come
>> in the Red Cross hospitals
>> under the fire of war and famine
>> in the white ambulance
>> under the red light and siren's song

"Oh, for Lord's sake, what in the world are you nattering on about?" Mother Mary Extraordinary hissed.

"I've just been thinking," Merry Berry demurred, her bright eyes agleam.

"We know you've been thinking. You are a noisy thinker. Out with it," Extraordinary demanded.

"There's no mention of cardboard boxes—in the litany, that is," Merry Berry enjoined amicably.

"Excellent observation, Merry Berry," interjected Sister Subordinary.

"My thoughts, exactly," chorused Extraordinary. "See to the revision, Mary Subordinary. Well, let's have it."

"In the first verse, between 'sterile hospital sheets' and 'down dark Calcutta streets' we can wedge 'in cardboard boxes' and the verse still scans nicely."

"Genius," Berry chirped.

That settled, the Sisters brought *The Litany of Infants* to its bold finish:

> they come
>> at the ocean's lip
>> in the valley's cradle
>> let them come
>>> with halo hair
>>> and soft eyes shining

Divine Mother, Sweet Protectoress
      shelter each foundling
      in the house of your infinite kindness
      in the womb of your joyous mystery
   Holy Mary, Mother of God
         teach us thy trade.

*Teach us thy trade.* Pause and consider what trade that might be, what Joyous Mystery played in the minds of the prayer-makers.

The Sisters were devotees of the oldest profession in the world—Godmothering. Now there was a deity in the house. They would be put to the test.

It had been a good long while since the Sisters of Immaculate Conceptions had made a revision in the order's sacred texts. The three surviving nuns said their God-blesses with lighter hearts that night in the year of unexpected bounty, grace, and gifts in a cardboard box.

# CONRAD EPPLER

THE BOY WAS GIVEN the unlikely name Conrad Eppler. The name was inscribed with loving flourishes in The Book of Holy Infants, the latest entry in the boys' column. Sister Subordinary had favored a Hindu name for the beautiful blue boy, but could hardly deny the name clearly marked on the tag that dangled from his anklet of bells: Conrad Eppler.

Still, it was such a plain name for such a resplendent boy. She longed to name him Pushpaka, after the Chariot of the Gods in the *Ramayana*.

Wasn't the baby exactly like that legendary bejeweled chariot, a veritable paradise compressed into one vehicle, a conveyance of rapture, a fountain of joy juice and abundant life, mirrored in all those glistening pearl-like drools?

The redoubtable Mother Mary Extraordinary had blanched at Mary Subordinary's frivolous suggestion and given Sister one of her ineluctable frowns, a frown of such ferocity that it could stop a room cold or drive a Cardinal out. Her thin lips seemed to bend all the way to her jaw line, giving the effect of a kabuki mask. So the boy was named Conrad Eppler, because the frown stopped any further discussion.

Pushpaka, indeed.

———

WHEN CONRAD TURNED FIVE, Sister Merry Berry pointed out that it was just as well that he hadn't been given a Hindu name, because he was no longer blue.

"Hasn't anyone, excepting myself, noticed?" Merry Berry chirped. "Conrad looks more like an Earth boy these days and less like a fallen deity."

She was secretly pleased to see Conrad take on a Columbian coffee-bean color, favoring her. Although in truth, she was more of a dark-roast café noir. Although when Conrad drew pictures of Sister Merry Berry, he liked to color her blue because she reminded him of a bowl full of blue berries.

On any given day, she and Conrad could be seen racing about the convent on their bicycles. Indoors, most of the time. Special protections had to be in place when Conrad ventured out, always in the company of one of the Sisters with the other stationed as a lookout, prepared to ring a warning bell should a Cardinal be spotted in the woods.

Outdoors, Conrad was never allowed to venture beyond the first line of trees and was always kept in view of a watcher. Entering the forest was forbidden. Always a mistake—might as well put a neon, roadside-attraction sign blinking over what has been expressly forbidden.

The convent itself was originally constructed by an extravagant railroad magnate, and thus enjoyed a prosperity ofluxe appointments. The ballroom and huntroom, emptied of furniture, became an enchanted race course. Even Mother Mary Extraordinary permitted herself frequent smiles at the sight of the two cyclists racing about under the Waterford crystal chandeliers.

Sister Merry Berry had modified her black habit to accommodate the demands of bicycling. Over time, she modified it to such an extent that she barely looked like a religious at all. She'd cut her skirts short, and then shorter, in the years of fetching formula to and from the 7-Eleven.

On a recent foray, she found herself admiring a floppy green, yellow, and red beret worn by the checkout clerk. She didn't realize that the young man had styled himself after Bob Marley; she only noted that his long dreadlocks were so much like her own tight aubergine curls.

"Wouldn't it be lovely," she mused, studying the clerk's beret, "to shuck the veil and let my hair fly free under such a spectacular ornament?"

In the next few days, her happy fingers crocheted a near-exact copy of the multi-colored floppy hat. Then Sister Merry Berry put away the wimple and veil and substituted her homemade beret, thinking she'd draw less comment. She was mistaken in that supposition.

Now she looked rather like a Rastafarian crossed with a plump, middle-aged schoolgirl. Her outfit took another remarkable turn when she ditched her black stockings and black lace-up boots for crew socks and a pair of florescent orange running shoes rummaged from a half-price bin.

Sister Merry Berry was beginning to look on the outside like the person she wanted to be on the inside, so her very appearance became a prayer for renewal. In fact, she thought of herself as a prayer-in-progress.

For weeks on end, she would mistake Conrad's happiness for her own. Then in the odd moment, Merry Berry would be shaken by an unspeakable loneliness. Until one day she realized that it was herself that she missed. Sometimes she worried that no creative dressing up would ever dress the wound that betrayed her joy.

With the deaths of her besties, the Sisters Mary Tuee and Sister Mary Josephus, it seemed she had lost some irreplaceable part of herself. But in truth, the piece had gone missing long before she entered the convent.

For better or worse, in her valiant and sometimes desperate endeavor to hold together the remnants of a girlhood barely recalled, she frequently helped herself to the excellent collection of vintage wines stored in the cellar beneath the convent. Her boosters, she fondly called the bottles, as if they were a following, forever clicking the "like" button on her page.

Not that there was a page or even a computer on the grounds. There was not. The three nuns mostly communicated by letter, when they communicated with the outside world at all, which happened so seldom it bordered on never. There were no screens in the convent. Not a cell phone, nor a Kindle, nor a Nook. No Netflix. No cable. No Apple TVs.

There was one landline telephone in the library, but it never rang. Well, almost never. They were a cloistered order, by choice and habit.

One piece of technology did make its way into Conrad's hands. For his birthday, the year Conrad turned six, he was given a walkie-talkie, also known as a handheld transceiver. This particular antique technology was developed during the Second World War.

The talkie aspect was more by way of optimism on the part of Sister Merry Berry. At six he still hadn't uttered a single word. Merry Berry would have been shocked to know that Conrad and the monkey frequently chattered mind to mind, and that one day it would be the monkey who would teach Conrad how to use the transceiver.

This afternoon, Sister Merry Berry was studying Conrad as he ran ahead of her down a garden path. Something was not right. In broad daylight, there was no denying that the boy had begun to fade again. She recalled how shade by shade the infant Conrad had lost his blue tint and lovely black curls. First, he had turned a luscious dark brown. And that was all right.

Now approaching age seven, he was the color of quartz-crystal beach sand, with sandy-colored hair. Sister Subordinary thought him most beautiful when he was blue. Merry Berry only wished he would stop losing color. Mother Mary Extraordinary had begun to call him her little Holy Ghost.

When Conrad stepped out on the marble decking one evening in the last days of his sixth year, he saw what he thought was an enormous white flower floating on the surface of the spring-fed pool. He was not allowed out beyond the terrace by himself, so he did not linger by the stairway that led down to the pool. But a few days later, curiosity overcame obedience and drew him back to the mysterious flower. This time the flower was moving across the pool. It had lost its circular shape and had more of the appearance of what it actually was: long white hair. And then, with a splash, there was Mother Mary Extraordinary climbing out of the water dripping diamonds, and he was struck for the first time with her otherworldly beauty.

"Oh, it's the little Holy Ghost. Come here," she invited, lowering herself back into the pool.

Conrad scrambled down the stairs and stood at the edge of the water."

"Now jump!"

He did.

This boy did not hold back. And so that very night he learned to swim in the spring-fed quarry pool. Every night thereafter, the two would take an evening swim. Among Mother

Mary Extraordinary's exceptional powers was an ability to absorb oxygen from water. Much to his delight, Conrad discovered that, like Mother Mary, he too could stay almost forever beneath the surface. Air was not their necessary atmosphere.

The Sisters created a spacious sun-drenched room for Conrad on the east side of the convent. This yellow room was the best room in the mansion. A wall of mullioned doors—four sets—opened onto the terrace, with its stairway down to the pool and the wide lawn with the laughing sundial.

Conrad kept a telescope on the terrace, where he studied the movements of the planets and stars. The telescope was his most prized possession, a vintage beauty on a tripod that Sister Merry Berry had found at Giltane's Antique Shoppe.

Star gazing was Conrad's particular enthusiasm. Where did I come from? That was the constant question he silently asked the sky, searching for signs of origins. The stars twinkled with tantalizing music, but it was the mysterious moon that seemed to be keeping secrets from him.

There was a comfy four-poster bed that Conrad refashioned into a sailing ship, with sheets raised to the masthead. He was indulged, never scolded, merely exclaimed over when he did something odd, like cut up his bedding to make sails for his ship. He did not ever imagine sailing on an ocean. Instead, he would throw open the four sets of double doors at night, and with a friendly breeze riffling the sheets, he'd imagine sailing to the moon. Wherever he went, in his imagination or in fact, the monkey went with him.

With one exception.

The monkey was not fond of water, so Conrad never took his furry friend swimming in the quarry pool. On those occasions, they would go their separate ways.

Mostly though, the two were inseparable. Conrad wore the monkey like a back pack, with the Velcro paws fastened at his neck. Like Conrad, the monkey was a seasoned sky-sailor, forever navigating imaginary oceans of air. He was Conrad's constant companion on the sailing ship.

So Conrad named his co-pilot Skipper.

———

SCHOOLED VARIOUSLY BY EACH of the three nuns, Conrad spent his first six years letting in without letting on how much he absorbed. He poured over his secret collection of comic books, memorized everything that was read out loud to him, copied illustrations and lettering. He had an eye for details. He was enchanted by the variety of typefaces.

When Sister Subordinary read the Bible to him, he wondered what font God used when he created the first word. When Conrad was on the verge of speech, he started to see his own thoughts in Courier.

Mary Extraordinary superintended his spiritual powers. She spoke in Times New Roman. For the most part, her lessons occurred underwater and entailed out-of-body travels. What she could not guess was how her teachings were cross hatched with Merry Berry's more whimsical contributions. Just yesterday, Conrad saw a comic-book bubble form above Mother's head and the word: "Indeed!"

Conrad had Sister Merry Berry to thank for his library of comic books. Merry Berry had appointed herself protector and curator of Conrad's normal boyhood. To that end, she read to him from Tom Sawyer and Huckleberry Finn. The boy sometimes wished he had a Huck Finn to teach him how to swear and spit, or build a river raft.

It was a guilty wish. Sister Merry Berry was the best of companions. They would sit under one of the pear trees with a picnic basket full of contraband goodies and books. Merry Berry gave him brightly colored candies and a dazzling assortment of comic books from a stash that she traded with the clerk at the 7-Eleven. The boy's collection included pristine archival treasures, stored in sealed plastic covers.

"Someday, Conrad," she whispered, "these will be worth a fortune! Keep them well hidden. You never know when the Magistere—" Merry Berry trailed off.

Sister Merry Berry always shopped as if she were on a treasure hunt. She could never pass by a yard sale or sidewalk sale—or the forlorn antique store, with its peeling sign and antique owner, Mr. Giltane. She found Conrad's walkie-talkie in Giltane's musty shop. She bought the boy sneakers, cowboy boots, and bubblegum with Pokémon cards. But it was the comic books that were a life-altering bonanza for a boy raised on sacred texts.

Each nun was convinced that she alone knew what was best for their beloved foundling.

Sister Subordinary saw to Conrad's grounding in the classics: Bible, Quran—there was a lovely passage in the Quran where Jesus makes a bird out of a lump of clay that was a particular favorite of Conrad's—the Bhagavad Gita, and the cherished Ramayana, plus some Euclid, Lucretius, Galileo, Hesiod, and Chaucer. It was an inextricable mix of myth, theology, astronomy and geometry. The Sisters' library also included a smattering of art folios.

During the historic persecution, the Magistere had marched off with much of their valuable cache of paintings, including all the Da Vinci folios and had left them with one measly oil sketch of Raphael's *The Annunciation*. The boy perfected his drawing skills copying that oil sketch. He once shocked Sister Subordinary with a remarkable color-pencil copy in which he "improved" upon the original. He'd added in a blue rocket and a pair of blue angels dressed in Indian dhotis. The charming boy could also write several alphabets: Greek, Sanskrit, Arabic.

His nursery courses were nothing if not eclectic. Not much of a scientist, Mary Subordinary might have been surprised at how Lucretius' *De Rerum Natura* anticipated modern physics. And Merry Berry would have been equally surprised at how closely the comic book world reflected the classic one, in a funhouse mirror sort of way.

"Nothing wrong with fun," Merry Berry would have enjoined, had she been willing to admit to the comic books.

Sister Subordinary made a special point of filling Conrad's head with tantalizing Hindu tales. After all, he was once a blue baby, and blue was the privileged color of divinities in the crowded Hindu pantheon. However, Sister's favorite character in the ancient *Ramayana* was neither divine nor blue nor

Hindu. The rebel Guha, the diminutive wild man in the forest who worshipped trees, held pride of place for the polytheistic nun.

From early childhood, Conrad demonstrated his enthusiasm for Guha's tale by scrambling over to the book shelf and reaching for the *Ramayana*. He would set the book on Sister's lap and flip through the pages until he came to the black and white drawing of Guha. He loved to hear how the Brahmin priests brought Shiva to the forest and demanded that Guha worship the statue. For Guha, the worship of an idol was an insult to the forest and all the world of living things. Logging onto the scene four-thousand years ago, Guha was the first Earth-first guru, a hippie among the ancients, the aboriginal iconoclast.

"Every day, rain or shine, Guha would give that statue a good kick—," Sister paused midsentence.

Conrad was Mary Subordinary's carefully watched clock. In the pause she would turn her gaze on Conrad, marveling because she could hear him finish the sentence in her mind's ear, word perfect.

*Even in the thunderstorms*, Conrad picked up the line. *Even when the statue was surrounded by wolves*, Conrad silently enthused and then stopped, just as she had done.

Sister Subordinary's ability to hear the inner voices of her beloveds and explore their hidden thoughts was her primary Mary power. Much to her credit, she rarely snooped. Conrad's silent reading voice was her favorite listen and altogether made up for the fact that he never spoke out loud.

Sister Subordinary picked up her cue and continued right where Conrad left off: "No matter the obstacle, Guha would give that statue of Shiva a good solid kick."

When Sister read to Conrad, her finger moved beneath the line of text. Conrad watched the sliver of a moon at the base of her fingernail as it skimmed along the passage. When she stopped reading and his inner voice picked up the storyline, that tiny moon would follow the text at his speed. When he stopped, the moon stopped. The pauses were clues dropped in a moonlit forest leading him deeper into literacy.

Conrad loved the part when Guha died and Yama came for Guha's soul, how Shiva refused the God of Death his prize. Moreover, and much to Yama's ire, Shiva restored the undeserving, disrespectful Guha back to life. At Shiva's bidding, the great white bull, Nandin, lifted Guha in his soft, grass-scented mouth and set Guha back down on Earth.

Yama swelled with indignation. Why was he, the Death Lord, to be deprived of Guha's soul? The wind began to blow through Yama's black hair and Shiva told the Death Lord that the wild man, Guha, was exceptionally beloved because he, among all worshipers, was the most constant in his practice.

Sister Subordinary loved to replay the memory of the first time Conrad gave her a goodnight kick, how the waterfall of Conrad's giggles splashed in her mind. She understood that her young charge had grasped a difficult paradox. She could not help but wonder if, in that moment of comprehension, Conrad was enlightened. And she, by dint of happy circumstance, was the chosen witness anointed in the splash of his laughter, the kick of his bare foot.

Later in chapel, Sister Subordinary checked her pride and tempered her expectations of the resident bodhisattva-in-progress. She knew full well that enlightenment itself is impermanent, possibly even over-rated. The trick is to string together a life of miniature enlightenments, less like the lonely flash of a single megawatt bulb and more like a string of holiday twinkle lights.

The stringing is the practice. And while practice makes perfect, perfection is volatile in this world of fluctuating realities. Fuses blow. Strings break.

Starting over is a necessary virtue.

———

FOR THE MOST PART, Skipper and Conrad got on famously, but as Conrad neared the threshold of his seventh year, the monkey became something of a problem. Not a day passed without the monkey urging the boy to explore the forbidden forest.

Conrad was well aware that, should he break promise with his caretakers and go venturing out of bounds, he could hardly blame a stuffed monkey.

*Stop being such a pest,* Conrad mindtalked.

*The woods are lovely, dark, and deep,* the monkey teased.

*That's just a silly old poem. Now hush,* Conrad reproved.

The marvelous toy refused to be bossed. The monkey kept chattering, messing with Conrad's beautiful mind. Clearly the relentless monkey longed for nothing so much as to go into those dark, deep, and dangerous woods.

The boy hated denying the monkey and was secretly sympathetic. He himself had begun to feel confined by the good intentions of his minders.

After nearly a year of resisting the monkey's nudge toward the wild, Conrad was beginning to wear down. Night time found Conrad dreaming of the forest's ancient evergreens. Day time found Conrad studying the mysterious woods through his telescope.

Then one rainy day it happened—a gap opened. The world paused, and Independence Day arrived with its trail of inevitabilities. Conrad's bicycle tire went flat. His ever-ready playmate, Sister Merry Berry, was laid up with a twisted ankle. Yesterday, she'd fallen, walking back from a tippling session in the Fairlane Chapel.

Lately, there'd been an awful lot of tippling and praying. And more worrisome, there were hushed conversations that stopped when Conrad approached. Everyone was occupied and preoccupied.

And last night, when he stepped outside to take his swim, Mother Mary Extraordinary was not in the pool. He jumped in and swam to their secret underwater chamber.

Not there.

Sister Subordinary toweled him dry and told him Mother Mary didn't feel well. The boy could not recall a single day when the ancient prioress was not up and about. Conrad gave Sister Subordinary a close look and watched her edit her thoughts. Then Sister tucked him in bed with an exceedingly brief story and a hasty kiss.

Only the monkey was alert on the morrow, when the rainy morning found the boy at loose ends. The monkey understood that loose ends were the necessary prelude to the sweet shift of a paradigm.

The shifty morning began inauspiciously. The sun winked on the walls of the yellow room. Conrad slipped Skipper onto his back. Then the boy fastened the Velcro paws and headed for the kitchen.

*Let's go exploring,* Skipper suggested.

*What about the cellar?* Conrad offered.

After all, the cellar was not out of doors. It was not expressly forbidden.

The hidden door to the wine cellar had been built into the back wall of the kitchen pantry during prohibition, when the railway magnate who commissioned the mansion needed a secret place to hide his illegal booze. The kitchen was conveniently located right next to Conrad's bedroom. Originally, Conrad's elegant digs had been one of several dining rooms, so at one time the juxtaposition of the rooms had made sense—dining room to kitchen to pantry. The repurposing of the dining room as Conrad's bedroom was a happy evolution for the boy. He often woke to the scent of freshly baked muffins.

Not this morning.

This morning the kitchen was still asleep.

Odd.

The boy and his monkey traveled unseen from bedroom to kitchen to pantry. He'd been in the cellar several times before, always in the company of one Sister or the other.

Never alone.

Remarkably, Skipper seemed mollified by Conrad's decision. The pestering about going into the woods stopped; the monkey climbed down from the jungle gym that he had so rudely erected in Conrad's brain and behaved himself for a change. The boy gave his friend an appreciative pat.

Conrad opened the cellar door, reached up and felt around in the semi-dark for the string that switched on the stairwell light. Almost immediately, he felt the thrill of crossing a threshold into an unknown. Something was different today. Down the creaky staircase, his hand skimmed the familiar roughcast wall; his nostrils tingled with the dank, tangy cellar musk.

Then familiarity began to wink out.

Bright before him was something he'd never noticed before—a gilded ormolu music box. Conrad took it down from the dusty shelf and lifted the lid. Spotting a crank on the side, Conrad began to turn it. The hypnotic inner workings moved, and the loveliest little tune tinkled in Conrad's ear. He was on the verge of proclaiming his joy out loud when he felt a hand slip over his mouth.

His heart stopped.

It was a small hand. A slightly furry hand. Turning his head to see over his shoulder, Conrad met the gaze of the white monkey, who was slowly shaking his head from side to side.

*NO*, the monkey mind talked, one finger lifted in warning.

The boy was so startled that he blinked several times. Finding his eyelids surprisingly wet, the happiest little tear spilled down his cheek. He knew it. He'd always known it. The monkey was real.

If the Gods had been watching just then, they would have seen an astonishing thing: love opened a secret chamber in the boy's heart. The monkey's eyes softened. He pressed one small paw against Conrad's chest, and the thrum of the boy's rapid heartbeat created a charged current. The monkey bowed his head. Tentatively at first, Conrad reached out and ran his fingers through the warm fur. Then, as if in answer to a fervent wish long denied, the small boy and the monkey explored each other's faces with their hands.

The boy floated on cloud nine, but the monkey was keen on exploring every curve and corner of Conrad's soul. The search was long and deep.

*Only mindtalk*, the white monkey tapped on Conrad's consciousness.

Then the monkey jumped from Conrad's arms and picked up the suspect music box and examined its inner workings. He quickly discovered the sound-activated recording device.

Somewhere, someone was waiting. Waiting and listening.

The song in the box was not one that either boy or monkey recognized. The tune itself was innocent enough. The Sisters would have known the childish words: *All around the mulberry bush, the monkey chased the weasel*. It did not end well for the monkey.

*I want to talk out loud.* Conrad only just realized this.

*Not yet. Tonight. Surprise Sister Subordinary.*

Skipper climbed back onto Conrad's shoulders and they continued their exploration in silence.

How warm the monkey's fur!

How noisy this new quiet!

The boy could barely keep himself from constantly reaching up to assure himself that there really was a small monkey riding on his back. Skipper's chin rested on Conrad's head, his paws folded at Conrad's collar bone. And the flick, flick of a monkey tail grazed the boy's backside.

Conrad lifted one of the monkey's paws to his nose and inhaled deeply. Wet grass, woodland oak, white musk, evergreen fir. The boy thrilled to a sudden flashback: he is being held in strong furry arms, high in a canopy of trees, snow falling—then without warning, the monkey plunges through the flurries.

The boy stumbled. The monkey jumped to the ground and brushed the dirt off Conrad's knees. Then he urged Conrad on deeper into the wine cellar, farther than the boy had ever been before. Soon they arrived at another door, a secret door. It was unlocked. The twosome pushed through and found themselves at the entrance of a dark underground tunnel.

*Now what, Skip?*

*Flashlight,* the monkey answered.

*Good plan.*

Tomorrow they would come back with a flashlight, and Conrad's world would be turned inside out.

———

UPON REGAINING THE SURFACE, Conrad paused in the stairwell with his hand on the cellar doorknob. A thrumming sensation let Conrad know that Skipper had reconfigured and was once again simply a stuffed monkey. Conrad reached for the string and turned out the light.

Emerging into the bright green kitchen, Conrad looked as guilty as any seven-year-old caught with his hand in the proverbial cookie jar.

"And what were you doing in the pantry?" The large wooden spoon in Sister Subordinary's hand stopped stirring the garden vegetable broth.

Conrad answered with a shrug, as if to say "nothing," which, of course, he did not say because he still hadn't spoken a single word out loud. Although Sister Subordinary was distracted by her steaming vegetables and much else besides, she did manage to send the boy a quick penetrating glance.

In the universal language of childhood, she understood that the shrug was meant to say "nothing" and she considered, for the first time, the possibility that Conrad had told a lie. If he had, he had also put up an impenetrable wall around his thoughts. Sister Subordinary immediately dismissed that uncomfortable notion, and Conrad deftly scrambled out of the way of further examination.

The boy had much to think over. As did Mary Subordinary.

———

WAS IT ONLY YESTERDAY that Mother Mary Extraordinary had rung for Sister Mary Subordinary? It seemed like a week had gone missing since the prioress asked Sister to fetch the book. That book. The one that bore the curious title, *What the Goat Girl Dreamed at the Holiday Inn*.

The memory of Cardinal Bunbury's hand on the copy had whisked across Subordinary's mind, but she whisked it right back out again. Somehow Sister Subordinary had never quite gotten around to mentioning the theft. It was not the original, only a copy. Why cause a stir?

As a caution, Mary Subordinary kept the original *Goat Girl* anthology locked in the aumbry, so when Mother made her request there was no immediate cause for alarm. Still, it was an odd moment. Mother Mary never called for the *Goat Girl*.

Until yesterday.

The unquiet had tip-toed into the chapel at morning meditations. Mother Mary Extraordinary was silently running the lines of poetry, when she noticed some words had gone missing. This had happened before. Sometimes whole lines would evaporate from memory. She knew how to repair the occasional cognitive glitch. She started over. A stanza went missing.

What in the world? She supposed she was finally feeling the effects of her great age. Her memory needed a refresher. She rang for Sister Subordinary.

Sister had been happy to fetch the gold-leafed book in its pink leather case, ribbons streaming from the bindings. It really was a lovely artifact.

A smiling Mother Mary slid the book from its casing, petting it with long boney fingers. Then she opened it and found herself rapidly turning pages, eyes ablaze.

The pages were blank.

Three additional copies, dutifully replicated by the circumspect Sister Subordinary as a failsafe, were immediately fetched from the aumbry. The handmade paper in each breviary was virgin white.

Terror struck two hearts.

The prayer eaters were back. Their tastes had always been eclectic; they dined on originality. No medieval texts for these spiritual vampires.

In the plague year, the predators feasted on the innovative scripts for Holy Mass that each Sister had composed so lovingly in her private theological bakery. When the order was in the flush of creative resurgence, Sister Mary Rose redesigned the calendar of Holy Days. December twenty-five was renamed Godchild Day and all infants were heralded as comings. In addition, each Sister was given a personal feast day and her self-penned prayer book was brought out to celebrate her Mass on her day, her way.

These individualized scripts were testaments to dazzling leaps of faith, metaphysical high jumps, theological caprice. Each Sister divined a Missal that mirrored the very shape and sense of her soul. Meticulously decorated transubstantiated cookies and freshly sliced heavenly loaves were served up at their communion rail. Not to mention the divinity wines. Ecstasy was commonplace for the Joyous Mystery Sisters in their brief renaissance.

Back in those glory days, Mother Mary Extraordinary was the conduit—all the announcing angels came through the gate of her soul. Each Sister waited in the corridor of angels to be visited by a personal muse, to be amused, bemused and then in turn, to create the spiritual amusements, also known as Holy Mass. Flush with inspiration, the books almost composed themselves.

Only two Sisters remained barren of book and so were spared the ravages of the prayer eaters. Sister Merry Berry still awaited her announcing angel, so she never conceived a personal Missal, and by this point she no longer minded being overlooked by the spiritual muses. Nor had Sister Subordinary conceived a Missal. There were too many contenders for her praises and for places in her personal pantheon. There were also times when, like Guha, she wanted to give the whole lot a good solid kick.

Mother Mary's book was singular—more marveled over than understood—and never ritualized as a Holy Mass. It had odd angles to it, much like its maker. And yet when she opened her book and in prayerful meditation perused the queer poetry, the nuns who knelt beside her in chapel could taste the very text on their tongues. And the word was made God, savored and swallowed. Holy communion happened with no bread at all.

When the first wave of Missals went blank, and death stalked the convent, it was a matter of some amazement that Mother's book remained inviolate. It was thought to be a testament to her personal power.

And now this.

Neither woman said the words "prayer eater" out loud. Sister Subordinary, who did not have a suspicious bone in her body, for the second time in her life considered the electrifying possibility that the ancient enemy was abroad and robed in red feathers. Could it really be that the Cardinals who had once ruled their lives and breviaries were not only oppressors, but murderers as well?

The timer went ding.

Sister Subordinary lifted a fresh loaf from the oven, set it aside to cool. Even in the kitchen, where the counter tops were altars and her cookery a Holy Mass, the unthinkable kept a constant knocking at the gate of her well-defended mind. She picked up a carrot and set to chopping it with unusual vigor. Putting her knife down, she was forced to consider a disheartening paradox—that the very mental strengths of which she was so inordinately proud might have betrayed her.

Her ability to tuck discordant information into neat piles and set aside judgment had left them vulnerable. How could she hope to fight an invisible enemy? With so many Gods crowding the heavens and religious zealots crowding the field, wasn't it best to let them sort themselves?

Yet, something evil was at large. And close by.

"Soup," she said to herself. "I know it's perfectly pathetic, but it's all I have," she told the pepper grinder.

Too bad she did not inhabit a world in which all could be cured with a nice warm bowl of vegetable soup. Still she must carry a bowl to Mother Mary, coax her to eat a spoonful or two. Then circle back and tend Conrad.

Mother Mary had survived the first night. None of the other Sisters had seen morning light once their pages had gone blank. Mary Extraordinary's deeper resources would save her.

That and soup.

———

BASKING IN THE AFTERGLOW of their underground adventure, Conrad and his monkey were happily bivouacked in a tent of blankets, unaware of the drama taking upstairs and down the hall.

Whenever Conrad wanted to give himself a good think, he liked to set himself up in bed with a flashlight and peruse his comic book collection. He found that when he shifted his focus to something other than his current dilemma, answers often popped up in unexpected places. He was especially intrigued by the way hidden solutions stepped out unannounced from the panels in his comic books.

Conrad looked longingly at his stuffed toy, willing Skipper to take an interest in the comic books. If only the monkey would come back to life, everything would be a perfect. Conrad was learning an unwelcome lesson; the monkey had a mind of his own. With a resigned sigh, Conrad let go as he was taught and offered up his wishes.

Mother Mary Extraordinary called this practice: "holding the empty cup."

With his mind cleared of I-wants, Conrad completely gave himself over to the comic book story of *Epic, The Etherworld Time Traveler*. Something looked different on the pages tonight. It had to do with the markings in the white balloons.

With a little gasp and happy shock, Conrad discovered that the words made sounds. His eyes skimmed the letters. Oh, the noise:

*Pow! Thwack!*

*Step aside, you demon.*

Conrad laughed out loud, as if he just learned a magic trick. The sound of his own laughter startled him. Change was afoot and quickening its step.

In the past, when he paged through a book that Sister Subordinary had read to him, *her voice* always accompanied the words. Because he knew those texts by heart, he never realized that he had long since learned to read. Now as he gleaned the words in the comic clouds, he began to hear the play of his own youthful voice.

An elation of speech brimmed, ready to spill. Conrad looked to Skipper.

*Not yet,* the monkey counseled.

Sister Subordinary rang the dinner bell.

The boy was miles away, lost in the marvels of his own mind. This was Conrad's hook up day. Over one billion synaptic connections were clicking away, processing and remapping at a staggering pace. A florescence of proteins winked in rapid sequences lighting up a tracery of multi-colored neural pathways. What a lightshow!

Sister rang the bell again. Louder, this time.

Vaguely aware of the distant bell, Conrad remained captive of the clamor of colors, sounds, and sense on the pages before him. All at once, the characters began to move. Epic turned and caught Conrad's unbelieving eye.

It was too much.

Conrad closed the book. When he opened it again, the formatting had changed. Now Epic took up two vertical panels and stood stock still behind a drawing of a familiar set of mullioned windows. Conrad peeked out from his tent.

Coast was clear. No one stood looking in at his window.

At a third insistent ring, the boy reluctantly put down his remarkable book. Then Conrad turned off his flashlight, ducked out of the tent and scrambled into the kitchen, Skipper in tow. He didn't notice the trouble Sister Subordinary wore on her brow as she served him a bowl of ordinary, garden-vegetable soup.

Conrad mindtalked his thank you and asked if she would please bring a bowl for Skipper. The accommodating nun placed a small bowl of veggies in front of the toy. Immediately Conrad set to generating a powerful wish. If only the scent of chopped carrots would bring his beloved monkey back to—.

Skipper interrupted Conrad's wish with a command. *Time to take your voice out of hiding.*

"What was that, Conrad?" a distracted Sister Subordinary inquired, misidentifying the source of the mindtalk.

Still silent, Conrad shrugged a dismissive "nothing" in response.

In truth, he was ambivalent about speaking out loud. He wished Skipper had let him try out his voice when they were alone in the cellar, or later, in the tent. Conrad was worried that once he spoke, he might belong less to himself and more to everyone else.

It wasn't until after supper, when Sister was settling Conrad into his covers that his words first met the common air.

Sister Merry Berry, who had skipped supper, was now deep in her cups. She tottered into Conrad's room on her twisted ankle. A birthday gift tied up in a pretty ribbon dangled from her hand.

"Oh, Bless me, Conrad. I forgot your birthday," Subordinary was abashed. No foundling-day cake. No candles. No gift.

Conrad didn't mind. Merry Berry always gave him the best presents. He quickly unwrapped seven plastic dwarves.

"I'm seven years old," Conrad smiled.

At the sound of Conrad's voice Merry Berry fell backwards, landing safely in an over-stuffed reading chair. Sister Mary Subordinary was so startled that for the second time in her life, her soul loosened itself and leapt into the air. Conrad laughed to see Sister scramble after her runaway soul. He cheered when she caught it, and clapped when she pressed it back firmly into her chest.

"This is the best birthday ever!" The joyful boy danced on his bed.

Conrad missed seeing the tear Sister Subordinary quickly wiped from her cheek when he crawled back under his covers and said: "Tell the one I like best, the one where you found me in the cardboard box on the porch steps."

Each time Conrad Eppler's small voice choired the room, the world seemed to topple over. Blue lights careened on the walls. A heightened consciousness teased shadows out of their corners. When the room settled, Sister arranged herself on the edge of Conrad's bed and repeated the story she had been telling him for nearly seven years.

It went like this.

"Godzillions of years ago," she began.

"Before the dinosaurs," Conrad interjected.

"Yes, way before then, when it was all just one great big Cosmic Belly. Eternity lay suspended in air like an ocean of water that never fell."

Images of the sleeping blue infant unfolded in her memory. This story was the one she whispered over his rising and falling breath as he slept in her drawer on that very first night, wrapped in the arms of the monkey. Sister Mary Subordinary stifled a sob and continued.

"Everything was absolutely still and absolutely silent. The Buddha sat with his great pink tongue extended, and not one drop fell from the ocean of eternity. No matter, Buddha had a diamond mind that could stop the rush of time. So he waited without waiting and defeated thirst and hunger. Life in the Buddha Belly had been suspended in an everlast of perfection ever since the Wheels defeated Chaos. Then one day, a sound interrupted the solitude and Chaos broke out of captivity."

Sister risked a glance at the toy monkey. And though his glass eyes gave away nothing, she felt rumbled.

"On this day, I mean on *that* day," she corrected herself, "the Cosmic Belly growled and became aware of its own hunger. After Godbillions of years of a never-changing perfect order, even the angels admitted they were bored. It was time to turn the Wheels. So amongst themselves, the Angels and the Belly and the Wheels agreed to let one planet in the Milky Way breed and be free and show them the way."

"And the planet called itself Earth. To rhyme with birth," the boy chimed in.

"Yes, it did." Mary Subordinary was elated, his words tumbling over hers, affirming what her heart had guessed. He had soaked up every pause, every nuance. There is nothing so gratifying to a teacher as the moment when a student claims his birthright. Conrad was a boy made of stories and would be ever after a seeker of stories. And the stories, in turn, would companion him and lead him home.

"Now say the part where you found me on the steps in the cardboard box."

"Well, that is skipping ahead quite a bit, but it is getting late. So, yes, there you were in a cardboard box."

"Skipper was in the box too."

"Oh, so the monkey has a name?"

She was being careful, covering her excitement, acting as if nothing unusual was taking place. Of course, she was afraid. He might speak just this once and then go silent for another seven years.

"Yes," Conrad affirmed in his perfect little boy voice, "Skipper, the Gospel Monkey. Go on with the story. Skipper likes it too."

She wanted to stop him and inquire: what gospel? But thought better of it and continued the story.

"I picked you up, and there was the universe dancing on your tongue, and a drool suspended from your chin considering whether or not to fall. Then you said—," she stopped and waited.

Conrad did not disappoint.

"Earth is the best place for love."

The birthday boy smiled. Sister Merry Berry hiccoughed. They had forgotten she was in the room. The sentence danced in the air with the hiccough.

"There. That proves it," Sister Merry Berry almost concluded before she interrupted herself, "only we don't know what it proves, do we?"

Then, oh so innocently, Conrad tugged on Sister Mary Subordinary's veil and said, "Skipper says you left something out."

That stopped her breath. Now they were on dangerous ground. She dared not look in the direction of Skipper. Each Mary had a power unique unto herself. So she took a deep breath, and in her mind she addressed the monkey. This is what she said:

"Hanuman, behave yourself."

She supposed that she had known right from the get go— from that first blink—that it was Lord Hanuman, best of monkeys, protector of free thinkers, poets and prayer-makers.

The collision of diverse deities in her personal pantheon had a long history. Her early, more orthodox Christian beliefs had been troubled and rumbled by other Gods since girlhood. She remembered the day she wished her adoptive mother, "Happy Ishtar." Her devout Irish-Catholic mother worried that her daughter had suddenly developed a singular lisp, especially when the wee Mary Dolan insisted that the colored eggs in her basket were Ishtar eggs.

That slip of tongue had been Mary Subordinary's first inkling that she might be some sort of entrance ramp on the vast spiritual superhighway, where free-wheeling Gods let themselves onto the Earth plane. There had been numerous visitors over the years. Now Lord Hanuman.

It seemed that no matter how carefully she tucked that white monkey away in her mind's most secure compartment, he was bound to escape.

Sister Subordinary was not allowed to linger over this mystery. The plangent ring of Mother Mary Extraordinary's bedside bell disturbed Sister's musings. Duty called.

Subordinary bid Sister Merry Berry stay and tuck Conrad in for the night. Conrad still knew nothing of the developing crisis, only that his swimming partner had been absent for two nights running. Sister Subordinary listened at Conrad's door for a moment, heard his sweetly spoken, "I love you too." She imagined Sister Merry Berry's smile and then rushed off to check on Mother Mary Extraordinary.

———

HIGH WINDS OF SPIRITUAL ANOMIE buffeted Sister Mary Subordinary as she ran down the hallway towards the unspeakable. Had she been in denial all these many years?

An unwanted memory unleashed itself. Hadn't she once knelt and kissed the ring on the hand of the enemy in the days of her youthful ardor? And hadn't the hair lifted on her arms? And wasn't there a twist in her gut when she caught the Cardinal's eye? Sister Subordinary remembered running to the bathroom to wash out her mouth, and then to the kitchen to scrub the copper bottoms of the pots until they sparkled like midnight stars.

Again, she heard the ringing of Mother Mary's bell, and she wanted nothing so much as to run back to the kitchen and polish the pots.

But she did not.

She took a breath, steadied herself, and pressed down the hallway. The updraft of memory pressed back. She flashed on that very first visit from agents of the Magistere Magisterium when boxes of prayer books were confiscated on the pretext of protecting The Great Church from—from what?

The words came back to her. *From the poison of revisionism, from the anathema of heresy.*

There had been warnings, rumblings, and rumors of a coming raid. Anticipating that day when their library would be rifled, they had made careful copies of the original texts and stashed the originals in the vault. Their precaution paid off. During the raid, only the copies had been snatched up.

The Sisters had been aware that they were dancing on the edge of an intoxicating mystery; but they had not realized the extent to which they'd become captives of the dance. Then a flight of Sisters took one grand jeté too far over the bounds of orthodoxy and conducted Holy Mass.

That night, Sister Mary Rose donned a red gown and danced on the altar to an original composition for viola. The dance embodied the ecstasy of female sexuality—the rose in bloom.

And that's when Mary Josephus fell forever in love with the beguiling Mary Rose.

One scandalized novice whispered in the ear of a visiting priest, who whispered in the ear of a concerned Cardinal. The Munificentissimus Divine Mallard of All Mysteries scolded the Sisterhood in a well-publicized encyclical. His scathing warning came too late. They'd gone too far afield in their green visionary dreams. There was no turning back.

By the time of the second official visit, the Sisters of the Joyous Mystery had settled amongst themselves that they would accept the Decree of Divorcement and Excommunication without protest, its recondite locutions charging blasphemy, heresy and witchcraft notwithstanding.

Damned to a hell they no longer believed in hardly signified. Sticks and stones can break our bones, they laughed amongst themselves, but words can never hurt us. So they dismissed the document nailed to their door, penned by the Divine Duck in his palace with the chalice.

They congratulated themselves on Mother's foresight. In her wisdom, she had kept them financially independent of The Great Church. Despite much importuning from a succession of earlier Hierophants and their various lackeys, the Sisters held onto the original deed to the mansion and its grounds. Excommunication meant they were no longer brides of The Great Church. They were free to espouse other Gods. Or each other.

For a while.

Ten years of rapture had wiped out the memory of the Magisterium. Ten years that separated the confiscation of the Missals and the deaths of her consoeurs had thrown Sister Subordinary off the scent.

Now here it was again—the problematic interval and the redolent memory; this time seven years had passed between the Cardinal's hand on Mother's book and the blanched pages of the original *Goat Girl*.

Those frankenscented monsters!

Sister Mary Subordinary was so practiced at mediating emotions that, at first, she did not recognize the hot white sensation. She leaned against the wall; the waves of anger left her breathless. She set her will against her better nature and refused to subdue the mental turbulence that beset her.

The ringing of Mother Mary's distress bell went unanswered.

Sister's vision tunneled, and she beckoned the onslaught. Overtake me, she bid the unfamiliar furies. Just this once she would open the door to a great gusting wind, let it scatter her neatly bound mental artifacts.

A squall of sensory data was lifted, dropped, then reassembled like a fresh crime scene neatly wrapped in yellow plastic tape.

As happens when one template is shattered and another shifts into place, the familiar became strange. The Document of Condemnation that was nailed to the convent door no longer looked like a mere conveyance of liberation. All of that ugly language: anathema, sacrilege, heresy—the order condemned to outer darkness, all light extinguished, its members damned to everlasting hell fire. Vile phrases hurled at the Sisters festered under the skin in secret like buried shrapnel continues its damages long after the guns are silenced.

Words mattered.

A confetti of shredded letters blew sideways in Mary Subordinary's memory.

Stolen words. Expunged text. Brought plague. Leeched the soul. Withered hope. Lines of poetry excoriated—killed the art and the artificer alike.

But how? Once the ties with the old church had been broken, how could the arm of the Magisterium reach surreptitiously and with such devastation into their world? Sister Subordinary bowed her throbbing head and covered her face. The puzzle would not resolve.

And what was the Magisterium's interest in the boy? Consider that, Sister. The Cardinals had known that a baby was coming to the convent, their calculations off by only one day. Or maybe not. What if they were right and the baby had arrived on Wednesday and Hanuman had kept the infant in the forest until the coast was clear? What if, even as the false Magi rapped on the convent door, Hanuman had been sheltering the blue baby in his strong arms?

And what of the Hierophant, His Holiness the Munificentissimus Divine Mallard? The Magisterium serves at the pleasure of His Holiness. The Sisters had always dismissed the Mallard of all Mysteries as lightly as he had dismissed them.

When they jokingly referred to the Divine Duck as His Quisling the Querulous Quack, had they been irresponsibly naïve, like schoolgirls making playground jokes about the principal, unaware of how powerless they would be against reprisals?

Had they underestimated his malice and intent?

Or, was the Magus at the heart of the dark mystery?

*Stop*!

She gave her head a violent shake in a vain attempt to settle herself. No time to clean up the mess now, she must attend to Mother Mary.

Sister rushed onwards, then she hesitated with her hand on the doorknob. Steady on, she admonished, before trying the door. Locked.

"It's me," Subordinary knelt and peered through the keyhole. "You rang for me."

"Prayer is dangerous!" Mother Mary Extraordinary's voice croaked. "Warn Conrad!"

"Mercy," Sister Subordinary exhaled and tapped lightly on Mother's door. "Let me in, please."

"Go away," Extraordinary rasped, "and do not, I repeat, do not dare ask if I am okay."

"Words matter. Words do matter, Mother. You know the *Goat Girl* poems by heart. Don't stop believing in your own words."

"Rags. Tags. Dustbin babies," the old nun muttered.

Sister Subordinary stood and leaned her forehead against the door. "Please, stay with us," she repeated under her breath.

The night before, violated prayer book in hand, Mother Extraordinary had cloistered herself in her convent cell to wrestle with the demon that fed on her poetry. She had won the first round, but it had cost her.

Mother Mary was diminished. Visibly so. Merely a voice in a pile of black rags. The beautiful pink leather-bound book rested on her chest, anchoring her soul. It would be so easy to float away. Her powers of mentation were compromised. Why linger? The ancient Mother Mary Extraordinary welcomed her incipient erasure. Her only concern was Conrad. She must not infect Conrad. He must not be erased. He must not pray.

"Mother—," Subordinary stopped short when she caught something out of the corner of her eye.

Oh, heaven forbid, here was Merry Berry swaying down the hallway. Why hadn't she told Merry Berry that Mother Mary's prayer book had been breached? Poor Sister Merry Berry had only been told that Mother Mary was under the weather. Under a death sentence was closer to the truth. As soon as Subordinary had a moment, she must confess the white pages to Merry Berry.

"Tell her the good news," Merry Berry bubbled. "Conrad speaks!"

"Noooo," howled the voice behind the door.

"Open up," Sister Merry Berry rattled Mother's door. "I've got good news, dear."

"Tell him *not* to pray! Warn the boy!" Extraordinary rasped.

"Whatever you say, dear." Sister Merry Berry gave Sister Subordinary a quizzical look and started down the hall.

"Sister, wait," Subordinary called out.

Sister Merry Berry turned and let Mary Subordinary catch up.

"You must forgive me," Subordinary began, "I wanted to spare you. Now I'm afraid I must give you a shock. The pages of Mary Extraordinary's missal have been licked clean."

Merry Berry hung her head for a long moment; then without a word, she headed straight for the wine cellar. Sister Subordinary watched her consoeur limp down the hall.

The hallway light flickered. Sister Subordinary faltered in the deserted passage.

*Heigh-ho the dairy-o, the cheese stands alone.* The nursery rhyme blew unwelcome through her mind, the playground taunts of bygone children who mistook her awkward solitude for snobbery. Despair was on the hunt, looking for purchase in the once orderly precincts of her mind.

She went back to the locked door.

"Mother!" Subordinary gave the door a good solid kick. "Recite your damn poems. OUT LOUD!" Subordinary kicked again.

She put her ear to the door. Was that a cough or a chuckle?

Sister softened, "Remember the one about Pan? What was the title?" She made a quick search through her mental archives. "Bless me. I found it. *Our Lady of the Royal Coach.* I'll start you. *Best Western—.* You can do this, Mary Extraordinary. Remember yourself!"

A faint voice on the on the other side of the door began to intone words penned decades ago:

Best Western Goddess
Holy Meretrix
Holy Medium
Remember
how the goat-footed God
kidded you
in the pagan days
& you birthed your half-
god
goat
girl
without blush or apology
Holy, holy, holy Godma
intercede for me tonight.

When Mother's voice wavered, Sister rallied her on. Through the long night, Subordinary sat on the other side of the door until Extraordinary reached her Amen and Ah She.

In the morning, the faintly inked ghosts of Mother's prayers were visible on the pages of her book.

Aware that she had survived an ordeal, Mary Extraordinary still suffered a vague apprehension that she had not yet accomplished some important task. Be that as it may, she no longer remembered what she meant to accomplish in this abidance on Earth. She only knew that she had escaped something and that something had escaped her.

———

WITH THE EXCEPTION OF Sister Subordinary, the household slept peacefully the rest of the night. Extraordinary dreamed of a missing pair of wings and a disorder of gem-toned angels spiraling through the blue beyond. Conrad's dreams sent him flying through a primal forest on the back of his monkey. Merry Berry took her bottle and the good news of Conrad's sweet voice to bed with her, and she slept like a rock-a-bye baby.

Mary Subordinary envied Merry Berry her consoling Cabernet. "To each her own consolation," Sister Subordinary sighed, giving up on sleep.

She thought about Guha's kick, how his practice steadied him, allowed him to thrive in a world that did not love its nonconformists, a world that often acted out violently in periodic fits of moral panic, spawning prayer eaters and violent oppressions.

Her faith in her personal practice wasn't shaken so much as it was riddled. No one likes to think they've conducted their life by a principle that did not altogether serve. Anger had proved an unexpected ally tonight. Anger flashed warnings, sharpened insight, bolstered resolve.

So be it.

She had always lived by the Socratic precept: let each one mind her own mystery. Just as she accommodated the monkey, she would accommodate anger and its chaotic inflations.

Sister Subordinary reached for her black boots, got out the tin of polish and the brush. Wax on. Wax off. Immaculate Mind was revealing some of its darker facets. As a concession to the furies, Sister allowed that she was proud of her kick. Then she pulled on her sturdy boots and tied the laces.

Down in the basement she emptied the dryer and performed a laundry meditation, scenting the sheets with vetiver, folding each towel with care. An unobserved celestial, who had taken up residence in the wine cellar, passed through her and she caught her breath.

*Stay with me, little breath,* she prayed.

Back upstairs, she performed a dish washing meditation, mindful of each cup. And for good measure, she mopped the kitchen floor.

Sister Subordinary was conducting Holy Mass her way. As she ordered the world about her, so she ordered her interior world.

There were quotidian Earth matters that required a becalmed mind. Someone had to bake the muffins, steam the broccoli, wash the dishes, tend Mother Mary, and tell a little boy goodnight stories.

# INTO THE WOODS

CONRAD COULD BARELY hide his disappointment when Sister Subordinary and Sister Merry Berry showed up in his room at the first peek of daylight. He and Skipper had been scheming in the predawn hours, devising plans and gathering supplies for their much-anticipated daytrip down to the newly discovered tunnel.

The Sisters brimmed with their own nervous expectations. They were anxious to hear Conrad speak again and affirm yesterday's miracle. They were eager for any spiritual tidbit or telling aphorism that might fall from Conrad's lips, any word to lighten what would most likely prove another arduous go-round—caring for a sick and increasingly cranky Extraordinary.

They waited.

They hovered.

They did not guess that, for Conrad, the advent of speech was not such a big deal, especially when compared to a secret tunnel. The Sisters would have been floored had they known that Conrad had plans for the day that did not include them. Rather big plans for such a small boy.

He had always been such an easily managed child, adapting to whatever regimen of study Sister Subordinary proposed, no matter how rigorous. He dutifully wrote out his letters—Greek, Arabic, Sanskrit—with the colorful felt tip markers provided by Merry Berry. He never balked at his chores or prayers. All in all, he seemed content to live according to their bells and whistles.

Adults reliably forget that all children lead double lives. As beautifully as Conrad had been curated, he had begun to chafe at the confines of cloistered life. To forbid him the forest, much less the world, was tantamount to an invitation. The boy had just turned seven, and it is axiomatic that a healthy boy of imagination, turning seven, must be in want of adventure.

This latter-day Huckleberry was a lively, skinny, sand-colored boy, with a smattering of freckles. Startling blue eyes were the only remnant of his former brilliant coloration. Sister Subordinary didn't love him any less, but she did miss her blue baby. Sister Merry Berry thought him most handsome when he was a dusky brown. Still, he was a perfectly attractive boy going on white, even though his head was a little large for his wiry frame.

"He will grow into his head," Merry Berry assured herself.

Sister Merry Berry was the keeper of Conrad's measurements. By default, she became his wardrobe mistress, seamstress, and shopper. The boy was easy enough to please. He only wanted pockets.

Merry Berry, on the other hand, believed in the art of aspirational dressing. The perfect pair of socks could be a prayer. She outfitted Conrad in brightly-colored drawstring pants and pullover t-shirts. She made the dyes herself, doing her best to compensate for his regrettable loss of color. Inspired by illustrations of happy childhoods in second-hand story books, she knitted bright winter caps and cardigans. She scoured yard-sales and thrift stores for jackets and footwear. The boy wore boots in bad weather, ran barefoot in mild.

Then last week, Merry Berry surprised him with a pair of factory-made cargo shorts with a delirium of pockets. This morning, he'd already stuffed the pockets with a boy's worth of necessary enchantments: an Indian-head penny, a plastic T-Rex, a matchbook, a dwarf figurine from the birthday pack—the dopey-looking one—a mini-flashlight, several apple seeds, three crystal rosary beads, plus a sketchy map in one front pocket and a florescent green water pistol in another.

"Sister Merry Berry," Conrad smiled, "have you got any extra batteries for my flashlight?"

It is true that it was a grammatically correct, nicely constructed, complete sentence, but altogether disappointing nonetheless. No great reveal or pronouncement. Not even a hello or good-morning.

"I *do* have batteries," Merry Berry exclaimed with an accompanying hiccough, her bright enthusiasm at odds with harsh realities. Quite possibly Merry Berry was setting a new, early morning record for that first sip of wine.

"I was hoping we'd have time to bicycle today," Merry Berry buttoned Conrad's cardigan. "I've managed a nifty bandage for my ankle. Alas, poor Mother Mary Extraordinary will need constant watching. Death came a-knocking last night."

"Sister!" Subordinary did not think death was a suitable topic.

"Batteries. I'm right on it." Merry Berry took the hint and positively beamed at Conrad as if batteries were the exact antidote to death's knock.

"Is Mother Mary Extraordinary going to die?" Conrad's question, so direct, took Mary Subordinary aback. Still, she managed to match his frankness and go him one better.

"Not today," Subordinary asserted with a ruffled finality, sounding a good deal more imperious than she intended.

Sister Subordinary was surprised to find that, once the words were hung out to dry, she actually believed herself. That small belief was going to make the day possible: Not today.

"Can I visit her?"

"Not today," Subordinary re-applied her handy bromide. "Conrad dear, I'm afraid you'll be on your own until dinner and Evensong. I've left a fresh loaf on the counter."

"I'll make peanut butter and jelly," the boy offered, "I can take care of myself."

Conrad felt the monkey approve of his take-charge attitude. And with a rush of happy anxiety the day broke loose, like a frisky kite freed of its string.

It wasn't so much that he was dismissive of Mother Mary's critical condition. Conrad vaguely appreciated that death was an important matter, but Shiva had restored Guha, hadn't he? And wasn't Mother Mary Extraordinary a much more illustrious personage? She was certainly the most powerful person in his world. He briefly pictured the great white Bull Nandin lifting Mother Mary in his soft, grass-scented mouth, and realized in that fleet vision that she had traveled far to come to this planet. He lingered on the picture of the bull setting Mother Mary back on Earth.

He knew she'd be fine.

————

TODAY CONRAD MEANT to tend business of his own. It was time to explore the mysteries of the convent he called home. In short order, two new batteries were snapped into his flashlight. Two peanut butter and jelly sandwiches were made. One was consumed. Conrad kept nudging the other at Skipper, extolling the virtues of the freshly baked bread. They needed fortification for the project ahead, the boy insisted.

"It's really good, Skip. You're missing out."

Exasperated, Conrad attempted to force feed the monkey. Nothing doing. Skipper was uncooperative, stubbornly remaining a toy. And yet the boy was certain the monkey was a willing co-conspirator in this venture, ever urging him on. He wrapped Skipper's sandwich in wax paper and stuffed it in his back pocket.

At the cellar door, Conrad felt the thrill of crossing a threshold. Adventure beckoned its crooked finger. He reached up for the string, gave it a tug, and the dank stairway swelled under the bent light. Making his way quickly down, past the racks of wine, past the music box—had it moved? No time to entertain that thought—he raced to the unlocked door that opened onto the underground tunnel. He turned the latch. And suddenly he was there, where every child wants to be, at the gate of a good story.

Conrad felt the tremor of myriad possible future lives blink out of existence—this reconfiguration of futures always happens when a milestone choice is made. He briefly wondered: where did those other lives go? And then he entered the story that would become his own.

One day he would run back to this moment, just before he stepped into the tunnel, when none of it had happened yet.

Conrad flicked on the flashlight. A circle of grey light barely illuminated the long cool tunnel. He tested the tunnel's depth with a half-hearted, "Hello?" in Courier font.

Then a louder, "Hellooo," in Excelsior.

His hellos echoed and broke up. He watched the letters tumble down the swallowing dark.

Gulp.

Conrad was moving more slowly now, less certain, more aware of the downside of not being missed. Brushing away what felt like a spider's web, he patted the Velcro-tabbed paws at his neck for assurance and marched on in his cowboy boots.

After trudging on a good long way in the stuffy, mold-ridden tunnel, Conrad came to a Y and sat down to massage his achy legs. Too late, he remembered the sandwich he'd stuffed in the back pocket of his cargo shorts, now a goopy mess.

Why hadn't he thought to bring water?

No going back now. He made his decision, got up and took the left branch of the Y.

It seemed he'd been soldiering on forever, when Conrad found himself at the disappointment of a dead end. He gave the wall a good solid kick. That's when he felt the monkey's soft paw slide down his arm. Then the small furry hand resting on top of his hand flicked off the flashlight.

Conrad's heart went thud in the sudden dark.

A twinkle of light in the pitch black made Conrad look up. There was a door above them, with a chink that let in one narrow stream of light, a beckoning light. A metal ladder secured to the roughcast wall made the decision easy. Conrad scrambled up the ladder, pushing his small determined weight against the wooden door.

The door gave way and swung open with a soft thud against the leafmeal forest floor. And they were out the hatch and into the woods—the very woods that they had both studied from Conrad's window and explored through the lens of his telescope. Dwarfed by the cathedral of trees, an amazed boy and his monkey drank in the oxygen-rich air.

The dizzying freedom of standing in the old-growth forest loosed a wild cry from the boy's throat, and in a shake Conrad was much more alone than he ever thought possible. The monkey leapt upwards with an answering screech and flew from treetop to treetop, bounding away at an astonishing speed.

Gone.

Conrad laughed and spun round and about, calling out, "Come back, Skipper. Wait for me. Teach me to climb!"

No answer.

"All right then, be that way, Monkey."

Conrad picked up a stick and tossed it as high and as far as he could. He was determined to take on one of the trees. He gave it a running start, quickly scrambled up to an impressive height, and just as quickly found himself lying on his back in the leafy mulch, a dreamy smile on his face.

What a revelation. The forest was full of music. He listened to the leaves chatter, felt the tingle of industrious life underneath him, and heard the primal song in the canopy of trees above.

Looking upwards he noticed a beautiful scarlet-colored bird on one of the lower branches. He reached out his hand.

"Come here, little bird. Tell me your secret."

There was a low rumble in the forest, and the sound of huge wings harassed the air with forceful repeated thwaps. The light around Conrad tightened like shrinking cellophane and then blew apart. Standing before him was a red-robed Cardinal.

The man was powerfully built; his robes snapped in the wind, a wind that seemed to belong to him alone. The rest of the forest was absolutely silent—no cricket trills, no bird calls, just the restless snapping of the Cardinal's robes.

Not daring to stand up, the terrified boy scrambled backwards, pushing his boot-heels against the dirt. He allowed himself one quick look upwards.

Mistake.

The man smiled. In a way it was an attractive smile, if perhaps a trifle wide. The square athletic jaw looked as if it could unhinge and possibly swallow so insignificant a thing as a boy. There was the signature red-feathered hat, with the yellow beak jutting out from the forehead. The Cardinal's eyebrows were shaved, and he had four deep, luminous eyes, only one pair human. It was the Magus.

Conrad was not meant to know of the existence of this terrifying four-eyed eminence, but the Sisters remained oblivious to how frequently and with what rapt attention Conrad tuned in on their conversations. It had worried Conrad that his caretakers withheld crucial information about matters concerning his welfare. Here was dismaying confirmation.

The boy's dread was inextricably mixed with fascination. Conrad could not look away.

At first fright, the dark sockets carved in the cheeks of the monstrous segregant appeared to be embedded with faceted orange gemstones too alien to be real. At the center of each glistening orb was a distinct reptilian ovoid lens: black, dilating, and very much alive.

Birdlike, the man tilted his head to better take Conrad's measure. To the boy's shock, it was the orange eye of the cassowary that focused in on him. The muddy-purple human eyes gazed inward on some unfathomable mindscape. But it was the hand reaching toward Conrad, with its lizard-like scaly skin and its three black talons that made Conrad think—raptor. In that last desperate moment, he regretted that he had left his battery-operated submachine gun stashed under his bed.

There was a velvet sack in the Cardinal's human hand, and as the large man-beast took a step towards him, Conrad knew beyond a doubt that the Cardinal meant to stuff him into that sack and haul him off to the Sanctum Avesticum Quoborium.

Just as the Cardinal was thinking—*Why do all small boys smell like peanut butter?*—a thunderous roar filled the forest, punctuated by the deafening cracks of breaking tree limbs.

The Magus froze.

Shielding his eyes from falling debris—it seemed the forest itself was shaking apart—Conrad dared an upward glance.

An enormous white monkey plunged out of the sky. He landed with one foot on each shoulder of the red-robed intruder. Cardinal Cassowary's jaw dropped, and he squawked in fear. His cape contracted. Then the Magus shrank into a small red bird and darted into the tangle-wood. The monkey screamed at the fleeing bird, exposing long gleaming incisors.

Conrad's heart beat wildly as he fought back angry tears. Who was this white monkey?

A wave of violent tremors shook the forest floor. The primal trees voiced their umbrage at the red intruder and acknowledged the white giant. Lord Hanuman was home. The trees bowed low in solemn rows, and then sprang back—tall elegant elders, the watchers in the woods. The sky shivered, and in whiplash increments, the monkey shrank to his normal size.

Once again, the woods trilled its familiar chorus.

The small monkey leapt onto Conrad's back, chattering monkey noises in urgent bursts. Conrad, still shaken, stumbled his way back to the tunnel, furtively checking over his shoulder.

When they reached the trapdoor, Skipper gave the all clear and Conrad ducked inside. The monkey leapt over Conrad's head to the tunnel floor. The boy closed the door overhead and slid down the metal ladder, his legs gone all rubbery. Then the boy sat in the dark safety of the tunnel until his hammering heart eased up. The monkey continued its urgent chatter.

"At a time like this, you want lunch? Really?" Conrad snarked between gulps of air, hastily brushing away tears.

*I'm starving.*

Conrad fished out the PB&J from his back pocket, now an unappetizing mash folded in wax paper. The monkey went at it, munching away, pausing briefly between bites to offer a critical comment.

"Crunchy?" Conrad was incredulous. "Next time, you want crunchy? I just nearly got snatched by a red beast with two extra orange eyes, and you want to talk about peanut butter? You're thirsty? Tough luck."

Sometimes a monkey is just a monkey. He reached into Conrad's pocket, grabbed the green water pistol, aimed for his mouth, gave himself a few squirts, and passed the proxy canteen to the boy. Conrad studied his friend, trying his best not to appear awestruck.

"That was some trick you pulled off in the forest," Conrad ventured, aching to know the monkey's secrets. Conrad was beset by an odd mixture of gratitude, admiration, and betrayal. He fired off a barrage of questions, both out loud and in mindtalk. He tried out various fonts.

The monkey munched away, glancing up occasionally.

*Crunchy,* was all the monkey had to say.

*Silly, stubborn monkey.*

The silly, stubborn monkey finished his meal and leapt onto Conrad's lap. He held the boy's tear-smudged face in his paws, and Conrad knew a sweet new sensation. He was beloved by a wild thing. The boy made a valiant effort to hold back his tears, and that effort made his heart feel a little crunchy.

On the way back through the wine cellar the boy stopped, puzzled. The music box was gone. That curious fact was set aside for later reflection on a day riddled with astonishments.

———

THAT NIGHT CONRAD dreamed of riding on the back of the white monkey and sailing through the trees. He was as happy as he had ever been. High in the branches of one of the pines, boy and monkey gave themselves up to star gazing. The monkey said his name was Hanuman, but he didn't mind being called Skipper.

"Lord Hanuman? I know your story. I've seen your pictures in the *Ramayana*. I used to copy the ink drawings. You're on page 186, 224, and 431. How did you—? Why did you—?"

"Go on. Ask your question." Lord Hanuman spoke out loud for the first time, his deep voice resonant and kind.

Conrad took a breath; his brain was a crowd of jostling questions, but one question butted in at the head of the line:

"Are you mostly Skipper, the Gospel Monkey? Or are you mostly Lord Hanuman?

In the morning Conrad would remember exactly what the monkey told him.

"He is that, so I may be this."

"Am I imagining you?"

"Yes," the monkey answered. "Creating guardians is a holy act of the imagination. Good job."

"Do you belong to me? I mean—who are you *really*?"

Hanuman studied the question. Then he picked a leaf from the boy's sandy-colored mop of hair and let it fall to the forest floor.

"What is one leaf among so many? And who am I?" The smiling monkey left the questions hanging and searched Conrad's eyes. Hanuman tapped the boney cage over his own monkey heart. "It is like this—your name, Conrad Eppler, is written on my every bone. It has been thus ever since I first heard the scratch of a pen inscribe your name on a cardstock tag. And thus inscribed, who am I?"

"I don't know," the mystified boy whispered.

The monkey let the moment linger until he could taste it on his tongue. Then he solemnly spoke: "When I do not know who I am, I serve you; when I know who I am, you and I are one."

The riddle tumbled through the boy's mind and scampered off.

"I want to fly some more, mystery monkey," the dreaming boy said.

So they did.

But life is not all flight and fancy. The boy would need to know how to make his way on Earth. And this boy had enemies.

Now that Conrad had been spotted by the Magus, another kidnapping attempt was sure to follow. Conrad's existence and his whereabouts were known facts. The boy would need to be hyper-vigilant. It is wearing on the adrenals to be in constant danger, the monkey explained to Conrad. Vigilance constricts the mind, and the mind of a boy needs to range wide and free.

"And fly," added Conrad, loosening his grip on the flying monkey, relishing the freedom of being airborne.

"Sometimes," the monkey cautioned, circling the treetops and then landing in a clearing.

Sitting side by side on a lichen-speckled log, Hanuman took the boy further into his confidence. He explained that his powers came from the forest. Inside the convent, those powers were constrained. Indoors, Hanuman could bring himself to life for limited intervals, and he could use his reserves to touch the boy's inner ear with human words.

Conrad took in each teaching the monkey tossed his way and turned the teachings over in his youthful mind. He understood that he could not always count on Lord Hanuman for protection. The solution was obvious.

"We could live here, in the forest." Conrad's mood immediately brightened. "We could build a fantastic tree house, and sometimes we could visit Mother and the Sisters and—"

"No," the monkey interrupted the boy's fantasy.

"Why not, Monkey?" Conrad challenged, uncomfortably aware that he was no longer running the monkey.

"Answer me this, Boy. Isn't it true that you have a desire tucked away in your heart, so secret that you never speak of it? Not even in prayer?"

The monkey's gaze made Conrad squirm.

"I don't know. Maybe I do. Maybe I wish that you could be real whenever I want you to be real."

"Not that wish. I know that wish. You are constantly pestering me with that wish. I'm talking about the wish that you keep right here." The monkey reached over and tapped his hard monkey finger right against Conrad's ribcage.

Conrad burst into tears. That tapping finger was bruising his most guarded thought. It was his most deeply felt wish, and it was the wish he was most ashamed of—Conrad wanted parents. He was so loved, given so much, that this longing seemed like a betrayal of the Sisters. Yet there it was, right under his breastbone. And the monkey found it.

"We are going to shake out that wish tomorrow. Give it an airing. Do you know what a radio wave is?"

———

THE NEXT MORNING, Conrad lay snug in his own bed rummaging over everything that had happened yesterday.

Yesterday was enormous.

Yesterday was filled with secret tunnels that opened onto secret worlds. Conrad had reached for what he believed was a little red bird, and a Magus in a red sateen robe had reached for him with its raptor claw. His own Skipper had grown to three times the size of a man. And then there was the dream that wasn't a dream. He had flown through the air on the back of Lord Hanuman. Arms wrapped around the monkey's neck, his nose had nuzzled in that soft, musky fur. Then there was the long discussion in the forest where the monkey had discovered the secret hidden behind Conrad's breastbone.

The boy looked over at the little stuffed monkey on his bed and smiled. Truly, this was a marvelous world.

The kitchen was filling with happy smells that wafted into the yellow bedroom. Conrad grabbed Skipper and fastened the Velcro paws around his neck. Everything seemed brighter this morning when Conrad sat down to tea and toast and jam with Mary Subordinary and Merry Berry. The two Sisters assured him that Mother Mary Extraordinary was recovering, and he could visit with her in the afternoon.

No one noticed the pretty little red cardinal outside the window. Except Skipper.

After breakfast, Conrad crawled under his bed and recovered a walkie-talkie from its hiding place behind the dust bunnies. He listened carefully to Skipper's instructions. They were operating in their familiar mindtalk mode. The monkey explained how a sound could travel great distances on electromagnetic waves. In no time, Conrad was operating the transceiver. That part was easy.

Now for the difficult matter of giving voice to Conrad's secret, teasing it out into the open, blowing the dust bunnies off the wish. It needed shaping up—this hope, this someday-maybe, this wouldn't-it-be-great-if, this unlived desire that had stayed tucked safely away behind Conrad's breastbone.

According to Skipper, the particulars of the wish would determine the attraction of the message. No one would be holding a receiver on the other end of Conrad's prayer.

*Why not?* The boy wanted to know.

*The message will magnetize the receiving medium.*

*The what?*

*It's all about the clarity of the picture you hold in your imagination*, the monkey simplified.

This was a problem because the boy's secret wish was more of a pang and less of a picture. Conrad had never actually seen or met a pair of parents, so he didn't have a lot to work with.

At inception, when a wish is barely born, there is a catalytic event in the imagination. Under the monkey's guidance, Conrad traveled back to that breakout moment. It was an instantaneous mental reconnaissance. Zeroing in on his comic book library, Conrad located the original mind-flash—the critical convergence when he first caught the scent of the story he wanted to make his own. He knew the dad he wanted down to the buttons on his boots, had recognized him the first time he slipped the comic book out of its archival plastic case and began to follow this man on the flimsy pages.

"My father is a cosmic hero in the etherworld!" Conrad beamed at Skipper. "Just the other day, he gave me a sign. On my birthday! His name is Epic and—"

*Mindtalk*, Skipper cautioned Conrad. *Tonight, when you take out your wish, send up a few test signals first. You don't want just anyone to catch hold of your prayer.*

*Right*, Conrad agreed. *Tonight. I can't wait!*

*Did you forget something?*

*No. What?* Conrad gave Skipper the innocent eyes.

Skipper waited. Conrad played dumb. It was a stare down. Conrad blinked first.

*How about we skip the mom? I mean, I don't really need a mom. I've already got three.*

Conrad had no inkling why, just as he was running quickly in the other direction, his thoughts ran directly into Sita. She felt the bump. Sita—the blue Goddess in the *Ramayana*—slowly opened her illustrious third eye. She bent close to the wondering boy. *You are Sitananda,* her voice chimed, *Sita's joy.*

Hanuman gently pushed that image from the boy's mind.

*I almost had something. Now it's gone. Did you do that?*

*Keep trying,* the monkey coached.

Conrad considered various comic book women. None of them seemed exactly right. Imagining a mom was so much trickier than choosing a dad. There were only two things he knew for sure. She was beautiful, and she could fly.

"I've got it Skip! How about an angel for a mom?"

*Mindtalk.*

*Sorry!*

*What sort of angel?* The monkey wanted details.

*A nice one. I don't know,* Conrad replied with a shrug.

Conrad stared out the window, gauging the exact spot where the moon would be tonight. He thought he saw the faintest outline of a morning moon. But it was slightly out of place and veiled in a pink haze.

"Surprise me," he addressed the visitor moon.

———

WHILE CONRAD WAS working up his wish, Sister Merry Berry tripped down to the wine cellar to refresh her happy purple haze. She stopped at a certain shelf and, like Conrad, noted that the music box had gone missing from its usual spot. Out of the corner of her eye, she saw something move. She whirled around and nearly dropped her cup.

O.

My.

Godma.

He was magnificent—tall, trim and beautifully turned out in black leathers.

*Am I hallucinating?* Merry Berry wondered, shading her eyes. For all his black clothing, he gave off considerable light.

Just then the outlandishly accoutered angel was enjoying a Moulin-à-Vent Beaujolais and listening to a nursery tune.

"May I refill your cup?" the angel lifted the bottle.

A speechless Sister Merry Berry held out her cup.

There had been rumors of a comeback, rumors churning in the great prayer mills of the Gods, rumors spun like cotton candy under the cosmic big top, sweet and sticky divine dish broadcast from the star-chambered press box. Notices of electrifying thrills posted on billboards drawing the crowds to the celestial circus, audition calls summoning all bright beings—the holy high-wire walkers, metaphysical tumblers, prayer-ball jugglers, mosh pit angels, olio intermissionaries, theological clowns, Talmudic tricksters, crystal-ball gazers, tarot readers, Jesuitical mentalists, and silver-spoon benders.

Showtime!

Concession stands were doing brisk business, offering an epicure's buffet of transcendent treats at the Supernal communion rails. Celebrity deities arrived in droves and hung out in the sacred groves. Someone spotted the Buddha sucking up a slurpee of subatomic deities from a giant red plastic straw. There was Krishna downing a holy berry milkshake, surrounded by his gorgeous gopis, while the white bull Nandin grazed on a nearby slope. The gopis sent surreptitious winks and air kisses to Dionysius, the original Greek party boy, who had just arrived from the seventh coast with a boisterous and thirsty entourage, Bota bags of wine slung over their hunky shoulders.

They'd heard it through the grapevine: Lucifer was back and better than ever.

Take a wild guess. How many angels will dance on the head of a pin when Lucifer enters the big top?

Answer: Still counting.

Whatever that exponential number, the angels were jitterbugging now.

O jubilation city, the juke joint was jumping.

What glorious good news! Lucifer had reached the midway: planet Earth, Humboldt county. The celebrants were tuned in and turned on. The wine cellar at the Convent of Immaculate Conceptions was *the* planetary hot spot tonight. The whole etherworld was watching.

Sister Merry Berry's heart went boom when Luce crossed the room to fill her cup. Thankfully, her gift of sight did not desert her. She knew that beautiful bad boy right off. He could have struck a match on the rock of her unreason, the moment was that combustible.

With a mighty effort, Merry Berry cooled herself down to planetary scale. Back in the temperate zone, the modest nun gathered herself to an immoderate greatness. She refused to be daunted by the comeback illuminato, no matter how extreme his glamour or how fine the cut of his sleek silver-studded leathers.

"I see you've been enjoying the wines in our cellar. I have to ask: Did you or did you not also help yourself to Mother Mary Extraordinary's prayers?"

"Not."

If he was lying, he was awfully good at it.

"Prayer is for the birds." Lucifer teased and turned on his slow smile, the one that started with merriment glittering in his green eyes.

"Ah, the birdmen," Sister Merry Berry wavered, but she wasn't won over. "I would think Mary Extraordinary's prayers might appeal to someone more advanced, more—shall we say lucid? Besides, Mary Extraordinary's prayers are so very innovative, and the Cardinals are so very behind the times."

"Never underestimate the power of those who live behind the times," Luce topped off her cup.

Lucifer knew whereof he spoke. It was not uncommon for outmoded Gods and angels to dig in their heels and refuse the call of evolution. The more resentful among the passed-over deities often became saboteurs. Those that history tried to forget plotted in back-alley cafés in the outer burbs of the Milky Way.

In the not too long ago, Lucifer himself had tossed back espressos with spiritual desperados in the demimonde—an overcrowded theatre in perpetual conflict, rife with wily agents, promoters, provocateurs, and rebranding consultants hooking up with counter-revolutionary deities on the remake, retooling their resumes, and counting on comebacks.

For reasons of his own, Lucifer didn't want to bring up the biblical Demiurge, possibly the most powerful figure operating behind the times.

"Many of the parallel worlds harbor leagues of Gods, archetypes and angels mired in belated attempts to catch up with their times. Your Cardinals are hardly alone in their re-tardiness." He raised his cup, "Your wine collection is remarkable."

"Next time try the Château Latour. A votre santé," she raised her cup.

"May I offer some friendly advice? Lose the florescent orange running shoes."

She gave the infamous hell's angel a recondite but elegant curtsy, purposefully pointing the tip of her orange tennis shoe just so—a sassy demonstration of her independence of mind. She was confident that her improvised etiquette answered nicely to this puzzling visitation by such an august, but still evolving angel. Then with a slight merry hic, she rushed off to her duties, the bothersome twist in her ankle completely untwisted.

Throughout the long day, Sister Merry Berry thought about the Angel of Light; wasn't that dashing illuminato the perfect patron saint of all dashed hopes? The ultimate fallen? And his comeback, the quintessential comeback?

Hope is a powerful elixir. The convent occupied but a miniscule corner of the plenum. And yet, it mattered. Measured against immensities, the revolutions of the great Wheels are always a local story.

A novel idea snuck up on Sister Merry Berry. She tried it out in a sentence, "The Cardinals might not be winning."

———

SISTER MERRY BERRY'S COCKTAIL of hope and high spirits might have been severely shaken had she been privy to Cardinal Cassowary's preparations. A seven-year imprisonment had afforded his mind the opportunity to wander at large, and the preponderance of his explorations had not been along avenues of retreat.

Now that Cassowary had served his time, he slouched in the corridors of the Sanctum, feathered and clawed, tending his mental hatchery, provoking caution and curiosity. In the Australian rainforest, it is the always male cassowary who sits on the egg and cares for the young hatchling until it reaches maturity. Like his self-selected totemic bird, Cardinal Cassowary was a dedicated egg-man, constantly brooding over his great nest of plans.

Lately, Cardinal Cassowary was seen showing off a photograph of a certain seven-year-old boy sitting on the forest floor, eyes wide with terror. "A hatchling," the Magus remarked.

The Holy High Magus claimed he had snapped the picture with one of his modified raptor eyes and downloaded the image from his own brain. He passed around the detailed digital print to a small coterie of skeptical Cardinals. "The eye is a camera," he noted pointing to his orange eye with a black talon.

When his claim was questioned at an impromptu gathering, the Magus offered to take the doubting Cardinals to his lab.

"You need proof. I understand," the Magus remarked affably, ready to assure his erstwhile enemies that bygones were indeed bygones.

The Magus caught Delacroix's eye, saw interest. "There's proof aplenty. If you come to my lab, I can show you a holographic video of the boy complete with sound and scent. Its authenticity is, by any standard, self-evident upon viewing."

Had there been a thought cloud above his head, it might have read: *applause, please.*

"I'd like to see that clip," ventured Delacroix. He had a hunch that the much-examined photo of the boy was indeed the genuine article. If there truly was a deity being raised at the convent, this time Delacroix wanted a look at the evidence as well as a seat at the table of deciders when the plan of action was drawn up. There would be no repeat of the Magi debacle.

On the appointed day, the Holy High Magus opened the door to his former prison suite and waved in the arriving party, "Welcome, confrères. Come in, come in. Enjoy the view."

Bunbury and Oolumbo entered the tower suite. Delacroix followed with his personal Budgies in tow.

Every Cardinal of means kept a pair of servants smartly turned out in Budgie livery, one to act as footman and the other as factotum. In Delacroix's case, the Budgies served as official ferret ferriers and devoted minders of the unhappy Felix.

The Budgie pairs were as close as The Great Church came to accommodating man marriages—unofficially, of course. One day Delacroix's Budgies, Reynaldo and Pierre, would adopt Felix, and their little family would finally know happiness.

The select birdmen soon gathered around a circular table that featured a projector mounted overhead. The Magus queued up the hologram. It was a stunning artifact, high definition, lasting mere seconds. A sandy-haired boy in cargo shorts scooted backwards; the tip of the Magus' talon was briefly visible as it reached for the terrified child. For a split second, a wild roar rent the air and threatened to splinter the sound system. The Magus cut the power. And the holograph disappeared.

"What was that, that screech?" Bunbury choked.

"A glitch," the Magus smiled.

"I'm not convinced," Oolumbo stated. "For all I can tell, the hologram is a computer-generated fake, a clever simulation. I won't be hoaxed again."

"Let me download an image from one of you. It's a painless, noninvasive procedure. You merely hold an image in your mind. Whatever suits. You pick. Any volunteers? Delacroix?"

"I choose the image. Have I got that right?" Delacroix was understandably wary.

"Be assured," the Magus addressed the room, "the machine cannot reproduce any image that our volunteer does not wish to share. I myself will place the control in the subject's hand."

Presently, the Magus led Delacroix to a comfortable chair. He removed the Cardinal's red biretta, "Perfect. Freshly shaved." He rubbed a minted-scented salve on Delacroix's bald pate. Then he fitted Delacroix with a fine mesh cap. "Are you comfortable?"

"Yes," Delacroix swallowed.

A row of little pink lines raced across a slate-grey screen.

*Lizards,* Delacroix silently identified the screen savers.

*Pink Iguanas,* the Magus corrected, giving Delacroix a jolt.

*Tricky bastard,* Delacroix countered.

*Indeed,* came the invasive reply. *Don't worry, I have no interest in your thoughts.*

Delacroix was too shaken to register the insult.

Placing the control in Delacroix's hand, the Magus gave a final instruction. "When the desired image comes to mind, just press the green button."

The Magus dimmed the lights. The room went still.

An overpowering desire fired off millions of neurons in Cardinal Delacroix's visual cortex—if only he could see his wife and son alive again. Victims of the power wars that broke out before the current Hierophant was elected, Delacroix's illicit family had been blown to bits in a car bombing. He had no wish to revisit the explosion that still haunted his dream life. But there was another day, on the beach—a perfect day—when he sat watching his then-secret wife and his beautiful son play in the surf, the boy's ferret running back and forth at the water's edge. Melissa turned and waved to him.

Cardinal Delacroix pressed the green button.

Melissa turns and waves. Delacroix waves back at the holographic image of his wife being chased by a breaking roller. The sea foam curls over his son, who springs up paddling his arms in the surf. The sound of the boy's laughter tears at Delacroix's heart. Felix jumps from the arms of his Budgie minder and scrambles onto the table where the hologram jitters out.

A brief reprieve of darkness settled the room. Then the Magus turned on the lights.

"Your wife and son. I am so sorry. A tragic loss. So, now you see how it works. Have I made a believer of you?"

"Felix!" Delacroix tore off the mesh cap. The ferret jumped in his lap and bit his hand. "Thank-you," he stroked the furry head. Then he gathered up his dignity and left the laboratory.

———

AN EMERGENCY MEETING was convened at the request of His Holiness—a formal conclave.

The colloquy of Cardinals gathered in the gloomy beauty of their great hall. Blue light slanted through the stained-glass windows onto a long, resin-polished wooden table, a single slab cut from one of the forest giants. A bowl of sunflower seeds was set at each place. Each Cardinal stood behind his designated chair. Upholstered in red velvet, the high-backed chairs featured wooden frames with intricately carved wings. Expressions unreadable, the standing Cardinals waited for the entrance of the Munificentissimus Divine Mallard of All Mysteries, His Holiness the Hierophant.

Notoriously late, the current Hierophant was indifferent to protocols and politics alike. Unlike his brethren, he did not love the trappings of power. He loved napping.

The Cardinals had been repressing their annoyance for nearly an hour. Colorful Budgies flitted in and out keeping the wine goblets filled.

Members of the Order of Budgerigars were a familiar presence at all formal occasions. They came in three colors. In full livery, they donned either bright turquoise, pale purple, or lemony-green cropped jackets with matching puffy pantaloons.

The jackets, with pearl buttons in front and long tails in back, were tightly fitted over white shirts with stiff collars and black string ties. The ensemble was topped off with a fluffy black and white feathered bonnet. Prosthetic beaks were de rigueur on formal occasions. They worked in pairs and tended to roundness as they were given free access to the larder.

There were two seats of power at the conference table. At the east end, there was a black-upholstered cathedra, trimmed in orange and deep blue, the throne of the Excellent Holy High Magus, His Eminence Cardinal Cassowary, Magistrate of the Magistere Magisterium and Court Astrologer. He alone among the birdmen had a double avian identity. He alone was a shape-shifter.

Long before the Magus had begun his disastrous morphological experimentations with cassowary stem cells, he had perfected an unseemly ability to change from human to cardinal and back. He was both envied and resented for this disconcerting piece of conjury. It was said that he had picked up his penchant for atavistic magic from the quasi converts he had made among the Australian aboriginals.

All rumors concerning the Magus were weighed and measured by the collective Sanctum Avesticum. He was an eminence constructed out of hearsay. His resumé had never been vetted. Supposedly, he had once served as a Bishop in an obscure corner of Queensland. No one quite believed the story. No one guessed the truth.

More than one Cardinal of The Great Church shuddered, contemplating the malign forces that might have shaped the four-eyed segregant who so rudely outranked them. His orange replicant eyes with their reptilian ovoid lenses let no one forget that he had never been and would never be one of them. In the hallowed halls of the Avesticum, there were many who held the entire continent of Australia in contempt, with its appalling array of evolutionary oddities—platypuses, echidnas, cane toads, and cassowaries.

The colloquy of Cardinals shook their collective capped heads at how swiftly the unlikely and unlikeable foreign Bishop had risen in their ranks, first to Cardinal, and thereafter to the lofty station of Magus. Now he outranked everyone at the conclave, excepting the Hierophant.

When the unknown and unknowable Bishop first approached the head of The Great Church, those who were present at the secret synod were quick to leak insider information. The oft repeated tale—how the highly impressionable Hierophant had been taken in with a mere parlor trick—surely evidenced an enfeebled mind. It was said that the Munificentissimus Divine Mallard of All Mysteries had laughed like a child, and clapped his hands when the Australian Bishop turned himself into a little red bird. The bird had only to hop on the delighted Hierophant's finger and the promotion to Cardinal was a done deal.

Now His Eminence Cardinal Cassowary, was about to reprise the offensive bit of conjury and irritate the entire consortium of Cardinals at one fell swoop. The eastern doors of the great hall were opened by two Hooded Crows, and the

Magus made an aerial entrance in the guise of the distinctive North American Cardinalis, flying about the room in widening circles, before perching on the backrest of his throne, behaving for all the world like an innocent bird—preening his scarlet feathers, tilting his crested head.

"Look at him," hissed Cardinal Delacroix, "I wish I had a poison-dart gun.

"He has the attention of every man in the room," observed Bunbury as the little cardinal took flight again.

"He's mocking us," Cardinal Oolumbo reached for a handful of sunflower seeds. Just then a glop of wet bird shit splattered the back of Oolumbo's hand. "Landica!"

While the 'c' word would never pass the fastidious lips of the African-American Cardinal, all foul speech became fair when translated into the ritual language of The Great Church. The offended Cardinal held out his hand, and a lemony-green Budgie rushed forward with a warm damp towel.

The consortium waited. And then it came—that heart-stopping contraction in the atmosphere when the Magus reconfigured himself as a man.

"I hate it when he does that," one of the purple Budgies remarked to his partner *sotto voce*, "flapping his cape in that ridiculous wind he carries around with him."

"What was the Divine Duck thinking—mentoring such a beastly throwback?" his purple partner twittered.

"This is a church, not a freak show," a lemony-green Budgie huffed.

"That claw of his is the epitome of bad taste," another Budgie tsked.

The Magus let his feathered cape fall open, displaying the much-dissed claw. Then he made pointed eye contact with the critical Budgies, who blanched, puffed up, feigned indifference, and tightened their sphincters so they would not poop their puffy pantaloons.

"Bad taste?" His Eminence Cardinal Cassowary blinked his long-lashed raptor eyes flirtatiously. Then he gave one of his raptor nails a lascivious lick.

Unwilling to wait any longer upon the Hierophant, the Magus made an unprecedented break with tradition. He seated himself first. The gloating Cardinal Cassowary took in the murderous glares of the standing Cardinals, and then His Eminence began to slowly tap his notorious middle talon on the table top, signaling his growing impatience at the non-arrival of His Holiness.

Tap. Tap. Tap.

The currently tardy Divine Mallard of All Mysteries had been elected by the Cardinals as a compromise candidate after a year of bickering that had escalated into violence, salacious publicity, and widespread public disapproval. Even though indulgences were promised in exchange for support, the number of *likes* on the Cardinals' Facebook pages took a ruinous downturn during the election and had never recovered.

Each *like* from a believer was worth one year time off in purgatory—where souls tossed in fiery pits were purged of past offenses before being admitted to the holy environs of heaven.

The time-off coupons could be saved up and cashed in at death, a bargain for the light sinner with a quick finger.

*Click. Click. Click.*

Nonetheless, there were few takers, even when the value of a click was increased to five years time off.

In the weeks leading up to the election of this Hierophant, the illustrious birdmen had turned themselves into tabloid sensations. One exposé after the next had parishioners unfriending the Cardinals in droves. The headlines were lurid. Two Cardinals had been poisoned, one knifed, and Cardinal Delacroix's secret wife and only child had been killed in a car bombing.

In his grief, it was Cardinal Delacroix who had proposed they elect the sickly seventy-seven-year-old Cardinal Matsuki Makindo and put an end to the assassinations. A bookmark Hierophant, he was meant to hold the page until the scandals faded from public mention and memory.

To the Cardinals' collective dismay, His Holiness proved resilient and beloved of the people. The scandals faded, but Matsuki Makindo endured. This whimsical Divine Duck became an indefatigable advocate for the disenfranchised. He auctioned off Quoborium treasures at Sotheby's and gave millions to build housing for the destitute. Already a groundswell movement was underway, pressuring the College of Cardinals to declare this Hierophant a saint.

Unlike the Cardinals' pages, the Munificentissimus Divine Mallard's page was well-liked on a daily basis. *Click. Click. Click.* This Hierophant was a hit. The laity posted moving little stories of his benefactions. His funeral would, no doubt, prove exorbitantly expensive, unless the constantly plotting Cardinals could involve His Holiness in some provident scandal.

Now the College of Cardinals was being held hostage to the Divine Duck's desultory politics. They could never guess where His Holiness would land on any given topic. He rarely arrived at the point. Off topic was his rhetorical specialty. His voting record was erratic. And for all that, he wielded considerable power. His word was TFW, The Final Word. If he called Hierophant's Prerogative, it meant he was speaking Ex Cathedra, and any declaration he made Ex Cathedra was considered Holy Writ.

The Word of God. Debate over. No voting necessary.

Finally, the western doors to the great hall were opened by two Sanctum heralds, Order of Balearica Regulorum, the incomparable grey-crowned cranes. The heralds inflated the red gular sacs under their chins and honked energetically.

In came the emaciated, tottering Hierophant, leaning on his staff, his astonishing iridescent cape trailing behind him, an array of mallard greens and browns, with luscious black and white trim. That cape was the envy of every Cardinal in the college.

Matsuki hated it. Walking was challenging enough without the impediment of a fifty-kilo cape dragging behind him. And the hat, with its gold-plated mallard beak pointed straight up to the heavens, made it near impossible for the Hierophant to hold his weighty head steady on his skinny neck. The golden beak was constantly jerking his head forwards.

At last he sat and arranged himself as best he could with the help of a pair of doting Budgies. Head bobbling, the Munificentissimus Divine Mallard of All Mysteries raised his hand and blessed the convention. At his signal, the Cardinals seated themselves.

"Hierophant's Prerogative," Matsuki declared.

Immediately Cardinal Delacroix was on his feet. He must stop the Duck from making a declaration.

"May it please Your Holiness, the discussion has not yet begun."

"Of course, it has. I'm not an idiot. There is only one topic. The boy."

"Point taken, Your Holiness," interjected Cardinal Bunbury. Then at a discrete signal from the Magus, Bunbury continued "I am pleased to announce that the Excellent Holy High Magus, His Eminence Cardinal Cassowary, has produced a picture." Bunbury held up a copy of the digital printout. "All signs indicate that this boy is, in point of fact, the prophesied Avatar, as His Eminence Cardinal Cassowary originally, and with acute foresight, foresaw. Our eternal and humble apologies to Cardinal Cassowary for the seven-year confinement," Bunbury licked.

Tap went the talon and the anxiety in the room was ratcheted up another notch.

"At this very moment, the boy is being raised by that rogue order of nuns—the self-styled Immaculate Conceivers. Can't say, really, what banner the witches fly under these days," Bunbury wiped his brow.

Tap.

"We are much obliged to the most Excellent Holy High Magus, who has seen the boy with his own eyes. All four of them," Bunbury bungled onwards, doing his groveling best to keep himself in the good graces of both the Magus and the other Cardinals of the Magistere.

Tap.

"We can all certainly agree that if we do not take charge of the boy and his education, the chances that he will break with doctrine are—," Bunbury risked a glance at his master.

"Chances?" cautioned Cassowary. "Why speak of chances? It is a certainty."

The Munificentissimus Mallard's head bobbled forward, and his chin rested on his chest, the heavy gold mallard beak now missing its heavenly mark by a good forty-five degrees. No longer aimed skywards to channel The Word from above, the axis mundi of the Holy High Hat, the conduit between the Heavenly Father and the Earthly One, had lost its bearings.

It slumped.

It sagged.

The convocation of Cardinals began to relax as the golden beak drooped further until at last, it thunked on the table and the divine dozing duck floated away on the blessed river of oblivion.

The Cardinals sent up silent Pater Nosters of gratitude.

The Prerogative sidestepped, the discussion quickly came to a point. The Holy High Magus, Magistrate of the Magistere directed Bunbury to pass around copies of the photograph. Delacroix testified favorably, jockeying for a favorable position.

All agreed the arrival of a foreign divinity in the Americas was a dire threat to the authority of The Great Church. Something must be done.

The collective concern, as always, was the corrosive of change. Over the centuries, as consciousness evolved and paradigms shifted, the birdmen did not like to massage their set credos and vintage ideologies. It was awkward to refit doctrine to the whims of science. It was painful to acknowledge error or admit doubt. If only those damn dinosaur bones had stayed buried. It confounded the legion of followers when the Keepers of the Truth had to amend the certainties. It cast doubt upon the Cardinals' connection to The One Great God, The One Universal Supreme Being.

One God was plenty. The Church and its God were either everything or nothing.

The tragedy of these religious was that they existed in a perpetual state of spiritual deprivation. Their prayers had grown stale from hundreds of years of repetition. To put it bluntly: they were starving. Their invocations, Paters and Aves no longer nourished, leaving the Cardinals prey to powerful addictions. They wore gold snuff boxes on chains and occasionally allowed themselves what they called "preventative sniffs" of purloined prayers.

The Holy High Magus had recently test-marketed a new prayer elixir, a spritz and sniff maximus. He named his perfect drug Humboldt Snow #7 in honor of the unprecedented snowfall seven years back, in honor of seven productive years in the tower, and in honor of a certain seven-year-old boy.

Word of the sensational designer drug had been circulating in the Sanctum gossip mills for weeks. The creative chemist had saved his extraordinary product for a politically rainy day. Now a storm was coming on.

The Excellent Holy High Magus, His Eminence Cardinal Cassowary, Magistrate of the Magistere Magisterium and Court Astrologer stood up. The room went silent. At his signal, a twitter of white-gloved Budgies carrying silver trays entered the meeting hall and stood at attention, pearly buttons shining, puffy pants ballooning. The trays were filled with heaping mounds of white powder. The Cardinals shifted in their seats, eyes glued to those beautiful white hills.

Cardinal Cassowary feigned indifference to the row of immaculately groomed Budgies with their loaded trays and made his play, "We must regroup forces and prepare an offensive. Take the convent by siege and rescue the boy from damnation. I will draw up the plans. Delacroix, Oolumbo, Bunbury will meet with me informally tomorrow in my apartments to finalize the details."

The Holy High Magus made no mention of the giant white beast he had encountered in the forest.

"I trust there are no objections," the Magus concluded.

There were none.

All attention was fixed on the white hills.

"Free samples," Cardinal Cassowary smiled, "Good God trip, my good fellows."

———

HIS EMINENCE CARDINAL CASSOWARY, had long harbored a secret wish behind his breastbone. Unfortunately, there was no monkey to tap it. Not even the Magus himself suspected the existence of this untapped desire. As far as he knew, what he most wanted was power. He wanted to run the greatest show on Earth. He wanted to be Hierophant. He had no clue whatsoever that the votes he tallied up in his dreams would never satisfy the hunger that growled in the pit of his being, that prowled under his night dreams, that curled like a sleeping cat in his unconscious.

He thought of himself as a self-propelled wheel, the ultimate free agent. In truth, his secret desire ruled him. It fueled his every compulsion to remake himself, to invent scientific marvels, to create miracle drugs, to rise in the Church hierarchy. It seemed counter-intuitive that he would choose the life of a churchman. Not particularly religious, he didn't so much want to worship as he wanted to be worshipped. His great unappeased longing was for devotion—a pure devotion, untainted by fear, resentment, or jealousy.

Yes. The monster wanted to be loved, revered, doted upon. And in the kaleidoscopic dance of retributions and just desserts, the wish granting dervishes, the cosmic imps of fate who spin the Great Wheel of Fortune and Misfortune, who turn the heavenly Carmina Burana, who engine the Divine Ferris Wheel of the Stars, conspired to give the Magus exactly what he didn't know he wanted.

Viewed at a celestial distance, His Eminence Cardinal Cassowary, was a tantalizing spiritual enigma, a near miss, a brilliant failure, an intriguing karmic puzzle. One by one the infinitely slow pieces were coming together, forming a picture that included a variable array of disparate futures. It was a carefully watched queue of futures—the lineup of probables and possibles vying for that simple twist of fate.

Then twist happened.

One day the Magus had broken down and wept in his prison cell. And on that day, the fates moved a few select futures into the realm of likelihood.

For seven years, impelled by a mysterious attraction, the Magus had returned again and again to Mary Extraordinary's breviary, *What the Goat Girl Dreamed at the Holiday Inn*. Each time he made the decision to destroy the book, the decision would unmake itself. Over and again Cassowary would find himself perusing the poems, sometimes strangely uplifted, more often disturbed by their mysteries.

Nearing the close of his prison term, Cassowary had torn out page after page from Extraordinary's prayer book, brushing hot angry tears from his human eyes. He cut the pages into strips, boiled the paper to a mush, squeezed out the potent elixir, added a few secret ingredients, dried it and ground it to a fine powder.

As he cooked, he wept and breathed in the fumes. A molecular conversation took place between his amygdala and the scent of a different story. Under the influence of the *Goat Girl*, drafting compass in hand, he drew up plans.

New plans.

Garden plans.

Beautifully drafted, beautifully crafted, the scrolls were unceremoniously tossed aside in Cassowary's prison suite.

He couldn't destroy them. He couldn't forget them. He couldn't keep himself from taking another look, from making just one more tiny tweak. A day arrived when the beauty simply became unbearable and he handed the drawings off to Bunbury.

"Get rid of these scrolls," the Magus instructed.

Bunbury, who loved nothing better than courting the favors of those in high places, was granted an audience with the Divine Duck. And so it came to pass that the plans landed in the hands of His Holiness, the Hierophant, who was also perplexed by the unbearable beauty of Cardinal Cassowary's drawings.

The Magus was simply glad to be rid of *The Goat Girl* and the scrolls. A habitual maker of plans, and for the most part certain that he was king of his own cognizance, the industrious Magus refused to understand that his drawings were syncretic transcriptions of Extraordinary's prayers and were, in great measure, an answer to those prayers.

Unfortunately for the ancient prioress, there was a downside, and the downside was steep. The extracted drug had a tapper on her soul. It was her essence, after all. And a powerful essence it was, made even more potent when kinetically linked to the deprivations and desires of the user. The addictive effect of Humboldt Snow #7 would be exponentially intensified by the spiritual longings of the malnourished birdmen.

Not many heavenly loaves have a shelf-life of eternity, no matter what additives promise fortification, no matter what enchantments are muttered over the communion crusts. For the ecclesiastical birdmen, longtime eaters of wonder breads long past their expiration dates, one whiff of the freshly milled powder was all it took. The free samples had them hooked.

Cardinal Cassowary's designer prayer-inhalant hit the market with a bang and a good deal of whimpering. As a sly nod to its source, Humboldt Snow #7 was given a handy acronym by the Magus: GOAT—greatest of all time.

Got Goat? became an opening salvo, pandered in whispers in the sacred halls of the Sanctum.

Spiritual orgasms were achieved in record numbers. Demand was high. Return business was brisk. For a precious sum, Cardinal Cassowary refilled the gold amulets of his confrères. Uninterested in money, he was generous with loans. Everyone was his friend. No one loved him.

Back in the early days of chemical cookery, the Magus had distilled the works of poets and prophets, both the known and unknown. Over time he developed a connoisseur's taste for originals; the mythic voice, the hermetic koan, the unmistakable enchantments of innovation. Then during the historic Inquisition of the Sisterhoods and the consequent ransacking of convent libraries, Cassowary lucked onto the homemade prayers of the Sisters of Immaculate Conceptions. That iteration became the famous Prayer Juice series #9, only recently surpassed in the realms of higher hosannas by the incomparable Humboldt Snow #7, aka GOAT.

Through the years, the Cardinals remained unaware that they were hooked on the prayers and aphorisms of literary outliers and spiritual rogues. They were caught in a maelstrom of hunger for the very substances they condemned, virtual prisoners of their own dogma, cuffed and jailed by their own thought police. Their dry papery souls thirsted for the homemade moonshine, the divine ecstatic expostulations and holy ejaculations of soul-sprung verse.

Denied.

Trapped in ancient orthodoxies, these priests could no longer range freely on the evolving spiritual frontiers. Under the Golden Duomo of the Sanctum, no priest dared admit he had been abandoned by the deity he professed to adore.

Just keep praying. Just keep swallowing the wine and wafers and bird seed. The very thought that others were nibbling on pink-frosted metaphysical cookies, sanctified soufflés, consecrated truffles, or spiritual shrimp toasts was infuriating.

Back in the days of inquisitional rigor, storm-trooper priests had stomped out the bright fires that the luminous Sisters of the Joyous Mystery lit on their newly-minted holidays, closed that chapter of heretical lunacy with a satisfying slam. Now the closed chapter insisted on opening itself up again, opening its doors to a foreign deity. It was an outrage that burned in the Cardinals' veins and pumped venom into their hearts. These men of rules and holy orders would rather murder a world than expose themselves to change.

It is a terrible condition to be tantalized by what you revile. In this dark tumult, the holy men had stumbled upon the perfect formula for making monsters of themselves.

They were the prayer eaters.

# FIRST CONTACT

AT THE FIRST SCINTILLA of twilight, Conrad opened the four sets of double doors and stepped out onto the terrace. He lifted his arms in a semaphore of universal greeting, letting interested parties know that the runway was clear. Then he extended the aerial from his walkie-talkie.

"Hello. Hello. This is Conrad Eppler calling from station Earth. Conrad Eppler attempting contact. Hello. Hello. Anybody out there?" Conrad scanned the bowl of sky from horizon to horizon.

No unusual glimmer. No unusual ripples or riffs of star-song. The celestial DJ was playing oldies. All patterns holding. Each star in its place. The hum of the universe unchanged.

He'd try again after dinner. Skipper warned him not to put any specifics out on the airwaves because a wish was very like a prayer, and there were hungry spirits abroad who feasted on prayers.

*Stray prayers,* cautioned the monkey, *are peanut butter and jelly for the spiritually starving.*

This notion sounded preposterous to Conrad. However, the boy was schooled to suspend judgment, schooled to consider the unlikely—more than consider, he was encouraged to relish the unlikely, the unknowns and improbables. So he examined the monkey's proposition further.

Perhaps if the jelly in your jar had gone bad, and if the bread in your cupboard had gone stale and no one baked fresh loaves, someone might be jealous of another person's PB&J. He could see that. Or maybe Sister Subordinary's bread might have special ingredients or was combined in a unique way. Something to think about. He trusted the monkey.

———

LATER THAT NIGHT, when Conrad stretched out the aerial on his walkie-talkie once again, he gave no hint of the inner shape of his prayer. He held the images of his longed-for parents in the privacy of his beautiful mind and simply repeated:

"Hello. Hello. Conrad Eppler calling. Conrad Eppler, waiting patiently. Hello. Anyone listening?"

No response.

Conrad sat on the edge of his bed and flipped through a copy of X-men. He'd always been good at this, putting his mind in the elsewhere with the help of his comics. He studied a drawing of Storm. She was his favorite female character, with her power over the weather. Her long white hair reminded him of Mother Mary. He missed Mother Mary Extraordinary, missed their nighttime swims, their long meditations under water. He guessed that she still hadn't completely recovered from death's knock.

Losing himself in his comics was proving difficult tonight. Waiting for someone to answer his radio signals and simultaneously trying not to wait for new parents made him uncharacteristically antsy.

He hopped over to his telescope, checked the night sky. It was the same maddeningly beautiful winking display, his intimate familiar, memorized over nights of study and longing. He tried the walkie-talkie again and added the walkie part; this time he paced back and forth on the terrace while dialing up the universe of air. He paused, held the transceiver to his ear and listened for an answer.

A slight movement in the night sky caught his eye. A star was missing. Eclipsed. It twinked back on. Something was moving awfully fast out there. He ran back to his telescope. Three bright objects were coming closer.

And closer.

Conrad raced back inside and sat expectantly on the edge of his bed, an orphan on the verge, riding the swerve of a continuously revamped future. He would have been perplexed had he been able to hear the conversation taking place just then between the three glowing spheres.

"What a slippery atmosphere," one orb commented.

"Ew, the clouds are wet. I'm not going to appear like this. I've ruined my dress," another huffed.

"Spin dry, delicate cycle," a third sphere teased.

Two of the glowballs gave the one in the wet dress a shove and sent her tumbling in a spiral of giggles.

From his perch on the bed, Conrad watched one star grow brighter and cartwheel out of control, radiating whorls of fractured light, a Fourth-of-July pinwheel of prismatic sparkles. The boy was all heightened expectation.

"I'm here," Conrad urged under his breath. "Come on down."

The carefully watched sky-riders happened to be an adulation of adolescent angels out and about. They'd been giving planet Earth a cruise-by when Conrad's radio signals hit the airwaves. These three high-octane hopefuls were fly-bys, fireflies, gem-toned glow sticks, skylarks out larking, dressed to the nines and tens and elevens—groomed to the ends of perfection. Flush with slumber party anticipations, the transcendent trio had slipped past their minders unseen. It was their big night out. Holy! Holy! Holy! *In Excelsis*! Angel babes on the loose in the galaxy.

For a while there, back on planet Grace, they had been caught in a tangle of clichés—all dressed up with nowhere to go, pixilated pixies with nowhere to post, twitters with no followings. All those pink puffs of prayers and all that lovingly detailed prep, from the tip of their wings to their star-dusted toes, was all for naught until Aletheia said, "What about Earth?"

An appearance was the very thing these spiritual glitterati needed to release all that pent up Pentecostal juice. These pre-orgasmic babes were on the hunt for a magic red-carpet glide where they could strut their star stuff, light up the zoom lens of an eternal camera roll with break-your-heart smiles.

Too bad they overshot the Hollywood sign. These wing siblings would have adored being chased by paparazzi—flashing lights, write-ups and exposés in magazines, dust-ups posted online—all OMG and LOVE and not a MEH among them. They were divine baby stars, so nova and ultrafine, they had the step and rhyme. Decked out in designer gear, they were the ultimate angel flash, the original dreamgirls, singing out *discover me.* Litanies of look-at-me. Searchlights on high beam, sky-scanners announcing the big event: coming soon to a theatre near you!

Or a convent.

When Conrad aimed his telescope at those three bright orbs hovering over Humboldt County, they felt that first electrifying thrum and surge, that gleam, that gift, that golden moment of being observed. Like Schrodinger's hello kitties, their subatomic particles got a wallop.

And they fell, skidding to a stop in the sky just above the terrace outside Conrad's window.

Then, they saw him—so unprepossessing and small.

"Look."

"Where?"

"There. Isn't he pretty?" Aletheia, the emerald angel undulated as she spoke.

"What in the seven worlds is it?" Epiphany, the rubellite angel questioned with palpable disdain, shifting her colors from red to shocking pink, then settling on magenta.

"It must be one of their young," cooed the Periwinkle, the amethyst angel, oddly taken with the curious, colorless creature.

There was a crackle of static, and the angels bent to listen as Conrad shot another transmission into the starry night.

"Come on. Let's do it. He wants us," the emerald angel teased.

"We don't know what he wants. We'll get in trouble," the amethyst angel demurred.

So the gem-toned beauties paused for a micro-mini fraction of a second as a concession to the unknown and possible trouble. Then kissing caution adieu, they revved their mighty flighties.

"Wings up," the green angel signaled.

"Angel lights on," the magenta powered up.

"Brakes off," exhaled a breathless purple.

The blithe emerald-green dreamgirl led the way down the star step. With a plosive pop, she passed through the portal of materiality and stood on air, rippling inside the plate-glass window. She was still a flat screen transparency when she whispered, "Conrad, we're here."

"Show time!" The magenta angel was standing right at his shoulder, her vocal tintinnabulations spiraling down his ear canal, molecular imps on a waterslide. Splish. Splash. Splish. "Heads up, Conrad."

The startled boy was just starting to make out the shape of the green angel in the glass when the magenta angel's atonal waterworks filled his ear. Fractal by fractal, the angelettes were taking on material form.

"Incoming angel!" The purple angel miscalculated and found herself crawling out from under Conrad's bed.

"Periwinkle. Really?" The magenta dreamgirl turned away.

Conrad looked down and there was a pale purple angel pushing herself inelegantly on her back, right beneath his dangling legs. A shy, embarrassed "hi" bubbled on her glossy lavender lips.

"Sorry, Epiphany. Can I try again?" Periwinkle did her best to recover dignity and made a show of puffing up her ruffled feathers.

"You spoiled our first appearance!" Epiphany was miffed. Preening magenta wings, she scoffed over her shoulder, "How could you?"

The collective illuminati had all but forgotten the boy sitting on the end of the bed, when his small voice tapped the air with a quiet, "Hello."

The three angels turned in unison and studied him.

It was a difficult moment.

Of the four, Conrad was the most troubled. He had been imagining parents for so long. The father was drawn and detailed with absolute clarity in the boy's mind, their future meeting carefully rehearsed in Conrad's waking dream life—a man whom he already loved, someone around the corner, almost tangible, certainly more real than the comic book hero that inspired his invention.

Now, here were these three jewel-toned creatures, breathtakingly beautiful, but silly and impossibly young. He regretted not giving the mother more thought. Perhaps, because he already had three mothers, the want was never keenly registered, so his desire never took on a definitive thought-form.

He should have asked for Silk Spectre or Storm. Those comic book heroines weren't very mothery, but at least they had powers and a certain fierce dignity. Conrad was convinced that Skipper had misled him. It was a mistake not to be more specific with the wording of a prayer.

The angels were not any more copacetic with the developing scene than Conrad. They were embarrassed by Periwinkle's clumsy entrance. An entrance is supposed to entrance.

Truth to tell, they were even more embarrassed by their collective existential impasse. They had dreamed this moment for eons. Their first appearance. Being seen. The show. Every angel in the knest anticipated what they called a "fly up," even though the cosmos was a spiraling affair without ups or downs.

Just now, the three angelettes were suffering from a severe failure of imagination, precisely because they had never bothered to imagine the moment that came next.

After the entrance. After the beguile. There was supposed to be a prestige. Something for the Holy Books.

They didn't want to admit that even though they had managed to arrive, they were still just adolescent angels, all dressed up with no place to go. Dreamgirls without a clue. Star-struck by their own audacity and riddled with stage fright.

At last, the green girl broke through the dilatory silence, running an improvised script.

"We're special angels, at your service," she offered tentatively. "Level one. First appearance."

"We heard your prayer tonight, and right from the start it went straight to the heart." Epiphany chimed in, getting her groove on, flashing the magenta charm.

"And you knocked us right out of the sky." Periwinkle finally broke through her tongue-tied stage fright.

There was a collective sigh of self-approval. Then silence.

Awkward moment happening again.

"WOW!" Conrad quoted from a comic book.

The perplexed boy really wasn't all that wowed, but he felt they needed encouragement. He actually saw the "wow" in a jagged thought balloon, inked bold and black, all caps, with a nice fat exclamation point. He had been repeating this caption over and over until it finally jumped out of the balloon and into the room.

"WOW!" he tried again, warming up. "So? My prayer knocked you out of the sky. And you landed in America. Did you know that? This is America," Conrad rambled on, doing his best to be a good host. "And this is my room. And this is my monkey, Skipper, the Gospel Monkey. He was in the box with me when the Sisters found me."

The angelettes listened in baffled silence.

Conrad beckoned his visitors, "Come here. No, really, come on," he coaxed. Finally, he had an inspiration.

Conrad crawled under his bed, clearly expecting the angels to follow suit. They stood, dumbfounded by this vocal creature, until Conrad reappeared pushing a small trove of comic books out in front of him. He passed them around.

Periwinkle, blinking tiny purple lights, sat enchanted by the drawings.

"Wow," said Periwinkle, imitating Conrad's vocalization.

"Silk Spectre," Conrad told Periwinkle, tapping the page. "She's amazing." The boy hopped over to the magenta angel. "That's Storm," Conrad instructed Epiphany.

Epiphany studied Storm, unimpressed.

Conrad guessed that the green one was in charge, so he signaled her to sit next to him.

"Here, you can have this one," he urged, flipping open the book to a well-worn, sun-faded page. This is a picture of the dad I want. His name is Epic. Here, take it. You can have it. For keeps. A present."

Aletheia instantly put up her guard, rapidly changing shades of green. "Oh, no. We absolutely cannot accept gifts."

Thinking quickly and belatedly about the consequences of bringing contraband back to Grace, she snatched up the comic books from a nonplussed Epiphany and a disappointed Periwinkle. Then she handed them back to a puzzled little boy.

Conrad, however, demonstrated some amazing bounce and immediately got his hopes back up where they belonged.

"I bet you have a photographic memory just like me. Am I right?"

Baffled silence.

He changed tack. "Isn't there a message? Something you're supposed to say *unto* me?"

More silence. Existential doubt was sneaking back in. *What were they doing here?* Each angel wondered. Their collective unconscious shrugged, and the boy sensed he was losing them.

"Don't be shy," Conrad encouraged. "I'm glad you're here. Want to play?"

"No, we can't stay," the green one glimmered at him. "We just dropped in to say—." She glanced at her sister angels, who glanced away. Then the emerald angel plucked a message out of the shimmering air, "Blessed be Earth boys."

"Yes! Bless, bless," Periwinkle and Epiphany echoed. Happy with their exit lines and satisfied that the appearance had ultimately taken a graceful turn, the purple and magenta angelettes twinked out.

"Don't go!" cried an alarmed boy.

Conrad was just warming up to his new friends. They filled his room with such giddy effervescence, like shaken soda bottles bubbling over, popcorn hitting the lid of a pan, caramel crackling, bubble gum snapping. They might not be mom material, but they sure looked like fun.

The green one lingered, caught by the longing in the Earth boy's blue eyes. So he had time to say, "I don't even know your name. What's your name?"

"Aletheia. Next time, Starfriend."

In a blink, she was gone. And with her, all the color drained from Conrad's room.

When illuminati depart, they have no idea of the gray world they leave behind. Conrad noticed that the sunny yellow had drained from his bedroom walls. His bright blue jammies were now a pallid gray. It was as if the angels packed up the rainbow when they left. He'd been robbed.

It wasn't fair.

————

Luckily, He'd Shown the presence of mind to ask for Aletheia's name before she dashed away. It is a considerable power to be able to call an angel by name. But Conrad figured there were sure to be unknown risks.

He wondered if angels needed colors for fuel to get back home. He wondered if he'd ever see his familiar surround restored to its former color-saturated loveliness. A disconsolate Conrad tried to engage Skipper in a mindtalk parlay. He wanted explanations. The walkie-talkie maneuver failed to yield the hoped-for results.

No Epic. No Mom. A world gone gray.

*Skip, why did the angels leave? I wish you'd talk to me.*

Skipper was not being responsive. He seemed stuck in his toy monkey act just when Conrad needed consolation and guidance. Conrad guessed that the monkey might be reserving spiritual juices, recharging his karmic batteries. But it was all surmise and speculation. The monkey wasn't talking.

Conrad was partly right in his guess. The monkey did need to recharge, but he also meant to test Conrad's ability to draw from inner resources.

Alone was a huge unexplored territory for the boy. The divine issue of two ancient lineages, worlds apart, an illegitimate son, unacknowledged, he was heir to nothing but his spiritual genome. And that genome was a doozie. The child was endowed with exceptional resources—to create, to destroy—rich veins the boy had yet to tap. The monkey wanted to see how Conrad handled a dark night of the soul.

"Who is this boy," Lord Hanuman wanted to know, "when things do *not* go his way?"

For the next couple of days, Conrad was pretty much left to himself. The Sisters spent a good deal of time in silent meditation and urgently whispered conversation, just the sort of corner-conferencing that makes a boy curious enough to listen at doorways. He felt the danger and heard the talk of prayer eaters and soul sickness. Conrad understood that Mother Mary had had a close call. He guessed that the Sisters had retreated into silent meditation to protect themselves from some celestial shark that preyed on hopes and dreams. Why else all this silent prayer and whispered urgency?

His eavesdropping, combined with Skipper's previous warnings about hungry spirits, made Conrad cautious. He'd been warned against scenting the air with spiritual PB&Js. He did not want to attract the bad guys. His one close call with the Magus had been close enough.

As much as he longed to raise up the aerial on his walkie-talkie and offer clarifications, as much as he wanted to make sure that the angels understood the particulars of his request for parents, he dared not give voice to his desires. He was stuck in an uneasy abeyance—bombarded with second thoughts, unable to fall asleep, picturing a huge, hungry celestial shark circling the night sky.

Conrad was on the brink of changing his mind. He felt bossed by all the warnings, whisperings, and confidences withheld. He did not like being circumscribed by caution.

Rebellion stirred.

His finger was on the walkie-talkie button, and he was sorely tempted to risk calling on the green angel. The call would be a powerful one, especially now that he knew her name: Aletheia. The Greek spelling came easily to him. Conrad wrote her name in a comic thought balloon: Ἀλήθεια.

The boy hesitated, the inscribed thought hanging above his head in a perfect white cloud. In that moment's hesitation, Mother Mary's deep meditative voice reached him, and the silver linings of the cloud were illuminated.

*Let me mind the cloud. Your thoughts will be safe with me,* she offered.

*What about me? Who will mind me?* Conrad questioned.

*Look for the gift in the empty cup.*

*I'd like to give that cup a good kick.* Petulance clouded the boy's blue eyes.

*Your choice.*

Though it wasn't the answer he was looking for, Conrad recognized the call for what it was—an invitation to dive into a mystery.

*Come with me*, Conrad entreated Mother Mary.

*I'll mind your thought cloud. You take a flying leap,* she chuckled. *Imagine that your soul is a quarry pool.*

Conrad took a deep breath. He saw a pool in his mind's eye.

His pool.

His soul.

And he jumped. By himself. Then he spiraled down a sheer wall of blue. When he came back up he knew what he must do.

Nothing.

Sitting on his bed in lotus pose, a picture-perfect Padmasana, Mother Mary came back to him, a vision as real as his living breath. She handed him the cloud that was floating above his head.

Again, he saw what he must do. He erased Aletheia's name from the thought cloud. He let it go, let the empty cloud drift away. He bowed his head. Tears fell into his cupped hands. After a while, the tears dried. His breath stilled. His heart quieted. His longing dissipated.

Freed from desire, Conrad dropped deeper into his own diamond mind. He entered a cave and came to a stream. With a staff that he found leaning against a tree, he changed the course of the water. Following the water's new course, he came to a grotto. A small overflowing crystal cup sat balanced on a ledge. He reached for the cup and drank deeply.

And there it was: the gift at the bottom of the empty cup— emptiness. That same maddening gift. Or was it?

This cup wasn't just any cup, nor was it some universal idea of a cup. It was the cup in his hand. All at once he understood that you could never hold the same cup twice. He saw that there was a particular emptiness in this cup, in this moment—a call.

He was being asked to step back, to give the universe some room to work its magic.

The universe did not like being bossed.

The very notion of a boy running an angel, or a monkey, much less the universe, was ridiculous. Conrad laughed out loud and immediately came home to his body.

He let himself sink into the exquisite happiness of being a boy, sitting Padmasana on a bed, with a stuffed monkey in his lap, a boy repeating his mantra—*Earth is the best place for love*—a boy on a bed on a spinning ball, hurtling through the big blue mystery.

Coming out of his meditation and picking through his new discoveries, Conrad knew three things with a rock-solid certainty.

One, that he was brave.

Two, that he was free to choose and not choose.

The third certainty made a mystery of the second: All had been settled in the long ago.

By whatever distant arithmetic the Gods make their calculations, the green angel was his chosen, the one meant to adopt him. He could change the course of that stream, and so could she, and so could many others besides. But right this minute, the light was green.

A portal had been opened. The universe had chosen for him.

Humbled by the insight and newly awakened to the knowledge that a generous gift that had been offered, Conrad deeply regretted thinking that Aletheia was silly. Before he fell asleep, he remembered his manners in time to whisper, "Thank you."

When the *thank you* left his lips and flew out the window, he cautiously allowed himself to fall a little bit in love with the emerald angel.

In the morning, Conrad could see colors again.

# Malicious Trespass

CONRAD WAS STANDING on the terrace the next morning, glad to be a boy in a world filled with color, when he heard the bells. Not the deep sonorous prayer bells, not the silvery foundling bells. These were striking, insistent clangs of warning. Cardinals had been sighted.

Conrad ducked inside. Instinct made him close and lock the four sets of double French doors. Risking a glance or two out the mullioned windows, trying to spot the enemy, he moved quickly from one set to another. His fingers felt stiff and clumsy. The strident bells continued their jarring clangs. Conrad jumped onto his bed, tore back the covers. His heartbeat thudded in his ears. Where was Skipper?

Mother Mary Extraordinary came charging in, her veil undone, her white hair tangled in the air. In one motion, she grabbed up Conrad and unlocked one of the doors. Out and down the steps, she flew to the edge of the quarry pool and tossed an amazed boy into the pool.

Mary Extraordinary was back in Conrad's room in a flash. She and Sister Merry Berry made quick work of stripping the room of any evidence of boy.

Conrad swam to the bottom of the pool. In the deepest part, there was an underwater cave. Conrad could remain in that dark water-filled cavern indefinitely; he shared a deviant genomic inscription with Extraordinary that allowed him to breathe water. They had rehearsed this drill many times. It was a game Conrad enjoyed tremendously, back when it was just a game. Let's play *The Cardinals Are Coming*.

"Now jump!" Mother Mary would order. And Conrad would embrace the cold water with a running leap. Then he'd make his way quickly down. He had a strong kick. Guha strong. Over time, they outfitted the water-filled cavern with comforting accessories. Underwater flash lights. A weighted belt, so Conrad could stay down without effort. Snacks that could be sucked down through a special straw. Although once Conrad achieved a state of suspended animation, he no longer experienced hunger.

This time however, he didn't want to let go of consciousness quite so fast. This was the real deal. He sucked one of the glucose snacks out its foil packet. His instructions were to sit in meditation and slide gently into a deep alpha state. More difficult to achieve when your heart is racing.

He was worried about his friends. Everyone he loved was up there on the surface. He knew that a pulsing wave-like signal would stir the water when everything was safe again. What if the signal never came? What if he emerged and everything he knew and everyone he loved were gone? And when had he last seen the white monkey?

His mind was a turbulence of questions, like a washing machine agitating a load of colors—red, black, magenta, periwinkle and green thoughts chasing each other in circles. Cardinals. Nuns. Gemstone angels. He started to feel dizzy and short of breath and realized that he was approaching a danger zone. He struggled to restore an even, rhythmic breath cycle: inhaling water through his nose, exhaling hydrogen through his mouth. If he gasped for breath, he would inhale a great lungful of cold water and die.

Conrad looked into his heart and sought out the green angel from the tangle of multi-colored thoughts. He heard her say, "Next time, Starfriend," and he let go.

Now he sat Padmasana, three inches above the cavern floor, at peace—his trust in the green angel exquisite and complete. There would be a next time, and that was enough.

———

ON THE SURFACE, all was turbulence. The Convent of Immaculate Conceptions was under siege. The invading forces were divided into two wings, one approaching from the front, the other from the rear.

The forest contingent was led by the Magus. For this occasion, he was decked out in his full cassowary regalia, with the addition of a brass and silver Roman helmet, its transverse of horsehair bristles dyed orange. Acting as self-appointed Commander-in-Chief, his vanity had carried him to new heights of dominance display.

Commander Cassowary was counting on Conrad Eppler making a break for the woods. The velvet sack for the prized boy was at the ready. This time he was prepared to make quick meat of the monkey.

Inside the convent, three breathless nuns gathered their collective will for the confrontation. Sister Merry Berry, all nerves, had argued that they really ought to call the secular police. The Cardinals had no authority over the Sisters, had lost that authority when the charter was revoked.

Still there was the question of the boy, Sister Subordinary cautioned. Conrad had never been registered with the state. This objection merited further consideration, but there was no time for further considerations. Nor was there time to pursue another question of interest: who had sounded the warning bell?

The second contingent, led by Cardinal Delacroix, was stepping quickly up the drive. The front gate had been breached. The enemy was lined up on the porte cochere.

Sister Merry Berry opened the door.

Cardinal Delacroix made no effort to repress a look of studied repugnance. His Eminence took in her unorthodox appearance one jarring increment at a time—starting with the large floppy rainbow-colored Rastafarian beret sliding off her exuberant tangle of dreadlocks, pausing at her habit's immodest hemline, his gaze finally stopped at her fluorescent running shoes.

This was no convent. This was a covey of lunatics. The ferret on his shoulder seemed to disagree and began dooking, an affective little cross between a quack and coo.

Cardinal Delacroix shushed the animal. Then he swallowed his disgust and prepared to push his way past the inconsequent nun, his posse of Cardinals in tow.

"Don't you dare!"

Straightening up, the Cardinal met the cold gaze of Mother Mary Extraordinary. Unveiled, her tent of long white hair gave her a striking appearance, but it was her ineluctable scowl that stopped him. In fact, her Kabuki stare backed up the entire regiment of Cardinals. The would-be trespassers tripped over their own red robes, knocking into one another. A set of topsy-turvy red dominoes, they tumbled, hats knocked askew, kohl-circled eyes wide and blinking.

Mary Extraordinary kept her eyes locked on Cardinal Delacroix, and when he finally roused himself to return her glare, she literally stopped his heart. Instinct made him grab his chest, and his hand found the amulet suspended from his neck. Unscrewing the golden vial in two awkward turns, he lifted it to his left nostril and took a deep reviving sniff.

Mother Mary Extraordinary immediately fell unconscious to the ground.

The salve of her prayers massaging his malevolent heart, Delacroix allowed himself what passed for a smile. Then he stepped over Mary Extraordinary and entered the convent. The unkindness of Cardinals grabbed their hats, righted themselves, and followed suit, stepping over the fallen nun, red capes flowing like a river of blood through the convent door.

"Go," Subordinary urged Merry Berry, "I'll tend Mother Mary."

The short, round nun pushed her way through the flock of red capes and made as if to lead them on a tour of the convent. Oddly enough, they let themselves be led.

Cardinal Oolumbo paused in the Chapel and snapped several pictures with his u-phone but missed the trick panel that hid the aumbry.

There was an uncomfortable moment in the pantry. Merry Berry's concern mounted. They might spot the door to the wine cellar. To her relief, the shelf of pots hastily rolled in front of the cellar door when the alarm sounded held up as camouflage.

Now, swinging through Conrad's room, they verged on more dangerous ground.

Sister Merry Berry's heart raced. Thankfully, the nuns had been thorough in eliminating any outward sign of boy. *Fool*, Merry Berry rebuked herself. She deeply regretted not admitting to the hidden stash of comic books and boy toys—the cache of Conrad's happy childhood no longer seemed a whimsical delinquency. If one of those priestly intruders bent low and looked under the bed-skirts, the game would be up.

"The guest room," Merry Berry managed to slide in a half-truth, eyes wide. "Your ferret looks hungry. Perhaps we should go back to the kitchen. Do ferrets eat carrots?" she trailed off.

Cardinal Delacroix smelled boy in her evasion and once again studied the ridiculous nun, "I suppose you have a vault where you've secured the gold that we gifted your order on our last visit? Was that seven years ago?"

"Yes, seven and no. That little bag of gold is long gone."

"Little?"

"Taxes," Merry Berry improvised. "Bless you and bless the Hierophant, His Holiness, the Munificentissimus Mallard. He must have guessed. We owed a pontiff's ransom in back taxes. Such munificence!" She smiled.

With cunning foresight, Merry Berry had taken the red velvet bag of gold and stashed it in the wine cellar. In the event the Magistere discovered the location of the vault at the back of the tabernacle, they would find it empty but for a couple bottles of wine that Merry Berry liked to keep at hand.

"And the music box?"

"Such a beautiful object, much too much for our simple ways. But, a perfect wedding gift for Alyssa Rosaria Dante." Sister Merry Berry had no idea it was so easy to lie.

Cardinal Delacroix knew the seven-year-old boy was still in residence, tucked away in some hidey-hole. The Magus had seen him, had recorded the image with his replicant eye and had produced a high definition hologram of the boy seated on the forest floor, his blue eyes full of terror.

It was all a game, of course—the parlay betwixt nun and Cardinal. A high-stakes game.

Both Delacroix and Merry Berry knew that the three gifts delivered seven years ago were meant for a baby divinity whose existence the nuns dared not admit, not seven years ago and not today.

"And the incense long since burned, I assume," Delacroix carried on the charade.

"Exactly. Frankincense, such a favorite among the heavenly host," Merry Berry played along.

Then abruptly, the Cardinal announced he would spend the night in the guest room, a preemptive move in this dangerous game of hegemony.

"I counted twenty empty cells on our tour. Plus, this nicely appointed *guest room*," he paused for effect. "Twenty-one Cardinals will stay the night. Hopefully an extended stay will not prove necessary. We'll leave after we visit with the boy."

Sister Merry Berry's newly discovered facility for lying deserted her. She said nothing.

"Perhaps you should check on your Mother Superior," Delacroix concluded.

With that dismissal, His Eminence moved out onto the terrace, and made as if he were taking in the view like any ordinary tourist on holiday. He admired the quarry pool, a mere twenty steps down from terrace. Scanning the vista, his attention was arrested by a rusting, turquoise and white Ford Fairlane parked at the far edge of the field. Was that a monkey waving at him from the driver's seat?

Delacroix's contingent had followed him outdoors and arrayed themselves along the balustrade in clusters of twos and threes. A murmur of Cardinals whispered in one corner. Oolumbo took out a pair of opera glasses, trying to determine exactly what was going on in the woods with the self-entitled Commander-in-Chief. Cardinal Cassowary's Roman helmet had put Cardinal Oolumbo in a twist the moment he laid eyes on it.

Cardinal Delacroix moved over to the telescope. The casing was sticky to the touch and he caught a whiff of peanut butter. He had to raise the tripod and it struck him that it had been the perfect height for a small boy. He focused the telescope on the Ford Fairlane. No monkey. It had been a long day.

Back in the library, Merry Berry was holding a court conference in her head. She really should call the police this very instant, shouldn't she? If by any chance the Cardinals nabbed Conrad and made off with him, it would be too late to place the call. The Cardinals had only to deny that such a boy existed, and who could prove otherwise?

The toys under the bed would hardly suffice as evidence that a boy had awakened in that very room just this morning. However, the stash was sufficient evidence to keep a predatory Cardinal on the scent. If she called the police on the Cardinals before the boy was discovered, she'd be in the clear. She made her closing argument and sent the jury out to deliberate. She'd poll them later. For now, she'd better check on Mother Mary and let her consoeurs know that twenty-one Cardinals planned to spend the night, one of them in Conrad's room.

———

MEANWHILE, BEYOND THE GARDEN and the laughing sundial, a fight of a different order of magnitude was gaining momentum. From the first flicker of daylight when the vigilant monkey spotted Commander Cassowary leading his wing of Cardinals into the woods, Lord Hanuman knew that blood would be shed before day's end.

No matter—the dauntless monkey was prepared to make any sacrifice. Lord Hanuman had once battled an army of demonic Rakshasas back in the glory days when he fought beside Jambavan, the Bear King, in defense of the lovely Sita. What did the peerless monkey care for a mere cassowary and a clutch of cardinals?

First things first. The monkey had raced back to the convent and rung the warning bell at the first sign of danger. Then back again to the break in the woods.

Lord Hanuman liked to loosen up before a battle, so dealing with the ostentatious Magus would have to wait while the monkey had his fun. Purposeful fun, of course. There was always a method to his mischief. He swung from tree to tree, menacing and teasing the Cardinals, driving them deeper into the woods, relieving them, one by one, of their precious drug-filled bejeweled amulets. Look up. Look down. Easy pickings for the swift and agile creature.

Then the white monkey turned his mind to what most intrigued him—the raptor-like claw that had reached out to grab Conrad. The claw that could rip his white fur to shreds was also the key to Cassowary's defeat. Instinctively, the monkey understood that the deadly claw was a weakness as well as a weapon.

Like every adept, Commander Cardinal Cassowary was at the mercy of his mighty ego. Past failures rankled him, pushed him into the darker recesses of scientific experiment and necromancy.

Cassowary's deep and abiding regret at the extinction of the dinosaurs was almost pathological. It was a heartbreaker when all of those impeccably designed giants went down.

Any child who has ever played with a set of miniature plastic dinos understands this. Any seven-year-old, given the chance to create a world, would want a T-Rex menacing a landscape fraught with volcanoes and meteor showers, not to mention vast oceans of creatures hunted by Megalodons.

The Magus dwelt in that mindset, delighted in it, thus his affinity for lizards, birds and all the precious remnants of the age of giants—the halcyon days of beautiful monsters: some benign, some bloody.

Every time the Excellent Holy High Magus looked at a chicken his heart went thwang. What a come-down! What sad retributive karma for the incomparable Tyrannosaurus Rex. A chicken. So many dinosaurs gone to the birds. Oh, well.

Even the Magus considered his ability to transform himself into an avian cardinal a mere parlor trick. A useful parlor trick, to be sure—it impressed the childlike Hierophant, and won him the coveted Cardinal's cap, not to mention the advantages of sudden flight and camouflage.

But it was the flightless cassowary that soared in the imagination of the Magus, far above and well beyond all other existent reptilian relations. The history of this singular obsession was complicated.

A native of his beloved Australia, this powerful and regal creature, descendant of that rock star of the mid-Jurassic—the Velociraptor—was one of the incredible Dromaeosauridae, the feathered running lizards. When the Dromaeosauridae ran, that blade-like middle toe never touched the ground. It was held aloft and slightly retracted, at the ready to slice off a leg or eviscerate an enemy.

Flipping the bird was no laughing matter for a sickle-clawed raptor—a insider joke the hermetic young Bishop liked to share with his Australian flock. Yes, once upon a rainforest the Magus preached exclusively to the birds and the reptiles. He regaled his listeners with legends of a fall from a Jurassic Eden. And oddly enough, it was love that had set him headlong and heedless on the path of self-transformation. It all began on the fateful day he adopted an orphaned hatchling in Queensland.

"Give us a shake," he'd say to his pet cassowary.

The bird would balance on one leg and offer a claw to his admiring master. How the Magus loved that marvelous claw.

He daydreamed.

He sketched.

He coveted.

While sitting at his makeshift desk back in the Daintree rainforest, the Magus would press the forefinger and ring finger of each hand against the eucalyptus planks, keeping the middle fingers lifted until he felt the enlivening surge in his brain stem, the acute chemical charge when the reptilian part of his brain went on red alert. Pressing down harder with the tips of his human fingers, his shoulder blades locked, his head bowed, his mind merged with the cassowary who looked in at him from a window.

This meeting of the minds was a signal moment for the reptile-besotted Bishop.

The very day his pet cassowary died, the bereft Magus brushed away steamy tears and began splicing genes, cloning and grafting stem cells. He kept the remaining cassowary parts in a deep freeze of his own design. By no means the first in the annals of science to experiment on himself, he was one of the more successful practitioners of the art of self-modification.

In the months after he was made Cardinal, he had successfully implanted and connected the optical nerves of the cassowary eyes to his occipital lobe. Then, during his years of imprisonment in the Sanctum Avesticum Quoborium, he worked on controlling the claw.

Almost by accident, he discovered how to become the big bird, flightless wings and all.

The bird wasn't all bad. Middle toe aside, that sometimes-terrifying beast had also evolved some positively endearing genetic qualities. The male cassowary was an exemplary father, an egg sitter and unabashed single parent. It might have been those very hyperbolic parenting genes that triggered Cardinal Cassowary's obsession with the boy in the first place. Conrad was something of a misplaced egg, after all.

Among the tallest and fastest of the two-legged flightless birds to have survived the Paleocene, the cassowary was arguably the most mesmerizing. Definitely an eye-catcher, with its shimmering black coat trimmed in turquoise and bright orange. A boney crest topped its small head, giving the long-necked creature its distinct noble bearing. Its large orange eyes hypnotized with their reptilian stare and lush lashes, beautiful and threatening all at once.

But to Commander Cardinal Cassowary, it was the middle toe, with its nine-inch black dagger, that defined the proud beast. One rip from that powerful claw and the coming fight was as good as over. Anticipating victory, the Magus had already designed a handsome commemorative medallion.

Lord Hanuman studied the enemy from his perch in one of the tall trees.

In full battle regalia, the Magus was truly a magnificent opponent. He wore a fitted iridescent turquoise jacket with a winged orange collar. One of the sleeves was striped black and gold to highlight the raptor claw that he held to his heart. His bronze and silver crested helmet, with its distinctive orange bristle gave off the stately aura of a Roman General.

Lord Hanuman appreciated the display, but he did not wish to fight the man with one claw. He meant to coax out the ancient Jurassic beast.

The Holy High Magus was in accord—he also meant to engage the monkey beast to beast. His great shamanic achievement—the ability to change himself into a full-blooded cassowary—would be put to the test. He welcomed the coming contest, had dreamed of this engagement in his prison suite, and had prayed for a worthy opponent.

Now the Commander stood in the exact spot where the boy had escaped after Lord Hanuman had shaken the forest and pounced in a surprise attack. Today would be a day like no other; Commander Cardinal Cassowary was primed for glory.

One critical caveat played on the mind of the Magus: the kill must be quick. In the heat of battle, his limbic system fired by blood lust, the Magus could not risk more than sixty seconds to make minced meat of his enemy. Beyond that brief interval, he could easily disappear into the bird, never to return.

A calculating man, caution was his watchword. Just once, he had let anger overcome reason, and the result was the permanent loss of one of his human hands. He did not regret the raptor claw; he only regretted that it hadn't been his choice.

Control was everything.

Commander Cardinal Cassowary would have to keep his guard up and operative in his towering neo-cortex if he wished to remain a big-brained primate for the duration of this incarnation. If he were provoked, the neo-cortex could be short-circuited; if the provocation were sustained, the reptilian part of the brain would be flooded with an aggression-inducing chemical cocktail of catecholamines.

The monkey meant to stir up that killer cocktail and keep his adversary's adrenals pumping. To that end, Lord Hanuman drew himself up and assumed the size of a three-hundred and fifty-pound gorilla, then thought better of it and reduced himself to the size of a man—a more tempting prey for a cautious adversary. Not so large as to intimidate, the clever monkey wanted to be a risk worth taking. He'd learned a valuable lesson from his last encounter. He didn't want Cassowary to shape-shift into a small cardinal mid-battle, dart off and reconfigure elsewhere.

The monkey's plan was simple. Provoke an attack. Then, prolong the fight.

Letting loose his signature call— the deafening primal cry of the wild—the monkey hurtled himself from branch to crackling branch. Then gathering his wits, he descended from the canopy with supple grace. This time the forest floor did not tremble. This time Lord Hanuman tilted his head inquisitively as he landed with a soft thud on the leafy mulch.

Mere inches separated the adversaries. The monkey and the Magus locked eyes. Lord Hanuman grunted and smiled, showing off a pair glistening incisors.

The reaction was instantaneous and bloody. The Magus drew out his one claw and raked it across the monkey's chest. Three red rivers bloomed on the white fur. The center cut went all the way to the bone. The monkey bellowed, hot spit dripping from his incisors. The reptilian part of the cassowary's brain inhaled the sweet rusty scent of fresh blood. In that instant man became bird—all fight and no flight.

Now there were two sickle-shaped retractable nine-inch nails at the ready. The bird jumped five feet in the air, lifting its claws in classic attack position. The monkey sprang back, just outside the deadly strike zone. The cassowary missed. Hanuman made himself a little smaller, a little more tempting, a little out of breath. Let the enemy smell victory.

The bird made another jump and slash. The monkey sprang back and faked an injured leg, tempting the confident bird to come in closer.

Next—the game changer.

The monkey leapt onto the cassowary's back and began to jump up and down, laughing while the furious bird tried to shake him off. Then Hanuman grabbed the base of the bird's neck, barred his long incisors and bit down into a jangle of nerves. That's when the cassowary broke from the woods onto the Sisters' lawn, hitting his top speed at thirty miles per hour.

Game over.

He was all bird now. His crested head bent low, his orange wattles flapping. The flightless bird was at a full run. Any memory of having once been an emissary of high magic had gone down the bird brain.

One of the Cardinals on the terrace gave out a shout.

Sister Merry Berry, who had been seated by the quarry pool, rushed out onto the lawn to see what the hubbub was about. There was a cassowary running towards the convent with what looked like a monkey riding on his back.

———

THE TICKET-TAKERS at the celestial circus were doing a landslide business. The Convent of Immaculate Conceptions was center ring and the featured act was a show stopper.

Hanuman rode on the back of the Demiurge. The Hindu gopis were chiming their finger cymbals. Krishna blew holy ragas on his flute. The heavenly host went wild. Guha kicked. Shiva laughed. The Buddha belly shook like a bowl full of jelly. Holy mackerels, sweet honey in the rock, what an ontological upset at the all-star ecumenical rodeo. The eight-second bell rang out loud and clear. Bring on the cosmic clowns.

Much like the celestial audience, the Cardinals on the terrace were struck with wonderment. Could it be their cassowary?

The wing of red-capped Cardinals who had been under Cassowary's command, could be seen emerging from the woods, all of them drawn to the spectacle on the lawn. All of them reaching for their missing amulets. They watched the monkey jump off the back of the cassowary and head for the trees. And just like that, the show was over.

Catching sight of Sister Merry Berry from his perch on the terrace, the bespectacled Cardinal Bunbury made his way down the stairs to the lawn.

"Was that your monkey?" he inquired.

"Was that your cassowary?" she countered.

Both Bunbury and Berry held their own consul.

"I say," Bunbury rejoined, "you seem to be running a zoo."

In that moment, it occurred to Merry Berry that she was not running anything at all. It seemed rather that the convent had been overrun by an invasive species of birdmen.

"You should be ashamed of yourself," Merry Berry stated flatly and walked away.

At least Conrad was safe for the time being. Extraordinary claimed he could remain underwater indefinitely. Indefinitely seemed a stretch to Sister Merry Berry.

———

IT TOOK SOME SORTING, but finally the convent settled into an uneasy sleep. Twenty-one Cardinals bedded down. The remainder, including Cardinal Cassowary's contingent, headed back to the Sanctum after making a cursory search for their erstwhile Commander-in-Chief. All they found was his bronze and silver helmet. The befuddled invaders, already feeling the effects of drug withdrawal, were most anxious to get back to their stashes at the Sanctum.

As the cataclysmic day inched past midnight, only one person remained awake. A vigilant Sister Merry Berry found herself sober and brooding. The very thought of those despicable men sleeping in the convent cells was an insult to every Sister who had died and been denied her priesthood. Without giving it much thought, she put on her florescent running shoes.

Murder crossed her mind. Had these very Cardinals somehow been responsible for the deaths of her friends? Murder re-crossed her mind going in the other direction. Could she? She smiled at the absurdity. The consideration of murdering the uninvited guests was so briefly entertained, it could hardly even be counted as a near occasion of sin.

Newly awakened to the news that divine mischief was afoot by the auspicious appearance of Lucifer, Merry Berry's own rebellious nature was stirred. When she wandered into the library, she could not deny the unaccustomed deliciousness of being the one left in charge while others slept. She revisited the impertinence of Cardinals. How dare these entitlement-riddled churchmen assume they were safe?

Merry Berry was conducting her existential brood like a symphony. All at once she pointed her baton at the brass section. When the French horns blared, topped by an attack of trumpets, she discovered how much she did not like being dismissed as if she were an irrelevant school girl. Then came an insinuation of oboe, and she found herself eyeing the telephone. She polled the jury of flautists. The verdict was unanimous. She picked up the receiver and dialed O.

"This is Sister Merry Berry and I have twenty-one Cardinals sleeping in my house. Exactly. The others took off. No, I don't want the animal shelter. They are not birds. I want the police. Yes, this *is* an emergency. What? Nine, one, one? No, thank you. I can dial it myself."

The world was full of magical numbers. Nine, one, one. Twenty-one. 7-Eleven. Three o'clock in the morning. Sister Merry Berry forged on. It was a lot like praying. You sent out your message and waited for answering angels.

She reiterated to an incredulous dispatcher that, "No, the Cardinals are not birds. They are ecclesiastics from the Sanctum Avesticum Quoborium. It is an affront. Twenty-one uninvited men, sleeping in the Sisters' beds. Yes, intruders."

Two officers tanked on caffeine took the call from headquarters.

"We'll check it out. If it's not a prank, we'll call for a couple vans at the crime scene," a skeptical officer told the dispatcher. "Crime scene," he joked with his partner, "how likely is that?"

Sister Merry Berry met the police at the door and insisted that they absolutely must remove the Cardinals. At once. One of the intruders, the purported leader, was asleep in the guest room, just off the kitchen. The remaining twenty were in the east wing. There was a gravely ill elderly nun and her attendant in the west wing and they were not to be disturbed.

"I don't get it. Did you invite them in?"

"Absolutely not. They knocked out Mother Mary Extraordinary and stepped over her unconscious body. I don't know what you would call it, but I call it malicious trespass," and then as an afterthought, she added, "with intent." She was a voracious reader of crime novels.

"Intent to what? To sleep over?" Again that mocking tone.

Merry Berry missed the jest, paused and danced around what for her was a slippery question. She was not about to say, "intent to kidnap."

"I have absolutely no idea what their intentions are, but you can be certain that they are up to some foal malevolence. For one thing, they released a wild dangerous bird on the property."

"A bird, Ma'am? Fowl play?" The officer raised an eyebrow.

"Yes," Merry Berry beamed at the officer, "a cassowary. Well, go on then, write it down."

"Yes, Ma'am."

"The birdmen of The Great Church are not above the law," Merry Berry stood firm on her legal grounds. "I intend to press charges against the unrepentant trespassers. This is our property. We pay the taxes."

The two doubters became reluctant believers and called for back-up vans.

By the time the Cardinals were roused and cuffed, dawn had also arrived with its rosy fingers dressing the strange scene with a holy-card luster. It certainly seemed like a biblical moment to the proud Merry Berry, who stood on the porte cochere daring His Eminence Cardinal Delacroix to make eye contact with her.

Just then His Eminence was a riot of barely contained rage.

"Do you not know who I am?" he was repeating at increasing decibels to an indifferent officer who shoved him into a waiting van. Cardinal Delacroix and his wondering ferret observed what happened next from the safety of the police van.

"There it is!" shouted Merry Berry.

And there it was in all its glory, strolling leisurely through the tanglewood. The beautiful feathered beast plucked a wild pear from one of the trees, and everyone stopped to watch the bulge descend that long elegant neck.

Cardinal Oolumbo, whose chipmunk cheeks were puffed up with repressed expletives, suddenly could contain his "futuos" no longer. His Eminence let loose a vile string of Latinate profanities.

The cassowary blinked its large orange eyes with their enviably thick fan of dark lashes—the second significant blink in the course of this narrative.

Oolumbo paused mid-obscenity. The bird tilted its head. Surely the bird did not remember that Oolumbo was one of the signatories on the order to arrest Cardinal Cassowary, if in fact this bird was their Excellent Holy High Magus.

Yet here came the beast at a leisurely lope, gradually picking up speed. The queue of cuffed Cardinals stumbled backwards, beaks bobbing, clutching at each other's robes. Once more the red dominos went down, red robes puddled in disarray.

Oolumbo alone remained standing, wide-eyed, sweat beading on his forehead.

The next explosion of profanities from Oolumbo morphed into a scream when the cassowary came bounding towards him. One of the officers drew a gun.

Sister Merry Berry launched herself into what was to become the beginning of a great friendship. Belly to belly, as agile as any sumo wrestler, she toppled the officer and stayed the execution. The quick movement of the flying nun and the fruity orange of her running shoes caught the cassowary's eye. He turned his majestic crested head and his orange eye locked on Merry Berry, who was just then dusting off her short skirt.

The bird gave out a characteristic low-frequency, throaty cry.

Was it a warning?

No, it was not. It was mating call. Love was in the air.

High in the trees an injured monkey laughed. And higher still the celestial audience chortled in their joy. The cosmic clowns of karmic justice granted the cassowary his fondest wish. He was given a devotee. Just one look was all it took.

Not even with Merry Berry's considerable gift of sight could she glean any trace of the magician in the bird. The Magus was quite gone. Well, ninety-nine-point-nine percent gone.

Although Merry Berry was a bit off her game, she did pick up something: an allure, an intrigue. She gave him her best smile, the one that dimpled her chin and showed off the gap in her front teeth. He was unquestionably attractive. And the bird was clearly smitten.

They made quite the pair.

From Merry Berry he would learn the secret of reciprocal devotion, the holy oil that graces the Wheels of the Universe. She would pluck pears for him, preen his feathers, stitch up the nasty monkey bite and invite him to sleep indoors on a lovely pile of quilts. He would become her faithful guardian, following her everywhere she went. Like Mary and her lamb, their devotion would become legend.

Merry and her cassowary stood side by side and watched the officers load up the peevish miscreants, some of them praying, some of them grousing, others plotting vengeance. One dooking ferret looked longingly out the window of one of the vans.

Twenty-one Cardinals were arrested that morning on charges of criminal trespass. They were hauled off in two unmarked vans, unceremoniously finger-printed and booked. Behind bars, they awaited the inevitable arrival of the Sanctum

Legal Eagles, who would show up in due course impeccably dressed in bespoke suits with bond money and a carefully worded statement for the press written by an underpaid law clerk.

These lawyers were the epitome of brand: eagles engraved on their gold cuff links, they were ivy-leagued, off-shore banked, custom-tanned, shoe-shined, manicured, lint-free, teeth-capped and smiling at their great good luck—twenty-one rich Cardinals to defend. They assured their bewildered clients with elaborate ambiguities and movie-star smiles—everything was going to be just fine. For a price.

A staunch and smiling Sister Merry Berry watched the vans roll out of the gates. She was disappointed that Sister Subordinary and Mother Mary had missed her moment of glory. Had they really slept through all the drama? Slept through this momentous flushing out of the Cardinals? Perhaps they had, Merry Berry thought as she made her way to the west wing to find her consoeurs.

———

MOTHER MARY EXTRAORDINARY'S constitution had been given a grave shock when Delacroix inhaled her prayer essence. At times through that long night, she seemed to come around, although she never quite came around to this world. Earlier she had called for her Wing Sergeants and Sister Mary Subordinary improvised an excuse, assuring her that they would be back soon. Extraordinary was crestfallen.

"They never leave me. It must be a sign. But a sign of what? I have been safekeeping those Wings for eons. They're not mine to lose."

"I'm sure you'll find them," Subordinary offered, certain that Extraordinary had lost more than a pair of wings.

A blissful smile settled on Extraordinary's lips and she fell back to sleep musing on the magnificent one to whom the wings belonged. When Subordinary watched Mother Mary's frown loosen and become a sleepy smile, she gave up a prayer of thanks. At some point Sister Subordinary drifted off. Then she woke up rattled by a succession of foggy dream sequences—one near catastrophe morphing into another. A quick check of Mother Mary's pulse assured her that the prioress was not in any immediate danger. Then Sister Subordinary slipped down the backstairs and made her way to the quarry pool.

She had a favorite spot, a stone bench supported by carved angels and overlooking the water. Under the dome of sky, Subordinary summoned her wits in preparation for whatever the fates and furies might unleash next. The monkey chose that moment to drop from a tree onto the bench.

"Lord Hanuman!" Sister gasped.

Three bright red wounds crossed his chest. Without a word, she reached into her deep pocket, brought up the little jar of homemade salve she always kept at hand, and began to dress his wounds. The cuts were deep. And what was this? A name inscribed over and over in tiny letters on every exposed bone—*Conrad Eppler*.

*Who is this boy?* Sister wondered.

The white monkey felt her mind reach into his, but he was adept at keeping secrets. No one was going to mess with his marbles. So she only found the eternal om repeating in the monkey's infinite mind.

*Fine. Keep your secrets,* she messaged him.

Calling Hanuman her wounded hero, she touched his noble mind with her kindness. Thanking him for ringing the warning bells, she managed to knock one round glass cleary out of the cosmic circle of his perfect oms. That marble was currently arching its way toward a certain starry-eyed green angel in need of a wake-up whack.

Too exhausted to carry herself back up the stairs, a frazzled Subordinary nodded off on the stone bench. She dreamed of a blue Goddess on the other side of the other side of the world. The deity's back was bent over an intricately carved sheesham desk; she was inscribing something on what appeared to be a small card. After blowing on the ink, the Goddess carefully attached the card to an anklet of bells. She stood and turned. A large tear fell from her third eye and rolled down the side of her nose. Lord Hanuman held the infant while she fastened the anklet.

Merry Berry gave the dreaming Mary Subordinary a gentle shake. The waking nun was startled to find herself sitting outside, the tearful gaze of the Hindu Goddess still upon her, the dream reluctant to dissolve.

*Mercy on my poor beleaguered soul,* Sister Subordinary realized that Hanuman had revealed Conrad's mother.

"There you are," Merry Berry brought Subordinary back to this world. "Couldn't imagine where you'd got off to. Such a relief to find Mother Mary Extraordinary sleeping peacefully," Merry Berry beamed at Subordinary, her story all wound up and ready to spring.

"Have the Cardinals awakened yet?" Subordinary asked.

"Well, yes they have. But not exactly voluntarily. You see, when they decided to spend the night—how rude was that? Some of them, possibly, sleeping in the very beds of the women they may have murdered. What was I supposed to do in the name of decency, in the name of our dearly departed Sisters? Besides, we could not leave Conrad in the deeps indefinitely while the prayer eaters stayed on. And on. Yes, I said it. Out loud. Prayer eaters. You never take me into your confidence, but I can put ten and ten and one together, thank you very much. So don't blame me. I did the only thing I could do."

While Subordinary waited on Berry's explanation of all things impossible, the perplexed nun noticed a small stuffed monkey on her lap. Recollecting the bloody wounds, she ran her fingers through the toy monkey's fur.

"What luck! You've found Skipper," Merry Berry brightened.

"Yes, I suppose I have." A wide-awake Subordinary quickly pushed the monkey and the vision he sent to the back of her mind. "Dare I ask? What did you do about the Cardinals?"

"Why, I had them arrested."

"What!?"

It was hard to give Mary Subordinary a shock, and Merry Berry relished her moment.

"And guess what?"

"Please, Sister. I am all suspense."

"I have a new pet. A white monkey chased a cassowary right into our yard," Merry Berry trilled.

No, the monkey did not, Subordinary wanted to insist, feeling as if more than one parallel world were running amuck alongside her ordinary one. Must she really include a cassowary in her accounts? She tried to hold the story still, but the words whipped in the wind like a kite tail; erratic gusts sent the story in deep dives and sudden ascents. She wondered, not for the first time, if anyone was holding the string.

"After the Cardinals were tucked in, I found myself both aggrieved and inspired. I think it was the oboe that pushed me to consider extremes, but the jury of flautists decided me."

"Decided you what?"

"Oh, I never thought I'd see my hand on the telephone. Two calls. I made two calls last night," concluded Merry Berry's brief but incoherent history of the evening. Then with a swell of belated pride, Merry Berry thought to mention her own heroism. "I saved the cassowary's life."

"Mercy on my soul. Have you been drinking?"

"Not yet," Merry Berry twinkled, "first things first. Now that the coast is clear, Conrad will need a rising up."

Sister Merry Berry struck the all-clear bell, sounding the watery depths. "Song waves," she called the signals.

Up came Conrad, swiftly through the miracle of blue. Sister Subordinary stood poolside with a big fluffy bath towel that she plucked from the clothesline. She wrapped up her dripping boy and hugged him tight.

When Conrad's body heat was restored, he asked after Mother Mary. Both Sisters assured him that the danger had passed. But had it? Sister Subordinary whisked the worry from her brow and kissed Conrad's forehead. Then she was off to check on Mary Extraordinary.

Merry Berry carried Conrad up the stairs, happy to have a bundle of damp, sleepy boy in her arms. He didn't protest when she plunked him down for a daytime nap. The boy was spent.

Merry Berry tucked the monkey in beside Conrad and he pulled his furry ally close. Straight away, he discovered three small tears in the monkey's chest and felt as if his own chest had been ripped open.

*Battle wounds*, Conrad guessed.

Sister Merry Berry set about mending Skipper's coat with a quick silver needle while she told a wide-eyed Conrad how she rid their world of Cardinals, and then—even more astonishing— how she stayed the execution of a cassowary and stitched up a nasty bite on the bird's neck.

"Here you go. All's well that mends well," Sister handed off the toy monkey. "It's been a busy needle."

Conrad knew there was a lot more to the story, but he'd have to wait on the monkey to hear the good stuff. Experience taught the boy that in the aftermath of a big adventure, Skipper refused all mindtalk, taking time out to recharge. The stitches hinted that the restorative interval might be longer this time.

The hours Conrad spent in his underwater cave had seemed like weeks. He had traveled far in that brief interim of clock time. Without really knowing it, he was looking for his adoptive father. His meditations had rocketed him onto a vast astral plane where he witnessed wondrous galactic vistas—multiple suns rising, intersections of moon settings, star signs, time tunnels. There was so much space in space. So much darkness between the bright spots.

Truly, Earth is the best place for love.

It was good to be snug and dry, tucked in his own bed. Even though his injured friend was silent, Conrad was pleased as pineapples to have those Velcro paws closed at his neck.

———

BACK IN HER ROOM, Sister Mary Berry made an astonishing discovery. In her top dresser drawer, there was a great pile of gold amulets, the happy result of Hanuman's thievery. Merry Berry did not pause to question either the provenance or providence of this glittering abundance nestled with her under-things. She believed in lucky chances. Almost immediately, an overpowering curiosity tempted her to open one of the bejeweled vials.

It seemed that Sister Merry Berry had no caution to cast to the wind. Not that she hadn't seen the consequences of a mere sniff. She remembered with absolute clarity that when Cardinal Delacroix inhaled the vapor from his gold amulet, Mother Mary had lost consciousness. Truth was, Merry Berry did not mind losing consciousness. A practiced imbiber, she was not a virgin when it came to passing out. A little wine, a little uplift, and at day's end, a little toast to all that was and will be. Amen and out. Her rule of thumb was to station herself on her bed when she took the sip that took her out. So she plopped down on the edge of her bed, prepared for whatever might eventuate.

As soon as she unstoppered one of the amulets, the fragrance shot right up Sister's nasal cavity and hit her beautiful almond-shaped amygdala with a smack. The hippocampus joined the sensory party, releasing a rush of associative memories that knocked her off the bed and onto her knees.

In a twinkling, Sister Merry Berry's convent cell was redolent with the scent of roses—pink roses blooming in a snow-dusted field. A beribboned, pink, leather-bound book opened its wings and flew through the garden. The rapidly turning pages sent Merry Berry chasing after dearly missed friends. They were all there—she was certain—embedded in the pages of Mother Mary's *Goat Girl* poems. She ran faster to catch the butterfly of a book, that flew on just out of reach.

Turning down a country lane, the prayer-smacked Merry Berry stumbled into a cluster of pink-robed Sisters—working, playing, sowing praises. A joyous rush cascaded from the top of her dreads down to the toes of her orange shoes. Choiring her voice, she joined the Sisters in ecstatic song:

> We know the garden, we know the gate
> The sunshine lights the path we take
> It fills the garden up with gold
> When winter comes, we're never cold
>> And we dance barefoot
>> Round the roses in the snow
>> Roses, roses, ring around the roses.

When the last note of the childhood rhyme skipped away, the Joyous Sisters began a recitation:

> Hail holy queen, Mother of grace
> Who tarried with the announcing angel
>> While the stage coach driver idled
>> And star bridled ponies waited
>> All the blue-winded night
>> To carry you over the moon
> Oh, Best Western Lady, ride
> Your Royal Coach down the sky
> Enter the Holiday Inn once more
>> Take us into thy convent
>> Into thy covenant
> Holy Mary Mother of God
>> Teach us thy trade.

———

WHEN MERRY BERRY TRIPPED back from her holy hallucination, Sherlocking among the evidence in her personal mind palace, she made a simple deduction.

"A reduction deduction," she laughed out loud.

During the plague year, the Cardinals must have distilled the prayers of her consoeurs. The gold amulet that she unstoppered most certainly held the essence of Mother Mary's prayers. How else could a mere whiff bring back such particular sights and sounds and songs?

Still, there remained several mysteries resistant to her detection. She understood why she and Subordinary had been spared. They had never put pen to page. But how had Mother Mary Extraordinary survived the white pages?

Merry Berry reviewed that moment when Cardinal Delacroix reached for his amulet. To all outward appearances it looked like a hostile act on the part of the Cardinal, but as Merry Berry turned the scene over in her mind, she approached a different conclusion. Perhaps it was the scent of her own prayer that had knocked Mother Extraordinary out when Delacroix unstoppered the amulet.

Merry Berry closely interrogated her arrival at this conclusion. She doubted that Cardinal Delacroix could possibly experience anything close to the vivid ecstatic vision of a true practitioner. Not one particularly given to metaphysical speculations, she noticed that the certainty she sought always hopped like a rabbit over the next hedge. Intellectually winded from running up and down the hills of her own mentations, she wondered if the wise ever gave up.

Perhaps they refrained from coming to conclusions altogether. Maybe they held all possibilities open, or tucked them between slivered moons of parentheses in a forever abeyance. She pictured judgments like so many jumpers suspended from bungee cords—a pride of suspended judgments never quite touching ground.

"What a merry mind chase," Merry Berry chuckled to herself as she carefully emptied out Humboldt Snow #7 from several amulets into a large bowl. Then she added three cups of Chateau Latour and stirred. The mixture gave off the scent of wet goat with low tones of pencil shavings and high notes of violet—not altogether unpleasant. She funneled the heady blend into perfume bottles from her personal collection of colored cut-glass atomizers. What a lineup of booty!

She locked the Cardinal's bejeweled amulets in the vault and tucked a bottle of the new, improved Humboldt Snow #7 into her pocket. It was a vintage, prismatic, cut-crystal bottle, with a blue crocheted atomizer and gold tassel, purchased at Giltane's Antique Shoppe. She'd always known the charming bottles would come in handy one day. Oh, and wouldn't Mr. Giltane pay a God's ransom for one of those gold amulets? Something to think about.

Occasionally, Merry Berry gave herself a few happy spritzes. In private moments, she would examine the puzzle of Mother Mary's allergic reaction to her own prayer essence. Or maybe it wasn't an allergy. Perhaps it was just the unexpected jolt of memory made unbearable by the great divide between what the order once was and what they were now. Clearly, this was not what they had aspired to be. And yet wasn't this something? Something that mattered, something vibrant, with its own unexpected turns of events and amazements.

"I wouldn't miss this for the world," she almost concluded before she remembered that she was practicing not coming to conclusions. It almost occurred to her that it was precisely her yes to the present that prevented her from being completely knocked down and out by the past, as had happened to Mother Mary Extraordinary. The eternal yes that haloed the world kept Merry Berry haloed as well.

Sister Merry Berry was so delighted with this turn of mind that once again she found herself chuckling. Never much of a thinker, she had developed no method of organizing her thoughts, so she promptly forgot the exalted notions that had tickled her brain only moments earlier.

She allowed herself a double dammit when she realized the thoughts had gotten away from her before she had a chance to register the lovely insights and lock them in. Aware that she was onto something of merit, a notion worthy of pursuit, she circled back. It wasn't a conclusion she was after as much as a theory that might illuminate Mother Mary Extraordinary's struggle. It had something to do with being overpowered by an unlived life, how an intended life could somehow diminish the given life.

Yes, that's it! Extraordinary is haunted by the ghost of the life she meant to live—and so am I. This unexpected realization gave Merry Berry pause.

It seemed to her that when a person gave up the ghost of the intended life and she's headed nowhere in particular, nowhere marked on any map, what was needed was an invitation to somewhere. She pictured the invitation arriving on a wind, in a small white envelope, with a crisp piece of tissue obscuring the lettering and logo. Then once again, Merry Berry saw the writing on the wall: *You are cordially invited to invent a new future.*

"Are there any further instructions? How do I go about it?"

"Oh, I'll have to get back to you," she informed the wall. "That's Mary Extraordinary's bell. I must be off. Keep me posted."

*Stay spritzed*, the wall replied.

———

NEITHER MERRY BERRY nor Mary Subordinary was much surprised when at the end of the day Mother Mary called them to her private chapel.

Mother Mary Extraordinary made no references to her difficult passage. She knew that she must act decisively in this blessed interval of clarity. The danger was over for now. But for how long? No one could say. She knelt at her intricately carved rosewood prie dieu in the tent of her long white hair. Sisters Mary Subordinary and Merry Berry stood silently before her. The prioress looked up at her two friends and held them in a long, loving gaze. She waited until she was certain that they knew what she was going to say before she spoke the words out loud.

"It's time we give up the little Holy Ghost." Then she bent her head and wept. And when she stopped, she was no longer the person she once was.

# LIES

MOTHER MARY EXTRAORDINARY fell fast and far into a chilly winter of decline, brief intervals of lucidity alternating with increasingly longer periods of dark rambling meditations. Approaching one hundred and fifty-seven years, she was extremely fragile, and yet her flares of irritability could be quite energetic.

A frustrated Merry Berry was hard pressed not to give Mary Extraordinary the tiniest spritz of Humboldt Snow #7. She had to keep reminding herself how badly the prioress had reacted to that first whiff of *Goat Girl* essence when Cardinal Delacroix unstoppered his amulet.

Just recently however, Sister Merry Berry found herself reconsidering her caution. It was her new favorite pastime, feeding tasty metaphysical morsels to a pet theory. This mischievous kitty of a theory meowed plaintively in her ear. Perhaps it was just possible, the kitty purred, to gradually re-introduce Mother Mary Extraordinary to her former self, one small spritz at a time. There would come a day when the nudging of that soft pink nose and soothing purr would prove a temptation too much. And Mary Extraordinary would get spritzed with wondrously mixed results.

The week following the invasion left no time to experiment with rehabilitations. The Sisters initiated a set of arrangements that took on an escalating momentum.

*Tonight*, they promised each other.

That particular morning found Conrad uncharacteristically listless, almost as if he sensed *tonight* hovering around the corner. No muffins baking in the kitchen, just a bowl full of pears left on the table.

Where was everyone?

Ever since he came up from the quarry pool, it seemed the planet had increased its tilt by some infinitesimal fraction, pulling everything slightly out of alignment. Conrad couldn't help but be aware that something important concerning himself was troubling the Sisters. They quarreled. One time the phone rang and Mother Mary Extraordinary took the call. Another time, they made an outgoing call, all of them huddled in the library.

All on the hush.

The boy was certain he heard his name mentioned, and he was certain he was being excluded from a conversation that was altering the course of his life. Apparently, it was something grown-ups did—made preemptory executive decisions and presented their faits accomplis, scotch-taped, packaged, and tied in neat ribbons. Instinct told him that the surprise awaiting him was something he did not want.

Worry is a contagion. No one is immune when a household goes into the doldrums, no matter how spiritually fortified. Conrad began to feel endangered by the people who loved him.

Every night that week, Conrad checked his telescope, hoping to see a certain brilliant object moving in the night sky. No such luck. A cloud cover blocked out the stars all week long. At daybreak he scanned the woods. He could not make himself feel safe, even after he went back inside and locked all the doors.

Doubt threw shadows everywhere in Conrad's yellow room.

Skipper, his absolute ally and defender, had always been a dependable warm spot. Surely, Conrad thought, Skipper must be recovered from his wounds by now. One week is a long stretch in the life of a boy. Convinced that it was time to remove Skipper's stitches, he cut off the knots with a Barlow knife Sister Merry Berry had given him.

He was ready to pull the threads when a vision of Skipper's stuffing blowing about the room stopped Conrad's hand. He cleared his mind. Taking a deep breath, he tentatively pulled out the black threads. *Please,* he prayed. Then slipping his fingers through the familiar fur, he examined Skippers chest.

Sweet relief—the rips in the monkey's fabric were mended.

*Skip, you're good as new! Skipper? Talk to me. Was it the Magus that ripped you?*

*Yes,* the monkey mindtalked, and Conrad snuggled him close, patting his furry head.

*There. There,* the boy said in perfect imitation of Sister Subordinary. *So? Tell me everything. What happened?*

At last the monkey relented and gave Conrad the front-row-center account, with all its gory theatrical detail. How the boy delighted in the fabulous story of Hanuman's brave battle with the Magus cum cassowary. Conrad trembled when Hanuman let Cardinal Cassowary draw first blood. He applauded the strategy designed to tease out the ancient raptor-like instincts and drive the Magus deeper into his animal nature. Conrad was quick to appreciate the happy irony that the bird was now Sister Merry Berry's devoted pet and that she, in turn, was devoted to the strange bird. And what a clever monkey—to catch a Magus. Then the topper—to imprison the magician inside his own sacred totem!

Later, at the monkey's urging, Conrad unlocked the doors to the terrace. Living in fear was not healthy. At Skipper's instruction, the boy fetched the bowl of pears from the kitchen and a jar of peanut butter.

The sun was lowering in the west when Conrad lined the balustrade with the tempting row of fruit. Three freckled pears gave off a faint luster in the pink dusk. Soon enough the cassowary was up on the terrace. The boy picked up one of the pears, holding it with an outstretched arm. Only a little more coaxing and the cassowary stepped into Conrad's room on raptor claws.

Click. Click. Click.

Conrad contemplated the two retracted middle toes.

What a bird! Nearly six-feet tall. The cassowary tilted its head and the dilating orange eye, with its ovoid black center, registered the boy. The boy repressed a shiver and held out a halved pear dipped in peanut butter. The awesome beast opened its beak and accepted the peace offering. For the first time in days, Conrad broke out in a smile, a broad radiant open-hearted smile, like the sun throwing off a cloud cover.

The convent, however, remained under that cloud. Despite Sister Merry Berry's deft routing of the Cardinals, all three nuns struggled to recover their former ease—and for good reason. They suspected that the birdmen would never give up.

They were right.

The Cardinals, now released on bail, were up to their beaks in plots and subplots—subterfuge was their daily bread. As they munched on their buttered toast, they left a trail of crumbs that led the conversation continuously back to the Convent of Immaculate Conceptions from which they had been so rudely ejected.

"Witches," Bunbury accused.

"The Coven of Misconceptions," Delacroix denounced.

"At least we are rid of the Magus," Oolumbo smiled and shrugged.

The Cardinals would try for Conrad again, failing to understand that it was a garden they longed for, a mythical garden that had rudely ejected them once upon an originating sin in a story ripe for revisions. They were birds looking for a paradise lost and settling on perches in all the wrong places.

The likely return of the red menace meant that the veil of secrecy surrounding Conrad must be lifted. If the boy should ever be kidnapped, it must be already established that there was such a boy.

The nuns faced a sad and sorry truth: Conrad must become a fact, an official person, with papers and numbers and suchlike. With a great deal of reluctance, Sister Subordinary had phoned the state social services earlier in the day and had begun the process of putting Conrad on the rolls of official children. The Sisters were teaching themselves how to give up the little Holy Ghost.

No longer blue, there was no justifiable reason to keep Conrad in a convent that was no longer a safe haven. He could live in the secular city and pass for an ordinary school boy, with a backpack and a cell phone. It was never meant that he should be their permanent charge, but at seven he still seemed awfully young and awfully small to be given up to the world.

———

CONRAD HEARD THE FOOTSTEPS of the approaching nuns: Sister Merry Berry's bouncy step, Subordinary's measured one, and trailing behind, the scraping uncertain footfall of Extraordinary.

"Intruders approaching. Quick, Skipper. To the ship."

Conrad shooed the cassowary out, scooted his comic books under the bed, and dived for the covers. He would pretend to be asleep. Everyone was acting like themselves, as opposed to being themselves, and Conrad hoped to skip tonight's performance.

How quickly and inexplicably all three nuns had become strangers. Merry Berry's false cheerfulness made him sad. Subordinary's careful reassurances made him wary. And to take matters beyond baffling, the most astonishing nonsense would tumble in fractured bits from Extraordinary's parched lips. He would watch the words break up in the air, letters cascading every which way, coherence becoming chaos.

When Conrad visualized Extraordinary's spoken words, the tiny black letters were still Times New Roman. That one consistency remained a small assurance that it was indeed her voice and not some malign ventriloquist controlling her speech.

Conrad sensed Sister Subordinary bending over him and reaching for his thoughts. He made his mind still as ice.

"Conrad, come out from under those covers. We have good news," Subordinary coaxed him in the very meant-to-be-comforting voice that alarmed him most.

"Took us by surprise. Didn't have a clue. Wouldn't you know it? Out of the blue," Merry Berry rhymed, nonsensically.

"Good Evening, Conrad," Extraordinary finally caught up with the others, bringing a strange, somber formality to what used to be a cozy after-swim visit, with Conrad wrapped in a warm towel, and Mother Mary feeding him enchantments.

"Good Evening, Mother Mary," Conrad offered, echoing her gravitas. He played along, uncertain exactly what this cold-voiced, distant Mother Mary meant to convey by her remove.

Something off.

Something on.

Something gone.

Something arrived.

"Like a bolt out of the blue," Merry Berry hiccoughed.

Mother Mary intervened, "Sister Merry Berry, I will deliver the news."

*Bad news,* Conrad was certain.

Much like a windup toy determined to walk right off the edge of the table top, Merry Berry ignored Extraordinary's appropriation and prattled on.

"Would I presume? To deliver your news? Not at all. Not a word. My lips are zippered up. Zip," Merry Berry mimed a zip and let another hiccough slip.

Extraordinary sniffed the wine-scented air and her eyes slid in Merry Berry's direction. When she was certain her disdain had been registered, she forged ahead.

"I have a grandniece of sorts, the daughter of the daughter of one of the circle of Marys—that would be the renegade Mary Mirabelle," Mother frowned. "Mirabelle had a daughter, Grace, thanks to that absurdly handsome idiot, Dagoberto Rosario Emilio Marquez, who rode around the convent on that damn yellow backhoe."

"Mother!" Sister Subordinary cautioned.

"What?!" Extraordinary snapped.

"The good news?" Merry Berry prompted.

"Exactly. Grace had a daughter, Alyssa. Alyssa Rosaria Dante. She married a river. Well, his name is Rios. Alyssa telephoned us. Impeccable timing, I must say. Right when I was at my wits end and wondering if there would be a rescue, she phoned and—"

Extraordinary stopped abruptly, as if she'd just awakened in a new world. Her heart went plummeting a thousand fathoms deep. Her voice went soft, buttery and familiar, "She asked to adopt you."

"She can't!" Conrad was desperate.

A rattled Mother Mary Extraordinary found her crankiness right where she left it.

"She most certainly can, and she must. Dear child, she's the best we could possibly hope for. Almost one of us. She's some sort of doctor," Extraordinary paused. "What sort?" she questioned herself. "Give me a moment. It'll come back."

They all waited for it to come back.

"There it is. A molecular geneticist and her husband is a— oh, holy merde. Who cares? It's a package deal. Parents. They were married on a beach, wearing flip flops."

The flip flops brought Extraordinary's monologue to another staggering halt. This time the ancient prioress knew she had missed her train; she was standing bewildered on the platform, watching her thoughts roar past and disappear into a dark tunnel.

Gone. Everything gone except two vagrant words: flip flops.

Then the screen on her inner cinema lit up with a startling moving picture. She tried to shake off the unwanted image of a naked couple emerging from the ocean, an aquatic Adam and Eve, dripping sea foam and wearing those ugly rubber sandals—flip flops.

She was desperate to get rid of the flip flops.

Conrad tried to help her break up the two offending words; the letters flipped and flopped in the crashing surf, then rewrote themselves on the wet sand.

The boy watched the ineluctable frown of disapproval drag at the ends of Mary Extraordinary's mouth while they waited for the wave that would wash the words away. He hurt for her. Conrad took in a deep breath and with eloquent simplicity, addressed his great old friend, swimming partner, and foster mother.

"Mother Mary Extraordinary, thank you very much for trying to find the perfect parents for me, but I'm afraid I'll have to say—no, thank you."

"No, thank-you?" The frown deepened.

"I can explain." The boy forged ahead.

"He can explain." Subordinary encouraged.

Silence.

"Well, then," Extraordinary took charge. "Let's have it. Mind you, Conrad, should your explanation fail to satisfy, the penances will be severe." She eyed a jar of peanut butter on Conrad's nightstand. "No more crunchy peanut butter. We'll put coal in your socks, fill your pillow full of rocks, and—"

Merry Berry interrupted with an explosive hiccough, and they all watched Mother Mary's fluctuating personality edge closer to the borderline.

"Sister Merry Berry, will you kindly stop staring at me?"

"Staring? Am I? Not at all." Merry Berry fluttered nervously and then landed on a perfect improvisation. Much like that magnificent blue butterfly, the Queen Alexandra's Birdwing, she teetered on the slender stem of a Mimulus filicaulis, "Rocks? Socks? A burst of creativity on your part."

Then blue butterfly took wing, "Impressed? Yes. But staring, no, no. Never. Not at all."

Encouraged by Merry Berry's aplomb, Conrad began to trot out his explanation in stops and starts.

"Something happened," he stopped.

Conrad did not like to share his intimate epiphanies. He would never tell the Sisters about his magical adventures with Skipper, nor mention the encounter with the terrible claw. His reticence in these matters was very like the Marys. Each Mary liked to keep her own council in all matters respecting the etheric realms. It was the rule of the order that each religious had a right to the privacy of her personal mystery.

Conrad was stalled at the precipice. He needed to take a leap of faith, of trust. He needed to stop this adoption process, throw all his little weight in front of this awful gathering momentum. But first, he must face a troublesome truth—the angels had promised him next to nothing. The green one, who called herself Aletheia, had even refused the comic book drawing of the dad he dreamed of. He was going to have to give the story a bit of a spin. So he began by hedging before leaping.

"Skipper was with me, and he saw them too."

"Saw whom?" The old nun came alert.

"Three angels appeared," Conrad ventured further out.

"Three angels did what?" Her frown twitched at the corners.

"They appeared *unto* me. Like in the Holy Book. And guess what?"

"I'm not in the mood to guess," Extraordinary's eyes narrowed.

"They answered my prayer. You don't have to worry about parents for me because the angels promised to take care of everything."

There it was. Conrad lied. Nothing had been promised. The cup was empty, but for an intangible assurance that had made of Conrad a believer—*Next time, Starfriend.* What might be, would be. He stood firm.

Mother Mary Extraordinary knew how flimsy the bridge was that Conrad stood on, how wide the span between belief and the heartbreaking world. Her heart literally clenched at the mention of angel promises. She had buried her visionary utopias and strictly forbade her memory from straying to those long-gone days of grace, those halcyon days when she lived in an illuminated world. She had opened the door to hope and heartbreak for the last time when the blue baby arrived in his cardboard box. And she had firmly slammed that door shut when she decided to give the boy up.

The room waited.

Mother Mary Extraordinary was speechless. She was vigorously stomping out the flames of her fury when that stray image of a naked Adam and Eve had the temerity to wander across her visual field again, kicking up beach sand with their offensive flip flops. The little slappity slap of rubber against their heels, as the lovers traversed the wet sand, might as well have slappity-slapped her burning cheeks. How many times must she dismiss these naked children, these recalcitrant visual intruders?

"Get dressed, for Lord's sake," she finally hissed.

The vision obeyed and now the young woman was wearing a long tulle veil, trailing in the sea foam. Exasperated by the strange beauty of her unmanageable visions, she practically growled at her stunned consoeurs.

"I've lost my way. Help me out, damn it. Sister Subordinary, will you please let Conrad know my thoughts about angel appearances. Well, let's have it. Heaven forbid I should be the last to know. What am I thinking?"

"You're thinking about a naked bride on a beach." Sister Merry Berry chirped happily. Merry Berry hadn't meant to spy on Mother's mental picture show, but the images were so bold and enticing.

"Not that! What about angel appearances and promises? What is my position on *that*? Sister Subordinary? My thoughts, please."

Subordinary forced herself to draw on her infrequently exercised skills of invention. Improvisation was not her métier but she looked deeply into Extraordinary's troubled mind, past the naked couple and came up with something almost prescient.

"I imagine it occurs to you that if you were the brightest angel most supreme, and if any of the lesser angels stepped out of line, well—I suppose you would take immediate disciplinary action."

"My thoughts, exactly." Mary Extraordinary was impressed, pleased to be so concisely sorted.

"The angels meant no harm," Conrad was quick to their defense. "They were tremendous, like nothing I ever imagined.

Green, magenta and purple—three amazing color-crayon angels. For real. When they blinked their lights, they looked like birthday candles. I made a very important wish. It was my seventh birthday. The angels were the way my wish came true. They were my come-shining-through. They even forgot to say: *be not afraid*, but it didn't matter because I wasn't. I was glowing on the inside."

"Don't lie."

"I'm not."

"I know just what Conrad means—about the glow inside," Merry Berry temporized, "Sometimes when I pray I get this surprise filling, and I feel just like a Hostess Twinkie."

Too late, Merry Berry realized she might have misspoken. Lately, she was becoming increasingly aware that she had a few small substance-abuse issues—the wine, the Twinkies, the atomizer of prayer juice that she kept in her pocket. She had to admit, she never felt altogether like herself unless she was feeling that inner glow.

"Twinkie? I don't like the sound of it. Not one bit. I feel the devil drawing near."

Subordinary interrupted, "Mother, remember yourself. We don't believe in the devil."

Extraordinary ignored her, "Conrad dear, only a very, very wicked child would make up the kind of lies I've heard from you tonight. Every time you tell a lie, the devil who lives beneath the cellar stairs takes another sip of wine. If you should get him drunk enough on your lies, he might climb up the cellar stairs tonight and—."

Merry Berry gave out three loud hiccoughs in quick succession. Extraordinary swiveled, sniffed the air and caught the scent of a 1998 Châteauneuf du Pape.

"Sister Merry Berry, have you been drinking?"

"On the whole, probably not. Possibly a drop. Putatively a sniff. The merest whiff. Ahhhh, the fullest bouquet. In short, I'm positive I couldn't say," Merry Berry concluded with a brilliant smile.

"Brevity is a virtue, Sister."

"Yes, bless me. Did I ramble? No harm meant. No disrespect. Brevity is my motto."

———

IF THERE WERE A DEVIL beneath the stairs getting drunk on lies, this night would surely put him under the table—sloshed, totaled, completely wasted.

Conrad lied about what the angels had promised him. Merry Berry lied about her drinking, glossed over how frightened and appalled she was by Extraordinary's outbursts, and tonight she pretty much paraded an altogether fraudulent cheerfulness. Mary Extraordinary, for her part, was so riddled with lies, she couldn't begin to think straight.

Only Subordinary managed to skirt the orgy of lies, probably because she kept all things so neatly compartmentalized. Once her thoughts had been blown apart, they had settled nicely into their new arrangement. She had no intention of stirring them up again. Besides, the monkey's blink was always there to remind her that divine mischief was alive

229

and well and running footloose in the green and gold fields that quilted this tilted planet.

And what a quilt it was!

The world's story was infinitely patched and varied, made and unmade in every mind, at every moment. Poetic licenses were passed out freely at birth. This incredible story had a story of its own: a meta story, an über story, an underscoring, a subscript, an interlinear, a back story, footnotes, a foreword, and countless epilogues. The entire quilt was a busy crosshatch of inventions, visions, evolving sciences, imaginative leaps, and speculative fictions.

As Plato once said, "The poets always lie."

What the great sage didn't know was that angels pick and choose among the many lies, sample them like forbidden fruit, like spiritual truffles. And every now and then an angel tries to make an especially tasty one come true. The most delectable stories are selected out to be bred, genetically modified, spiritually diversified and versified until something unexpected happens between the lies and the lines of poetry. Sometimes among the canonized and imprimatured, indexed and library-of-congressed, some slim volume appears out of alphabetical order.

A pamphlet. A chapbook. A prayer book. A song.

Or a boy and a monkey in a box.

It is not at all surprising that on this night of lies, some truth seeped out, albeit truth of a tougher, chewier sort. Not all truth is palatable.

---

"THE ANGELS DON'T come here anymore, Conrad. And even if they did once upon a time, I wouldn't trust them with my happily-ever-afters."

Once Mary Extraordinary found her subject, she had much to say.

"At the behest of an immature deity, untrustworthy, miscreant angels, came bearing swords of fire and burned the Garden of Eden to the ground, if I recall my Genesis, and I assure you I do." Mother Mary unwittingly sampled a bit of urban apocrypha in her biblical mix and did so with a remarkably assured, demented élan. Then she finished off with a fragment of nursery rhyme. "I suppose I could put a rosy ring around it, but it's still ashes to ashes. Even the children know— we all fall down."

It was remarkable how quickly Mother Mary Extraordinary moved from doddering to fierce, how her fuzzy outlines could abruptly turn bold. One thing was certain; angels were not a happy subject for her, so she turned back with one more piece of bitter advice before she left the room.

"Be careful when you call on angels, Conrad. Unanswered prayers are most times the greater blessing."

Lit by the inner fire of her own anger, Mother Mary exited the room with considerably more energy than when she had entered it. It seemed her black habit was gaining in volume, almost as if she had grown dark wings.

Conrad was shocked.

The erratic swing from threats of peanut butter deprivations to angel warnings was dizzying. This was the same glorious Mother Mary Extraordinary who had explored the underwater world of the quarry with him, his small hand in hers, the two of them propelled by her strong flutter kick until he found his own.

Somersaulting in the blue deeps, she had taken him down into a lustrous dark eternity of meditation and lifted him skyward into the bright highs of astral projections. This same Mother Mary had wrapped him up in soft, warm towels and called him her little Blue Burrito. And when he lost his color, her little Holy Ghost. Where did she go?

Sister Merry Berry tried to explain it to Conrad with one of her new pet theories; how sometimes when you are very old or even not so very old, you can be haunted by an unlived life. And this lovely might-have-been can be more deeply missed than something that actually had been. When a dream dies, a big-dream believer is left with a big dream-sized hole in her heart.

Subordinary saw Mother Mary's heart, not so much blown apart, but pierced by so many arrows of desire.

"She was a revolutionary idealist, Conrad." Subordinary picked up Merry Berry's thread, working it into the weave of her own thoughts. "Really, it would not be an exaggeration to say that Mary Extraordinary was something of a visionary zealot in her day."

"That she was. She was forever accusing me of entertaining doubts. She'd say, 'Sister Merry Berry, I see you are dancing a little jig for your doubts today. Shall I hire a fiddler?' "

"I'm afraid Sister Merry Berry is right; Mother never allowed room for doubt. She held fast to her vision. Even after the plague year, she remained certain that the young novices would come, fill the choir back up, and bring the garden back to flower. They never came. We are the last of a dying order, and when we are gone there will be no one left to carry on. Her dreams, Conrad—they deserted her like the flights of angels that once kept her company. She is the loneliest woman in the world."

"Are angels her Kryptonite?" Conrad ventured.

Sister Subordinary, a master linguist, was boggled by this strange non-sequitur. Subordinary had always been most particular with Conrad's reading materials. Sister Merry Berry glanced down and saw the edge of a comic book peeking out from beneath the bed. She knocked it back with a quick covert kick.

"Conrad, let us not speak of *crypts tonight*," Merry Berry blinked rapidly, hoping her wayward remark would knock the word Kryptonite clean out of the room. Conrad caught on and dropped the K word out of his mind, so that when Subordinary glanced back at him she only saw a waterfall of giggles, like some postcard from his happy childhood. She never saw the glowing green mineral that Conrad sent orbiting into outer space.

Merry Berry allowed herself a private puff of pride when Subordinary took up the explanation where she'd left off.

"The angels that used to visit Mother Mary Extraordinary gave her a great vision of the future—an Earth haloed in clear air, sun-kissed and rain-gardened. Now she knows that the vision was a fantasy, a beautiful make-believe."

Merry Berry stepped in confidently at this juncture. "And when she stopped believing in her make-believes, it made her grumpy, and grouchy and mean."

"Sister!"

"But a nice kind of mean, as it were. A very pleasant sort of mean. I mean it's a pleasure to see someone be so mean in such a pleasant way."

Only the most perceptive among cognoscenti could have heard the censure under Merry Berry's bouncy retort. Her hand slipped into the pocket of her modified habit. It was a lovely deep pocket. And at the very bottom of it was the atomizer. Maybe a few spritzes of *Goat Girl* would change the atmospheric pressure and steady the emotional weather.

Subordinary was assuring Conrad that somewhere deep inside, Mother was still the person she had once been, when Merry Berry turned her lovely round backside to them. Facing the mullioned windows in Conrad's room, she surreptitiously spritzed the air.

The effects were almost immediate. Conrad began to reminisce about a yesterday that was only weeks old, and yet felt far away. He spoke of how Mother Mary used to tuck him in and ask him if he'd said his prayers. He remembered further back to when he was a blue boy, toddling about in diapers, how she sat him on the balcony and talked about a garden that used to grow just past the terrace, right outside his window. She promised him it would bloom again one day, if he prayed.

Mother Mary Extraordinary was the one who taught him that prayer was a palace of visualization. She encouraged the speechless boy to practice his mind pictures. Over time, he achieved an astonishing virtual clarity. He practiced his art with a pure devotion until the world he saw in his mind palace made him shivery with happiness.

Occasionally, Mother Mary would walk into his visions and critique them. Sometimes she would let Conrad stroll through hers.

Spritz.

Spritz.

Spritz.

Merry Berry quietly doused the air, then dropped the atomizer into her deep pocket and turned around.

"So many roses," Merry Berry encouraged the nascent memories, "magenta, gold, and emerald green. The green rose was our pride of invention. The green-rose wine—it sparkled on the tongue, crisp and minty with a note of lemon grass. And the trees bore fruit like you've never seen—the most spectacular, audacious pink pears. What sassy holiday pies we'd bake," Merry Berry laughed.

Subordinary, who almost never indulged in nostalgia, found herself riding on the carousel of Merry Berry's memory. Mirrors and bells and calliope music—round and around and up and down, Sister Subordinary went galloping off on a bejeweled pony. She experienced such a sudden onset of unaccustomed euphoria that her soul flew out from her before she had a chance to catch it.

"Mercy," Sister Subordinary expostulated, observing her soul hovering near the ceiling, well out of reach. She shot a look of dismay over to Merry Berry who was still chattering away in spritz-induced ecstasy.

"We came so close to paradise, we thought we saw the gate!" Merry Berry chimed. "The habits we wore were tickle pink. We made the dye ourselves, from home-grown beets."

"I see them!" Conrad was jumping up and down.

Merry Berry went to the French doors and flung them open wide. All three observers rushed from Conrad's room out onto the terrace. Then whoosh, Mary Subordinary's soul fled through the open door and was out of sight.

"My soul," Subordinary sobbed.

"The pink Sisters! The garden!" Merry Berry clapped.

And there it was—a ripping holy-hosanna-in-the-highest hallucination! It was a re-mastered miracle, a super-saturated color wheel of kaleidoscopic blooms, an exoticum of tantalizing edibles. This celestial stir-fry sizzled. This holographic paradise, paint-by-divine-numbers bingo card was coming up all heavenly sevens. The dice-rolling deities were hot tonight. A jubilance of pink-robed Sisters, equipped with rakes, hoes and shovels, whirled like dervishes. A delicately-wrought garden gate swung open and the cassowary casually strolled onto the scene. A hovering pair of Raphael cherubini offered the elegant fowl a perfect peach.

"My cassowary!" Merry Berry blinked, trying to hold the tremulous outlines of the visionary field in focus.

In the distance, Sister Subordinary's soul was being tossed about by beribboned, sandal-footed angels. One of the angels gave a running start and drop-kicked that beautiful prayer-ball of a soul. It was airborne and flying high, a rotating globe shedding pinwheels of light, spiraling towards the startled nun.

One hand on the balustrade, Sister Subordinary reached up and caught her soul.

Cheers went up from the angel host.

Was that the former Sister Josephus sitting in her beloved Ford Fairlane, laying on the horn? And it certainly looked like Sister Mary Rose sitting there beside her.

"This is too much," Sister Subordinary pressed a hand against her chest, lest her soul jump free again.

The Gabrielline trumpeters let loose a fanfare, and pairs of angels hovered, bearing holy day garlands. A light snowfall glazed the scene and a choreography of swaying nuns broke out in a heavenly choir of hallelujahs.

"Can you hear that?" Conrad asked.

"YES. I know that song." And Merry Berry lifted her velvety deep voice:

> We know the garden, we know the gate
> The sunshine lights the path we take
> It fills the garden up with gold
> When winter comes, we're never cold
>> And we dance barefoot
>> Round the roses in the snow
>> Roses, roses, ring around—

Sister Subordinary caught Sister Merry Berry's eye and the song died. Here comes the butterfly stomper, Merry Berry grumped to herself, dodging Subordinary's long look.

It was the universal preemptory look of those who know best. With some effort, the pragmatic Subordinary seemed to be successfully throwing off the trance. No more soaring to dizzying heights, if she could help it. Spitting out the madeleine of memory, she resolved to keep her Earth-boots more tightly laced from here on out, thank you very much.

Merry Berry was frantic to keep the good vibrations going and pleaded with Subordinary, her voice knotted with longing.

"The holy day snow! It used to fall on our garden, our very own customized micro weather, our personal Humboldt snow. Then seven years ago, it fell again on the day before Conrad was delivered unto us. Now this vision. Surely some mystery is upon us." Merry Berry didn't like to beg, but she was close to tears.

"Shake it off, Sister." Subordinary did not want to be sucked into a vortex of nostalgia. She felt mocked by the memory. It was soul bruising.

Merry Berry's hand was on the spritzer. Why could Mary Subordinary never admit to transcendent realities? Sister Merry Berry desperately wanted to spritz Sister Subordinary's straight Gaelic nose, give that nose a good drenching. But she paused, and with newly acquired acumen, Merry Berry's mind sprinted ahead to the quizzing that would inevitably follow the reveal of her secret potion. So her hand remained stuck in her pocket.

Ultimately, Subordinary's doubt and redoubtable will killed the vision. Every last trace—gone.

Merry Berry was inconsolable.

"Conrad, you saw them—dressed in pink. Our dearly departed. How they danced in the snow."

Conrad tried to broker a peace between the two Sisters, but he would not deny the vision. He backed up Sister Merry Berry and stood by his claim. The boy was nothing if not steadfast. He really did see the Joyous Sisters; he heard them sing, and no one would ever convince him otherwise.

He's just like Mother Mary, thought Subordinary, more is the pity. All this precocious visionary sky-larking was putting his tender young mind at risk. And for what? Their past had nothing to do with his future. Sister Subordinary was shaking her head ruefully, signaling her consoeur that the conversation was at an end. Over and out of bounds.

Subordinary might do her worst, sending her intrusive messages, but Merry Berry was not receiving just now. Merry Berry was miffed. She could feel her dark curls tightening about her head. She continued to press Sister Subordinary.

"You must admit that you felt, at the very least, a sudden *small* something stir the air. Just that much. It is a miniscule admission by any standards. A stir." Merry Berry caught the stubborn refusal in Subordinary's eye and felt a tear rush down her cheek. "Are you going to deny it?"

Subordinary denied it, claimed she felt nothing whatsoever. There it was. A lie had fallen from Subordinary's lips. She turned to the boy.

"Conrad, this place—it's all fogged up with memories. It's all about yesterday, and it doesn't have a tomorrow. But you have a tomorrow," Subordinary soldiered on, ignoring her consoeur.

"I have a tomorrow," Merry Berry protested, "and so does the cassowary."

Subordinary redoubled her effort to rise above these Berry interruptions.

"Conrad, tonight we'll tuck you up tight, and you just have to believe that everything will be all right."

"What about the devil under the stairs?" Conrad worried.

"Some of the things Mother Mary says these days are beyond belief," Subordinary huffed.

"I believe her. I've seen him down there myself," Merry Berry folded her arms and dared Subordinary to contradict her.

"Sister! Oh, please. Perhaps you should go to the chapel and pray."

"Whatever you say," Merry Berry bounced off, her hand in her pocket, fingering the atomizer.

Someday, Merry Berry promised herself. She had her own unanswered prayers, unwritten chapters, and possibly even untraveled roads. Why must everything be given up to youth? She loved Conrad as much as anyone, but she was not at all ready to start digging her own grave.

———

TONIGHT WAS AS CLOSE as Conrad had ever come to witnessing the enormity of a parental quarrel. He found it riveting, full of noise and muted furies, like worlds close to collision, one near miss after the next. His head was full of the sound of cataclysms not making a sound.

Merry Berry's exit had left a dismaying void. And Conrad filled it with the perfectly wrong question.

"Sister Subordinary, what do you believe in?" Conrad turned his penetrating gaze on her.

Sister Mary Subordinary had just bent over to retie the laces on her boot. Now she straightened up.

"I believe in the vegetables—the beets and the broccoli. And I believe it's time to say goodnight. I must go tidy up my feelings," Sister paused. "I'm afraid I've not been at my best tonight. No matter what, Conrad, please remember that you are beloved beyond all measure."

Conrad's mind skipped right over "beyond all measure" and took up with "no matter what." He didn't know how to unpack that capacious phrase. He set it aside, but "no matter what" would come back to trouble his imagination as soon as the lights went out. Sister was waiting to hear his prayer, and he went ahead with a short litany of the usual I-love-yous and then tossed in a couple new ones.

"I love you and Sister Merry Berry and Mother Mary Extraordinary and Skipper. And the cassowary. And the garden. And the snow. And my planet. And the three angels, especially the green one. And the parents she promised me. Bless my special angel and the cosmic hero and all the heroes from here to eternity."

"Heaven help us, Conrad."

Her hand reached for the switch and the lights went out.

# REBEL ANGELS

AS SOON AS SISTER closed the door, Conrad rolled out of bed, counted to ten, and then turned the lights back on. He was wide awake, mulling over "no matter what," taking into consideration the undeniables. He had stretched things a bit in his retelling of the angel appearance. Was it possible he had lied in the stretch? He was left with the uncomfortable notion that a certain fallen angel underneath the stairs was getting drunk on his lies.

Not very drunk. The lies were after all, if lies at all, smallish sorts of lies. More like wishes. Still, it was best to be cautious.

Conrad raised the pillowcase flag attached to one of the bed posts, and he formulated a plan.

"Skip, I think I better do a security check. You guard the ship and I'll go make sure the wine cellar door is locked."

Conrad inched along the hallway, feeling his way towards the kitchen light switch. He wasn't so much worried as he was engaged in a boy's game of dare, his trusty Mattel at his side.

He flicked on the kitchen light.

A crash of thunder shifted the equation, hanging more weight on the worry side of the scale. A second lightening clap took out the lights.

Steady on, Conrad braved the darkness. He made it to the pantry, a little breathless and wishing he'd brought Skipper along. A third crack of lightening briefly illuminated the small pantry where Conrad stood puzzling over the strange interior weather.

Then bang! The cellar door at the back of the pantry blew wide open.

Conrad flew out of the pantry, down the hall, and into his room. Never stopping, he grabbed Skipper and dove under the bed. He was certain that he'd seen a figure standing at the open cellar door.

Moments later, a cheery, sing-song male voice made certainty a reality, "O knock, knock. Anybody home? Ain't nobody home, Boss."

"Out of my way," came the reply.

Conrad listened to the footfalls. Two intruders. The boy held himself still as a stone.

"Hey, Boss, look at that."

*That* was Skipper's tail sticking out from the hidey-hole. And that tail was twitching, seemingly itching for a little mischief. In one swift motion the boss bent down and yanked Skipper out from beneath the bed.

The monkey played dumb.

Conrad was so startled by this quick turn of circumstances, there was no time for him to get a grip on his monkey, much less stifle his impulse to cry out.

"Skiiiiiiiiiiiiper," the boy's cry hit the airwaves with an embarrassingly pathetic whine.

Conrad immediately realized his mistake and reached for his submachine gun. At least he had a grip on something. Just in time, because someone grabbed hold of his foot, and he found himself involuntarily sliding out from under the bed on his back. As soon as he cleared the bed, he sat up and aimed his gun.

A startled pair of eyes met his.

The intruder backed away, hands in the air, palms up. A happy realization struck Conrad. It was just like in the comics; you aim the gun and hands go up.

"Hey, Luce, the kid's got a gun."

Conrad saw the Latin spelling: l-u-x. He wheeled around and aimed his gun at the scintillating black-clad astral being who carelessly dangled Skipper by the tail. Conrad noted the meticulously crafted leather wings attached—like military epaulettes—to the jacket's sleeves. Could this be the lie-drinker?

"Okay, Mister, game over. Give me Skipper back." Conrad was grateful that his voice didn't shake.

Lucifer studied the bold child and smiled. It was an ambiguous smile, a mix of merriment and sneer. The smile seemed to dare Conrad to make a try for the toy.

"Luce, give the kid his monkey back," the figure whose hands were still in the air addressed his lustrous partner.

"You don't know who you're dealing with," Conrad steeled his voice, momentarily confounding Luce because it was true. Lucifer did not know who or what this child was, and the Eppler enigma bothered him a great deal more that he liked to admit.

Conrad glanced at Skipper, urging Hanuman to take the hint and *do something*. While the boy's attention was riveted on the toy monkey dangling from Lucifer's hand, Kilowatt carefully inched his way closer from behind. Conrad sensed the sneak attack and turned quickly, ready to fire off a warning shot. The curious, less illuminated, stranger reached into his pocket and pulled out a notepad.

"What kind of gun, you got there, Earthworm?" he asked, casually lifting a stubby pencil from the shelf of his ear.

"It's a Mattel," Conrad answered without thinking.

Conrad took in his interlocutor, the friendly crooked smile and dimpled cheeks, the strange aviator helmet and goggles pushed up on his forehead, the long-sleeved black and white stripy t-shirt. This oddball intruder wasn't the least bit intimidating. No weapon. No talons. Just a pencil poised at his writing pad.

"Look kid, ain't nobody gonna hurt your beanbag, okay? So put down the Mattel. Is that one 't' in Mattel or two? For the record."

"For the record, he's not a beanbag. That's Skipper. Skipper, the Gospel Monkey," Conrad worked up his indignation.

The boy swung his gun back toward Skipper's captor, giving the one called Luce a boy's measure of menace. For a seven-year-old, he was doing a pretty good job of imitating super-villain Bruno Mannheim's square-jawed grimace, but wishing he had something more intimidating in his small repertoire. Wolverine's steely claw came to mind.

What in the world was Skipper waiting for? Conrad's brain was jammed with mind signals and distress calls.

*Pick up. Pick up*, he kept signaling Skipper.

At a time like this, why was the monkey being difficult? Why didn't he use his Hanuman powers, shape-shift and take care of these intruders who were treating the glorious monkey like a dumb joke?

"I mean it," Conrad advanced on the menacing angel.

An outsized switchblade slowly materialized in Luce's hand. One click revealed an impressive steel cutting edge that appeared oddly translucent at certain angles. Conrad thought about his Barlow knife, small peanuts by comparison. Lucifer's knife had an unearthly gleam, and Conrad was wondering where the light came from when he realized that the tall man who held the blade emitted his own soft pulsing radiance, and that everything he touched shared that pulse and radiance.

One moment Luce seemed as solid as any Earthman, dressed as he was in slick black leathers. The next moment it seemed as if he were made of geometric light particles; moonstone grays and shadowy silvers, rolling with intermittent waves of gold.

Shifty, Conrad thought. Not entirely solid. If Conrad turned his head at a certain angle, he could see through the beautiful stranger. The boy took another step closer.

Lucifer's green and gold eyes seemed to measure each moment against eternity. He had an angular face and molten-blond hair—slicked back, it had the appearance of combed gold. At times Luce gave off a disconcerting feminine aura, as if daring any label to constrain his magnificent variety. His mouth was both sculptural and sensuous. He always seemed to be tasting something delicious, always on the verge of smiling, even when angered, even when he put the point of the blade to Skipper's throat.

"Drop the Mattel, Earthworm, or we spill the beans," Luce deadpanned.

Conrad caught the pun.

"Not funny," the boy said.

*Beanbag*, Conrad steamed silently, *if you only knew.*

Luce casually tossed Skipper Conrad's way. The perplexed boy dropped the gun and plucked his furry friend out of the air. He suddenly realized that this was one of those times that Lord

Hanuman had warned him about. He was on his own. Conrad let that cold stone sink in. The boy straightened his spine. He would rise to the occasion, impress the monkey.

*Don't worry, Skip. I got this.* "Who are you two guys? Are you good guys or bad guys?"

Instead of answering, Luce tore off a strip from Conrad's bed sheet, set one foot on the bed and bent to remove a smudge of Earth grime from his boot. The elegant black wing that extended from the boot drew the boy's admiring eye.

"Know anybody around here named Conrad Eppler?"

Conrad took in a quick breath. Determined to sound like a tough guy, he quickly sorted through a catalogue of comic book retorts. He could picture the balloon of inked words above his own head when he said, "Yeah. That's me. Who's asking?"

Lucifer straightened up. "You know who I am."

"Maybe I do."

Kilowatt was impressed. The kid was a player.

"Hey, Eppler. Is that one 'p' in Eppler or two?" Kilo still had his pencil poised at the notepad.

"You'll have to pardon Kilowatt. He suffers from a mild light deficiency."

"Hey, Luce, I don't need this abuse." Kilowatt firmly believed that his status as a minion deserved its portion of respect, especially considering the luminary he served.

"Earthworm, may I offer some friendly advice?" Luce paused. There was a hint of a smile. "Don't do drugs."

"What? Are you good guys or bad guys? Who are you two guys?"

"I'm Lieutenant Colonel Kilowatt," the note-taker offered. "It's true, I dropped some acid in my misspent youth, but I am so over it. No worries."

"Okay," Conrad said, assessing the situation. "I don't mean to be rude, but this is my room, and I'd like to know what you're doing here."

"Earthworm," Luce leaned on the edge of Conrad's desk, "this isn't about you, or your minders. It concerns Supernal matters. This investigation was authorized on high. On very high, I might add. I am tracking down some miscreants in my capacity as Chief of the Angel Police. I think you can help."

"Angel police." Conrad was genuinely puzzled. "Is that Bible or comic book?"

The black-clad illuminato rippled with laughter, and Conrad had to smile.

"The kid's a comedian, Kilo."

"Do you mind if I see some ID?" Conrad thought to ask.

Without hesitation, Luce pulled a clear folded wallet out of the nowhere and handed it to Conrad, who flipped it open to expose an impressive hologram. It was a silver police badge that spun in the air on rapidly-beating, tiny gold wings. Shattered light constantly broke from the metallic surface, making it difficult for the boy to make out the embossed lettering.

Conrad was officially dazzled. He couldn't help but covet the impressive badge that he reluctantly handed back to the Chief of Angel Police.

"One small request. I want you to help us identify some offenders." Luce held out his hands palms up—a gesture meant to be disarming.

"Offenders? Maybe I can help. Can I have a badge?" Conrad opened the negotiations.

"Sure, kid." Luce gave him the all-inclusive smile—the one that said, we're all pals here.

"But first," Conrad hedged, "before I join your special forces, I need to know what side you're on."

"We're all on the same side." Again, that smile from Luce.

"What side is that?" Conrad shot back. Maybe this high-ranking officer could help him defeat the Cardinals, avenge the Sisters.

"The side of the angels," Luce said.

Kilowatt saw how keenly Conrad wanted the badge. The kid only needed some assurances to feel right about helping out. No slouch in the minion department, Kilo began to extol Luce's many virtues, went so far as to claim that Luce was a one-hundred-percent-bona-fide good guy.

"Look kid, Luce took a fall. He did some time, but now his star is on the rise." Inspired by his own enthusiasm, Kilo burst into song: "It's a very moving story, a tale of love and glory—"

"Kilowatt! Thank you for not singing. We came to take the Earthworm's deposition."

"Right, Boss. I'm on it, Boss. Eppler, take a moment before you answer. Have there been any unusual happenings around here lately?"

Alert to the possibility that the two strangers had come to investigate the Cardinals, Conrad began to open up. But as it turned out, The Great Church was not in their jurisdiction. Conrad was dumbstruck when Kilowatt informed him that their investigation *only* concerned angels. And some unusual appearances in the vicinity.

"How many?" Conrad swallowed.

"Let's say three—three light attractions in the night, if you know what I mean? Ring any celestial bells?" Kilowatt inquired, his pencil hovering above the pad.

"I'm not talking."

"Whoa, kid," Kilo looked crestfallen. "Don't clam up on us. We picked up a trail of angel dust. And guess where the trail led? Now we got reason to think you called the delinquents down. Anyway, we got a transcript of your prayer request. We just need confirmation."

Luce reached behind Conrad's desk and placed an ornate ormolu music box on the desktop. "See this? It is a remarkable artifact," Lucifer's eyes glittered. "It puts me in mind of a certain artificer. Care to comment."

Conrad shrugged. He immediately recognized trouble. It was the voice-activated recording device that Skipper had warned him about. He wondered how long it had been hidden behind his desk.

"All around the mulberry bush, Eppler," Kilowatt shook his head. "You been holding out on us. For some unknown reason, the original remote listeners abandoned their posts."

"I didn't talk for seven years, so I guess the original remote listeners got bored."

"Who got bored?"

"The Cardinals. The enemy," Conrad added with some vehemence.

"Okay, kid. This ain't about them. So anyway, me and Luce, we requisitioned the box from your cellar and changed the channel. Guess who was doing the not-so-remote listening in the not-so-remote past? You know, someday I'm gonna have to try a Twinkie."

Conrad squirmed.

"Play back time," Kilo pressed a button.

They all listened to Conrad say: "They appeared *unto* me. Like in the Holy Book."

Kilo pressed the pause button, "Want me to fast forward to when you tell the black habits that the birthday-candle angelettes promised to grant your wish? And find you some parents?"

"No, that's okay. I remember what I said."

Dismay deepened as Conrad took in the particulars of Kilowatt's rambling disquisition. They had all the evidence, or so Kilo claimed. They knew that the angels were in Conrad's room; there was angel dust everywhere. The appearances were unlicensed, the entries illegal, and all Conrad had to do was identify the delinquents. They just wanted names. Three names.

Conrad was cornered. He had no idea how to defend his prayer or his answering angels. The allegations were perplexing, but the appearances were personal. Conrad felt protective of the lovely gem-toned visitors, especially the green one.

The boy looked over at the mostly silent, mysterious being who was currently peeling an apple with his switchblade; the peel hung in a loose unbroken spiral.

"Want a bite?" Lucifer offered.

"No, thanks."

The apple disappeared.

Kilo lowered his voice, "Eppler, there's something you should know about the boss."

"What's that?"

Lucifers's dazzling smile came all the way out of hiding. Then he spoke the words that Conrad had seen hovering overhead, "I am the Angel of Light."

"You could've fooled me," Conrad folded his arms.

"Yes, I could have. But I didn't, did I?"

"That's capital T, capital A of capital Light." Kilo explained, unhelpfully.

"I know that. I can see the letters. The Angel of Light talks in Times New Roman just like Mother Mary. Your font is Futura Sans," Conrad told Kilo. "That's short for Sans Serif."

"You're a weird kid. Anyone ever tell you that?"

"No."

Luce shot Kilo a look.

"Forget I said that. I'm one of those guys that's always got room for improvement. Futura Sans, huh?"

Conrad turned to the Angel of Light, "I've seen you before. In a comic book. But when I went back to look for you—you were gone. You left the story. And there was one other time— when I was little. I thought I dreamed you."

"You remember that?" Lucifer's gaze turned inward. "Traveling far on a cold dark night, I followed a wandering star and came to a convent covered in new fallen snow. I looked through a window on the second floor and saw a blue glow emanating from an open dresser drawer. So I slipped inside for a closer look."

"Why were you watching me?"

"I like to keep abreast of extraordinary events. Who knows? Maybe you're the coming Avatar."

A sudden hot surge made the Angel of Light almost unbearably bright. Conrad blinked, then watched incredulous as the matchless illuminato began to revolve in the air. In another blink, the Angel of Light broke up into a scatter of translucent flakes, like gold hammered to an impossible thinness. Then he was gone.

"Don't you love the way the boss does that? He was the best and brightest of his generation. He was state-of-the-art."

The boy sat on the edge of his bed, speechless. Comic book pages fanned before his eyes. He thought about how Epic's rocket accelerated in hyperspace, planet hopping from one galaxy to the next at the flip of a comic book page. Maybe that's how the angels traveled—an invisible page turned. In his brief life, the boy had encountered four angels. Maybe five. He wasn't sure about Kilowatt.

"You seem like a nice kid. If I was you, Eppler, I wouldn't go for the Avatar gig—all that crazy Vedic whoopla. People expecting you to crack wise at the drop of a Namaste. Besides, you're not blue anymore. Now me, I'd rather be a rock star."

"What's a rock star?"

"You don't know what's a rock star?" Kilo shook head in disbelief.

Kilowatt played a few classic licks on his air guitar. It was an astonishing instrument. The sound system was light-years beyond what currently passed for state-of-the-art on Earth. An itinerant musician at a crossroads might be tempted to sell his soul for such an instrument; but according to Kilo, the electric air guitar was not up for grabs.

Conrad had lots of questions about the air guitar and rock and roll, but they would have to be saved for a rainy day. Kilowatt was steering the conversation. The lowly angel noted that the Sisters had neglected crucial aspects of Conrad's education. Clearly, the kid needed a mentor.

"Where's your computer?" Kilowatt asked.

"My what?"

"This place is screen-free?" Kilowatt tossed the idea around. "I kinda get it. Me? I'm partial to a graphite pencil."

"Me too."

"But the graphite pencil has limitations. No laptop. No Google. No video games. No Bloodborne. No YouTube. No stupid skateboard videos. No spell check. Hey, how come you know the names of fonts?"

"Sister Subordinary and I made a chart. Your font has the best lower case 'g.' I'm a pretty expert copyist. Plus, I can write Greek and Sanskrit letters, but my specialty is comic book."

"Comic books rock, Eppler."

"So, what happens now? Are you going to grill me?" Conrad asked.

"Nah. Luce was probably just testing your mettle. Sizing you up. We got the music box, the dust. This convent here, it's a hot spot. A lot of etheric energy. We're thinking it's you. Or, it could be the old lady. Luce'll work it out."

Kilowatt started to head for the cellar door. He had a jaunty walk, his chest puffed up, his arms swinging rhythmically. He called it the stride of life. One day Conrad would imitate that walk, much to Sister Subordinary's dismay.

Kilowatt turned back. Conrad was about to make an unlikely friend, the first friend he had ever made on his own.

"So, Eppler, how about we make a deal for your Mattel?"

"What'll you give me? The air guitar?"

"Nah."

"The music box?"

"Nah. How about we say, I owe you a big favor?"

"Do I look stupid?"

"It's always in your best interests to have someone on the inside what owes you a big favor."

Conrad wanted to know exactly where and what side the "in" side was on. Was it in a different dimension? Did Kilo live in hyperspace? How do you get there, and where exactly was *there*? Did someone have to turn a page? Could Kilo describe it mathematically? Could he draw a map? And where did angels go when they left you?

"Whoa, whoa, whoa, kid. Now you're grilling me. I feel like a metaphysical cheese burger. So chill with the grill. How about this? Imagine you're a sturgeon."

"I don't want to be a sturgeon."

"It's a metaphor."

"I know it's a metaphor, but I don't want to be a sturgeon in the metaphor. I'd rather be a hammerhead shark."

"Geeze, okay kid. You're a shark. You're in the sea. You got no notion of the world above you. Glimpses maybe. Well, that's where me and the other angels abide. On the inside what's above you, there's a planet called Grace. A nice place. Period. Now do I get the Mattel?"

Conrad was enjoying this. This was the first time he'd ever experienced what it might be like to play with another boy you happened to meet in the neighborhood.

"Tell you what. I'll give you three comic books, down payment on the big favor. Then when I call the favor in, you get the gun."

"Done deal, kid. Anybody ever tell you, you're not so dumb?"

"I know that."

Conrad crawled under the bed to retrieve his stash. Pushing comic books out onto the floor, Conrad emerged dusty and eager to share.

A gleeful Kilowatt plucked up a *Superman* original. Conrad saw the "wow" in a jagged balloon above Kilo's head. The minion was also a big fan of *X-men* and *Watchmen*. The two readers them found themselves sitting side by side, lost in time, pouring over Conrad's collection.

Skip nestled in Conrad's lap, vicariously enjoying the camaraderie, his tail twitching occasionally. Things were working out well, at least according to the monkey.

"There might come a time, kid, on life's checkered highway when you're going to need more than one big favor."

"I'm open. Let's deal." Conrad was happy to trade up. "What makes Luce think I'm an Avatar?"

"Beats me. Luce isn't a big talker."

Before Kilo left, Conrad thought to ask if the Avatar was a good guy or a bad guy.

"Depends on who's running the Avatar," Kilo shrugged.

Kilowatt's answer gave Conrad pause. And the pause created a roomy space for Conrad's first big thought—the possibility that he did not entirely belong to himself.

## Book Two

# PLANET GRACE

LET US HOPE
IT WILL ALWAYS BE LIKE THIS
EACH OF US GOING ON
IN OUR INEXPLICABLE WAYS
BUILDING THE UNIVERSE.

SONG OF THE BUILDERS,
MARY OLIVER

# Deep Background

Planet Grace Is a Diamond in the sky, albeit a sky in an alternate fold of reality. A place of cold, austere beauty and stark purple sunsets, the pressurized carbon atmosphere produces storms of diamonds that whorl endlessly across the plains. Cyclone clusters stampede in herds of shimmering funnels—lifting, dropping, rarely stopping. The diamond planet hosts a continuous cataclysm of spectacular weathers, convivial perquisites for the elite celestial inhabitants.

A perfect place to breed infant illuminati, planet Grace is renowned among the hierarchy of Archangels, Thrones, and

Powers for its kaleidoscopic Angel Knest—a cylinder-shaped pod with discs revolving inside of discs. At dusk, when the kaleidoscope spirals across the matrix of crystal plains—its cargo of embryonic angels tucked in cozy modules—a tidal music swells in successive waves that tower and roll through the dimensions. The array of orchestral themes varies from crashing symphonic tsunamis to delicate subatomic hums and clicks. An ever-rearranging light show of flowering symmetries blinks in time to the tubular harmonics.

The celebrated Knest, long considered one of the marvels of the plenum, recently saw Conrad's three gem-toned visitors emerge from its portals. By comparison, the wet blue jewel in the Milky Way galaxy, with its plethora of strange warring organic beings, comes off as a planet somewhat aesthetically and morally suspect—possibly an experiment on the verge of failure. Its designer and builder, a youthful but gifted second-tier deity, almost abandoned his project at the point when dinosaurs ruled the Earth. Perfectly happy with his reptilian creations—the scaled, the clawed, the plated, the beaked, the horned—on day seven he was ready for a rest. And some well-deserved applause, or so he imagined.

As it turned out, not everyone was pleased with the life forms. Instead of the expected slap on the back and good show, the Supernals asked for a do-over. The artificer's eager younger brother, the incandescent Lucifer, made an attention-getting project of eradicating the misshapen crawlers and flyers, hurling meteors at the planet, triggering an ice age—and then for fun, the young Lucifer reversed the magnetic poles. The brothers fought, a classic clash between creator and destroyer—one for the holy books.

The unhappy Demiurge was commanded by one of the Wheels to try again—and this time not to be so stingy in the brains department.

Expectations ran high. The Demiurge was well known in the omniverse for the wildly inventive nature of his creations. He was equally renowned for his adolescent temper tantrums and sulks. With a great deal of prompting, he got back in the game and made one final effort to fill the new world with life forms. This time the fledgling deity created mammals, including the much-anticipated primates. Again, the Supernals were less than impressed.

"They'll evolve!" the Demiurge screamed at his critics and stormed off.

Occasionally he sneaks back to his creation and attempts a few tweaks. But for the most part, his world wobbles on unassisted.

Not surprisingly, the sentient beings presently in ascendance on planet Earth are riddled with abandonment issues, subliminally aware that their creator jumped ship. The struggling human inhabitants labor under the burdens of several myths of irreparable loss, myths that retrofit an Edenic oasis in the apocryphal long ago when all was briefly bliss, an imaginary moment in a time before their temperamental deity looked upon them in disgust and took a runner.

The origin myth got increasingly muddled in successive retellings. It was never paradise, never a happy valley of bliss. It was a violent show from the get-go. Despite the revelations of science, the denizens remain beset with visions of a perfect paradise.

This teleological paradigm is virtually embedded in their DNA. It was meant to be aspirational. Instead it became a false memory. Nostalgic by nature, the Earth-born can't help but hanker for a pristine inviolate pastoral postcard that never was—lions lying down with lambs in an ephemeral sunlit nudist colony, festooned with ferns and fig trees.

Asheilstarte, Mediatrix of Grace, Queen of Angels and High Consul to the Knest, knows an abiding compassion for the myth-saturated planet. She has a soft spot for its inhabitants, and pities them their beloved postcards and fables and Edenic fantasies. Over the eons, She-Who-Sees-Everything watched successive generations come to consciousness crushed with the disappointing news that their planet abides in a hopelessly degraded state. How disheartening it must be for new arrivals on Earth when they learn all too soon they have arrived too late. Barely out of their cribs, they are told that they already missed all the good stuff.

Many of Earth's young achieve literacy virtually teething on stories of a fall. They look out their nursery windows on a variety of unhappy landscapes and feel themselves to blame, as if some collective sin created the forlorn vistas—the muck of oil spills, the wreckage of super storms, the grimy air, the urban cityscapes replete with plastic bags and empty candy wrappers blown up against the chain link fences.

Stalked by a mysterious sin so bleak and original, all neonates arrive tainted before a single breath is taken. Born with an almost indelible smudge on their newly minted souls, the little ones are obligated to be born again. She-Who-Mothers-Creation is vexed by the legends of babies born with original smudges.

Asheilstarte's special area of expertise is origin myths. She is on intimate terms with the big bang, the injurious fall, and all the subsequent fallout. She tastes the spew and miasma of conflicting origin myths that keep the tribes endlessly pitted against each other. She visits the apocalyptic visions that keep the survivalists terrified, armed, and bunkered. She frequents the dystopian fantasies that keep the rhetoricians dependent on drip-lines of creeds and screeds.

She wants to untangle the knot of keeps and keepers.

She knows that some promises are prisons.

Asheilstarte examines the promises of varietal redemptions. Heavenly bread and circuses for the downtrodden. Virgins for the martyrs. A palliative of soundbites and celebrity for the hysterical Cassandras and buttoned-down doomsayers that stalk the media, sounding alarms, laying the blame. The ancient tower babbles on. So much terror on terra firma. The violence is enervating.

She is shaking the Tree of Knowledge with her mighty wind. The windfall apples cover the land. This vision gives her hope.

Overhauling the myth of the fall and its cast of archetypes is her current personal project-in-progress. Lately, She has been turning the Eden myth over on the rotisserie of her diamond-pointed mind. One imagination at a time, Asheilstarte works her way into human consciousness.

She-Who-Rules-Grace wants to syncopate the myth of a lost paradise to her personal pulse, and march Eden into the future where it belongs. Her star-chambered heart is the primordial different drummer. Lie on any sun-bathed patch of Earth and you can feel her beat, her heat.

She dreams of a garden yet-to-be: Not a paradise lost on Earth and subsequently found in heaven. Not a wish fulfilled in a next life. Not a replicant garden, built on some revolving space station cum Elysium. Not located in the outer burbs of Andromeda. Not arrived at tunneling through some Einstein-Rosen wormhole. Not on Mars. Not on Neptune's moon, Triton, nor on any other alternate site favored by those hankering for a galactic off-planet ride and hide away.

She redlines all relocation plans. She envisions a home-grown paradise on Earth. She wants to ignite hope of a muscular variety. Hope that roles up its shirt sleeves, muddies its boots.

*Gardens, gardeners, guardians.*

She conceived Grace as a gateway planet, a platform for myth-minders and archangelic overseers. Myth is the entry point to the permeable consciousness of humankind—cave-painters, story-makers, star-gazers. Among the tools of mythcraft, She privileges visions, daydreams, insights, incarnations, appearances, and the occasional flyover and drop-down. Her current appearance on Grace is a staging maneuver. She is not appearing as herself. She rarely does.

Her enterprise is vastly complicated by the fact that the renovation of a myth requires the co-operation of the mythic archetypes involved. A further complication in the shifting of a mythic paradigm is the measure of belief that sustains a prevailing myth-cluster at any given juncture in the space-time continuum.

She means to smash the current cluster with a soft hammer.

The Tinkerbell Paradox holds that prayer is a critical function in the reset algorithm. Homage is the dream-catcher.

*Praise me,* she whispers to the lonely planet.

She speaks in wind and rainfall, her voice surges on ocean whitecaps, crashes down mountainsides in bridal veils, sluices over river rock.

*Paint me. Dance me. Make me a paean.*

Poetry is the insurrectionist's artform. It is the soft hammer. A countervailing wind of new song must ruffle the waves of orthodoxy, loosen the hold of old beliefs and clear out the clogged sloughs of dogma to make room for fresh acts of the imagination.

Asheilstarte works her renovations in concert with a vast array of prayerbenders, artificers, insurgents, and messengers. Engagement—this is the calling of all angels turning the kaleidoscope of dreams in the diamond night. Knest work.

*Bemuse the dreamers,* she counsels her angels. *Tease out their stories.*

She is made of stories and remade by stories. She is every child whispering:

*Tell me a story.*

There are no direct experiences in her epistemology, merely shifts in the patterns of signals, the electric flash dance of dendrites that link and ignite identities and narratives alike, link and ignite all the infinitesimal points of consciousness. Her personal nirvana is to submerge herself in the illuminated minds of other beings, bathe in the ecstatic effusions of sentients flooded with insights, riddled with game plans.

*Once upon a planet. . .*

———

NOW IT IS MOONRISE on planet Grace. Asheilstarte has just completed her diurnal review of the Knest. All angels tucked in, She allows herself a momentary bathe in the pleasures of self-satisfaction.

A three-headed, tripartite illuminata, She is formally addressed as High Consul. She has two flanking Wing Sergeants, each sporting one powerful wing. Stretching out her enormous wings, She is preparing to address herself. She is, in fact, her own address, located resplendently in the environs of self.

"So lovely. Such exquisite paradigms of innocence. This is possibly the best litter of angels we have produced yet. Still, the prophesied Earth Angel has yet to reveal herself."

The right Wing Sergeant pursued that thought, "There might be one or two Thrones among the neonates."

"Thrones among them. Maybe even a Power," the left Wing echoed.

The three heads turned simultaneously at the entrance of the Angel of Light. On planet Grace, Lucifer's leathers were an impossible diamond white. The impeccably clad illuminato hesitated.

"You may approach us," the Trinity surged, towering above Lucifer, casting streamers of particulate light, a show of appreciation for the legendary celestial celebrity, the quintessential link in the angel chain. When the exultation reached its zenith, the tripartite illuminata contracted to a more hospitable size and opened herself to receive Lucifer's appreciations.

"High Consul, Chair of Divinity, Chair of Wisdom, Chair of Paradox, Angel Most Generous and Supreme Ruler of Grace."

"Eosphoros," She called him by his Greek name, "you interrupt my reverie and salute me with praises dipped in irony and barely concealed irreverence."

"Noted," Lucifer shrugged.

"Kilowatt, will you address us?"

Lucifer's minion was taken off guard. He considered himself far enough beneath notice that he could count on going unnoticed in the presence of the upper echelons of angels.

"Hello, Kilowatt," She tried again.

"Hi, Consul," Kilowatt ventured. "I mean *High* Consul. Chair of—of true value and quality, quality discounts and fine leather upholstery," Kilo improvised.

The Trinity surged with a contented harmonic om.

*A fool*, the superluminary mused in the semi-privacy of her trifold mind, clearly taken with the quick-minded salvos of Lucifer's minion.

"High Consul," Luce stepped forward, "one small request and we'll leave you to your meditations. With your permission, I would like to inspect the Knest."

"Permission withheld. We've just reviewed the Knest and everything's in perfect order."

"I happen to know otherwise. Three of your angelettes took an unlicensed flight."

"Is that possible? Wing Sergeants?"

"The review could have been illusion," Wing I responded.

"Illusion," Wing II echoed. "They are amazing little adepts."

The illuminata preened with Knest pride. Beatific smiles lit her three faces, and the diamond-studded gold monocle set over Asheilstarte's right eye clicked two degrees narrower.

She may have been laughing. Lucifer was uncertain.

This tripartite mutant angel had not been around when the Angel of Light had last soared in the etheric realms. Lucifer's canonical clash with the Demiurge had sent him tumbling into a fathomless dark hole, only to reemerge into a world of unfamiliars.

She was an unknown. He wore his history on his sleeve.

Lucifer glowered in silence, taking her measure before he set his intentions and made his play. There had been a revolution in the heavens while he'd brooded in the darkness. That much was clear.

"Let us praise the angels emergent," the illuminata invited Luce to join her reverie.

Lucifer chose to risk dissent, "I am not sure praise is the appropriate response. There's been a violation. Unless I am misinformed, there have been no flight permits issued to the Knest. As Chief of Angel Police, I strongly advise you to issue a search warrant, so I can proceed with the arrests."

"Arrest whom? Do you know their identities?"

Kilowatt stepped up at this juncture, music box in hand. "We got the music box and we got the dust. May it please Your Honor," he added as an afterthought.

"Dust?"

"Angel dust, picked up right on the premises." Kilowatt produced a baggie of rainbow-hued dust.

"And listen to this," Kilo pressed the wrong button, and the box began to plunk out a tinny melody. It was the tune to a nursery rhyme concerning a monkey that chased a weasel.

"Give me a sec, Your Majesty." Kilowatt felt Lucifer's heat burning holes in his back. "Sorry, Luce," he muttered as he retreated to fiddle with the cranky machine.

"Eosphoros," High Consul's voice billowed in the diamond night, "I am baffled by your investigative techniques. Amusing to be sure, but primitive. Truly, I expected something more sophisticated when we engaged your services. Let us begin again, shall we? I am confident that were you to make even slightest effort, you could *imagine* the identities of our miscreant angels. Allow me to assist you. It would be a pleasure to share my insights with you—by intuitive transfer."

"There will be no intuitive transfer, Your Divine Complacency. Let us apply Occam's Razor, shall we? And cut to the chase." Lucifer no longer bothered to dissemble his disdain. "Who are they?"

"I imagine that the first to leave the Knest would be Aletheia. They're young, Luce—these things have a tendency to happen. Wing Sergeants, who would follow Aletheia?"

"Periwinkle."

"Epiphany."

"My thoughts exactly. Wing Sergeants, call them up."

The Wing Sergeants emitted a coded series of sound waves that triggered a confetti toss of sparkling particles inside the Knest. Almost immediately, Periwinkle and Epiphany appeared at Consul's station, answering the call with a show of their own magenta and purple sparks. Again, pride brightened the Trinity.

"I will confess them, bless them—"

"You mean, I can't arrest them?"

The Wings ignored Luce's outburst and signaled High Consul that that the search was complete. Aletheia was missing from the Knest.

"One missing," She mused out loud, "the tendency to happen would appear to be happening. Periwinkle and Epiphany, you may approach me."

"Chair of Radiance," Periwinkle's tiara twinkled.

"Chair of Mystery," Epiphany's aura glowed.

"I will hear your confessions."

"Bless us, Reverend Mother. We dutifully confess—one flight unlicensed and one appearance unauthorized," the angels bowed down low and lower still until their noses brushed the diamond dust. Kilowatt made note of the elaborate bow.

"May it please Your Grace," Periwinkle embellished, peeking up to see how their confessions had landed.

"Forgiven," the Mediatrix of Grace bid the angels rise.

The sigh of relief from the adolescent angels only served to further infuriate Luce, who was backing up and attempting to keep the pulse of his moonstone lumens from giving away his dark mood. The angelettes were giggling by this point, but the gold flecks in Luce's green eyes were giving off dangerous glints.

The Mediatrix let the neophyte angels absorb her absolutions. Only when they had their fill of grace did She pose the question of the moment, "Where is Aletheia?"

"I bet," the amethyst angel offered by way of a helpful guess, "she is examining her conscience."

The rubellite angel seconded Periwinkle's guess with a flutter of her downy plumes.

"I'm not interested in speculations about her current spiritual activities. Where is she, dear ones?"

The gemstone angelettes were forced to admit that much to their regret they had lost Aletheia somehow, somewhere out there, on the way back to Grace. With that admission, they immediately felt the full force of High Consul's attention.

Periwinkle and Epiphany, enjoying the spotlight, shook out a curious story about a ship and happily laid the diverting tale before the Mediatrix—how the ship had pursued them, darting every which way among the stars.

"We stopped at the edge of the Cloud Canyon, and we turned around. The ship looked like a bent featherless silver wing. It came within inches of us and hovered," Epiphany relayed the story with barely repressed delight. "Then suddenly the silver wing cut Aletheia out of our flight triangle."

"Whoosh," Periwinkle embellished.

"Aletheia sped up, and the ship gave chase," Epiphany filled in.

"Then poof!" Periwinkle added an exclamation point.

"Poof?" High Consul tasted the strange word and spit it out.

"Poof. She was gone. Quite." Epiphany clarified.

The Mediatrix instructed her Wings to make a sky search in the fourth quadrant of the Cloud Canyon.

"Casting, casting, casting," the deeply layered vocalizations of the Wings rolled out in resonating waves. "Full sweeeeeeeep. In the net."

An electric crack rent the night. Then a cluster of scintillant facets broke apart, creating a hole in the dense atmosphere. A fragmented Aletheia stepped out of the opening. She sparkled in the diamond light until her emerald green luster reconfigured and solidified. Then she shuttered her wings.

"Beautifully executed, Wing Sergeants." The Mediatrix gave Luce an admonishing glance. She was teaching him their ways. And he was reassessing her on a tilt of resentment.

"Aletheia, you may approach me."

"High Consul, Chair of Eternal Recurrence."

"You know your Nietzsche."

"May it please your High Consul. I choose not to confess."

"You *do* know your Nietzsche," the illuminata beamed.

"I have examined my conscience and I cannot find my regrets."

Aletheia was performing perfect concentric circles of primary enlightenments. The tripartite divinity intensified her penetrating high beams, her monocle now focused exclusively on the emerald angel. Luce darkened, but at the same time allowed an indefinable attraction to the sassy green neophyte under examination.

While Luce appraised the outward attributes of the emerald angel, High Consul explored the contours of Aletheia's inner workings. He learned nothing. She made an interesting discovery.

"Tonight's was not a virgin flight, was it? You meant to visit the child, didn't you?"

Epiphany and Periwinkle discharged purple and crimson flares, incensed by Aletheia's betrayal. Aletheia had led them on—her own littermates, her wing siblings—all the while pretending it was an improvised lark.

Aletheia immediately shifted the blame to Conrad, betraying her immaturity. She described how she'd slipped out of the Knest one night to practice solo flybys and felt an unexpected tug when she passed over planet Earth.

High Consul silently noted that Aletheia failed to question her initial attraction to Earth. With a slight nod, She encouraged the emerald angel to continue her tale.

*Tell me a story.*

"When I flew off with Epiphany and Periwinkle, we were just going to appear. And disappear. Mainly disappear," Aletheia wavered.

Then her story took on the speed of her increasing uncertainty. "I never meant to touch down. It was the boy who meant me to, bent me to *his* dream. A powerful electromagnetic current grabbed me, grabbed all of us and kept pulling us closer until we were in his clouds. Then the boy grounded us. Personally, I'd venture to say that he's some sort of love battery." Aletheia smiled, pleased with her conjecture. "Then we bounced around his space, flashed him a little and charged him up. He's all right, isn't he? We didn't do any harm, did we?"

Consul concurred that most of the time, when angels appear to a child in the material world the vision fades rather quickly, and no harm is done. Usually, parents can be counted on to reinforce doubt, dismissing visions as acts of the imagination, as if the epistemological products of the imagination were somehow of an inferior provenance.

*It's only your imagination,* parents like to say. At some point the child-book of wonders is put away on a dusty shelf and forgotten. Memory revises itself until the past aligns with the prevailing realities in the present.

"The only time any real harm is done by angel appearances is when promises are made and subsequently broken," Asheilstarte counseled the green angel.

"No promises were made." Aletheia looked to Periwinkle and Epiphany for support.

They turned away from her, tossing off silent amethyst and rubellite retorts. The message from her wingsibs was clear. Aletheia was on her own.

Dutifully, the emerald angel re-examined her conscience. She had said, "Next time," when she was leaving the boy. Did that imply a promise to return? No. *Next time* just meant *sometime* around the big bend. Right now, the important thing was to control the presentation.

And yet here was that ridiculous sidekick of Lucifer's, confidently coming forward with an enchanting looking music box as if it held some evidence against her.

"May it please your Royal Highness," Kilowatt made an awkward attempt to imitate the low and elegant bows of the angelettes.

With one arm sweeping the floor and the ormolu music box tucked under the other, Kilo wobbled until he nearly dropped the box. Then catching it with both hands, he placed it on the edge of High Consul's platform, and straightened himself up. Ignoring the giggles from Periwinkle and Epiphany, he managed an appealing dignity for all that.

"Here's a transcript of Eppler's prayer." Kilo pulled his notepad out and ripped off a couple pages. "He made two requests, to which the angelettes gave a definitive yes and yes. I did the math myself. The kid's request is recorded in various places. This is from when I think he was talking to the monkey. Let me press this here button and—"

"No! That's not the way it was. I mean, we never really listened to the boy's prayers."

"How careless," Consul's monocle made a delicate adjustment.

Aletheia felt a twinge. A small one. The reprimand spoiled her perfect presentation.

"But you are curious now, aren't you? You do want to know what the boy wished for," the Mediatrix persisted.

"Well, no. Not really. Well, maybe just a little curious. Was it something big?"

"Big? He was able to pull three etherics out of our world into his world, by your own account."

In a flashback, Aletheia reviewed the appearance. She remembered surfing on the radio waves, Conrad's sweet voice on the walkie-talkie, the comic book he tried to give her.

"May it please your Grace, I've changed my mind. I do want to know what prayer I answered," Aletheia bowed.

"Kilowatt, enlighten us."

"Here's the lowdown: the kid wants a comic book hero. And an angel."

"He asked for an angel? You mean like a guardian angel? I can do that," Aletheia brightened.

"No, Aletheia," Luce scoffed, "you answered a prayer for parents."

Flaming with indignation, the Chief of the Angel Police turned on High Consul, "It's a damn disgrace, the way you run this place!"

Immediately Kilowatt was on guard, looking up, down and over his shoulder, certain the lightning was about to strike and blow his two bits back to kingdom come.

"Your uh, her uh, Royal-Indulgence-Divine-Kindness-Illustrious-Management. Luce here, he didn't mean that."

"I meant it."

Kilowatt advanced on Luce with urgent whispers.

"No, you didn't, Luce. Listen, I don't want to get cast out. I hate being cast out. I hate it."

Kilowatt turned back to High Consul, "Excuse us for a sec, Your Royal Above-It-All, me and Luce need to discuss how much we like these new jobs we got." Kilo shook his head ruefully and faced down his boss. "I'm telling you, Luce, I ain't going back with you into the black hole. I had it with the black hole, Luce."

The Angel of Light pushed Kilowatt aside. "High Consul, I come to your planet Grace. I offer my services. But you don't seem to appreciate what I can do for you. I've been around. I know the score. I can help you clean up this mess. You won't let me arrest the angelettes? Fine. There are other ways."

"What do you suggest?"

"Right off the top of my head? Earthquake." Lucifer almost laughed.

Instead he produced that luminous all-attractive smile, as if there were nothing in the world more satisfactory than the earthquake on offer. This delight in mischief suggested a lingering adolescence. Clearly Luce's historic animosity towards all things Earth was still a flashpoint in the angel's catalogue of resentments.

Aware of Lucifer's serpentine history, how his reputation suffered the exigencies of various belief systems in need of an arch enemy, the Mediatrix paused the proceedings to conduct an archival search.

———

ASHEILSTARTE QUICKLY SORTED through the many mythical threads that reified Lucifer's existence. She noted that the cartography of his myth was drawn with multiple permeable borders. Ironically, the myth that most closely matched her memory had Islamic roots. The Quran records how the angel Iblis was banished from the heavens for refusing to worship Adam. She laughed to herself, recalling Lucifer's initial reaction to Homo erectus.

Adam, in those first days, was a disappointment to all etherics—a hirsute violent creature of questionable intelligence; and with that sloping forehead, he was not very appealing to behold. Lucifer, brilliant and beautiful, cannot really be blamed for being underwhelmed in the presence of the first man.

Yes, the mammals were an improvement over the reptiles. Still, the humble, grunting, hunch-shouldered Homo not-quite-sapiens that emerged from his cave was hardly cause for rapture. Lucifer had let loose a world-rattling snicker when he first caught sight of the sorry creature. The infamous snicker could still be heard rolling through the outer burbs of the plenum.

If it weren't for that snicker, how differently the story might have gone!

Not one to admit that he was embarrassed by his own creation, the Maker picked a quarrel with the Sparkler.

Prototypical brothers, thought Asheilstarte as She meditated on these ancient grudges and rough beginnings. Maker and Sparkler—long forgotten nicknames from a raucous childhood that left its mark, its ineffable brand on planet Earth.

For his part, Lucifer remained convinced that had he been invited to collaborate at the drawing-board stage, creation would have been a glorious success. But when the Wheels called for a design, the Sparkler had nothing to bring to the table but visionary swagger.

The Maker had won the commission to authorize Earth's life forms by dint of hard work, with a beautifully rendered series of drawings and simulations. The industrious firstborn was happy to go it alone. He did not want his younger, shinier brother snarking over his shoulder while he worked his wonders to behold.

Long upstaged by the flashier sibling, the Demiurge relished his turn in the spotlight. He petitioned for total creative control. He got what he asked for, and along with it, all the blame when Earth woggled off course.

To make matters more fractious, Lucifer had been quick to spot flaws in the original design. Thus, earning the dubious right to say, "I told so."

By Lucifer's considerable lights, the pastoral Eden never really had half a chance. He pointed out that if the creator-of-record had truly been interested in a peaceable kingdom, he would never have placed the lovely long-necked Apatosaurus in the same world as the Tyrannosaurus Rex. And while T-rex battled Triceratops, battle lines were drawn in heaven.

The lesser angels took sides, and there was a great inconclusive conflagration. The Angel of Light and his illustrious minions battled the Demiurge and his band of followers until it was clear that both sides were losers.

Afterwards the creator, whose ego never recovered from the snicker, skulked off to some distant corner of the plenum. He took his pieces out of the game. Earth would get no further aid from its maker for the next two-hundred-thousand years.

"Let them eat prayers," he was heard muttering as he took his exit.

The Angel of Light stepped into the gap, into the not-quite paradisiacal garden. Begrudgingly Lucifer had to admit—if only to himself—that the ferns were spectacular, and the beaches were beyond compare. Lucifer entered the legendary scene with admirable intentions. He wanted to give the lowly human-like creatures a little stimulation in the frontal lobes.

Myth attributes this upgrade in intelligence to an apple. Luce is fond of the apple metaphor; however, he abhors the way his role in evolution has been degraded over time. Especially painful to watch was the gradual distortion of his image until he was reduced to a claw-footed red ogre with a tail. The tail was a particularly unfortunate turn, because it was precisely the tail that he most disliked in those first appearances of the primates. Without consulting the runaway designer, Lucifer made certain aesthetic modifications. He removed the vestigial tail and tweaked the frontal lobes.

The brothers fought again, this time one on one. This time over copyright. In view of his belated contributions, Lucifer wanted credit as co-creator. The Demiurge protested on the legal grounds that no one had invited Lucifer to upgrade the minds of humankind. Besides, Lucifer was already credited in empyrean annuls for the big blow out that initiated the material universe. The extended cosmic brawl over copyright on Earth's lifeforms nearly caused early-onset apocalypse.

Asheilstarte caught the final comet that Lucifer had hurled at planet Earth back when he unilaterally resolved to obliterate the offensive rock. A quickly convened mediation of Supernals tossed the reactive Angel of Light into a black hole for a lengthy cool down.

Later, more secular-minded generations on Earth speculated that a visit from aliens explained the great leap forward in intelligence. Others attributed the growth in brain power to meat. Meat? The planet was constantly adding insult to Lucifer's injured but resurgent pride.

———

"LOOK AT IT MY WAY," Luce entered the caesura with no idea that She had just been looking at it his way.

"Go on," She encouraged.

"Every spiritual disorder running rampant on planet Earth can be traced back to unlicensed angel appearances. My appearance in the garden being the exception, of course."

"Of course," the Trinity agreed, giving Luce an unexpected boost.

"Don't get me going on the Angel Moroni. Look at the mess he initiated. Utah? Major case of angel infection. And California? You've got your channelers, your televangelists, your Scientology. And now you've got Conrad Eppler with a major case of angel infection right up the coastline in Humboldt County. Forget the Earthquake. How about I fire up that sleeping volcano under Yosemite? Wipe the slate clean."

"Somehow, I don't think that is the path I wish to take."

"Why not? I'm talking one stop, quick fix, miracle services."

"I was hoping for something more visionary and less aesthetically obnoxious."

"You got it. How about an apocalypse? Now that's aesthetic. Imagine the beautiful noise. Imagine the fireworks. Nuclear fission, planets in collision blown to smithereens, star-guided missiles, modernist steeples slicing through the stratosphere, blasting every, everlasting human artifact off the surface of the material plane."

When Luce projected his ecstatic visions, he didn't seem much of an improvement over the artificer and his raptors. And yet, High Consul remained intrigued.

"Things have changed since you've been away. There have been revolutions in the heavens. The great Wheels have turned ten thousand times."

"Therefore what? Earth is just a stopover planet. They know it. We know it. The best among them are doing time until they can climb onto a higher plane. The rest of them are squeezing all the juice out of it. You have to admit, it's not the green dream-baby the Wheels had in mind."

"We see Earth as it was in the beginning, a great potentiality, a gleaming jewel, the pearl of peace, the ground of love—the sparkling hope of heaven."

"Are we talking about the same planet?"

"The heavens were locked in a perpetuity of frozen perfection until we set one planet free and let it breed. We let Chaos rumble the plenum, but you pushed it too far."

"Danger gave humankind desire and reach," Luce defended himself, "the spark of the divine."

"That spark was an immeasurable gift, Luce. You touched the mind of Eve and opened the gate."

"One of my more brilliant days," Luce caught a glimpse of someone reaching for an apple on a switchback in his memory.

"You can be the illumined one that you were once destined to be."

"What does that mean?"

"Earth is tragically enmeshed in legends of a paradise lost. The founder's myth trumps all hope. You cannot initiate a creation with a failed paradise and finish with an apocalypse. It is an unworkable story. That is the text we most wish to revise."

"Look, all I am saying is that if you let me blow it up, we get to start from scratch. It gives the Wheels a chance to work the kinks out of the original design," Luce slipped in a gratuitous dig at his brother.

"We prefer to work through one imagination at a time."

"That could take forever."

"Then we have all the time we need."

The Trinity bent its light to pierce Lucifer's armor and magnify his brilliance. Things were heating up.

"What better work is there, than the audit of an imagination?" The illuminata's effulgence infiltrated the scintillant membrane of Lucifer's soul; "Every imagination I inhabit enlightens me."

Too late, Lucifer became aware of her presence in his mind. He tried and failed to throw her off.

"Your imagination has always intrigued me, Lucifer. How enlightening! I see that you are picturing yourself on my throne, wearing my wings, the future Supreme Ruler of Grace."

The Wing Sergeants snapped to attention.

"Damn straight," Luce came back.

Kilowatt blanched, but Luce engined on.

"I won't have to lift a finger because you are giving the power away. If you don't get the angels of Grace under control, the Wheels are going to cast you out. And you are going to say, Lucifer tried to warn me. Luce tried to set me straight."

With that, Lucifer shifted dimensions, leaving a fall of gold particles in his wake. The silence would have been profound, but for the intrusion of Kilowatt, who made his way quickly towards Consul's platform.

Time for damage control.

"Your Honor, I just want you to know," the minion straightened his sleeves, "I'm on your side, whatever side that is. Blessed be. Blessed be."

Kilowatt made second attempt at a formal bow. This time he pulled it off. It was a classic Restoration obeisance; one hand fluttered to the ground and rose again in a graceful sweep. Then with his arms held out at his sides, he improvised a rolling motion with both wrists as he backed away, his hands swimming like happy fish. Finally satisfied that he'd made a good impression, he stepped backwards into the next mystery.

The tripartite celestial began a deep resonate chant. Slowly, the two powerful Wings enclosed the effulgent being at their center.

Periwinkle and Epiphany were relieved that they had been forgotten during the great exchange.

"I'm glad She's gone." Periwinkle whispered. "High Consul gives me the spooks."

"But don't you love the Angel Police? I wanted High Consul to let them arrest us," Epiphany teased.

"High Consul should kick them off Grace. Who needs police?"

"Have you ever read their thoughts?"

"No. What do they think?"

"They think about us."

Periwinkle and Epiphany spilled giggles, each one amping up her personal radiance, putting on quite a spectacle, aware that Aletheia was approaching. They agreed not to speak to her. As Aletheia came closer, they made a great show of not seeing her, puffing up their feathers, tossing an impenetrable ring around their intimacy.

"Don't say a word, Periwinkle," Epiphany warned.

"Guess what happened in the Cloud Canyon?" Aletheia meant to draw them out and pull them back to her.

"We're not speaking to you, Aletheia," Periwinkle couldn't resist saying *something*.

"You're not trending anymore," Epiphany added with a sorry little shrug.

"The two of you are just jealous of me because—"

An embarrassed Aletheia paused, momentarily perplexed. Inside that pause there was just enough time for a certain marble, a cleary of some renown, to finish its journey. It had been traveling ever since it was knocked out of the monkey's perfect mind by Sister Subordinary. At last it found its perfect target.

"Ouch!" Aletheia put her hand to her forehead. She spotted the marble rolling away and bent to pick it up.

"I'm waiting," teased Epiphany. "Why are we jealous?"

"You're jealous because I have a *destiny*," Aletheia shot back, wondering where in the seven worlds that notion came from as she tucked the offending marble into a pouch at her waist.

"Destiny!" Periwinkle was immediately stung with jealousy. Near tears, the amethyst angel called out to the departing Aletheia, "Destiny? When did you get a destiny?"

Epiphany, determined to pull Periwinkle back into her circle of influence, brimmed with lucent insistence. "Let her go. Just wait and see. If she breaks one rule too many, the hierarchy will take away her wings. She's not as smart as she thinks. Let's get back to the Knest."

So the threesome parted ways. Aletheia lifted herself up with rapid wing strokes as her littermates tucked themselves into the kaleidoscopic Knest.

At High Consul's station the hum from Asheilstarte reached a high pitch. The Wings opened and stretched from horizon to horizon.

"Ah, bright Wings," High Consul addressed her flanking guardians, "so it is Aletheia, after all. Eve has revealed herself unwittingly. We have traced her transmigrating soul, time and time again. Her pattern holds. She is always drawn back to Earth. Her destiny."

"Brave soul," Wing I praised.

"Mother of beginnings," Wing II proclaimed.

"And now, O valiant wings, Lucifer has shown himself again."

"Do you think he's ready for the transformation?" the right Wing inquired.

"Ready for the transformation," the left refrained.

"As ready as ever. Imagine all that power harnessed to a higher purpose," Asheilstarte intoned. "Two more players and the cast is complete. Another chance to reset the dance."

"Chance dance," the Wings echoed.

"The great Wheels spiral down the halls of time and changes," High Consul declaimed. "Between times they rest in the everlast."

"Everything changes," affirmed Wing I.

"Nothing is lost," averred Wing II.

Asheilstarte stoked her great wings and the Trinity ascended into the deep purple midnight.

# Cloud Canyon

Back When the Ship First Appeared like a featherless silver wing slicing across the star-speckled dark, the three angelettes had been caught off guard. Cruising and arguing their way back to the Knest on Grace after their unlicensed appearance on Earth, Aletheia was flying lead point in a spiraling triangle with Periwinkle and Epiphany at her flanks.

Without warning the ship had swooped down, wedging itself between Aletheia and her wing siblings. Then with decidedly aggressive maneuvers, the silver wing herded the emerald angel off course.

Testing herself against the speed of the machine, Aletheia had accelerated to her personal max velocity. In a twinkling, her Knest mates and the silver airboat that chased her were mere shimmers trailing in the stardust. That was the reported whoosh-and-poof explanation offered up by Aletheia's jewel-toned cohorts when questioned by the Mediatrix on Grace—an accurate report as far as it went.

Flashing her emerald greens and self-possession, Aletheia had seen no reason to confess to High Consul that she had purposefully ditched her wing siblings. Her only regret was that she had also lost the curious ship that had initiated what she imagined to be an intriguing game of air tag.

"Game on," the intrepid angel had called out to the unknown flyer, before she engined her wings.

"Catch me if you can," she teased and sped off trailing a splashy froth of luminescence; she imagined the silver wing surfing the towering waves of light she left in her wake.

When she finally braked and made a showy but graceful turn-around, the ship had been nowhere in sight. Either her pursuer couldn't keep up, or she wasn't of sufficient interest.

Disappointed by the lackluster chase and unable to shake off the sense of being tagged by a mystery, the emerald angel had circled back. Concealing herself in a cloud, she watched the ship touch down on a floating island in the valley of clouds. The figure that disembarked headed for a makeshift campsite. She was studying him with keen interest and considering how best to approach the rocket man, when the Wing Sergeants had rudely relocated her back to Grace.

That would not happen again.

296

Heart spinning like a prayer wheel, this time Aletheia left Grace and the Knest far behind in the existential been-there-done-that. The self-emancipated angel soared in successive widening parabolas, alert to nascent chances, gliding towards some tantalizing indefinite, the marble of enlightenment tucked in a downy pocket at her hip.

The freedom was electrifying.

Aletheia set her intentions and headed for the floating island where she'd last seen the intriguing figure emerge from his ship. The volatile notion of a destiny ran every which way in her quicksilver mind. Calculating the critical difference between a destination and a destiny proved a misery. So she simply shrugged off all doubt and made her move.

"Easy does it," she coached herself and rolled into the Cloud Canyon.

Convinced that she was the agent of her own becoming, she never guessed that ancient algorithms outside her angel arithmetic were already in play. She didn't know that yesterday's glimpse of the rocket man was swinging like a wrecking ball in her wayward angel heart.

Coming into view below her was the campsite: a flimsy lean-to skinned with foil sheets, some vintage electronic devices she recognized from holographic files in an anthropology class back in the Knest—historic bobbles, outlier curiosities.

There was no trace of the rocket man himself. Unobserved, Aletheia slipped down to the surface and began to prowl among his artifacts. She liked shiny things and was presently drawn to a galvanized metallic chest with leather straps and enchanting diamond rivets. There was no lock on the hasp, she noted with a smile.

As her various mythic threads untangled and reshaped beneath the radar of her awareness, Pandora was only the faintest whisper in her ear:

*Open the box.*

Happily unaware of inconvenient subtext, she lifted the lid. Soon she was sorting through a collection of curios—tools and artifacts from other worlds, she supposed. The emerald angel had just selected an intriguing gizmo—an electronic wrist cuff—for further inspection when she felt his presence. Then she heard his voice.

"Hello, there."

"You startled me," she accused the voice. Then she put the shiny object back in the chest, closed the lid, spun around, and gave the owner of the voice a disapproving look.

"No, please, don't let me interrupt," the rocket man stepped aside.

Was he mocking her? Disconcerted, the emerald angel turned back to the metallic box to give herself a moment to recover from the shock of the stranger's attractiveness. It seemed just plain rude to be that roughhewn and good-looking. She liked to think of herself as the bedazzling one, the eye-catcher. Here he was, not emitting a single photon of light, and yet he was breathtaking.

Aletheia was determined to take her breath back as soon as she could catch it. She bided her time. He could wait until she was good and ready.

With her back still turned to him, she pretended to concentrate on the multi-colored glowing disc that she lifted from the chest while she sorted her impressions of the unkempt stranger. His unfortunate outfit—the mirror opposite of her own carefully appointed ensemble—was haphazardly constructed of metals and leathers and not altogether clean or in good repair.

The young man was definitely more anthropos than angel; he had no wings and was probably dependent on his antique machine for flight. Yet clearly, he was an etheric of some sort, possibly an old soul, possibly lost. How else to explain his presence in the Cloud Canyon's cold, thin atmosphere?

"It's not every day you find an angel rummaging through your personal effects. This must be my lucky day."

Nice diction. A pleasing, deep voice. Possibly the right material for a destiny. First however, she must take charge of herself and somehow shift the balance of power. She turned and faced him.

He studied her carefully occluded gaze, "I don't know if I should trust you or arrest you," he bantered affably. "I've got a wrist cuff exactly your size."

"Just try it," she dared him. "I was already almost arrested earlier in the time belt."

"Perhaps I can come up with something more original." He leaned on the word *original*, and again a strand of her personal mythos stitched itself into the fabric of her identity.

The word *original* was knocking around in her conscience, wreaking delicate havoc, when he smiled at her. He was blessed with that rare sort of smile that seemed to say that this moment was the very best moment and seemed to insist that you agree.

It was a maddening smile because it approved of everything within its circumference equally: the angel and the island, the canyon and the clouds and the campsite. Then the smile broke into laughter at the great good luck of it all.

Irrationally pleased to be a part of his great good luck, Aletheia gave him a closer look. Now she saw something behind the laughter and the smiles. His eyes brimmed with yes, and she felt his yes down to the dance of her subatomic photinos.

It happened fast. And against her will. Aletheia fell so smack in love that she was certain the stranger had put her in a mindcast.

"By the way, that disc you're holding—it's a map," the smile spoke.

"I know that," she said witlessly. She had forgotten that she was holding anything at all.

"Can you read it?"

"Of course, I can."

"Then you must be pretty good because you're holding it upside down."

He leaned over and turned the disc around. When Aletheia glanced down, a disconcerting set of images flickered on the surface of the disc.

"Oh, I can't look at this," she handed the disc back. "To see the future is to be blinded at the gate."

"The future-reading function is not very accurate. Too many free wills involved. Would you rather see the past?"

He began to reset the disc.

"I have no past."

"According to this reading, your past timeline looks fairly epic."

"It's wrong, then. I am all present."

"It looks to me like your past is about to catch up with you. See this intersection?" He held up the disc. "Your past is crossing my present right here."

He reached for her.

Alarmed, she stepped back.

He took in her perplexed look and concluded, "You don't know anything, do you?"

"Yes, I do. I know everything." Aletheia realized it was a preposterous claim, but now she was stuck with it. She prattled on, sounding exactly like the recently born, barely-schooled angel that she was. "The Seraphim are raised to be Archangels, the Thrones rule the Archangels, the Principalities govern the Thrones. Then come the ninety Powers and above the Powers, there are the Seven Wheels," she concluded her awkward recitation.

"I'm a Wheel," he teased.

"No, you're not." Aletheia stepped out on the shaky ground of her limited knowledge, "The Wheels are—." She stopped, uncertain.

"What are they?" he pressed. "Rumors? Whispers?"

Was he taunting her? Or was he denying the existence of the Wheels altogether? She couldn't decide.

"Catechism #1: The Ontological Order of Being," she was happy to be back on book. "And I quote: *The Wheels are the original prime movers of the plenum.*" She was hiding in memorized bits, trying to get a purchase on this tricky destiny that had a mind of its own.

"The original artful dodgers," he shot back. "The runaway deities."

"You're a God-chaser," Aletheia guessed, immediately certain she was right.

"No, I'm just a guy kicking the Buddha stone, looking for a few good answers.'

"Am I your answer?"

"You tell me. Look at you. An angel! Who would have believed it? It's an astounding contradiction—Eve, the original bad girl, decked out in wings."

"Eve? That's not my name. My name is Aletheia."

"Okay, then. Aletheia. Let me assure you—Aletheia," he repeated her name, bemused if unconvinced, "I would know you by any name: Lilith, Pandora, Adamah, Lakshmi, Embla, Chang'e. Am I ringing any bells? No? Fine. All you need to understand is this—I don't intend to spend the next forever tracking you and chasing you and courting you and losing you. Consider yourself found. I'm on a mission. I want you to come with me."

He waited, then prompted her, "Say yes."

"I might say yes. I want to say yes. What mission are you on?"

"I'm going to find the Wheels."

"In a blink, we'd be enclosed by the infinity. And that map of yours? It's pathetically inadequate. No one finds the Wheels. They find you."

"I'm going to make it easy for them. Take the dare, Aletheia."

With the invitation reframed as a dare, Aletheia was hard put to refuse. On Grace she was the daring one, the one willing to leap out of bounds. This role reversal had her in a spin. Taking her miscues from the pitiable ship he arrived in, Aletheia was unprepared for this contest of wills.

Flush with designs of her own, she couldn't let herself be swept into his plans. She threw him a classic come-hither look, with no idea in the world how good she was about to get at what she used to do so well.

"Frankly, I'm disappointed. This is not the way love is supposed to be," she opened the parlay.

"It isn't? Okay, angel heart, I'm listening. How is it supposed to be?"

"I'm not absolutely certain about this, but I think we're supposed to—kiss."

She waited. He studied her.

"Close your eyes."

And there it was—the kiss. The one she was born for. The one she didn't know existed, until it struck with the force of eternal recurrence.

In an instant, what was foreign became familiar. She had expected a jolt of the exotic. Didn't happen. Instead she bent to the thrill of a cosmic intimacy. The kiss knew her. Knew her in ways she didn't know herself. How was that possible?

She had every intention of running her own destiny. Now her destiny grabbed her by the hand and was running her faster than she'd ever moved before. She needed to brake before she fell any further.

"Who are you?" She managed to stall, hoping to parse the ontology of the kiss.

"Don't tell me you don't remember."

"I don't remember."

Another kiss. A gateway kiss. This one intrepid, exploratory, full of messages and awakenings.

Roica pulled away, appraised her. He was smoothing her silky green hair away from her face, waiting for the gate to open. Then his voice grazed her forehead, "We came from a garden."

Enraptured and wary, her curiosity pulled her closer to the mystery of herself, a mystery that she had been resisting ever since she laid her angel eyes on him.

"What garden?"

"We stood on a promontory, clouds at our feet, awe-struck by a wild green world that rolled beneath us. We watched a river run to ocean-raised whitecaps splashing against a forever sky. It was an enchantment and a damnable lie. But you were lovely, dressed in light."

"I love wearing light," she teased playfully. And without aforethought, she slid blithely into his vision of the garden.

He was so open to her, so easy to enter. She couldn't stop herself. She let his mindscape enfold her. Drunk on her first sip of enchanted air, she ran through the garden. The pounding surf beat its ancient rhythm, and she became the rapture of oceans, the strength of primordial forests. Then memory shifted, and a fear grazed the back of her neck.

"Wait," she steadied herself, "Something happened to us."

He hesitated at the gate of sorrows, his voice stark; "Death happened."

"What is death?"

He moved carefully over this untested ground, concerned that a sudden crowd of memories might scare her off. He began with a story, searching her eyes for signs of flight.

"We were caught in the crossfire between a menacing angel and a jealous God—the angel went down. We watched this magnificent descending spiral of feathers and light. Then the falling angel seemed to stop midair. I swear he caught my eye just before he took his vengeance out—for whatever unfathomable reason—on us." Roica momentarily got lost in the recollection.

"What happened?"

"The angel tore away the veil that shielded us from time. The garden changed, and it was not a pretty sight. What had briefly seemed endless ended and was riddled with endings. We were robbed of immortality, or its illusion." He let that sink in. "And I failed. I failed you. I wasn't capable of—"

"—of what? Not capable of what?"

"Of loving what was brief."

"What do you mean by brief?"

"Bracketed by time—a look, a life, a falling leaf."

"You mean bracketed by death."

"Yes."

She took in a quick breath, "I do know what you mean. I visited a planet the other night, and I watched a leaf lose its little life. My wing barely brushed it, and it fell."

"There was a fall, all right. And then we were swept into an endless cycle of incarnations. A myriad of lives tumbled like a plague of fallen leaves. Death after death after death. Always one of us bereft and left behind. Sometimes eons would pass before we'd meet again. You're not easy to find. Now we've got chance at eternity, Aletheia. I found a gate. One hundred and nine ultraviolet moons point the way. I'll give them to you. My wedding gift."

"Have you got a name, God-chaser?"

"Call me Roica."

"I haven't got any moons to offer, Roica. But I have a life to offer, a destiny really." Finally, she was getting a grip on herself, taking the lead. "It would mean all the world if I had your yes. Will you come with me? On *my* mission? Will you follow me into a mystery?"

Roica gave her a rueful look. First the kiss, he was thinking, and I'm bonded to her again. Now this.

He watched her drop her diamond thoughts on the smooth surface of his mind, and he traced how the ripples moved in widening circles, enveloping his intentions. She may be an angel in this confluence of time, but she hasn't changed all that much, he noted with a shake of his head. He began to raise an inner shield.

"Roica? Am I losing you?"

"Historically speaking, following your lead has not always been in our best interest. We've been slung off course, taken countless wrong turns—all at your insistence."

"I must have done something right—back when I was dressed in light. Why else would you chase me through time after time?"

By infinitesimal increments she altered her green dress. It became wet and sheer and frothy—white-capped ocean waves rolled soft over her shoulders, splashing over her breasts, running in rivulets down her legs. Sea foam curled at her feet. Wind lashed her hair. She opened her arms.

The emerald angel was tempest and temptress all at once.

This was an aspect of Eve he knew all too well. And he was having none of it. "Okay, spit it out. What've you got? The Apple of Omniscience? The Apple of Immortality?"

"I found an orphan." Her dress calmed down.

"How did you manage that?"

"It was an accident."

"There are no accidents."

"Of course, there are. I accidentally answered a prayer for parents, and then you coincidentally came shining by in your silver ship. You got here just in the nick of time to be the cosmic hero, the one who adopts Conrad with me," the angel rushed on. "He's an enchanted boy who lives on a spectacular blue planet in the material world. It calls itself Earth."

"Earth. I've heard of it. Clue in, Aletheia, that's where we lost paradise. Earth is the dream crusher."

"Take the dare. Tomorrow night, Roica. Planet Earth."

"I won't be there."

"Oh? Does that mean I'm obliged to give up all those ultraviolet moons? How many were there? A hundred and nine? Maybe I'll keep just one, for a souvenir. See you next lifetime, Starfriend."

With accelerating decisiveness, she mounted the air. A contrail of shimmering green particles—water turned to ice—laced the sky, now empty of angel.

The hot ice pelted his campsite. He stood confounded and aggrieved by the beauty of her weather. Then he gave the metallic chest a solid kick. It answered with a few pathetic bleeps.

# EARTH MATTERS

ON EARTH THE ILLUSION of one-way time, clocking the short lives of its sentient beings, inhibits the conception and stalls the launch of farsighted visionary projects. Why bother beginning when there is always the possibility of clocking out before completion? No problem for the enterprising deity who can see forever; however, when that same off-world Supernal takes on an incarnation, time is scaled down to the circumference of a human life even though the visionary project remains scaled to eternity.

The crunch is often painful for both the vision and the visionary. Infused with mytho-poetic enthusiasms and an ambitious garden renovation project to boot—as was the case with Mary Extraordinary—Earth culture came as a shock to the well-intentioned deliverer.

The various indigenous societies have always been considerably more resistant to deliverance than eager Avatars anticipate. The visiting adepts who attempt rescue missions time and again underestimate the challenges of material existence and habitually overestimate the reach of their own omniscience. The mission always looks deceptively easy from afar, but invariably materiality takes its toll. Beset by serial rude awakenings, even the most spiritually fit ultimately wear thin.

Earth is tough, coming and going. And Mother Mary Extraordinary was going.

Her Earth incarnation was as close to failure as the Wheels could allow. It was time to take her out. Mission unaccomplished.

Her journey had begun with such high hopes and high purpose. But gravity and the enemies of innovation had given that high, hopeful purpose an existential thrashing. She was a wreck, almost an embarrassment. Fortunately, no reputations were at stake; her incarnation was unheralded and her origins unknown.

Much had been expected of Mary Extraordinary's descent into the material world. Dangerously close to expunging the very lovely postmodern beings that were evolving in so many promising ways, the planet needed someone to press its refresh button, to lean on that button, someone to fire up an ontological orgy of innovation, someone to inspire the homegrown heroes, someone to cultivate a new generation of gardeners along with the organic tomatoes. A great galvanizing soul might rejuvenate the host of Renaissance workers—the visionary vanguard who keep the wayward planet hospitable, hanging out welcome signs and practicing the wide embrace.

The Joyous Mystery Sisters, under the guidance of a young Mary Extraordinary, at first astounded the Supernal watchers. A collective of different dreamers who marched to dream beats of their own invention, The Convent of Immaculate Conceptions seemed a perfect place to launch a new love story—a bright green story.

Abiding in a cloistered world of their own making, over the years the Sisters had filtered out the roar of information—most of it dire—from the news industry. One journal after the next, Sister Mary Rose canceled their subscriptions. Reading about the monoliths that sucked oil out of the Earth and spit out legions of automobiles or keeping tabs on the great round up and rodeo of industrial farming was too dispiriting.

It didn't serve to muddy the mind. Muddy the boots instead. Hand on the plow.

"Love what touches you," the young Mary Extraordinary bid her consoeurs, "the Earth underfoot, the infant in arms, the Sister who kneels beside you."

The matter of making Earth matter became their guiding mantra. Their reconfiguration of the fall as a fall into a mystery was the sacred heart of the Joyous Sisters' trailblazing psalm—the fall into being, the falling in love with being, the song of material being—The Magnificat of the Miracle Mudball. A magnificat that gloried the Earth—the greatest love story ever untold.

The celestials who monitored the declining trajectory of Extraordinary's incarnation were at a critical juncture. They did not like to abandon Earth to its own devices, much less abandon the material world to the oligarchs who sucked out the Earth's marrow and priestly cargo cultists who aimed to move believers up the celestial stairway to some bright future in a heavenly elsewhere, as if there were a cupboard of goodies in the sky just waiting for the lucky few who traded on the future by behaving themselves in the now—paying duty to the oligarchs and tithing to The Great Church.

Mother Mary Extraordinary had once been an ardent believer in the greatest love story untold, in its second becoming, in its nascent poetry, in its daily practice, in the practical magic that makes something tangible out of the notional. Not merely a believer, she herself was a Renaissance worker. Mary Extraordinary was not one of those etherics who visit Earth on a tourist pass. The risks are minimal for those spiritual Earth divers, bouncing about on their astral bungee cords, offering preachments, prayer cloths, mantras, mental cleansings, and the like.

Nothing ventured, nothing lost.

Extraordinary had ventured much and lost nearly all. Her soul was badly scuffed, worn down at the heels like an old shoe. Aware that she'd been hobbled, that she might not even have the wherewithal to cross the bridge to the other side, she narrowed her sights.

One last obligation—Conrad Eppler.

Then let them toss out the old shoe. See if she cared.

However, now that her connectivity to higher echelons blinked off and on erratically, there was an unmistakable disconnect in even her best-intentioned endeavors.

Her knock at Conrad's bedroom door was tentative. It had taken considerable effort to arrive at his door, so even though she couldn't remember her purpose she was reluctant to turn around. There was something important she meant to tell him or give him. Half-formed thoughts dropped into a sea of oblivion—plink, plunk, plop. Momentarily enchanted by the music of loss, she drifted into Conrad's room and gave the sleeping boy a shake.

Conrad had tumbled into bed in the wee hours. He had spent a succession of lonely nights searching the sky for three bright stars that never reappeared. Earth evenings empty of angels were becoming unbearable eternities. Last night, he'd stayed up practically until dawn.

Mother Mary Extraordinary gave Conrad another shake.

"Good morning, Conrad. I missed you at morning prayers. I've missed our nighttime swims. Wake-up, you little Holy Ghost. You mustn't miss breakfast. Sister Subordinary set aside a nice big bowl of curds and whey."

"Curds and whey?" Conrad sat up rubbing his eyes.

Mother Mary Extraordinary was a jittery presence, as if she no longer had the energy to maintain solid outlines, much less produce the reliable set of gestures that make a person recognizable to their friends. The personal was being deleted from her personality.

She was breaking up.

"Do you know what Miss Muffet said to that nasty old spider?" she queried the groggy boy.

"No, not really." A puzzled Conrad noted that this Mother Mary was oddly chipper, silly even. Conrad was to learn that there was no way to anticipate what version of Mother would show up on any given day. Just now he watched her lose her way and prompted her, "What did Miss Muffet say?"

"It is mildly absurd when you fall into the curd, but it is rude to get in the whey." Mother Mary's chuckle quickly turned into a cough, "I'm sorry I got in the way." She suddenly looked impossibly sad but somehow solid once again.

"Mother Mary Extraordinary, are you okay?"

"Oh, bright new day, the Lord hath made, let us be glad and," she trailed off searching for a conclusion she couldn't find. Reaching into the deep folds of her voluminous habit she pulled out two packages, sloppily tied with kite string and immediately looked alarmed, "What are these?"

"They look like presents," Conrad offered helpfully, worried that at any moment she might topple over.

"My thoughts exactly. Let's see. Yes, it's coming back to me. These are for you and the monkey."

Conrad was wary, but raised a flag of false cheer, "O boy, Skip, I wonder what we got?"

Conrad tackled the smaller package first. The string was a knotty tangle, tightly wound around the brown paper. Mother Mary was growing impatient. Her black gown seemed to be growing in volume along with her irritability.

"What is it? What did you get?"

"Are these from you?" Conrad asked as he pulled out a pin cushion and a measuring tape from the package.

"Of course, they're from me. They're supposed to remind me of something. And they do! I wanted to make an adoption suit for Skipper to match the one I made for you, but I didn't have the monkey's measurements. Open the other one up. There it is—your adoption suit. One must make an effort to look appealing to the prospective parents. Go ahead. Try it on."

Mother Mary Extraordinary's attempt at tailoring was not half bad. Conrad held up a white seersucker sports coat, then fished out a pair of matching Bermuda shorts. It was a sort of tropical variation on the traditional First-Communion suit.

Mother was proud of her workmanship and taken aback when Conrad firmly vetoed the odd-looking getup. He didn't care much about style. It was the mention of adoption that decided the boy against the suit. He had no intention of being adopted by strangers, much less dressing up for the occasion.

"These clothes are really nice, but they're not my size," Conrad smiled, trying not to be unkind.

"No matter. We can let the suit out. We can take the suit in. Unfortunately, there is time for alterations. There's been a delay. It worries me. Give them too much time and your adoptive parents might do something rash."

"Like what?"

"Like make a baby of their own. God forbid."

"They can do that?"

"Yes. It has something to do with a kiss. Don't ask. In any case, there have been setbacks in the adoption process."

The promise of a reprieve made Conrad sit up taller.

"Setbacks? Like what?"

"There are legalities involved. The state wants proof. I spoke with a certain Ms. Margaret Demeanor. She needs proof that you belong to us before you can be legally adopted by my great Goddaughter. Or anyone else, for that matter."

"Can you prove it—that I belong to you?

"I might as well try to prove that angels can dance on the head of a pin. They can, you know. But proof? The proof is in the pudding. Or is it in the curds and whey?" Extraordinary's eyes narrowed. "Ms. Demeanor will rue the day she crossed me. I'll gladly give that woman a piece of my cane."

"What does that mean?" Conrad was genuinely puzzled.

Extraordinary demonstrated by lifting her cane and shaking it at Conrad in a manner that tried to be threatening but only managed to give Extraordinary a dangerous wobble.

"Ms. Demeanor said there is going to be an investigation to determine if I am fit to be an interim foster mother. The impertinent twit. What's that tapping at your window?"

An elated Conrad ran to one of the glass doors that opened onto the terrace.

"What is it? Is someone out there?" Mother Mary squinted at the window, looking straight through the emerald angel.

"Just a little fresh air," Conrad quickly improvised, "I think I'll let it in."

For the briefest interval, Aletheia was taken aback at the sight of the old nun in black.

"High Consul? Is that you?" The startled young celestial thought if you added Wing Sergeants and subtracted the volumes of black and placed a diamond-studded monocle over one eye, it very well could be the Mediatrix of Grace.

The monkey's tail twitched.

"No," Conrad corrected his personal angel in an urgent whisper, "*that's* Mother Mary Extraordinary."

"Extraordinary, indeed. When I catch myself in a mirror these days, I can't tell who is looking back at me. My faith, Conrad. I don't remember losing it. It seems rather that it left me. What a nuisance. It's like a missing sock, the one in the drawer always reminding you that there used to be a pair. The faded pages of a book, reminding you there used to be a prayer. But you have enough faith for both of us, don't you, Conrad?"

"Yes. Yes, I do and if you could just believe there was an angel in this room standing right next to you, you could see her too."

Mother Mary remembered how Conrad loved the story of Peter Pan. In fact, they both loved that story once upon a time. Clap if you believe in fairies.

"Shall I clap, Conrad? Is Tinker Bell in the room?" Mother Mary's frown began to pull at the ends of her mouth and she turned on him with unaccustomed rancor.

"Conrad! You must *stop* this. There is a difference between faith and fantasy."

Then she turned on herself, "And what about you, Mary Extraordinary? What makes you think you're the queen of heaven? Carrying on like some big wheel. You are nothing but the oldest tree in the forest. Prepare to fall!"

With a startlingly loud clatter her cane hit the ground and she began to gasp for breath.

"My heart. Tight as a fist," she rasped, tilting wildly.

Aletheia rushed to the crumbling nun and in an instant propped Mother Mary Extraordinary back up.

Conrad slipped his small hand into Mother Mary's old one, "Please, don't die."

"Just a dizzy spell. It's that damn draft. What is this?" She picked up the adoption suit where Conrad had dropped it on the bed. "Where did you get this suit?"

Before Conrad could answer, Merry Berry careened through the doorway with two vintage bottles of wine, both uncorked.

"Sister Merry Berry," Mother Mary reproved. "Have you lost all sense of decorum?"

"Mother Mary Extraordinary, cheers to you," Merry Berry took a swig from one of the bottles. "I have such good news. The red devil is a fake. There's been a terrible theological mistake. The all new Angel of Light is a nonesuch, a nonpareil, a paragon, a luminary, a liberation for libation. You should make a visit. He's quite amenable to sharing a tipple," Merry Berry slurred and sat on the floor.

"Sister Merry Berry, please deport yourself immediately," Extraordinary ordered.

Undismayed by the reprimand, Merry Berry beamed, "I think I shall deport myself. Or rather, it is the devil that has been deported, or as it were, debunked. And I have been exported by virtue of this divine Pouilly-Fuisse which has been imported to export me into the next ecstasy. Would you care for a drop?"

"I would not." Mother Mary sat on Conrad's bed utterly perplexed, as was Conrad. The world was being tossed on a carnival tilt-a-whirl.

"Ah me, I see," Sister Merry Berry squinted at Aletheia from her spot on the floor, then unsteadily pulled herself up.

Somehow the besotted nun managed a tipsy little curtsy.

"How do you do, Miss? You must be the social worker. We were exporting you at noon—I mean expecting you so soon. Oh, do let's be social and work on this divine Pouilly-Fuisse! Or would you prefer the Beaujolais?"

"The Beaujolais, I think. Thank you very much." Aletheia accepted the bottle and took a tentative swig.

"O. My. Godma," Mother Mary expostulated and grabbed Conrad's hand. "The bottle. Look! It's floating in the air, turning itself upside down."

"Aletheia, stop! Put the bottle away. Here. Give it to me."

With bottle in hand, Conrad assured his old friend. "See. Everything is okay."

That was exactly the moment irascible fate chose to have Sister Subordinary enter Conrad's room with the actual social worker, Ms. Margaret Demeanor, trailing close behind.

"There you are, Mother Mary. We've been waiting for you in the library," Subordinary coached.

Ms. Demeanor immediately locked eyes on the uncorkcd bottle of wine that Conrad held in his hands. The boy managed a blurry smile.

Everything and everyone seemed blurry in the presence of Margaret Demeanor. In stark contrast, she was focused and in focus.

A sharp looking young woman, her hair was wound into a smart knot, pinned at the nape of her neck. Everything about her seemed pressed and pointed—a pointed nose holding up a pair of pointed glasses, pointed nails tapping pointedly against her sleek gray skirt, a tight-waisted suit with a pointed collar, and a pair of red, high-heeled, pointy-toed patent leather shoes set in ballet position number two. And her lips, painted glossy red, presently hosted a pointed little smile.

Extraordinary immediately counted up the points and sneered, "It's that interfering twit."

"The feeling is mutual," pursed the glossy lips.

"I suppose you have a pointy little pencil in your purse and another form for us to fill in," Extraordinary glared at Ms. Demeanor.

"Please, excuse Mother Mary. She is not altogether herself these days," Subordinary mediated.

"Then who, pray tell, am I?" the prioress questioned. "Speak up. Don't keep me in suspense. It's disconcerting—the way my identity slips off these days. Any help securing it would be most welcome. Well, Subordinary? Who am I?"

Margaret Demeanor was taking notes, her pencil skritch-scratching across her writing pad.

Mary Subordinary, desperate to deflect attention from Extraordinary's strange volatility, made the mistake of introducing Sister Merry Berry, who immediately lifted her bottle of Pouilly-Fuisse.

"Cheers, Ms. Demeanor. Why, I seem to be seeing you in doubles."

"No doubt," came the curt reply.

Conrad noticed the curious fact that Ms. Demeanor was capable of speech without moving her lips.

"How jolly of you to have arrived twice," Merry Berry beamed at the social worker.

Realizing something was not quite right, Sister Merry Berry pointed to Aletheia, "What are you—?" Then abruptly, she swung about and pointed the rest of her question at Ms. Demeanor, "—doing over there?"

Aletheia immediately repositioned herself closer to Ms. Demeanor.

Merry Berry relaxed, "Well done! It is ever so much easier to look at you now that you are beside yourself."

"Beside myself? I am that and more," Ms. Demeanor straightened, and the room straightened with her. "I am appalled. This place—it is not remotely suitable for a child. I will not wait upon the adoption. I will speak to my superiors immediately and make arrangements to remove the boy."

Just then the cassowary, who'd been watching from the terrace, poked his crested head in at the open door and blinked his orange eyes. Ms. Demeanor's red pumps suggested certain plump ripe fruits of a superior organic brand, polished to a startling perfection. He could not know that he had fallen for a pair of Manolo Blahniks.

Margaret Demeanor glanced at the large bird who was stretching his long neck towards her shoes, and pronounced with a chilling finality, "Pack up the boy's clothes. I will be back."

"Is there no mercy?" Mary Extraordinary cried out.

"Ms. Demeanor, can't you see? You're upsetting Mother Mary." Conrad appealed to a better nature that was nowhere in evidence.

"Classic case of child abuse," the social worker announced, then diagnosed, "Stockholm Syndrome. The boy has identified with his tormentors."

The red lips twitched.

Aletheia stepped behind Ms. Demeanor and lifted her gorgeous green wings, fanning the air. It was her way of cooling down Ms. Demeanor's rising ire.

"Merged at last," Merry Berry sighed, reassessing this new version of Ms. Demeanor. "Has anyone ever told you that you have the most exquisite pair of wings?"

"This is a madhouse," Margaret Demeanor snapped and turned on her pointed heel.

"Ms. Demeanor," Merry Berry called after her, "come back! You seem to be leaving yourself behind. Wait up, dear. I'll show you the gate."

"I can find my own way out," Demeanor tossed back over her shoulder, striding away from the interview with brisk determination.

In a blink, the cassowary took off after the disappearing Blahniks. The click of Ms. Demeanor's heels on the marble floor quickened. Squeals echoed down the hall. A door slammed.

"This is going well," a flat-voiced Subordinary addressed the ceiling. "I have no doubt she will return with papers and take Conrad from us."

"Papers," spat Extraordinary.

"Don't worry, Mother Mary Extraordinary," Conrad soothed, "I'm not going no place with her. No way." He rested a hand on Skipper's paws, securely velcroed at his neck, and felt reassured.

Sister Subordinary noted the deterioration in Conrad's syntax. Then she reached out to Mother Mary, "Come, let me take you back to bed."

"There are bugs in that bed," Mother Mary confided.

"We'll clean them out," Subordinary assured in an even tone that belied her many worries.

"Don't you just hate it when the spider sits down beside her and frightens Miss Muffet away?" Mother Mary Extraordinary grinned, lifting her white brow as if she knew exactly what her nonsense implied.

In the morning, Merry Berry would find a pair of red high-heels in the hallway, just outside her bedroom. Ms. Demeanor had kicked them off in her frantic sprint to escape the cassowary. After the bird had determined that the Blahniks were inedible, he left them at the door of his friend.

## Hello Again

CONRAD WAS NOT CONCERNED with Ms. Demeanor or her pointed threats. His answering angel had returned. Now that the two of them were left alone, Conrad could finally speak his heart.

"I watched for you every single night. I knew you would come shining through. What happens next? Is there a plan? Are you going to be my mom?"

"Don't you think I'm a little young to be your mom?"

"How old are you?"

"In Earth years? I'm not sure. Ten thousand and twenty-one. Maybe a good deal older. There are some things I don't remember. But I met someone who does remember. Or at least, he says he does. At first, I was convinced he was my destiny. Now, I'm not so sure. Maybe I fell in love with the wrong one."

A breeze ruffled her feathers, and Aletheia turned towards the glass door and closed it.

"You fell in love?" Conrad wasn't sure if this development was a positive or a negative.

"Yes," the angel spun around, and her glimmering green gown swished with frothy ocean waves, mirroring her emotions. "I fell in love." Silently she settled her heart with a promise that she would reverse the fall, and her green oceanic dress settled as well.

Conrad was just about to declare *his* love, when out of the corner of his eye, he caught a series of movements on the terrace. It looked like an invisible paint brush was rapidly filling in the colors on a comic-book page.

The impossible was happening. And accelerating.

The two-paneled drawing of Conrad's wished-for hero had become a three-dimensional reality. There he stood, outside the closed door, one hand pressed against the glass, as if he'd stepped right off the page of the very comic book that Conrad had once tried to give Aletheia.

"It's Epic," Conrad whispered, his heart beating double-time.

Unaware of the drama taking place behind her back, the emerald angel heartily agreed with what she took to be

Conrad's insight into her dilemma. Her personal crosscurrents were exactly that—epic.

"Unbelievable," the boy marveled.

"It's more than unbelievable," Aletheia huffed, "It's irritating. Love—who needs it? It's like losing a part of yourself. Now, I want that part of me back again. But I can't have it because he's got it."

Conrad had no idea what she meant, but there was no time to read the shifting tides on her oceanic gown.

"Look. Behind you," he prompted. "It's the super hero."

Aletheia turned to look, then immediately turned back to Conrad. He watched a tsunami wave coruscate down her dress and splash on the floor. The boy jumped back to avoid getting soaked.

"Omygosh. That's him." Aletheia recomposed her weather. Slow rollers, evenly spaced, splashed down and bubbled at her feet. Sunshine sparkled on her bare shoulders. "Get ready, Conrad."

That Roica showed at all, when he said he wouldn't, was gratifying evidence that she had more power over him than she thought. She was glad that she'd dressed in ocean. It really was her best look.

Still, she warned Conrad, "He is not much of a hero, really. He's more like—oh, I don't know—a broody poet."

"I like poetry," the boy let her know, as he opened the glass door.

Roica stepped in. Conrad stepped back. Immediately the room seemed smaller.

"So, this is your Earth boy?" His tone was casual, mildly dismissive.

"My name is Conrad. Conrad Eppler."

Had ever such a young boy held so much personal dignity in the face of such an extraordinary event? There was his galactic cowboy, standing right before his startled eyes, a living breathing wish-come-true. Conrad Eppler seized the moment, side-stepped Epic's skepticism, and laid his claim.

"And this is Skipper," Conrad continued his introduction. "I know you thought there was just going to be one of us. But there's not. There's two. Me and Skip. We're a team. You can't break us up." Conrad took a breath. "I can't believe it's you."

"Sweet stars above me. How do you know me?" Roica was ever alert to karmic traps.

The boy disappeared under his bed and missed the looks that flashed between Roica and the angel. Conrad emerged with the comic book, flipped to the page that held his favorite drawing, the one that took up two vertical panels.

"Got it right here. Look. The evidence. You're Epic, the galactic cowboy and time traveler. That's you—Dad."

"Whoa. I'm not Epic." Roica was quick to assert, although he could not deny that he and the drawing bore a striking resemblance. "And I'm not your dad."

"I know that. But you're going to be," Conrad insisted with ingenuous confidence.

Roica looked up at the green angel, his eyes sending messages to Aletheia that Conrad could not read, except for the obvious. She was the one that Epic sought out. Not him.

"Aletheia promised you to me," Conrad declared, putting himself in the middle of the silent tug-a-war that was taking place between the angel and the time traveler.

"She did, did she?" Roica experienced a gravitational pull generated, he supposed, by the charismatic boy. It felt just like Earth karma—sticky. And the galactic cowboy didn't like it. Too many times, he'd been caught in the broken world, stumbled through its ruined cities and despoiled continents. Why on Earth would anyone choose Earth?

"I'll tell you what, Conrad. If you'll agree to come away with us—with Aletheia and me—I'll give this family thing a try."

"Count me in," Conrad beamed. "Where are we going?" He was a boy always keen on adventure.

"We're going to find the Wheels that turn the universe."

"Don't scare him," Aletheia cautioned.

"I'm not scared," Conrad scoffed. "I want to see the universe and search for the Wheels—but Earth is my home planet."

"Earth isn't my home," Roica stared the boy down.

"Yes, it is too," Conrad insisted. "There's an abandoned garden here that needs tending."

"Damn."

Aletheia frowned at the rocket man and turned to Conrad, "Tell me about the abandoned garden."

"Earth is the abandoned garden. Earth is an orphan just like me, and my planet needs parents just like I do. And I know you are the ones."

"What if he's right, Roica? What if we are the ones? What if we are two gemstones falling into our perfect setting?"

"Falling into a perfect trap is more like it." He saw that he'd offended her, but he plunged on. "At first, I thought your memory loss was an advantage, but now I see we'd be better off if you remembered just how devastating it is when we are stuck on Earth, ravaged by time, robbed of hope with no means of lifting ourselves out of the mire. Now we have the advantage of flight, the freedom to move between realms."

Conrad was all but forgotten as the two primal forces clashed.

"One lifetime," Aletheia persisted. "What is one lifetime measured against the immensities?"

"Once you are Earthed, you are caught in the cycle of birth and death. Then what? If we say yes to one incarnation, we don't know how many lifetimes we're buying into. Or if we'll be separated. Or when. Or how. Or why. Or for how long. I want answers, Aletheia."

"Oh, right, the God-chaser. The unknown belongs to the Gods."

"Don't mock me. I'll have my answers if I have to shake down the vaults of heaven."

"What a strange sort of love this is," the angel frowned.

"Believe me, Aletheia, nothing has ever or ever will diminish my love for you. It drives me from star to star."

"I don't want star to star. I want one happily-ever-after on Earth."

"There's no such thing."

"But Conrad's vision—"

"It's illusion."

"No, it's not," a small voice entered the fray.

"I know the planet's in trouble. Big trouble. But we can't just leave it. I know there's other galaxies and solar systems.

I've seen them. But it's cold out in space. And there's no place out there that's as good as this place. We're in the Goldilocks zone."

"The what?" Roica studied the boy, his poise, his gravity, his bright tinker-toy enthusiasms.

"The Goldilocks zone. Where everything is just right. Not too hot. Not too cold."

The keen edge of Conrad's green hope laid open an old wound. A boy's hope is a dangerous thing. Roica cut the conversation short. "Conrad, I've made you my best offer."

"This is a great planet. The sun's always on time," Conrad was scrambling for enticements. "We've got monkeys. And the best forests. And a disappearing moon."

"Roica, please," Aletheia's eyes went soft with sorrow. "Don't make me choose between you and Conrad. I've made *promises*."

Conrad charged back into the argument. "Earth is the best place for love. It's the best place to grow the dream garden."

"Got that much right, kid. It's a dream."

"Love can make it real," Conrad shot back.

"Ahhhh," a little piece of Aletheia's heart escaped her. Enchanted by Conrad's loyalty to his tiny planet, she let his enthusiasms fill her and spill over. Her dress became a storm-wracked sea crashing against the stony cliffs of Roica's refusals.

"Don't forget the oceans," Aletheia surged, infusing Conrad's plea for his world with her own ungoverned passions. "I love the oceans here," she let the rising tsunami gather to a greatness at her back. The wave hovered but did not break.

"Be calm, my seas," she softened and breathless, her arms dripping watery stars, she reached for Roica.

Stirred by the beauty of her volatile changes, Roica knew he had to get away before the angel and the boy could bind him to a destiny he was dead set against. "Make up your mind, Aletheia. Bring the boy along or say your goodbyes to him. I'll wait outside."

Too late, he regretted how his harsh words sounded in the ensuing silence. He had managed to break free, but at what price? It was a dejected Roica that walked out the door, certain that he'd lost her to the boy.

He was wrong.

Conrad watched a fat droplet of a tear get ready to spill down Aletheia's cheek. At all costs, he had to stop that tear from falling.

"Go with him!" Conrad blurted, and the startled tear dissolved. "I know about broken dreams. My great friend, Mother Mary Extraordinary, lost her faith. Maybe it's like a tag team, because now I have the faith. This is my planet. It needs me. I can't leave."

"There must be something we can do. Look at him standing out there, like a fallen wish-upon-a-star. He loves me. He came this far."

"Too bad the old garden went to seed. If only the garden was more like the one in my dreams, then I bet he'd want to stay." Conrad picked up Skipper and hugged him close.

"Describe it to me," she encouraged Conrad. "Tell me how the garden grows in your dream."

Conrad went quiet, so very still and so very unsure. How could he possibly describe the electrifying moving pictures that made up his wild and ever-changing dream garden?

The monkey's tail switched back and forth.

Instinctively, Aletheia reached into the rolling surf on her dress and retrieved a certain destiny marble. She folded the mysterious cleary into Conrad's small hand.

"Find the words, Conrad."

The first word that flew from Conrad's mouth and out the open door was—*yes!* Then fonts erupted like fountains, and the fraught air that surrounded a startled Roica was littered with sprays of little black letters. Words swarmed, and the shape of the land shifted. Tree by tree, bloom by bloom, a boy's version of a primal garden broke through the membrane that separates the imaginary from the sensible world.

Conrad's garden teemed with life and danced with angel trees. One by one, the trees sprouted swaths of diaphanous leaves and clusters of luminescent fruits. A white monkey ran through the garden, jumped on Roica's back, then scampered off. For fun, Conrad added a family of foxes. Roica watched the baby foxes trot after the mother, a row of red plumed tails held high in the long grass. Roica turned to the sound of crashing surf and the cries of gulls. He stood amazed, looking over the very promontory where, once upon a memory, he and Eve spellbound watched the rebel angel battle the Demiurge.

"Look," Aletheia turned Conrad around. "See what you've created."

"Wow! I did that? It looks like a garden in a story book."

"What story are you thinking about?"

"I'm thinking about a story with a poisoned apple." Conrad wanted to impress Aletheia, so he improved on the Biblical tale. "There's a snake crawling through the garden like a red fuse. It's a rigged garden, all set to explode," Conrad enthused, getting carried away with dramatics. "Then a fiery angel appears in a flash of lightning."

Before Aletheia could interrupt Conrad's inventions, the word *lightning* flew out the door. The sky darkened, and a lightning bolt struck the ground.

Conrad ran out onto the terrace and was stunned when the Angel of Light appeared. He saw the words—*red fuse*—stretch out and snake through the forest. And as if he were watching the scene through a zoom lens, Conrad followed Lucifer who followed the red fuse all the way to the edge of the woods. Then the trap door to the underground tunnel flew open, and Kilowatt emerged, hauling an old-fashioned plunge detonator.

Conrad laughed, delighted with his inventions.

"It's all rigged to blow, Boss," the words were set in a comic book bubble. When Kilo looked up and spotted the comic bubble above his head, he grinned in appreciation of Conrad's visionary mash-up. Then a co-operative Kilo connected the plunger to the fuse.

Lucifer studied Roica, who stood at a distance, alone on the promontory.

"No!" Aletheia cried out, watching Conrad's vision veer dangerously off course.

"I know those two guys. They're good guys."

The green angel put her hand under Conrad's chin and held his gaze, "Don't think about the snake or the story, Conrad. Think about the sun."

As quickly as Conrad changed thoughts, the sun broke through the clouds. But Lucifer and Kilowatt were still in the garden.

"Please Conrad, take out Luce and Kilowatt."

"Don't worry," Conrad grinned, "I can fix it."

Conrad dropped a Tyrannosaurus Rex into the scene. As soon as Lucifer spotted the predator, he vanished in flash of self-generated fireworks.

Kilowatt watched the slick pyrotechnics of his boss, nodded in admiration, and then high-tailed it to the trap door, making a more quotidian exit down through the underground tunnel. The T-Rex sniffed the air and roared its displeasure.

"Get rid of that monster," Aletheia cried.

Perplexed that his solution did not please Aletheia, Conrad took out the T-Rex. The pastoral scene was restored, a perfect peaceable garden.

"Conrad, listen. You must be careful with your thoughts and your words. This is going to be dangerous for me," the emerald angel was at a loss.

She had not anticipated the sprawl of the boy's imagination. Incompatible realities merged in swift incomprehensible succession. The boy was a mix-master. If it had a text, he could picture it. If it had an image, he could text it.

The marble was clearly a powerful catalyst, but the boy needed tempering.

"Conrad, I am going to cross over into the vision that you created. I am going to try to capture Roica's heart for the Earth."

"You can do that?"

"It depends on you. You mustn't put any monsters in the garden. And don't let in Lucifer or Kilowatt. Make an enchanted garden, Conrad. Flora, fauna, light and oceans—all in perfect harmony. Can you do that?"

"Yes."

Just one more kiss and Aletheia believed she could bind Roica to her destiny. She took Conrad back inside and had him sit cross-legged on his bed.

"Now close your Earth eyes and hold the vision of a perfect paradise. No funny stuff. Don't let anything break the vision. Keep it in the Goldilocks zone."

"You got it," Conrad assured her. "You're covered."

He closed his eyes and watched her leave by his own inner astral light. And that's when he knew who had answered the call when he had dialed up the universe on his walkie-talkie.

*She's Eve,* Conrad whispered to Skipper.

*But she doesn't remember,* the monkey confided.

Skipper pulled apart his velcroed paws and slipped onto the boy's lap.

Conrad stroked the monkey's fur and sank into a deep meditative trance. As his breath stilled, Conrad entered an absolute Alpha state of mind, holding the vision steady to keep Aletheia safe.

Eyes firmly shut, Conrad watched Eve walk through a meadow towards the promontory where Roica stood waiting.

Conrad quickly amended the vision, adding a gossamer mist when he realized that Eve was dressed in nothing but light. Then he lost track of her.

———

STEPPING CAUTIOUSLY THROUGH THE MIST, this new Eve entered a swath of greenery—patches of mellow yellows shimmered on the dew-speckled grass. Soon vast streamers of sun louvered the surrounding forest, and she found herself running towards the cliff's edge where Roica stood against the forever sky.

Every step was impelled by a desire she neither questioned nor understood. As she drew closer, Roica lost all traces of his personal identity. He was simply man.

Although she was youth itself, an ancient memory stirred. Eve looked back on the fresh green breast of a new born world, and it became this world. Standing beside Adam, she experienced each scent and sight as if life were entering her for the first time.

Like trailing bridesmaids, two angel-trees followed her to the precipice. These sylvan nymphs, sporting multiple wings of diaphanous leaves, were dressed in folds and falls of petals. They made a silken music as they spun like tops across the meadow. Petals jettisoned outwards in spirals and left patterns in the grass to entertain sky dwellers. When their leafy wings finally settled, tangles of flower-dappled hair dropped over their sun-splashed shoulders.

The two maiden trees rooted themselves on either side of the lovers. And shaking out their branches, they offered glimmering fruit to the original couple.

"Earth is a garden to play in," the trees sang. "Taste the fruit that lights the mind."

A white monkey slipped from Adam's attendant tree and set a burnished pomegranate in the open palm of the first man.

"You can have whatever you design-desire-design-desire," the attendant trees chorused.

Eve took the proffered fruit from Adam's hand and broke it open, revealing its succulent interior. She lifted it to her lips.

And paused.

There are those romantic revisionists who want the story to stop here and let the garden remain pristine, free from any human stain.

That is not possible.

The garden that Aletheia and Roica are standing in is still a myth-in-the-making. It hasn't happened yet. And it cannot happen until stars, angels, archetypes, and deities align to touch the mind of humankind. The ecstatic vision is meant to flame desire and move myth to miracle.

Eve must open the pomegranate and bite down. She must break the skin, and feel the crunch, and taste the juices spilling down her chin. And Adam must join her in this infinite tumble into a future still unmapped—she falling from Grace and he from his outlier home in space.

Their eternally recurring Earth embrace keeps the garden spinning in a coming spring, a paradise whose time is a horizon not yet seen, a sun not yet risen.

So Aletheia becomes Eve on the brink of one among many dangerous crossings, on the brink of one among many manifestations, strung like prayer beads across eternity, or like holiday lights winking hope on dark winter nights.

Through the ages, artists and visionaries continuously reinvent Eve. She dances barefoot in Botticelli paintings, turns en pointe in Balanchine ballets, flies to the moon on Chinese silk-screens, unfolds from cornstalks, holds snakes on Cretan urns. Her image is fired in primordial clay, carved in Neolithic stone, enshrined on marble pedestals, painted al fresco on ancient walls, embossed in gold leaf, designer-dressed on runways, politicized in new age novels, scientized in academic journals, illuminated on silver screens, and fished online from digital streams.

Lately, she's been sporting angel wings. And every once upon an almost never, she is tempted to reify one or another ancient myth in person, to incarnate and become Earthed again.

Myths, like prayers gone stale, long to be reawakened and evolved. They get restless. They tug and rumble and tease, prompt heresies, monkeys and mad ideas, tempt prophets and poets, fools and angels alike. They sport themselves and, like seasonal blooms, shift shapes and colors over time. They are alive.

Eve lifts the ancient fruit.

The taste of the pomegranate seed rings the bells of time on her tongue. She closes her senses to everything but that familiar tang. She is entranced.

"Swallow the seed," the trees whisper.

The mystery quickens within her.

When she opens her eyes, Eve recognizes her long-lost mate. She sees Roica as Adam and Adam as everyman.

The great Wheels pause briefly and wait out the moment. If she remembers too much, she might refuse him the next kiss, the one that changes the story. Words tumble from her lips in a tracery of questions:

"How were we so wedded, that I knew you before time sounded its metered bell, shattered our dimension and settled us in space? Who are you that you know me so well? What was our first garden like, Starfriend? How did you love me then? Did we kiss each other with our minds? Did we become drunk inhaling air?"

"Myriad lover," Adam addresses her. "I have fought forgetfulness and forged your memory in the fires of loss. I have made the very scent of you immortal in my mind. I've searched out all the places where you hide in the labyrinth of time. I love the way you change, the way you shape in space. I love the boundless risks you take. I am the one who catches you when you fall from grace."

"Hello, gentle friend," Eve turns to him, her voice a song, "Hello again."

On that sweet refrain, the lovers bend to the kiss that always waits for them at the beginning of each invention of their ever-evolving story.

The monkey in one of the maiden trees hangs from his tail and embellishes the moment by his mere presence, by his curiosity, by his soft chattering.

The dharmic grove is charmed.

This historic kiss is slightly altered from all the rest, set apart by a subatomic increment, a prayer so small as to be almost nothing at all, a nothing that could make all the difference.

This monkey-blessed kiss could unlock the hope of heaven.

In the annals of eternal recurrence, there are rare flashpoints when an infinitesimal shift occurs. The lovers felt a sweet tremor in the ground of being. There was an almost imperceptible flutter in Aletheia's womb. The Wheels registered the flutter and resumed their great revolutions.

# LOST IN TRANSLATION

BACKING UP TO THE BEGINNING, the cosmological beginning, before the word got out, before all the begats piled up, before origin stories and oratories and oracles, before holy pamphlets and pamphleteers, there was neither a bang nor a whimper. It was more of a whoosh.

When scientists in the 1960s actually heard the primordial echoes signaling the beginning of the universe, their best guess was that they were listening to the sound of pigeons pooping on their very expensive aerial. Satisfied that they had discovered the cause of the mysterious hiss, they failed at first to recognize the whispering whoosh of a distant birth traveling down their ear canals and pinging the collective scientific cochlear, zipping along the acoustic nerve and entering the temporal lobes. Like babes in the womb listening to the whoosh of blood through their mothers' veins, they had no notion of what lay outside their happy ignorance. Imagine the moment the scientists realized their error.

What a turnabout!

After billions and billions of years, the whisper finally entered the human temple of scientific truth—and it wasn't just pigeon poop. Hark, the scientific heralds sang in their highly-respected journals.

The traditional run of divinities does not like to admit that the creation of a universe is a lot easier and more prosaic than most of the mystified residents on Earth are wont to suppose. No need to involve the Wheels or illuminati or first-tier deities. No omniscience required. All it takes is a smart chemist with a good lab. Creation is the easy part. It's in the maintenance department that the dream-baby worlds go awry.

The Angel of Light managed to pull off the creation of the material cosmos in his early adolescence when his stellar intellect was still in the formative stages. Piece of angel cake. It took less than a thousandth of a gram to get the wee bit of vacuum necessary to precipitate the big blowout of chaotic inflation with its billions of galaxies, eventually including the Milky Way.

Before the seraphic whoosh and great galactic light show, this proto world-shaker and pyro-technician was just a feckless winged deity, kicking about the plenum with nothing much to do. But with the spectacular initiation of a universe, the angel went from neophyte sprite to super nova headliner in less than a nanosecond. Trumpeted by the superluminaries, he was heralded, haloed, hailed, and proved worthy of his name—Lucifer, bringer of light—Eosphoros. Brilliant, beautiful, and beloved, he quickly found himself with a huge following of youthful rebel deities.

For three-hundred million years the local celestials enjoyed the fireworks set off by the Angel of Light. Wave on wave of five-star rave reviews kept rolling in on the wire. It was the longest running star-studded extravaganza ever.

Then it got old.

All it took was an infinitesimal flicker of boredom, and a new vacuum was initiated. Then the merest wish created another whoosh. Instantaneously wish became a chaotic inflation of desire.

"Break it up," the divine spectators cried. "Make it new."

This cry caught the attention of Lucifer's less shiny, slightly older fraternal twin, the jealous Demiurge, who had been brooding over the ascendency of the Angel of Light for exactly three-hundred million years. A long brood, even by empyrean standards.

The less showy but equally gifted Demiurge was, after all, the first to emerge from the womb of creation. He had an exceptional knack for design; he was a master draftsman and an admirable artificer.

The Angel of Light had always been more of a chemist. In his youth he was known as the Sparkler: handsome, charismatic, a bit of a pyromaniac.

The Demiurge was known as the Maker, always building models and mobiles and machines. He was careless in appearance and hermetic in his ways. The Maker was a bit plodding, geekish even, and had always seemed older than his years, as if born with a furrowed brow and knee-length beard coming on. With his domed forehead and ponderous brow, it was hard to remember he was only moments older than his eternally youthful celebrity brother.

The Sparkler and the Maker had been tumultuous littermates, competing for glories from the get-go, constantly squalling and brawling in the womb of creation. As youngsters, the Sparkler courted universal admiration, but the Maker only wanted the admiration of his fraternal twin. The one who was born with wings became the envy of the one who was born without.

Initially, Lucifer's wings were viewed as a birth defect.

"What are those odd little bumps on his back?" Asheilstarte was heard to whisper.

By the time the adolescent Lucifer created the material universe, his wings had become lustrous, envied instruments of flight. As his renown soared, the modification was widely imitated.

Wings became the rage.

All the young divinities of the succeeding generation wanted wings. With so many skies and galactic wonders to behold, winged flight became the ultimate in first class travel. Soon enough the GMDs (genetically modified divinities) formed an elite society among etheric beings—angels.

When the wish to set one planet free moved from desire to determination, the Sparkler and the Maker were launched on a collision course of competition. First, Lucifer struck the sun. The Demiurge, with a blueprint for the dinosaurs tucked under his arm, cooled the Earth. Lucifer hurled a comet at the Yucatan and knocked out the dinosaurs. The Demiurge worked up Neolithic humans from clay models. Lucifer scoffed and tweaked their frontal lobes to create the spark of consciousness.

And somehow, on the tiny planet, as the word became text, the Angel of Light was lost in translation and the Demiurge got all the credit for creation. The Maker left his mark. The Sparkler's artistry was ultimately attributed to The One God, The One Universal Supreme Being, as he came to be known in some Earth circles.

An incensed Lucifer curled into the darkness, withdrawing his limitless light from the unworthy and ungrateful. He dreamed of reversing chaotic inflation—The Big Crunch, he called his apocalyptic vision. He was willing to wait out eternity for a chance to compress the whole mess into a tight nugget of dark matter.

The Demiurge, embarrassed by a flawed creation, kept looking for a fix. He attempted numerous incarnations, some of them bungled, some of them admirable. At some point, he gave up on redemption and tried for less grandiose improvements; wings might be a nice amendment to the human form.

Privately, he regretted that he had evolved humans from mammals. He couldn't help but speculate how things might have gone better if humans had descended from birds. His creative urges were boundless, and he simply could not resist attempting the occasional do-over. There were setbacks and public fiascos—the unfortunate Icarus experiment, for one.

*My kingdom for a pair of wings*! He tried to laugh off his obsession.

As much as the Maker feigned indifference, he would always be jealous of Lucifer's wings. Willy nilly, this repressed yearning would find expression in the Maker's repeated incarnations, as well as in the ecclesiastical vestments of his devotees, most notably the Cardinals and other birdmen of The Great Church. Like phantom limbs are sometimes beset with ghost afflictions, the Maker's wingless Avatars, priests, and praise-makers were vexed by fantasies of flight. They translated their blight into a variety of sartorial simulacrums, genetic modifications, and engineered marvels.

While it is true that the Maker's attempts to fix the world were often riddled with unfortunate consequences, he did enjoy one wildly successful incarnation as a Renaissance man. The renowned Leonardo da Vinci, like his progenitor, was a tinkerer at heart. Entranced by secret codes and war machines, Leo also claimed bragging rights to a blueprint for an exquisite set of mechanical wings. He studied of the flight patterns of birds and obsessively painted angels with meticulously detailed wings.

The Maker was dumbfounded that humanity never copped to the Da Vinci Incarnation (DVI). Leonardo's celebrated notebooks—seven-thousand pages of drawings and inventions evidenced the spark of divinity from page one. Although some among celestials were heard to mock Leonardo's iconic painting, calling it the Bemoana Lisa, it pleased the Maker immensely that the painting still held pride of place in the Louvre. And the record-shattering four-hundred-fifty-million-dollar sale of his painting, *Salvatore Mundi,* salved his ego, even if it did not save the world. His brand endured.

Despite the sneers of his constant celestial critics, who pointed out that a few paintings and a trove of drawings hardly qualified as an Act of Salvation, the Maker was given an A+ for effort, a belated acknowledgement of his abiding willingness to get down in the muck of Earth matters. After all, Leo did fix the plumbing in the palace of the Duke of Milan.

The Angel of Light, on the other hand, did not like the messy world that failed to credit him. He much preferred the pristine environs of fire and ice. For the most part, the Earth interested Lucifer not at all. Until the curious arrival of the blue baby, eons had transpired without his giving the planet a second thought—apart from his recurrent fantasy of blasting the mudball to bits.

———

NOW A SEVEN-YEAR-OLD adept was busy re-creating a mythic scene in which the Angel of Light played a central role. The surprise of seeing Aletheia walk into a mist-shrouded garden nearly knocked Luce sideways. When Lucifer examined his memory of the green angel on Grace, he convinced himself that he'd known all along that she was Eve. It occurred to Lucifer that some powerful Supernal or consortium of Wheels was attempting to remaster the myth of Eden. And that meant a power shift was in the offing. He was a major stakeholder in the Eden myth and knew exactly how he'd change the outcome if given half a chance.

Where there was Eve, there was Adam, and he really despised Adam.

"Back to the garden," Lucifer hastened. But to the illuminato's utter amazement, he was unable to reenter Conrad's vision.

Moments later Luce was pouring himself a consoling glass of Château Latour and checking on his minion who had high tailed it back to the underground wine cellar. Oblivious to Lucifer's dark mood, Kilo gave Eppler's garden a rave.

"Made my day, hanging out in Eppler's virtual world. When I spotted the hand drawn, comic book bubble floating over my head, the Earthworm got a double thumbs-up from yours truly," the low-ranking angel flipped open his notepad. "Yeah, five stars for the mash-up. The kid's dreamscape was toon city. And that T-Rex? Seriously awesome."

Unlike Luce, Kilo had no prior role in the garden myth and no personal grudge against Adam. He didn't much care one way or the other how the storyline was revamped. He did, however, share Lucifer's delight in all things explosive. A sweet line of red fuse was still connected to a handsome bundle of dynamite, and he was eager to push the vintage plunger he'd scored at Giltane's Antique Shoppe. That is, once the Tyrannosaurus Rex was out of the way.

Lucifer was ominously silent, sipping his wine, studying options. "Follow me."

"Paradise should always come with a random-ejection warning," Kilo laughed, trying to lighten things up.

"I want you to go back in. Detonate the dynamite."

"I already tried another hack on the vision, Boss. Nothing doing."

"The little spoiler," Luce hissed under his breath.

Pride kept Lucifer from mentioning that he too had tried and failed to get back into the vision. The minion made his own surmises.

"You gotta hand it to the kid. He's got some juice."

Lucifer was not about to "hand it to the kid," or laugh off Conrad's ability to keep him out of the garden. Being chased by a T-Rex was a keenly felt injury to Lucifer's self-regard and an egregious offense to his personal aesthetics—the oversized head, the measly front claws.

Still fuming over the Earthworm's uncanny powers, Luce left Kilo at the hatch door that led from the underground tunnel to the woods, and he took a leisurely stroll across the lawn to get a better read on the precocious scene stealer. The angel of light climbed the steps up to the terrace and leaned against the balustrade where he had a clear view of Conrad's bedroom.

The boy sat Padmasana with that stuffed monkey in his lap, a perfect little bodhisattva minding his breath and his storyboard. Luce made a cursory effort to break into Conrad's thoughts, but the vision was locked up tight. The angel was convinced the boy was getting help. He had just decided to step inside and grab the monkey, when Sister Subordinary burst into Conrad's room and lifted the boy up. Lucifer studied the developing scene with keen interest.

"Wake up," Sister gentled.

Still in a trance, Conrad was forcefully yanked through inner space. Aware that Aletheia was counting on him to hold the garden vision steady, the boy resisted Sister's call with all his considerable might. His name—*Conrad, Conrad*—pinged repeatedly against his consciousness. And the mounting urgency in Sister Mary Subordinary's voice pulled him relentlessly back into this world.

"Conrad," Subordinary held him tightly, "I am so sorry. Mother Mary's had a heart attack."

"Noooooo!" the boy cried out and the marble slipped from his hand. As the cleary rolled away, the protective shield fell from the garden. Conrad wriggled out of Sister Subordinary's arms and ran outside onto the terrace.

Lucifer took his cue, slipped into Conrad's room unseen and scooped up the marble. With a flick of the wrist, he tossed Lord Hanuman's cleary out of this world.

Time for revisions.

The Angel of Light strolled into the boy's paradisiacal field of dreams. He spotted Kilowatt waiting at the edge of Eden. At a signal from the boss, Kilo stumbled back into paradise and fell on the plunger.

A world-splitting KABOOM shook the dimensions. The unhappy ending was back on the storyboard.

The angel trees burst into flame. Roica launched himself over Aletheia to shelter her from falling debris.

"Noooooo!" Conrad cried out one final time. Then he gave himself over to sobbing in the arms of Sister Mary Subordinary.

———

A RARELY DISAPPOINTED Asheilstarte, watched the garden conflagration from a distance, while at close range her own heart contracted violently in concordance with Mary Extraordinary's affliction. The heartsickness came over her in waves. Slowly, the tripartite divinity enclosed herself in the solace of her wings.

The history of an error was repeating itself. She had managed the prodigious task of placing three key players back into their story to give them a chance to save paradise for a reset in the future. The biblical founder's myth was proving stubbornly resistant to revision. If anything, She had made things worse.

Ensconced in the palace of oms, She consulted with her Wing Sergeants and contemplated letting go. Her other choice was an appearance. Personal intervention was a clumsy way to reset and always a last resort. Her Wings urged her to take the dive.

Chaos was an opportunity.

Unceremoniously, She lifted her wings and made her descent. A blast of Gabrieline horns announced her presence as She touched down on the scorched Earth.

Although unhappy to be reduced to cheap theatrics, She knew no one could best her when it came to putting on a show. At her command, everything that had been blown apart in the explosion came back together—from the lovely promontory down to the least little beetle. She slowed down the reassembly, the better to impress the watchers. It was a rare opportunity to appraise Conrad Eppler's artistry and its various effects. Asheilstarte noted the boy's ability to build a dream world that teemed with materiality. A boy after his father's heart.

A cassowary crossed her visual field.

"What is *he* doing here?" She questioned her Wings. "Look at those pathetic flightless wings."

"Wings, at least at last," Wing I choked back a laugh.

"Waiting in the wings for his walk-on," Wing II sighed.

Asheilstarte did not love this reminder that She was not entirely in control of the developing scene.

"Lucifer, you may approach me," the Mediatrix of Grace turned to the intervention at hand, promising herself She would come back to the cassowary.

"High Consul, Chair of Justice, I give you the original sinners," Luce addressed her with a self-satisfied smile.

The unhappy couple stood at the world's edge, bruised by the destruction and baffled by the swiftly reconstructed scene.

Aletheia broke from Roica and came at a run. "High Consul, Chair of Omniscience, you must have known I was destined for a fall. Knew I would yearn for Earth. Knew Roica would be drawn to me. It's all come too clear too late," her words streamed with tears. "I was blinded at the gate of my past. You stole my memory!"

"Dear one, the memory of a great love fallen into despair and suffering will overpower every urge to return to the scene of lost hope. Thus held hostage to the past, how could hope be restored? How could the lovers free themselves to find their way home and fulfill the promise of the future? Welcome home."

"Earth is not home," Roica cut in. "Earth is hell!" Undaunted by the powerful tripartite deity, he drew closer. "Hell," he repeated.

Asheilstarte struck sparks on the flint of Roica's reckless effrontery. Insights coursed through the circuitry of her trifold mind. She appreciated his fearlessness and admired the adamantine set of his intentions. She pried his history open, looking for a purchase in his storyline, looking for a way to lead him home.

"If the first man and father of humankind forswears the Earth, how then shall his children and their children embrace it?"

She saw her mistake too late. Roica had no interest in legacy. He shut her down before She could recalibrate.

"We're a long way from the gates of Eden," Roica advanced. "Accept my amazement. You had me on the brink—until your cardboard cutout paradise was reduced to ashes. I thank you for the timely explosion."

"That's thanks to me and Luce," Kilowatt barged in, "I pushed the plunger, with all due respect to the powers that blessed be." The intrepid minion executed an elaborate bow. Clearly, he'd been practicing. She waited for his idiosyncratic honorifics. Kilo did not disappoint. "Your Most Royal Electric Chair and Divine Ex Machina, all what I am saying is give a little credit where credit is due."

"Stand down, Kilowatt! I am not going to take the blame this time." Lucifer turned on Roica, "In the long ago, I ignited the human mind with the flame of my brilliance. I offered the fruit of enlightenment. And my reward? I was reviled. I will unmake that mythos."

"By violence?" Roica countered.

"The explosion? Think of it as a personal expression of my disdain for you, First Man. Think of it as a test and a reminder. You never did have the resilience to fight the inevitable setbacks."

Although aroused by the Angel's well-slung insults, this was not the battle or the battleground that Roica sought. He turned his back on Lucifer.

"Roica, don't turn away. Take the challenge. Prove yourself a hero." A frantic Aletheia urged her ungovernable lover into the fray. "What does it matter that we were played? Our love is our endurance. And Earth is the Eden of our destiny."

"This is Eden's eleventh hour, angel heart. Don't be fooled, Aletheia. What we witnessed here is the Earth speeding towards its inevitable destruction. The garden is a fraud, a false front, a conjuring."

"If it is a conjuring, so be it. Let paradise be a prayer," Aletheia reached for Roica, but the word paradise struck him first and struck him wrong.

"Paradise is a word best suited for neon signs on seedy motels, blinking false hope for the desperate. I am not desperate."

Aletheia was abashed, aware that she was complicit in creating that blinking neon sign, complicit in the come-on; she was the seduction. Now it seemed that Gods and angels alike were aligned against Roica. A quick examination of her conscious told the emerald angel the undeniable truth—she had set the karmic trap when she asked Conrad to conjure a perfect place. How could Roica help but feel betrayed?

The divide between the lovers widened in the ensuing silence.

"Let the record stand." Luce shot a missile into the widening rift. "If anyone is inspired to write a new testament, take note—it was Adam that refused the call. So Gospelers, remember this: the Angel of Light is clean."

Ignoring Luce, Roica challenged High Consul, "Do you compel Aletheia? Is she captive of your designs?"

"None of this matters one whit if there isn't free will," the illuminata conceded.

"There is your answer, Aletheia," Roica held out his hand. "Come away with me. We can be free of the myth that breaks us." He waited until his arm grew heavy.

Futures raveled and spun out.

"Forgive me, best beloved," Aletheia could not look him in the eye. "I am bound by my promise to Conrad. Go find the Wheels, Roica. Find your answers. I will leave the gate open, if only you'll promise—someday you'll come back to me."

"I can't promise that."

"You promised in the garden; you gave me forever."

"Apparently, it was a lie."

"Then lie to me again."

"To what purpose?"

"To give me hope. Give me a lie worthy of belief and I'll hold on to it and make it come true. It's something angels do. Give me your lie, Roica."

When the stone silence had done its quick damage, Asheilstarte sorted her players.

"There we have it. Each has assumed a position. Aletheia, you choose Earth."

"I do," Aletheia looked to her beloved.

"Roica, you choose to chase the Wheels. What? No response?"

By way of answer, Roica singed the air with anger. It came off him in waves, eating up the oxygen.

Asheilstarte sidestepped the coming confrontation with Roica and smiled benevolently on the minion. "Lieutenant Kilowatt, you choose to take the credit?"

"I do, Your Majesty, I do."

"And Lucifer, you are choosing, what? Your usual ambiguity?"

"No. I am unambiguous on this matter. I choose Earth. I release my claim on the apocalypse."

Kilo tried to mask his shock and disappointment, but his uncooperative jaw drooped in chagrin. "What? No apocalypse?"

Asheilstarte allowed herself a smile. Some progress had been achieved after all. The Angel of Light was advancing heaven's hope.

She addressed Lucifer, "Am I to understand that you plan to incarnate?"

"No. That's not going to happen. Ever." And there was that winning smile. "I choose the Earth metaphorically."

"As I said, ambiguity," High Consul countered.

"Have it your way," Luce conceded amiably. "I can live with ambiguity."

Roica watched this blithe spiritual exchange, marking time. He was wretched, and somehow these bliss-meisters were enjoying the spar. It was insulting. It was infuriating.

Roica advanced on the tripartite illuminata, "Who are you, and what is your interest in our story? What position do *you* take?"

"I am positionless in this matter," her Wings instantly erect, High Consul prepared herself for an attack.

"That's a bald-faced lie."

The Wings snapped on high alert; an electric current haloed the Mediatrix of Grace.

Roica was unfazed. "The Earth is a failure," he began, aware that all eyes were on him, "and you can't face it. So you continue to manipulate the angels and graces in the vain hope that they can somehow gloss the history of Supernal errors. I know your God. We've met. It is your own imperious ego."

She was stung. This beautifully evolved being had winged her. The Mediatrix recognized his speech for what it was—an annunciation, an act of self-emancipation. It must be honored.

"Escort Roica to his ship," High Consul ordered Lucifer.

"I'll leave when I'm ready," Roica shot back.

Asheilstarte lifted herself and stretched out her Wings, forcing Roica to look up. Galaxies seemed to float in the folds of her skirts. The wings beat furiously, and She brightened so that Roica had to shade his eyes.

The sea beneath the promontory whipped up its waves and pounded the sand. A flight of white gulls reeled and cried overhead. She heard the words of one of Earth's beloved prophets and bent his words to her purpose.

When She spoke her voice was everywhere, full of the echoing Wings and wind and water.

"The day will come, Roica, when after harnessing the winds and tides, the Earth will harness the energies of love. And on that day the heavens will bow down in praise of the wet blue and green jewel that hangs like an ornament of hope in the black skies of love's long winter."

Asheilstarte ordered her Wings to form a barrier between Roica and her intentions. Immediately, he was locked in a column of blue light where he would be held until Aletheia was safely on her way.

"Aletheia, you will be escorted to The Colony, a renowned spiritual spa where the ritual transition to the material plane will be enacted. When you are returned to Earth, you will have attained your humanity once again. We will not forget that for a while you lingered here, an angel among us."

"Among us," the Wings chorused.

It struck Lucifer that the game was getting away from him. He was not aware of any renowned spiritual spa or colony. Clearly High Consul had not put him in the whole picture regarding the estates of Grace. Information was power, his daily bread, baked in the sun's nuclear oven, the pane copia, the communion of the cognoscenti, broken and shared among the chosen few. As much as he disliked letting the limits of his knowledge show, disliked being seen to beg for holy bread crumbs, he had to ask.

"High Consul, you mentioned a colony? What colony did you have in mind? For Eve's transitioning?"

"The Colony of my choice, Lucifer," and with that, She dismissed him.

"Wing Sergeants, call in the Guardians."

A pledge of elite angels—Powers and Principalities—surrounded the triumvirate.

"Holy Guardians, whose work it is to protect the angels who fall through Grace into the material world, venerate and glorious chaperons, shield Aletheia in your divine kindness. Escort her to the blue launch that fate has prepared for her journey. Light her path. Let the great Wheels spin. Let the story begin again."

———

ALL THE WHILE Asheilstarte sorted the players, Conrad's world kept shifting and rearranging itself—possible futures blinking in and out of existence at a breakneck pace. As soon as his visionary garden had gone up in flames, he'd lost contact with his answering angel. Waiting while Sister Subordinary tended the unconscious Mother Mary, the boy wondered if the events were linked somehow: the heart attack, the explosion, the loss of Aletheia.

Now the blare of an ambulance could be heard approaching the convent.

Sister Merry Berry had elected herself to accompany Mary Extraordinary to the hospital. Her satchel was brimming with quickly packed necessities. Up in her room, she carefully wedged in an emergency supply of prayer juice—two bottles, each tucked in its own lime-green sock. She tossed in the red Manolo Blahniks as an after-thought, plus a tangle of prayer beads, a supply of Twinkies, a novel, her crochet notions, a Snow White figurine that she'd removed from the pack of dwarves she'd given Conrad for his seventh birthday, and lastly a bottle of Cabernet. On second thought, she put the bottle of wine back on the shelf. She needed to keep her wits about her.

Conrad and Sister Subordinary stood by helplessly as a feather-light Mother Mary Extraordinary was lifted onto a stretcher and slid neatly into a slot in the ambulance. Mary Subordinary thought the ancient prioress might be carried out of this world under the siren song of that white ambulance. What an unhappy irony that Mary Extraordinary's first time leaving the convent might be her last.

Sister Subordinary squeezed Conrad's hand. What in the world was keeping Merry Berry?

Mary Subordinary had just turned to call after her consoeur, when the panting nun emerged from the convent, awkwardly lugging a suitcase with both hands. Merry Berry sported florescent orange tennis shoes and a patchwork satchel slung carelessly over one shoulder. Her beautiful round berry of a bottom was given a helpful hoist by an ambulance attendant over the loud objections an indignant cassowary. Barred from entry, the agitated bird paced back and forth emitting mournful bleats.

"Now the suitcase, please," Merry Berry pointed to an old-fashioned, fabric-covered affair with nickel-plated hasps. She loved the springy noise they made when they flipped up. The suitcase was filled with cold cash. Her bargaining skills honed by years of bartering, she had managed to sell the cache of precious jewel-encrusted amulets for a queen's ransom. Then she managed to lug the cash-filled case all the way from Giltane's Antique Shoppe to the convent in a wheelbarrow.

Now, at long last, she saw a rare opportunity to do some serious shopping in the city.

"What've you got in here, Sister?" The medic grunted as he lifted the suitcase into the cab.

Ignoring the query, Merry Berry waved her friends goodbye.

Conrad, Subordinary, and the bird stood and watched the ambulance carry their beloveds off into that most confounding phenomenological category: what-happens-next—a constantly checked mental screen, host to conflicting storylines, repository of hopes and fears, the lottery of chance and the logic of guess.

Their collective best guess didn't even come close. Two imaginations flew ahead to the hospital and a funeral and then made a quick U-turn away from loss and elegies. When Conrad and Sister Subordinary simultaneously thought to change the course of their alarming projections, they pictured a happy ending: their beloved Mother Mary back in the convent, shaking her cane, beautiful and irritable and altogether alive again. They never thought to worry about Sister Merry Berry.

Only the cassowary worried about his friend that afternoon. As the ambulance disappeared out of sight, he issued one last mournful bleat.

Conrad and Sister Subordinary never thought to worry about themselves either. While their minds were awash with what was rapidly getting away from them, a sleek black Oldsmobile pulled into the circle drive.

The smoked electronic window hummed down, and a hand with red pointed fingernails shook a handful of papers at them.

"I've come for the boy. Here are the papers," said the red lips. Margaret Demeanor eyed the cassowary; she was understandably reluctant to leave her vehicle.

Subordinary's grip tightened on Conrad's shoulders. The cassowary poked his elegant crested head in at the open window. Ms. Demeanor gave that bird a sound thwak with the papers. The bird let out an angry squawk, grabbed the official documents and ran for the woods.

Taking advantage of the aleatory moment, Ms. Margaret Demeanor stepped out of the car and seized Conrad by the arm. Her pointy nails dug in, and Conrad dropped his toy.

"Skiiiiper!" the boy yelled as he was shoved into the back seat of the car. The door slammed shut.

With stunning alacrity, Ms. Demeanor hopped back into the driver's seat. Subordinary grabbed the door handle too late. Demeanor flipped the locks. It happened so fast.

"Buckle up," Margaret Demeanor snapped at a startled boy. Revving the engine with an impatient foot, she was unaware that this was Conrad's first car ride. Flashing him a look of irritation in the rearview mirror, she whipped around and secured Conrad's seat belt. Then she let the window down a cautious inch and hissed, "I'll send the papers in the mail."

The cassowary came back at a dead run and jumped on the hood of the Oldsmobile, raking it with his nine-inch nails. Demeanor backed out with a squeal of rubber. The cassowary bounced off the hood.

Subordinary stood dumbfounded by how quickly the world and her heart could be turned upside down. She bent over and picked up the small scuffed monkey, a rubber tire track laid across his belly. She remembered how beautifully it had all begun on that long ago snowy day. The white monkey. The cardboard box. Earth was tough on its inhabitants. The cassowary limped over to her side.

First, the telephone, she said to herself. Find out where that woman was taking Conrad. Next, the hospital. Ask after Mother Mary. Then what? Tend the cassowary with a liniment rub. And last? Launder the monkey. It was the sanity list of a saint.

Sister Subordinary looked down the empty road. When she turned to go inside, the cassowary followed her. She held the door and let him pass in front of her. She dared herself to lift her hand and thread her fingers through his lush plumage. It was oddly comforting.

Later, rubbing a witch hazel liniment fused with Mother Tinctures on the raptor's hip, she realized that the bird was saving her life. Caretakers need someone to care for. She put the laundered monkey on her pillow and fell asleep praying for all those she loved. She felt blessed by the length and depth of her list; her growing litany of beloveds had just increased by one cassowary.

While Sister counted blessings, the monkey on her pillow dreamed of his lost marble. He watched it soar through the heavens, enter the Magellanic Cloud Casino, and land with a musical plink on the Wheel of Chances.

# BOTTLED PRAYERS

TAKING A BREAK FROM CARING for Mother Mary at All Saints Hospital, Sister Merry Berry set off on a whirlwind excursion of Avesticum City, scouting the area on foot with a vigor fueled by necessity and guilty elation. It was her first walk-about in a metropolis. Swept up in the dazzling cityscape, her red high heels barely touched the ground. Avesticum City had so much of whatever you never even knew you wanted.

Merry Berry tried gelatos in fifteen different flavors and saved each miniature colored spoon for Conrad. She attended a

3-D movie. She treated herself to a manicure and a pedicure. Her nails were now bright blue, and a spare bottle of electric blue nail enamel was tucked in her satchel for repairs.

The adventurous nun avoided going anywhere near the Sanctum Avesticum Quoborium that menaced the metropolis from its hilltop perch, surrounded by a private heavily-wooded park. But she did attend a religious service at a mega church, where she listened to a charismatic preacher on a jumbo screen extol the virtues of giving away cash. She couldn't agree more. Afterward, she danced under a streetlamp to a steel-drum band and tipped the players handsomely. Then in the deepening twilight, she saw a sign. A sign unto her.

Vintage Cars. Cash Only.

Tomorrow morning, she promised herself.

When she repaired back to All Saints Hospital, Sister Merry Berry found Mother Mary stabilized and sedated in the ICU. Two days ago, a stent had been placed in her left coronary artery to increase blood flow from her wayward heart. Although not out of danger, the recovering Mary Extraordinary was breathing easily with the help of oxygen piped up her nose.

Sister Merry Berry checked on the suitcase that she'd hauled into the ICU over the objections of the nursing staff. Her stash untouched, she curled up on a lounge chair with a paperback novel and soon was sleeping peacefully to the music of hospital machines.

In the morning, Sister Merry Berry placed her hand on Mary Extraordinary's heart. The blood was circulating at a steady pump.

"Pump," Merry Berry repeated the word out loud and pictured a pump of a different sort.

Walking about the city last night, she had been charmed by the lustrous beauty of the gas stations. They made her think of celestial landing pads—the glowing pumps lined up like greeters, the headlamps on the automobiles zipping in and out like angels traveling in perfect pairs. The novelty of the image quickened her resolve. With highway visions streaming in her head, Sister Merry Berry opened the springy hasps on the vintage suitcase, scooped out several bundles of cash, and stuffed them into her satchel.

"I'll be back," she promised a sleeping Mother Mary Extraordinary.

Merry Berry had never questioned the provenance or providence of the jewel-encrusted amulets she'd found in her dresser drawer, certain that the treasure was meant for her, and certain that she would put the prayer juice and the amulets to good use. She never dreamed of owning a car until she traded in the jewels at Giltane's and saw the mountain of cash. Now she was ready to make the mountain matter.

"So many pretty Benjamins and Tubmans and Hamiltons," the used-car salesman beamed at the fistfuls of bills, bound in bright rubber bands. "It be a good day for Tremont Montress."

Not a novice shopper by any means—all that bargaining at yard-sales and negotiating at Giltane's had served her well—Sister Merry Berry struck an impressive deal. The enchanted salesman not only sold her a car, he readily agreed to sweeten the exchange.

Perhaps it was the match of their Rasta dreads that prompted Tremont Montress to toss in the driving lessons, or it may have been the red high heels that turned his head. For her part, Merry Berry had never met anyone with her same blueberry-hued black skin. The salesman looked good enough to eat in his yellow suit; yellow-cake-batter flavored gelato, she mused, and then got down to business.

"No questions asked," she admonished at the outset. "I need to drive it off the lot."

She pointed to a hand-painted sign in faded block letters—Drive Off Lot—and explained that she would need some help in that department. She had just been reading a similar scene in a Jack Reacher novel. Jack was a great role model for getting around on your wits, unlicensed, packing nothing but a toothbrush in your pocket.

"Two lessons should do it," she guessed out loud, projecting a confidence based on nothing but optimism.

"Sure thing, Dawta. Tremont Montress, at your service."

"One lesson this morning and one this afternoon. And if I can make it successfully from your lot to the parking garage at the hospital and back—I will pay seven, no, ten-thousand dollars cash for," she spun around on her red high heels and pointed, "for that."

It was an adorable yellow VW Bug that stopped Merry Berry's spinning wheel of fortune. The salesman, impressed with her bravado and finding her attractive in a way she'd never been found attractive before, offered her some friendly advice.

"Listen Dawta, that ain't no beginna car. No offense. Trust we. Beginna don't start small. Beginna start big."

"Big?"

"You want car that floats. One that almost drives itself. Lotsa steel protect beautiful beginna on the city street. Look we over here. If ever there were dread wheels for a dawta in red heels," he pointed to a vintage stunner.

Sister Merry Berry fell head over heels in love. The object of her affection was a meticulously restored, pink 1959 Cadillac Eldorado Biarritz convertible with white leathers.

"You be riding with Jah in the sky."

She sank into the soft leather upholstery, and it was true. She felt like she'd died and gone to heaven.

"Teach me to drive," Merry Berry smiled up at him, the dimple in her chin deepening, her skin too dark to show the rush of blood to her cheeks.

Backlit by a dazzling sun, Tremont towers in his yellow suit. Then he leans on the open door and feels like he is falling into her dark brown eyes. She feels like the sun just dropped into her lap.

It was a whirlwind courtship—several city blocks long. And then back.

At one point, they stopped to practice parking in front of a music store—Vinyl Attractions. Tremont explained to Merry Berry that her vintage ride had a state-of-the-art music system and she needed a couple CDs.

"We go inside," Tremont invited.

"And explore?" Merry Berry flirted unconsciously.

Tremont leaned in for a kiss and just in time, Merry Berry realized what was about to happen. She hopped out of the car and made for the store. Tremont was quick. He raced ahead of her and opened the door.

A tinny bell rang them in. The store smelled musty, like the wine cellar at the convent. Merry Berry was very aware of Tremont standing behind her, and for a moment she couldn't move. All she could hear was her heart thudding in her ears. She wobbled in her high heels, and Tremont steadied her, his hands on her shoulders.

Finally, an angelic voice broke through Merry Berry's inner tumult; someone was singing about stardust and a garden. A dazed Merry Berry bought a copy of Joni Mitchell's *Ladies of the Canyon* and on Tremont's recommendation, Bob Marley's *Exodus*.

"Side two, track ten," Tremont said to a baffled Merry Berry, inserting the Marley disc in the player when they were on the road again.

At the end of lesson one, they stopped for gelatos. Dipping their plastic spoons in a pint of caramel sea salt, they exchanged tiny spoonfuls of story. When Merry Berry told Tremont Montress that she was a dedicated Sister, he shook his head in despair and claimed his heart was broken.

Surely, he must be joking, she thought. "Don't tease," she said.

Back on board the Cadillac Biarritz, the top down, the world spinning to a reggae beat beneath the wheels, Sister Merry Berry pressed on the accelerator. A rush of wind lifted her rainbow-colored beret and sent it spiraling into the air.

"Slow down. Easy, Sistah," his voice was slow and easy. "Pump the brake."

That word again.

"Pump," she repeated out loud and laughed for no reason. She had never felt so alive in her downy places.

Sister Merry Berry was fortunate in her teacher inasmuch as he was unfortunate in his bright bespoken student, who had pledged herself to the Sisterhood and a potpourri boho beliefs. It was a pity to lose such a quick brown fox and natural born driver. Too soon he was demonstrating how to gas up the Biarritz, and they found themselves preparing goodbyes under a revolving Pegasus sign.

Feeling the fool, he asked for her phone number. She refused him. He asked for a kiss to remember her by. She offered him a colored gelato spoon.

"One kiss," he tucked the spoon in his pocket.

She teetered, then stepped back from the brink, her face full of laughter.

"Don't worry, I'll remember you," she declined the beautiful man in the yellow suit. "I belong to the oversoul," she added as a gentle reminder to both of them that she'd taken a vow of chastity.

"JahJah is rich, Sistah. Not gonna miss one kiss. But you gonna miss it."

Their love affair was brief—the circumference of a kiss.

And Tremont Montress was right. She would have missed it. It was better than all fifteen flavors of gelato. It was better than the 1928 Château Latour. It was a gateway kiss.

373

Never before had she felt so much like her namesake blueberry, all juicy on the inside, ripe enough to burst through her own skin.

He whispered in her ear, "Are you living the life you want to be *re*living, Sistah?"

That stopped her. She reached in her pocket and gave herself a protective spritz. She inhaled the prayers and exhaled a yes. "This is what I choose."

Sister Merry Berry beamed her best smile at him, the one that showed off the handsome split in her front teeth, saying "My life is a life worth many relivings, and I am so awfully glad to take your *one* kiss with me on my journey."

With a good deal of reluctance, she closed the gate on the gateway kiss—almost closed it. He managed to wedge his polished shoe in just before the latch caught on that tumble of possible tomorrows. Tremont handed her a card with his number and added one bit of parting advice.

"Dawta, just remember, Jah is the driva." Then he gave her his best smile, the one that lit up a world that danced to a reggae drumbeat. "One Love," he said instead of goodbye, and he rapped three times on the shiny steel hood of the Eldorado Biarritz. Then she was off, leaving behind the man in the yellow-cake-batter suit.

When she realized driving was her new bliss, Merry Berry named her beautiful blue ride Jah Bliss. To think she'd gone so long without experiencing hands-on-the-wheel power glide. Floating down the city streets was another nirvana to add to an exponentially growing list.

With the directions to the Department of Protective Services taped to the dashboard, she headed into the heart of the city. Confident that Mother Mary Extraordinary was on the road to recovery, Merry Berry set out on her chosen mission— she was going to rescue Conrad.

When Sister Subordinary had telephoned Merry Berry at the hospital that first night and described how Ms. Demeanor had snatched Conrad—the nerve of that woman—Merry Berry knew she had done the right thing, hauling all that cash with her in the ambulance. The local pickings in the neighborhood where she bicycled had always proved a disappointment. Nothing like Jah Bliss had ever come up for sale.

Merry Berry glanced over at the passenger seat. Riding shotgun on the white leather seat was a newly purchased temperature-controlled container of gelato, all the flavors Sister guessed that Conrad would love best: pink bubblegum, peanut butter, blue smurf, and stracciatella.

She pulled into the Department of Protective Services parking lot, surveyed the concrete-slab building, and bolstered herself for the task ahead. In the lobby, she gave her name to a bored young woman seated at a metal desk, and with all the authority she could muster, she said she'd come to pick up Conrad Eppler.

"Are you the mother?" the woman asked, stopping Merry Berry short.

"One of them, yes," Merry Berry beamed.

"Oh. LBGT?"

"Pardon me?"

"Lesbian, bi, gay, transgendered? You implied that there are two mothers."

"Three. I just want to take him home. He was kidnapped, you see. By your Ms. Demeanor, the one with green wings. I didn't say that," Merry Berry smiled, remembering that she had promised herself to say nothing odd or off-putting. Being sober wasn't as easy as it looked.

She started again. "What I meant to say was that I am his *only* mother, the other two are really, well, aunts, I suppose." And then remembering that she was blueberry-black and that Conrad was now sand-colored, she added: "His adoptive mother, of course. I mean now that he's white—he doesn't look at all—not that he was ever blue. Of course. He wasn't. Ever."

Merry Berry took a breath.

"What I meant to say was. Just one mother. Me. I'm it. The one who rode bikes with him and bought his comic books and cowboy boots and—Twinkies," she trailed off. Suddenly, she was lonely for her consoeurs. They knew when to interrupt her nervous rambles.

The receptionist fiddled with her mouse, and studied a blue computer screen. Never even glancing up at an increasingly distressed Merry Berry, the indifferent gatekeeper explained that the boy had been placed in protective services by a court order. It made no difference how many mothers the boy had or what color he was now or may have been.

"Is he here? May I at least see him?"

"We'll keep him here until he's been evaluated by our team of psychiatric social workers. Then he'll be placed in foster care.

I can let you visit for fifteen minutes, but his caseworker must be present in the room. I'll call Ms. Demeanor."

"Of course," said Merry Berry, realizing belatedly that the less she said, the better. These people were like the Magistere. No heart. All rules.

"I'll just slip out to the car. I've got a present for him. I'll be back in two winks."

Oh, how she hugged that boy and wiped away his flood of tears with the corner of her skirt. She made promises and fed him gelato and gave him fourteen plastic spoons. She made him laugh and reminded him of the safe place inside.

"Even without the quarry pool," she coached him, "you can travel far and away on the astral plane, where no one can harm you."

"I want Skipper."

"Skipper," Merry Berry wished she'd thought about the monkey.

"I'm so sorry, Conrad. I'd have brought him, but I came straight from the hospital."

"Is Mother Mary doing all right?"

"Yes, Mother Mary is fine, or she will be fine. All of it will be fine. I bought a new car." Merry Berry finally landed on something that truly was fine.

"You did?"

"Yes. I named it Jah Bliss. It's pink. Someday you'll ride in Jah Bliss. I promise."

"Are those my shoes?" Ms. Demeanor interrupted, bending closer. "They are!"

"Possibly. I suppose they might be. The cassowary gave them to me. Of course, I mean if they're yours, you may have them back." Merry Berry was slipping the shoes off her bare feet.

"No. Keep them. I insist," hissed the red lips.

Ms. Demeanor took note of the blue toenails and was certain she'd never met a more preposterous person, either in appearance or behavior.

"Two more minutes and this visit is over."

Merry Berry took the boy's hands in hers. "Conrad, I've got one last thing to say to you. I don't know how and I don't know when, but there will be a—," she lowered her voice, "rescue. Now I'm zippered up but for one last, one-more last thing. A little gift. To remember me by, though of course you'd never forget me, would you?"

And with that, she handed him a small bottle of Humboldt Snow #7, a spare, with a newly crocheted atomizer, a little pump—this one dime-store blue with a mint-green tassel.

Smiling sheepishly at Ms. Demeanor she said, "Perfume."

"Perfume? For a boy? How nice." The social worker dripped disdain all over the gift.

"It's so I can remember her," Conrad defended his friend, accepting a gift that even he found an odd choice from the person who bought him comic books and toy guns.

"Exactly," Merry Berry addressed Demeanor. "If he gets lonely. In the night. Spritz. Spritz, Conrad dear. Remember that."

"I want Skipper back," Conrad's voice cracked.

A water-slide of fat tears rolled off his lashes when he realized he would be spending another night among strangers who did not love him. Merry Berry was at a loss.

"This is why we don't encourage visits," Ms. Demeanor put in, taking Conrad by the hand.

Her cold hand gripping his, Conrad shivered and immediately stopped crying. Freshly awakened to the knowledge that his tears gave Ms. Demeanor power, he stood a little taller; he pulled his hand free and decided to take his power back. What he said was this:

"Sister Merry Berry, you should have seen the cassowary. He jumped on Ms. Demeanor's car. Crunch!" Big bold comic book letters banged against the wall in a jagged balloon.

Power shift.

"The cassowary did that?" Merry Berry brightened.

"Horrid bird!" The memory made Ms. Demeanor smaller.

"He's a beautiful bird," Conrad insisted.

"A monster. The thing dented my hood with those gruesome claws. Then the creature left a deep, three-foot-long gash. Somebody's going to pay for that!"

Conrad wiped the social worker's energy field from the room. Then he looked up at Sister Merry Berry with a confident smile and said, "I'm going to be okay."

As soon as he said the words, he knew they were true. And so did his friend.

Afterwards, Sister Merry Berry would go over that moment and could not fathom why she said it. The words just slipped from her lips.

"See you on the moon, Conrad."

In the parking lot, Sister Merry Berry found Ms. Demeanor's Oldsmobile and committed another first. Her first visit to the city was brimful of firsts. Rooting around in her satchel, she found the bottle of blue nail polish. Who knew that vandalism could be so satisfying? She dripped a nice glopping blessing of glittery blue over the gouge on the hood of the black Oldsmobile. And for the finishing touch, she squeegeed the bottle into the last glop—her signature, rapidly drying in the hot sun. Hard as nails.

Sister Merry Berry drove Jah Bliss back to the hospital, making one more gelato pit stop. I am such a bliss bunny, she thought as she steered down the city street. The last bite of yellow-cake-batter gelato was melting on her tongue, when she spotted a vagrant shape. She slammed on her brakes and her sweet reverie went skidding off the map, lost in the weeds. She'd have to get back to her bliss another time.

An unmistakable tent of long white hair was strolling down the sidewalk in a hospital gown. Merry Berry hopped out, waving enthusiastically at Mother Mary Extraordinary.

"Care for a ride?" she invited, swinging open the passenger door. "Oh, please, make this easy," she begged for roadside assistance from any celestial first-aiders that might be hanging about the neighborhood. Apparently, she was heard.

"Lovely vehicle. A Cadillac, how cush," said Extraordinary, slipping inside.

"Jah Bliss," Merry Berry smiled.

"Wipe that off your mouth."

"Jah Bliss? The gelato? What?"

"You know what."

"Oh. That." Merry Berry glowed. She delicately lifted the kiss from her lips, rolled it into a tiny ball and placed it in the dimple on her chin, giving it a few gentle pats. She planned on keeping that kiss. She explained to Mother Mary, "Jah is a rich man. He won't be missing one kiss."

"Point taken," Mother Mary replied affably. "Wouldn't Sister Josephus be just green with envy if she saw you tooling about in this streamlined, classic beauty?" Mother Mary Extraordinary was remembering their dear friend, now buried in the field under the Fairlane.

"Mother Mary, do you know—are you aware that you had a heart attack?" Merry Berry ventured.

"What? Do I look like a fool?"

"You look heavenly, actually, in your gown and white hair and paper slippers. But I think we should take you back to the hospital."

"*We* absolutely should not. Let me tell you something about death."

"What?"

"It's over-rated, that's what. It doesn't last, leastwise not nearly long enough. No one ever gets a decent rest. If you think that our dearly departed Sister Josephus is still resting peacefully under her Fairlane, think again. The last time I sat in the Fairlane and attempted to commune with her spirit, she was nowhere in the vicinity."

"Perhaps her spirit has ventured on into a new life," Mary Berry condoled.

"At least she managed to get under the ground for a few winks. My death was attenuated in the extreme. Seconds, a minute at most. I heard the death army marching in my heart. Ra-ta-tat, ra-ta-tat. Then, what do you suppose?"

Extraordinary paused for dramatic effect. "O, siren song, I was carried off at a reckless speed. Medics! Pins and needles in my arms, machines pumping my breath, machines pumping my heart."

"We should check you back in," said Merry Berry, pulling up to the emergency entrance.

"Can't you read the sign? Emergency. It's time to emerge, Sister." Mother Mary Extraordinary lifted her arm, preparing to give herself a little spritz from an all-too-familiar bottle.

"What's that you've got there?" Merry Berry trilled, remembering with an alarmed clarity that she'd left that very bottle on Mother Mary's bedside stand in the recovery room in a moment of distraction. She had been stuck on the eternal hamster wheel of Hamlet's dilemma, to spritz or not to spritz. Somehow the hamster had escaped the wheel in Merry Berry's absence. "O my Goddess, you spritzed! Give that here. Please. It's mine."

"No, it most certainly is not. I'd recognize the scent of my goat-got prayers anywhere, although there are unfamiliar hints of violet and pencil shavings."

"I can't think what—" Merry Berry trailed off, thinking of the Chateau Latour.

"In any case, it was given to me by a two-headed nurse," Extraordinary continued. "Damn drugs, I thought, blurring my vision. But no, she really had two heads. And she was

Vietnamese. Both of her, dressed in a pink habit, with a red cross emblazoned on the wimple."

"The spiritual twins! You've had a visitation. From the other side. Didn't you recognize them? It must have been the Mary Tuees. Had to have been. I'm so proud of you. You used to have visitations at the drop of a prayer bead. Now, look at you. Back on your game. The Sisters Mary Tuee. Oh, I miss them so."

"Twee, twee, tweedle-dee-dee," Mother Mary sang, nonsensically.

The twins had been among Merry Berry's closest friends; that is, before the prayer eaters got them. What could this metaphysical twist possibly mean? The deeply missed Sisters Mary Tuee were conjoined twins, abandoned at birth, and slipped through the foundling door by a homeless person who had found them in a dumpster.

The Mary Tuees flourished under the care of the Sisters, who eventually found adoptive parents them. By the time their new parents sought medical advice, the girls were old enough to make their wishes known and chose to remain together. They returned to the circle of Marys in their early teens.

Back in the days when the garden flourished, the Sisters Mary Tuee had been quite twee, from their China tea cups of chamomile tea to their Beatrice Potter garden hats, not to mention their charming ink drawings, replete with bunnies and cats and watering cans.

"I heard my name being repeated," Extraordinary interrupted Merry Berry's nostalgic reverie. "At first it sounded like my name was caught in an echo chamber—Mary

Extraordinary, Mary Extraordinary—but instead of fading out, the volume increased until I opened my eyes and saw the smiling faces of the two-headed nurse. She picked up the perfume bottle and spritzed the air. O happy spritz!"

"How did you get out of the hospital?"

"I simply decided it was time. Closing time. I got up and out of the bed. I pulled out the plugs on those infernal, beeping hospital machines. When I held that bundle of electricity aloft, I felt like the Statue of Liberty, and I prepared myself to fall off the pedestal. Now I am dead, I thought. And that is precisely when I knew with a certainty I was not. Dead. Something had thrown me into reverse. In truth, I feel quite spry."

"What happened to the nurse? With the two heads?"

"What nurse? It was the Sisters Mary Tuee. The spiritual twins. You said so yourself," Extraordinary exclaimed, clearly enjoying herself. "I was spritzed by spirits."

Sitting in the passenger seat of the Cadillac Eldorado Biarritz, Mother Mary Extraordinary slipped back and forth between uncanny clarity and happy confusion.

Sitting behind the wheel, still parked outside the hospital emergency entrance, the younger nun was stuck pulling petals off an existential daisy—to the hospital or to the convent? The petals of indecision piled up on her lap.

Finally, reason forced her to admit that there was no getting the bottle away from Extraordinary, nor was there any way to get the prayer genies back inside the bottle.

Merry Berry looked over at Mary Extraordinary.

"Drive on, Sister!" Her superior ordered.

"Jah Bliss," said Merry Berry throwing the Cadillac into reverse. In her mind she heard Tremont say, "Jah is the driva, Dawta."

Orphaned at birth, it gave Merry Berry a shiver of illicit pleasure to be called daughter by a man she had kissed. She let herself float in the bliss, and she experienced the strangest sensation—almost as if Jah were steering the Biarritz.

————

WHEN SISTER MERRY BERRY pulled into the convent drive, a disconsolate cassowary immediately perked up. What happy bleats greeted her return. Mother Mary Extraordinary was soon in the capable hands of Sister Subordinary, and Merry Berry was able to give her full attention to the grateful cassowary.

"Oh, dear bird, what an adventure I've had. And what absolutely lovely scars you left on Ms. Demeanor's car."

The cassowary puffed up, and Merry Berry gave him a closer look. It was not as if he understood the compliment. He may have. But that wasn't it. They were both clearly happy and relieved to see each other again. But there was something more. Something that hadn't been there before.

Merry Berry had the gift of sight. She brought the bird into sharper focus. Could it be that devotion had catalyzed a subliminal change? Clearly something was disturbing the finer filaments of a certain strand of DNA in the cassowary's brain.

How something as ginormous as love could penetrate something so diaphanous and impossibly small as a subatomic particle was perhaps no mystery at all. The body is a cosmic listening post, floating in an ocean of superluminal frequencies.

The etherics call it stardust brain, when the walls of the DNA molecules break up under the constant bombardment of photonic love.

Oh, Holy, Holy, Holy Higgs Boson. Oh, miraculous photinos, accelerating the pulse of billions of galaxies while one bird on one tiny planet experiences the look of love. Merry Berry looked again. Yes, there was something new. Something trying to get free.

Souls exhibit a tendency to migrate in clusters from one lifetime to the next. Each cluster holds its own unique assembly of sentient beings, sometimes including blood-born relations, sometimes not. A soul-cluster might include the grocer, the neighbor two doors down, your kindergarten teacher, the used-car salesman, the person standing next to you in the check-out line, the security guard, the members of your carpool or convent, a deity on the lam, the child that breaks your window, the thief that steals your laptop, the surgeon that places the stent in your left coronary artery, the family that adopts you, the puppy you adopt, the ersatz families of the heart.

These soul-clusters are like migrating astral wheels and embrace a diverse array of connections—from the merely incidental to the great loves who ignite the passions that free us and the very enemies who shape the angers that limit us.

The beautiful brother and ancient enemy that had shaped the cassowary's anger was currently sampling a spectacular vintage Bordeaux in the convent wine cellar. Both angel and cassowary would have been astounded to discover their proximity to one another, how geographically close each was to the primordial sibling who dealt those first fetal kicks, in the great long ago, when the two of them floated belly to belly in the womb of creation. The bird was currently at the foot of Sister Merry Berry's bed, napping. Just two floors separated the soul-cognates, two floors and eons of transmigrations, encryptions, redacted texts, evolutions and devolutions.

There are approximately two-hundred souls in each cluster, the size of a healthy tribe according to anthropologists, the number of faces it is possible to remember and recognize according to neuro-scientists and cognition experts. Some, like Merry Berry, are constantly turning the key in that cognition and recognizing familiars. Hers was a wandering spirit. Over the eons, she had transmigrated among more than a few illustrious groupings. Tonight, she would revisit one of her all-time favorite soul-cognates, from the glory days when she rolled with the divinities.

———

ONCE SISTER SUBORDINARY and Sister Merry Berry settled Mother in for a much-needed rest, they caught each other up on all their recent beings and doings. Merry Berry left a certain kiss out of her story, but allowed herself the pleasure of scandalizing Mary Subordinary with the vandalism of Ms. Demeanor's car.

Mary Subordinary gave Merry Berry a satisfying double take, "You did what?"

Subordinary admired the image of the blue bottle of nail polish stuck on the Oldsmobile, tucked it away, and then asked about Extraordinary's medications.

Merry Berry explained that Mother Mary checked her own self out, so they had no prescriptions to fill. Besides, she had never really been checked in. Officially, that is.

Like Conrad, Mary Extraordinary had no papers, no thumb print, no social security number, was in fact an illegal of a different ontological order. Merry Berry had artfully dodged plenty of questions in the hospital. If anyone from the hospital showed up at the convent, they'd best claim Mary Extraordinary never made it home.

"We could be appalled, you know. Out of our minds with grief and indignation. What? You've lost her? It's an outrage!" Merry Berry happily elaborated on this possible charade.

"But what about the medications? When I spoke to her nurse on the telephone about aftercare, I was told that quite a laundry list of medications was necessary after a cardiac event such as hers."

"That is a problem. She doesn't even really have a name, does she? In the ambulance, I was completely rattled when they asked for her name. I said her name was Jane Greystoke."

"Oh," Subordinary was at a loss.

They discussed a tentative plan for Conrad's rescue and agreed that the plan needed tweaking. They'd sleep on it. Sister Subordinary offered to sit with Mother Mary Extraordinary through the night, remarking that Sister Merry Berry looked like she needed a good rest.

"Exhausted yes, bless me. First the wine cellar, then off to bed."

Merry Berry made her way down the cellar stairs, calling, "Halloo, anyone about? Halloo. Oh, goody. I was hoping I'd find you here."

He offered her a glass of Bordeaux. She accepted. They sat on the bottom step, and reminisced like the old friends they were. Then they conspired about possible futures and possible favors.

Conviviality was enhanced by the excellent selection of wines. At one point, after they uncorked the second Bordeaux, Merry Berry explained that she needed some falsified prescriptions for heart medications and a driver's license.

The Angel of Light wasn't particularly sympathetic—that sentiment was still outside his range—but he was willing and more than able. Invariably, he enjoyed showing off his brilliance. Creating Earth forgeries would be a snap. A false driver's license for a fictional Jane Greystoke—he could do that.

The illuminato suggested that Merry Berry take on the pseudonym. The scripts would be in Merry Berry's assumed name with her picture on the license. Leave it to him, he'd figure out what meds and what doses. No problem.

"Easy peasy, huh?" Sister Merry Berry paused. "Now for the tough one—Conrad."

"Who am I?" he scoffed at the notion of a tough one.

"The Angel of Light."

He raised his glass, "At your service, ad infinitum."

"I knew you'd come shining through. Here," she handed over Skipper, "give this to Conrad, so he knows he can trust you."

"Perhaps you can drive the get-away car," Lucifer suggested.

"Oh, I'd love that!"

# PSYCHIATRIC SOLECISMS

THE SEVEN-YEAR-OLD Conrad Eppler rapidly gained a reputation in psychiatric circles as an interesting case. Diagnosticians of the mind habitually redraw the lines between the visionary, the highly imaginative, and the psychiatrically challenged. These modern-day epistemologists are universally enamored of genius and its measurements. Conrad's I.Q., however, remained speculative.

Although his linguistic skills were nonpareil, his education was most remarkable in its odd lacunae. There were sudden drop-offs where he proved clueless. A concept like "baseball diamond" left him baffled. A Pythagorean theorem kept him happily engaged for hours. He was seven going on seventy, with vast tracts of contemporary culture missing from the map of his known world. He was a paragon precariously balanced on the edge of a parallel reality.

This child would have to be carefully managed and catalogued. And, Ms. Demeanor insisted, placed in a foster home with scrupulously vetted caretakers. Margaret Demeanor occasionally admitted to her journal that she might be the only person on the planet qualified to raise such a boy.

Supposedly, the scores on the various tests he had taken were a private matter, but because the results were extreme, the files developed extreme leaks. Some enterprising fifteen-year-old even put up a Wiki page that described a phenomenon called the Eppler Effect. It had to do with the power of rumor based on nothing. Rumor ex nihilo. Or as became apparent in Conrad's case, based on the ephemera of rumored test scores.

One blogger wrote that, if there were not a Conrad Eppler, necessity would invent him. The world could not go without. One way or another, the magical-boy archetype would manifest, be he a fact or a fiction. The blogger was riffing on Voltaire's claim that if God did not exist, ethics would require his invention. A *her* was not a consideration for the French Enlightenment philosophe, the blogger parenthesized. A twinge of embarrassed misogyny caused the blogger to lift his fingers from the keyboard. He wondered briefly if magical girls were also a necessity; then he shrugged off the notion and wrote on.

Another Wikipedian pointed out that the Eppler Effect was cousin to Kant's claim that ethical agents in the act of willing the best possible world for all persons would eventually create an Eppler. The boy quickly became a categorical imperative, willed into existence by the collective fiat of logical do-gooders and positivist tweeters. The boy also became the subject in several popular chat rooms. Some of them decidedly unsavory.

Soon enough, a passel of fanfiction key-boarders were chomping at the bit of creation, ready to race to the occasion. One book, titled *The Examination of Conrad Eppler*, was already listed on Amazon. Although the book remained unwritten, preorders were racking up record numbers, giving a new twist to the notion of speculative fiction, or in this case— speculative faction. The anonymous author and infamous hacker claimed that her Conrad existed firmly in the canonical universe of the actual, a real person and a bona fide deity, with a known address where he was being kept against his will and probed.

Inevitably, word of Conrad Eppler's growing popularity made it up the hill to the Quoborium. Finally, the Cardinals had something more than a rumor; they had an address. Conrad was being kept in residence at the Department of Child Protective Services.

Several Cardinals, among them Cardinal Delacroix, were intent on making their own examinations. The existence of a living deity—speculative or otherwise—outside the auspices of The Great Church would be an intolerable theological embarrassment. What good was a supposedly *universal* church if a there was a living God on the loose who did not belong?

In his short stay at the state facility, Conrad had been examined by a host of celebrity physicians. The current examining doctor, a pro bono consultant with a Yale pedigree, was stylishly decked out in a loose-fitting, striped Dolce & Gabanna lounge suit, bare ankled and wearing white Gucci loafers. There was no way the state could afford the hourly fee required to cover this overly branded analyst. With his meticulously groomed blond ponytail and his designer eyewear, he looked every inch the couch doctor to the stars. No doubt there was a Julian Schnabel with puffy clouds in his lobby and a Motherwell inkblot painting hanging on his living room wall.

Seeing no Eames leather-clad chair, the A-list shrink reluctantly sat his beautifully tailored ass on the chipped metal folding chair provided by the state. Alternately, he shifted his attention between Conrad and the provisional diagnosis on the plexiglass clipboard he held in one manicured hand.

"So, you're the new kid on the chopping block?"

The auspicious interrogation began. The casual pun, meant to ingratiate, missed its mark. The boy frowned. A green glint flashed from the doctor's eye.

"Conrad Eppler?"

"Yes, that's me," Conrad composed himself.

"What's it like being institutionalized? Life in the convent must have been a paradise compared to this." He read from the official document. "Ward of the state. That's an unqualified comedown—from paradise to prisoner. Unless?"

"Unless what?" questioned the wary child.

"Just looking over Dr. Menger's notes here. He seems to think you were abused by the Sisters."

The psychiatrist waited.

"I wasn't ever abused. Except for one time, there was this Cardinal with a claw who tried to kidnap me."

"A claw? Interesting. Dr. Menger mentions that you sometimes fail to distinguish between illusion and reality. Care to comment?"

Conrad was aware that he was being tested, invited to elaborate on the magical realms, but he wasn't interested in arguing for his world.

"Where is Dr. Menger?" Conrad asked his own question instead.

"He stepped out to take the air. This is quite a rap sheet you've got here. Hallucinations, both visual and auditory. Preliminary diagnosis: schizophrenia. Possibly bi-polar. Precocity combined with emotional lability. What do you think about all that?"

"It just means I act like a kid and that I'm smart and sometimes I cry."

The doctor nodded.

"Still, if persons were to take Menger's word for it, your personal prospects might take a sharp turn for the worst."

"What is the worst?" Conrad was on the alert.

"Listen to this: therapeutic anti-psychotic drugs strongly advised. Ever hear of Thorazine?"

"No."

"Promise me something, kid."

"What?"

"Don't do drugs."

"I know who you are."

Conrad might have guessed the identity of his interlocutor sooner, but for the impeccable artistry of the disguise. In the next moment, a similarly dressed individual slipped into the room from a side door with the news that someone was all tied up, then immediately corrected himself when he saw Conrad.

"Tied up in traffic," the minion improvised.

In a smooth segue, the designer Doctor introduced his colleague as Dr. D. Witt and himself as Dr. D'Angelo D. Light. Conrad smiled. Was this the rescue? They were pretty funny, going through all these dissembling machinations.

Kilowatt took out his ratty old notebook right on cue. With a stubby pencil poised at the ready, he asked Luce, "How do you spell D'Angelo?"

Conrad jumped in, "Capital D-a-n, capital J-e-double-l-o. I know you, Dan Jello."

"No, you don't," Lucifer gave Conrad a warning look. It seemed to say that the performance was not entirely for Conrad, leaving the boy uncertain how to play the scene out until Luce surprised him and pulled Skipper out of the nowhere. Then the angel in the striped lounge suit flipped the monkey high into the air. An elated Conrad caught his furry friend and hugged him close.

Safe! Or safe enough. For now. If only he could find a way to get to the trusty woods, so Skipper could recharge.

"Sister Merry Berry asked me to give you the monkey as a sign of my good intentions. Now, I want you to tell me about your visions. Have you seen any gem-toned angelettes lately?" Luce asked, getting down to business.

"No, they don't visit me anymore. I lost contact when you blew up my garden. Can you please get me out of here? You owe me one."

"Tell me about the emerald angel. Aletheia? Has she been around?"

"No, and she doesn't have wings anymore. She isn't an angel. She's transitioning," Conrad offered cautiously.

"Mind telling me how you know that?"

"I saw it in a dream vision."

"Okaaaay." Luce waited. He was so close. He didn't want Conrad to shy away from the next crucial disclosure. "So where is Aletheia? The green one?"

Skipper's voice urged Conrad, "*Tell him.*"

"She's on her way to the moon," Conrad hedged then clarified, "the other moon."

"What other moon? Your planet's only got one, kid."

Luce wondered why Conrad was being cagey.

Conrad looked Lucifer in the eye, "You better be a good guy."

"I brought you the monkey."

"You ever heard of Sister Moon?"

"No." Luce was taken aback. Was it possible that the Earthworm had higher connections than he did?

"The Earth has two moons," Conrad said. "Aletheia hasn't arrived on Sister Moon yet. Her blue rocket is still headed for Virgo. The Oracle said that Aletheia's transport would make a stopover in Virgo and pick up two Thrones. Blue angels," Conrad added.

"I know what a Throne is, Eppler."

Kilowatt was scribbling notes and reassessing the Earthworm. He noted that Luce had gone uncharacteristically quiet.

"Eppler, when you "see" this Sister Moon, are you sleeping or are you awake?"

"Awake. I spritz Sister Merry Berry's perfume and windows to other worlds fly open."

"Perfume? I'd like to try some."

"Sorry, Mister Doctor D'Angelo D. Light," Conrad shrugged, "Ms. Demeanor took the bottle. Are you going to help me get out of here or not?"

"Keep your voice down," Luce cautioned. "I've got a plan. It's a good plan."

"Ms. Demeanor has papers—did you know that? So even if you get me back to the convent, she can show up with her papcrs ," Conrad trailed off

"Papers," Luce scoffed. "Trust me, I can take care of papers."

"What's my cover story?" Conrad pressed.

"How about I tell Ms. Demeanor that I'm DEA, and that you work for us?" Lucifer offered, barely able to suppress a grin.

"What's DEA?" Conrad wanted to know.

"Drug Enforcement Agency," the Angel of Light informed the boy.

"Can I have a badge?" Conrad brightened.

"Why not? Consider yourself deputized," Luce said, handing Conrad a beautiful gold-embossed badge that he plucked effortlessly out of the nowhere. The Angel of Light had come to believe that it was in his best interest to keep this powerful child on his side.

"Do I have any special powers?" Conrad slipped the badge in his pocket.

"I think that's pretty obvious, kid. What? You want a cape? A claw?"

"No, I guess not. Thanks for the badge."

"Kilowatt, get the kid some decent clothes. He dresses like a schmuck. If you're going to represent, Eppler, you've got to look sharp."

"Represent what?

"You tell me." Lucifer gave the boy an appraising look.

There was a rapping at the office door.

"Conrad, listen up. Your pal, Sister Merry Berry? She's parked down the block in a fancy car, all bright and shiny, waiting to take you and the furball back to the convent." Luce shifted his attention to the self-appointed scribe, "Kilowatt, make sure the Earthworm makes it home. Safe and sound. Got that, Kilo?"

More knocking.

"Now move it, Eppler."

"You got it, Boss." Conrad gave the Angel of Light a handsome salute, and then the newly deputized agent turned to Kilowatt, "Kilo, when we get back to the convent, I'm going to call in the big, big favor."

"Does that mean I get the Mattel?"

Conrad nodded yes, and Kilo was a kid in high cotton candy.

"Gimme a fist bump," the lowly angel beamed.

The knocking grew louder, insistent. They could hear Ms. Demeanor behind the door calling for Dr. Menger. And then—a telltale rattle of keys.

"Get out," commanded Lucifer.

Kilo and Conrad scooted out the back door.

———

Seconds Later Ms. Demeanor entered and froze in her tracks. Then she opened that luscious red mouth and screamed, giving Luce a nice view of her palatine uvula. He did not return the favor. Instead he flashed his mesmerizing smile.

"Who are you?" she demanded.

"Doctor D'Angelo D. Light," more smile, pouring it on, heating it up.

"Where is Dr. Menger? Where is the boy? What is going on in here?" Her words were rote, in pointed opposition to what she was rigorously trying not to feel. The throaty hush in her vocalizations told Lucifer another, more tantalizing story.

"Has anyone ever told you—?" He searched for a compliment. "You have the most beautiful—." The Angel of

Light found himself at a loss for words. Flirting was not his métier.

"The most beautiful what?" Margaret Demeanor folded her arms, her pointed red fingernails sequentially tap, tap, tapping their lusty impatience.

"Scream." The smile grew warmer.

"Scream? I do?" The ice grew thinner.

She kept melting, he kept talking, "The most sensuous, melodious—"

"—scream," she finished. Margaret Demeanor was a puddle.

Luce picked up the rhythm. "Imagine my surprise. I come by to see my old friend, Dr. Menger, and in walks this incredible dream with the beautiful scream."

Ms. Demeanor pulled a hair pin out and gave her head a shake. Her tight bun unraveled in an unsightly clump. She whipped off her pointy-framed eye-glasses. Now she was blind, as well as melted. Blinking furiously under the florescent lighting, her arms extended, she felt her way towards Luce, who backed up a step trying to think his way out of the rapidly-evolving scene. Her glossy red lips were puckered for the big starburst smooch. He thought about it, but he couldn't make himself go there. Her lips hung in the indeterminate pause.

"Command me," she begged. "Shall I scream again?"

And without waiting for an answer, she screamed. Luce screamed. The receptionist poked her head in the door and she screamed.

"Put your glasses back on. Please," enjoined Ms. Demeanor's contrite, erstwhile suitor.

Luce recomposed himself. And that's when she slapped him.

"Thanks, I needed that," he said agreeably.

"Should I call the police?" asked a perplexed receptionist.

"No," said Demeanor and Luce simultaneously.

"We can handle this. Please, close the door," she added.

The receptionist shot her a worried look, but complied. As soon as the door clicked shut, Margaret Demeanor went on the attack.

"Why you son of a snit, who in the hell do you think you are?"

"Don't be so upset. Your virginity is still intact."

"How dare you presume?"

He cut her off, flipping open his impressive holographic wallet, showing off an instantly modified badge, "Commander D'Angelo Übermench. Special Forces, Undercover Drug Investigator."

"I'll have you know that we are a state-licensed institution, and Dr. Menger is a state-licensed psychiatrist, and he is licensed to dispense drugs."

"I'll get to Dr. Menger in a minute. It's the convent we're investigating."

"I knew it! That perfume she gave the boy. It's a hallucinogen. I locked it in the desk drawer." She picked up her keys and unlocked her desk. "Here. Take it."

"Did you try it?" Luce queried, giving the air a spritz.

She jumped back and pinched her nose between two red-lacquered finger nails.

"Quite by accident." With her nostrils pinched tight, she sounded like a cartoon character on helium.

"It gave me terrifying nightmares," she confided. "I was being chased by a two-headed Asian nun in a pink habit. Another nun came after me with a gigantic stethoscope. I could hear a heartbeat. It sounded like a sonic boom. I'm still having flashbacks."

D'Angelo Übermench slipped the bottle in his pocket and made sympathetic noises. She's lonely. Where did that thought come from? A sharp pang of empathy opened a window for him, his first brush with human feeling. The perfume, he surmised. It gave Conrad visions, it gave Margaret Demeanor nightmares and it gave him—what? A glimpse into the human heart, into longing and loneliness.

Brushing the unsettling sensations aside, Luce quickly crowded Margaret Demeanor with a distraction of drug intelligence: how the epidemic abuse of prescriptive drugs was overtaken by a sudden uptick in a newer generation of designer drugs—now cleverly disguised as boutique perfumes.

Oh, the sweet power of invention. Lucifer was having fun. He pointed out to the social worker that in her profession, she needed to be on the lookout for religious orders—nuns breaking bad, fronting for drug operations.

"Always check out the kitchens," he advised the enthralled Ms. Demeanor.

A perpetual outsider, she was inordinately pleased to be privy to insider information. She should have taken that job with Homeland Security, she scolded herself. A quick inward survey told her she would be a much happier woman if she were tracking terrorists. She never was that into children.

The self-styled übermench explained to the intrigued social worker that Conrad Eppler was a plant. Working undercover, the boy was the centerpiece of a clandestine investigation and the source of a virtual mudslide of information.

"When you pulled the kid out of the convent, there went the operation."

"But the poor boy, he's sick. And his upbringing—calling it unorthodox would be a kindness."

"Kindness is not a bad thing," Luce stopped and examined the anomalous thought. The word *kindness* left an unfamiliar but not unpleasant taste on his tongue.

"The boy was never even allowed to play with another child," Ms. Demeanor continued to build her case. "He compensates by filling his world with imaginary friends."

"He does that, yes. It is a pretense, a cover. He is a very imaginative kid. Gifted."

"I've noticed."

"Exactly. May I confide in you, Margaret Demeanor? Conrad Eppler is a professionally trained secret agent. He attended a special school, where we train super-smart orphaned youth. He's a lot older than he looks," said the diabolically gifted liar.

"Well, he certainly fooled Dr. Menger, not to mention a host of other notables."

Ms. Demeanor could barely contain her delight when Commander Übermench told her that Dr. Menger was tied up in the supply closet. But she did contain it. She was expert at capping her desires.

"Dr. Menger is tied up?" The red lips quivered.

Her flushed cheeks told the angel everything he needed to know. Luce surprised himself, discovered that he wouldn't mind helping her out. It would cost him nothing to toss a little encouragement her way. Pragmatically speaking, being nice would work out well for him. Access to the Department's computer would make his job easier. There were certain files that needed deleting and court orders that needed to be vanished. The illustrious illuminato was aware that Conrad had already gone viral. The important thing was to get the real Conrad off the radar, erase him from the state records. Let the fictional Conrad, the rumor ex nihilo, live on.

The Angel of Light heard a replay of Conrad's admonishment: "You better be a good guy."

Luce took a deep breath, "Today could very well be Independence Day for Ms. Margaret Demeanor. Time to refresh your inalienable rights, Margaret, and pursue some happiness. Make it a good day for you and Dr. Menger."

"Commander Übermench, are you suggesting—?" she snickered.

"Call me D'Angelo."

"D'Angelo, are you suggesting I seduce Dr. Menger with my beautiful scream?"

"No. Don't scream." He gave it a moment's thought, "How about this? Get naked and act nice."

"Nice?"

"It's damn good advice," he congratulated himself. Luce took a quick glance into his own labyrinthine mind and experienced a mild sensation. A soft illumination of "nice" lifted some shadows in an unexamined corner of his dusty stack of lives.

"Trust me, I know whereof I speak. Underneath that dress, there's a woman who can compete with the best."

"D'Angelo Übermench, you see right through me. I must admit, it is rather pleasant, being seen. Thank you, for your wonderful advice."

"If you have no objections, I'd like to use your office for a minute. I need to reclassify the Eppler files."

"Of course. Take your time. Thank you, D'Angelo Übermench. It's been enlightening."

"Mutually." Lucifer watched her walk out, his hand in his pocket holding the bottle of prayer juice, contemplating the vicissitudes of nice.

———

WHEN KILO AND CONRAD scooted out the back door, they headed down Bayshore Drive until they caught sight of Sister Merry Berry's newly waxed Cadillac, gleaming in the sunlight.

A bit anxious waiting for Conrad, Merry Berry had given herself a spritz or two and turned up the volume on the Bob Marley disc. She was wearing her new ear buds, and Bob was jamming in the name of the Lord. When Marley sang the "Holy Mount Zion" chorus with its big hosanna finish heralding Jah, "Who siteth on Mount Zion, Holy Mount Zion," Merry Berry heard the Spanish word for apple—manzana—"Who siteth on Manzana, Holy Manzana."

She saw the Holy-Holy-Holy-on-the-Highest Red Delicious and pictured a resplendent Jah sitting on a gigantic apple, orbiting the sun. Jah was busy crocheting an oversize beret, the yarn spinning out in great multi-colored spirals. He did not notice an African-American Snow White, her dreads as dark as ebony, her soul as white as snow, her blue cape flying behind her, her arms extended like a comic book super-heroine, zipping across the panels of another reality. She circled the apple in happy loops, until she was close enough to take a bite. The missing bite threw the apple-sitter off balance. Jah went tumbling. And a very Merry Snow White came to his rescue.

Holy Manzana.

Coming out of her holy hallucination, Sister Merry Berry spotted Kilo and Conrad coming up the sidewalk, and for a split second the world was perfect. Then the perfect world slid sideways, thrown off balance by a strange commotion. She plucked out her ear buds and watched in stunned disbelief as Kilo and Conrad were swallowed by a flurry of red-robed Cardinals. Merry Berry gunned her engine and raced in the direction of the swirling patch of malevolent red.

Conrad was lifted above the melee and quickly pushed into the backseat of a waiting car, a nondescript grey sedan with discrete little Avesticum flags above the headlamps. The sedan accelerated, with Merry Berry in hot pursuit. She zipped past the red flock of curbside abettors, who were being soundly thrashed by a furious Kilo, birettas and feathers flying.

There would be black eyes and broken bones, but none of these injuries delivered by the usually peaceable Angel Kilowatt gave him any satisfaction.

Conrad was gone.

A rattled Kilo slunk off to recover from the brawl.

———

RUNNING RED LIGHTS, squealing on two tires in a round-a-about, and then gunning onto the freeway, it quickly became clear to Merry Berry that the sedan was headed for Exit 256 and the one-lane switchback that climbed the hill to the Sanctum Avesticum Quoborium. Fog was rolling in, but no matter. This road had only one destination, and Merry Berry had only one objective.

Aware that he was being tailed by a flashy pink Biarritz, the driver dialed a private number at the Quoborium. Delacroix picked up and made a few quick calculations. Seconds later, Brother Umbruco took a call from Delacroix. As soon as the Avesticum sedan ferrying Conrad was safely past the lookout at Martyr Maker Point, two black-hooded figures went to work.

Brother Umbruco emptied a twenty-five-gallon tank of water that pooled dangerously on the pavement at the hairpin turn. Numerous wooden crosses lined the hundred-and-eighty-degree curve. The steep embankment was a deadly one-mile drop. A graveyard of crushed vehicles lay scattered below, silent testaments to the unlucky.

Umbruco's cohort, Brother Stelvio, emerged from the woods and began spraying liquid nitrogen on the puddled water, creating an instantaneous and deadly ice slick. The hurried Stelvio slipped and righted himself just in time to fold into the shadows and turn on the projector.

Approaching the switchback, Merry Berry saw a magnificent white holographic stag emerge from the mist. He stood stock still in the icy road; his dark eyes blinked once.

Merry Berry's eyes went wide. She hit the brakes and pulled sharply on the steering wheel. Missing the stag, Sister Merry Berry entered the vault of heaven.

The wheels of the 1959 pink Eldorado Biarritz slipped the surly bonds of Earth, and the vehicle was miraculously sky-borne. Merry Berry pressed the accelerator when she found herself on that metaphysical mix-master, the super-illuminated multilane highway to the celestial unknown.

Joni Mitchell's angelic vibrato filled the cab, "We are star dust. We are golden. And we've got to get ourselves back to the garden." The bliss bunny was on her way, flying above the clouds, not certain of her destination, but loving the speed of her transportation.

So much beautiful life flashed across Merry Berry's mind. Moving swiftly backwards towards her beginnings, she had a memory that couldn't possibly be hers. She saw a teenage girl kneeling in the grass. The young mother was wrapping a baby— a chubby, doe-eyed Merry Berry—in a Princess Barbie blanket. Merry Berry watched her mother slide the swaddled infant through the foundling door. She perked up when she heard her name spoken. And for the first time, she knew that once upon a time she had had a name—Savannah.

She heard the foundling bell. She saw her mother lingering at the edge of the woods, holding onto a branch, quietly grieving.

Then the vision jumped, and Merry Berry was propelled into the scene. She was running across the lawn in her orange florescent tennis shoes, her dreadlocks flying as she tried to catch up to a mother decades younger than herself.

There was the matter of a hug that she'd been waiting for all her life. And there was her mother—the perfect age to receive the blessing that would absolve her and make her young life possible after abandoning her infant daughter at the foundling door.

Merry Berry had always been running towards this girl, had always been saving this one hug for her young mother. She realized how the hug had been a heavy burden to haul through a life, but a burden she could never put down.

In her current etheric state, she knew the absolute visceral reality of the moment, skin on skin. Its paradoxical crossing of time-lines did not diminish the hug. Instead, the juxtaposition gave a luster of plenary grace to a scene viewed at a distance and experienced up close and personal in a pluperfect present.

Merry Berry sailed home on that hug.

Although, the Biarritz would have its crash landing, the big pink would never be discovered among the other mechanical ruins at the foot of Martyr Maker Point.

Merry Berry had miles to go before she slept.

———

A CEREMONIAL PARTY of Cardinals waited for Conrad at the top of the hill. The Munificentissimus Divine Mallard of All Mysteries, His Holiness, Hierophant of The Great Church, the former Matsuki Makindo, sat under a hastily erected, gold-trimmed awning, awaiting the arrival of the prophesied Avatar.

The sedan pulled up. The driver hopped out and held open the back door. A small boy holding a stuffed white monkey emerged from the dark interior. Wearing cargo shorts and a homemade tee shirt stained with pink bubblegum gelato, Conrad stood in a patch of sunlight.

The Cardinals shifted. Delacroix bit the inside of his cheek. Somehow the Divine Duck had outwitted him.

The Munificentissimus Divine Mallard of All Mysteries stood and offered his hand. Without hesitation, the boy came forward and slipped his hand into the hand of the old man. The two entered the palace as if the scene had been choreographed according to a secret script known only to themselves.

# SANCTUM AVESTICUM
# QUOBORIUM

ALTHOUGH THE DIVINE MALLARD of All Mysteries was a devoted sleeper and to all appearances an indifferent leader, his was an impressively organized Hierophancy, especially in the area of security.

A matched pair of pigeons, the Divine Duck's personally anointed spies, had copped to the Cardinals' abduction of Conrad Eppler while it was still in full fury. The two devoted aides-de-camp—both tonsured monks (Order of Cooing

Columbiformes), both with impeccable spiritual credentials and skilled in the necessary arts of encryption and decryption— had been monitoring a digital worm recently installed in Delacroix's u-phone when they discovered the kidnapping-in-progress.

Dedicated birders, the anonymous Columbiformes liked to watch and to listen. They were under a singular vow of silence and communicated with each other via coded messages in a complex language of coos.

The day of the abduction, Delacroix sat grooming his unhappy ferret in the safety of his Sanctum apartment. Turning on his earbuds, unaware that his server had been hacked, he listened with delectation to the blow-by-blow description of the curbside fray and kidnapping that he had set into play.

Cardinal Delacroix never guessed he was being birded by the best when he spoke unguardedly with the driver of the Avesticum sedan and gave his marching orders.

Housed in a rooftop dovecote, the diligent spies cooed the incoming information into their decoder and relayed a transcript of the conversation to the Hierophant's secretary, Milton. As soon as it was confirmed that the Avesticum sedan was on its way up the mountain with its cargo of significant boy tucked in the backseat, a receiving canopy had been hastily erected on the front lawn.

The divine sleeping Mallard was awakened by his Cooing Columbiformes, dressed and hatted by his personal Budgies, and virtually shoved out the palace door by his Franciscan guards.

The kidnappers successfully foiled, the Mallard of All Mysteries took the first opportunity to apologize to Conrad for the abduction. He explained to a mystified boy that he had been abducted from his abductors.

"The driver's original message was scrambled, like an egg," His Holiness confided. "An omelet, really. The yolk and the whites inextricably mixed with bits of mushrooms, broccoli, and bell peppers. My personal pigeons, virtual wizards when it comes to codes, were able to unmix the inextricably mixed. Put the egg back together, so to speak. Humpty Dumpty? Not a problem for the pigeons."

Conrad studied this peculiar old man who spoke in riddles and eruptions, aware of an innate sweetness. The boy didn't bother to mention that he'd already been abducted from an abductor earlier in the day. Why take any glory from the Hierophant who seemed so proud of *his* abduction? Although he could tally the abductions, Conrad remained understandably confused.

"The Sanctum Avesticum Quoborium is beyond baffling for a beginner," the Hierophant added sympathetically. "I get that. I was once a beginner, at the beginning of my reign, wasn't I? Imagine my surprise, when I discovered the circles within circles of intrigue. Tricky business, those circles. Like detecting the intricate workings of a combination lock. Had to keep my ear pressed against the door of secrets—didn't I?—until I heard the click. The Sanctum is like a safe, except that no one is safe. That is my point. You are not safe here."

"What should I call you?" Conrad ventured.

"I was wondering the exact same thing. What are the protocols? Where precisely do you stand on the scale of eminences? No one seems to know. Your ontological ambiguity is ruffling feathers. We are all political birds here. No one likes a misplaced deity."

"I'm not misplaced. Earth is my place."

Brother Swallow and Brother Larkspur perked up. The boy did not deny being a deity. That was interesting. These two burley—but against all outward appearances supremely mild-natured—Francines would serve as Conrad's bodyguards for the duration of his visit. Their charge was to protect Conrad's life with the sacrifice of their own, if necessary. At all costs, the two Francine Monks were to avoid scandal. If this abduction became known, all that ancient history regarding the kidnapping of Edgardo Mortara would be rehashed ad infi-twitterdom.

"Perhaps we should both call one another *Your Holiness*," His Holiness suggested amicably.

In that way, the Divine Duck reasoned, neither would be higher or lower than the other. The Mallard was not concerned for himself, but he wanted to send a message to the obsessively status-conscious Avesticum community that Conrad was an eminence ranked above everyone in any given room, excepting himself.

"For example," the Hierophant instructed the boy, "I say to you: Your Holiness, you can't trust anyone in the Avesticum except yours truly, the Francines, and the Columbiformes," then added as an afterthought, "and the French chef. And my secretary, Milton. My Budgies are loyal, but they gossip. And there's the Ravens. They are a hermetically sealed, altogether clandestine lot and only interested in their own archival pursuits. They are called Raven with no surname because they eschew personal identity. In any case, you and I shall be His Holiness."

"I don't know, Your Holiness. I think it's too weird. Just call me Conrad. Or Earthworm. Or kid. And by the way, this is Skipper, the Gospel Monkey."

"What gospel?"

Conrad started to laugh, "Sorry, Your Holiness, Skipper says I should call you Ducky. Then if someone ever wrote a book about us, they could name it: *Ducky and the Earthworm*. Or maybe: *The Mallard, the Avatar and the Monkey*."

"The monkey has opinions, does he? I wouldn't mind being called by my actual name. Matsuki Makindo. I haven't heard that name spoken out loud in ages. The important thing, Conrad, is that we get you home safely and as soon as possible."

"Why did you kidnap me, Matsuki?"

"You weren't listening. I did not kidnap you. I unkidnapped you. Cardinal Delacroix and his band of reprobates kidnapped you."

"Why does everyone want to kidnap me?"

"There's a question for the ages. I have given an order that no Cardinal, nor any Hooded Crow, may approach you. And that is why you have bodyguards. That and because, in all likelihood, there will be another attempt. I won't get one wink of sleep as long as you're here."

"You should just let me go, then."

"If only it were that simple."

"It is. Just take me into the woods and I'll be safe," Conrad challenged the old man with his eyes. The boy knew that Skipper would rapidly increase in power among the trees and wild things. "Please, Your Holiness."

"Leave you in the woods?" His Holiness, the Hierophant, was at a loss. He was puzzling over this strange request when his secretary, Milton, rushed in and handed him a report—a car chasing the Avesticum sedan had driven off Martyr Maker Point earlier in the day.

The Hierophant repeatedly tapped one boney finger on the disturbing missive, "No, no dear child. The woods are definitely not safe."

His Holiness decided that Conrad should spend the night in the room adjoining the Divine Duck's chamber, with guards posted at the bed and guards posted at the door. Matsuki Makindo's enemies were numerous and deadly.

Within the halls of the Sanctum Avesticum Quoborium, His Holiness could provide a measure of safety—with the help of his allies. He could count on the Francine palatial guard, the cote of Columbiformes spies, possibly the coven of Ravens, plus the recourse of a divine authority that commanded at least the semblance of obedience, even if that semblance quickly dissembled behind closed doors.

The Munificentissimus Divine Mallard of All Mysteries very much wanted to get to the bottom of the mystery surrounding this purported Avatar, and now that the boy was within talking distance he saw his chance.

So far, Conrad Eppler struck him as remarkably self-contained, mischievous, alert, bright as a button, but altogether just a boy like any other. Matsuki Makindo was himself all of the above and did not think himself anything special. What a relief if Conrad were an ordinary boy, and all the rest turned out to be a murmuration of rumor run amuck.

Tomorrow he'd take Conrad on a tour of some of the art treasures in the palace, show off the place. In the course of casual conversation, he would conduct his own covert interview.

That night, after Conrad was safely tucked in, the Hierophant telephoned his Cordon Bleu chef and asked this French paragon to create a Baked Alaska Flambé as a surprise for the boy. Father Remarqué rolled his eyes. The Hierophant had such pedestrian tastes. Matsuki Makindo found that he was looking forward to tomorrow. Art and ice cream, his two very favorite things. He could not guess what other servings of just desserts were in the making.

A mostly uneventful night left His Holiness snoozing peacefully, dreaming of Leonardo Da Vinci. Conrad and Skipper slept in the cozy luxury of thousand-thread-count sheets and down comforters.

The guards did not notice when, late in the night, a white monkey fell out of bed, silently slipped along the dark corners of the chamber and into the adjoining room where the Divine Mallard slept. Hanuman tenderly placed his small furry hand on the old man's chest—so carefully, his touch barely disturbed Matsuki's dream. Nonetheless, the monkey found what he was looking for: The Hierophant's secret. Matsuki smiled in his sleep. Mona Lisa smiled back at Matsuki and gave him an enigmatic wink.

In the morning, a hazy sunlight pierced the criss-crossed leaded glass and made enchanting patterns on the walls. A chime of amiable bells announced Lauds. Brother Larkspur and Brother Swallow guided Conrad to the Hierophant's private chapel with its stunning gold-leaf basilica and stained-glass windows, a mini-cathedral fit for the prince that he was.

Conrad felt the age of the musty prayers when the Hierophant's circle of monks began their Latin chants. The boy understood that the words held a terrible beauty, words imbued with sacrifice and strife, threat and remorse, penances and over-comings. A fearful deity rumbled behind the prayers— prayers meant to hold the wrath of a jealous God in abeyance and, at the same time, to invite him in.

Unlike the prayers, the bread served at breakfast was a freshly baked, heavenly, crusty delight. Conrad tried his first frothy cup of cappuccino. The boy felt very grown up, wearing a milk mustachio, a traveler in a foreign land.

It was strange to be surrounded by so many men. The Hierophant moved at the center of a floating coterie of Francines and Cooing Columbiformes, with Geococcyx and Budgies flitting about the outer circumference.

When Conrad accompanied His Holiness through the great halls, with their vaulted ceilings and towering columns, he felt small again. Looking for reassurance, he patted Skipper's furry paws velcroed at his neck.

The Hierophant's entourage came to a locked double door, made of blackened bog oak, set in an archway nearly three times the height of a man. A black-robed priest sat writing at a gold Florentine desk, dipping a black feather into an ink pot. He wore the Ravens' signature shiny black-feathered beard and a black mask that featured a long narrow beak.

The silent scribe looked up and pressed a yellow button that gave out the distinct rok-rok of the raven. The doors opened, and the Munificentissimus Divine Mallard entered holding Conrad by the hand. The coterie of birdmen strained to get a look into the private gallery, but the doors closed behind the retreating figures of the Hierophant, the boy, and his monkey.

Artworks were stacked from floor to ornately carved ceiling. As His Holiness steered Conrad through the halls, a constable of velvet-slippered Ravens emerged from the shadows and joined them. The only sound was the swish of their stiff wide-skirted black robes, beautifully constructed of a proprietary taffeta moiré. The sensation of being swept along in a swirling black sea made Conrad grip His Holiness's hand a little tighter.

The Ravens were ranked above the Cardinals, but did not involve themselves in Avesticum politics. They served as conservators of the secret cache of treasures: artworks and books collected over the centuries by agents of The Great Church.

When Conrad stepped too close to a painting, one of the Ravens emitted a deep throated rok-rok, and the boy jumped back. It was dizzying taking it all in, so Conrad was relieved when Matsuki asked him to sit on a velvet-covered bench in one of the galleries.

Finally, they had arrived at the moment the Mallard of all Mysteries had been anticipating since daybreak.

His Holiness cleared his throat and asked if Conrad had heard of an artist called Leonardo Da Vinci?

The Ravens leaned in.

Conrad said, "No. But I like pictures. When you look at pictures, secrets come out of them."

"Indeed."

"I like to draw. And guess what? I can write forwords and backwards."

"Odd you should mention that. Leonardo was fond of writing backwards."

"Wow! I like saying wow. It's a palindrome. It's the same forwards and backwards. Did Leonardo draw comic books?"

"Comic books? Heavens, no. You've never heard of Leonardo Da Vinci? I should have thought, the Sisters, you know, with their world class library, their art folios—. Well." He cut himself off, suddenly remembering that during the great persecution of the Sisterhoods, libraries had been ransacked, art treasures appropriated.

His Holiness swallowed his disappointment. He'd wanted to impress Conrad with the astonishing fact that one of the paintings in the Sanctum private gallery was an unknown rarity—a striking self-portrait by the great Renaissance artist, painted when he was still a young man, experimenting with sfumato and already demonstrating a precocious mastery of the foggy shadings that came to define his iconic style.

The only other known Da Vinci self-portrait was a faded and still fading red-chalk drawing depicting the bearded genius in his sixties, looking more like ninety and markedly grumpy. That rarely-seen drawing was locked in a temperature-controlled vault in the Royal Library at Turin.

Matsuki had once held the original drawing in gloved hands when he was a University student—a life-altering moment for the young seminarian. Decades later, when he became Hierophant and privy to the secret galleries, he had his first look at the Sanctum's treasured Leonardo. For His Holiness, Leonardo remained the ultimate enigma.

There were only a few uncontested Da Vinci paintings in the world. The artist liked to experiment with pigments, often to disastrous effect. Many of his paintings disintegrated, much like the disappearing ink he invented as a tool for state-craft. Art historians never seemed to guess what Matsuki Makindo had long suspected—that Leonardo purposefully created paintings that would eventually unpaint themselves.

Now you see it. Now you don't.

A master escape artist, he left many of his works unfinished, much to the consternation of the baffled patrons who filled his pockets with gold florins.

Now you see me. Now you don't.

A closely guarded secret, the self-portrait had been acquired over five hundred years ago, according to one set of Avesticum records. Double records were often kept to obfuscate dates and places when paintings had been obtained by less than admirable means. Even in the privacy of the Sanctum Avesticum Quoborium, the existence of the Da Vinci was only known to the small inner circle of curator Ravens who catalogued the rarest among the rare art treasures. The Ravens were collectively shocked that the Divine Mallard of All Mysteries would even consider showing the painting to a mere child.

The Hierophant himself was uncertain of his motives.

"Our pristine Da Vinci is worth untold millions," Matsuki was trying his best to impress the boy. "It's the Avesticum's most valuable art treasure."

Conrad understood that the viewing was a special moment, and that he was being trusted with secret knowledge. The Hierophant's staff was treating him very well—the soft bed, the cappuccino, and now their very best painting. Conrad wanted to respond in kind, and so he decided to share a secret that he only just now realized might be of interest.

"Your Holiness, I know him."

"Who?"

"Leonardo. Well, not know him exactly. But I've seen him."

"Impossible. He died over five-hundred years ago."

Conrad asked for some drawing materials. In short order, the curatorial staff provided the boy with colored pencils and paper. They stood watching in disbelief as Conrad sat on the floor with his toy monkey and sketched a near-perfect drawing of the painting.

At one point, the boy asked for more light. At a nod from the Hierophant, one of the Ravens drew aside a heavy velvet drape and natural light poured into the gallery. Light was the enemy of preservation and was seldom allowed into this particular darkness. All the curators took this rare opportunity to breathe in the enhanced beauty of the Da Vinci self-portrait in a sunlit gallery.

One by one, they returned to view Conrad's progress. The boy had almost finished his remarkable drawing, inexplicably leaving off the jaunty Renaissance beret. Instead he drew a Cardinal's triform red biretta on Leonardo's head. Then Conrad stopped every heart in that room when he sketched in an extra pair of eyes. Cassowary eyes. The Ravens quickly glanced up at the painting, glanced down at the drawing, back up to the painting. There was no mistaking it: The Magus was a dead ringer for Da Vinci.

Now you see me.

The Hierophant and the curator Ravens did exactly what churchmen had always done in circumstances such as this. They swore each other to secrecy.

What was merely an astonishing puzzle for the feather-bearded Ravens who were present in the gallery that day was a revelation for the monkey. It made sense of the secret hidden behind the breastbone of Matsuki Makindo.

"Where did you see this man, Conrad?" The Munificentissimus Divine Mallard braced himself.

"In the woods, behind the convent. He had a raptor claw. He tried to grab me."

Skipper intervened at this juncture and told Conrad to change the subject. Every man in the room knew and feared that claw and each one had speculated and worried over the whereabouts of the Excellent Holy High Magus. The white monkey especially did not want Conrad to mention the convent's pet cassowary, not in front of this assembly. Only a few of the Cardinals suspected, and they had evidenced no desire to pursue the matter. These Ravens might prove more meddlesome.

*Ice cream,* Skipper prompted.

"Ice cream," Conrad said out of the blue, "I'm starving. Remember, you promised me ice cream."

"Yes," said a shaken Hierophant, "let us have ice cream."

All the while His Holiness had watched the masterful drawing materialize, he had been reviewing his conclusions about Conrad Eppler's ontological status. That, added to the concordance between Leonardo and the missing Holy High Magus created such a headful of dissonant static in his poor brain that the old man might have passed out from sheer mental fatigue but for the thought of Baked Alaska Flambé.

———

THE FLAMING DESSERT arrived on a silver tray and was placed on a small table in the soundproof safe room. When the flames were doused, the insignia of the Divine Mallard emerged in the crisp peaks of meringue; a bit of magic that Leonardo would have applauded just as enthusiastically as Conrad did. The Hierophant and the boy raised their silver spoons and dug in.

The sodium ion transport-carriers rushed an emergency supply of glucose to the aging brain of the Munificentissimus Mallard, and shortly he was back in conversation mode with his young companion. Conrad asked if the scene earlier in the gallery didn't remind His Holiness of the scene in the temple with the young Jesus.

"I hope you are not suggesting that you are an incarnation of *Jesus*?" His Holiness tsked in a hushed voice. That was precisely the sort of rumor that would send Cardinal Delacroix around the bend, with his murderous minions following him round in short order.

"No. I am Conrad Eppler. I meant the part about discussing spiritual matters with the elders in the temple. And his parents thought he was lost?" Conrad tried for a lighter tone, "I beat him. That's all I meant. I got here sooner."

"He arrived over two-thousand years ago," remarked an affronted Hierophant.

"I mean I beat him by four years. He was twelve, I'm going on eight."

The Mallard expelled a sigh of relief. This was just quasi-biblical skylarking, bragging lite, hardly a calorie in it. Conrad wasn't trespassing on sacred ground, he was just running around like a kid playing kick the prayer ball. This was as good a time as any to test some deeper spiritual waters.

As Conrad chattered on about the musical values of gem-tone angels, the algorithms of astral travel, divine transporters, and underwater meditation, His Holiness attempted to return Conrad to more familiar environs with simple queries into what the good Sisters had taught Conrad about the Bible.

Thus it began—the interrogation that would shake the Munificentissimus Divine Mallard of All Mysteries to the very square roots of his dazzling soul, a soul that would be sent spinning in ever widening gyres of Fibonacci spirals sometime in the very next quarter hour.

———

WHILE CONRAD AND THE HIEROPHANT tossed metaphysical pi and parsed biblical riddles, another dazzling elder, tented in long white hair and leaning on a staff, was making her way up the long and winding road to the Sanctum Avesticum Quoborium.

Yesterday morning, Mother Mary Extraordinary awakened to a worried Sister Subordinary and took stock. Sister Merry Berry had never shown back up at the convent. Conrad was gone. And no one was tracking down these beloved missing persons.

Extraordinary had no patience for Subordinary's attempt at mollifying explanations and palliative optimisms. The bottom line was that the whereabouts of Sister Merry Berry and Conrad Eppler were indeterminate. So be it. She should have questioned Merry Berry more closely when they were in the Cadillac.

Now she did what she probably should have done many years ago. Before a second thought could give her pause, she sallied forth barefoot. Still in her nightgown, she left the convent for the second time in her very long life. It was high time to deal with the Hierophant.

A few spritzes of Humboldt Snow #7 boosted her energy and confidence. Fortune blessed her with a ride to the base of Mount Quoborium. She had climbed to the halfway mark by nightfall and slept like a baby in the woods, lullabied by nature's symphony of night song.

The next morning, as the Hierophant and Conrad spooned Baked Alaska, she made her way slowly and determinedly upwards, enraptured by the beauty of the wildwood to one side and the incredible vistas that opened beyond the precipice on the skyward side.

She stopped at Martyr Maker Point to admire the breathtaking view of sun-dappled cliffs and canyons and falls— a paradise lined with the rusting carcasses of rides gone by. She found a perfect rock at the edge of the drop off to sit in Padmasana, meditate, and breathe in the astonishing beauty.

Canticles of praise for the artistry of creation radiated from her every pore. She was ablaze with awe. After giving herself a few cooling spritzes, the diaphanous veil of time was lifted, and she watched a certain pink Cadillac speed towards a nearly invisible moon.

———

THE HIEROPHANT SPOONED pistachio and bits of meringue while Conrad entertained His Holiness with tales of the Sisters' highly original unorthodoxies concerning all things biblical. What Matsuki Makindo found most curious was their quaint but presumptive belief that the story of Adam and Eve in Eden was misplaced; that it belonged after the New Testament, because it was really a newer testament to something that hadn't yet come to be.

The Hierophant looked sincerely puzzled.

"Paradise," Conrad said helpfully.

"The Sisters don't believe there was a paradise in the beginning?"

"Of course not. It was full of dinosaurs. And volcanoes. And later on, the Neanderthals. It was hot. It was cold. It was brutal.

Now we've got love and there's a chance to make the kind of Eden that matters," Conrad stopped.

Conrad was learning that it was tougher talking about such things to someone who thought you were talking nonsense. At home, such discussions were daily theological bread, moist and steamy. When everyone is building a belief together, the words don't catch in your throat. Conrad was not about to say that he had seen Eve in her garden and that the story was still under construction. He took a different tack. A parable.

"The story is a flambé, like the dessert," Conrad tried again, digging in deeper with his silver spoon, "You have to get past the fiery part, then through the pistachio, or you'll never get into the raspberry filling."

What Conrad could not possibly realize was that the Munificentissimus Mallard was desperately hungry for any least flambé of hope. He relished all the tidbits Conrad tossed about with such careless élan. The politics of purity, credos, and credentials—combined with the irregularities in the management of the Quoborium financial portfolios, piled on top of the damning sexual predations of the ordained, and the persistent rumors that that GOAT caused hallucinations of outlawed deities, many of them female, most of them pagan— the whole rotten compendium was driving the Mallard close to despair. No wonder he took refuge in art, ice cream, and giving away money and property to the poor.

He hated his mitre, with its golden mallard beak, that sat heavy as doom on his throbbing head. One of his Budgies had removed it before Conrad and the Divine Duck dug into their ice cream mountain. It was such relief to get out from under that six-aspirin topper. The headaches were for the most part manageable. The much-despised hat and the weighty feather cape were mere symptoms and symbols of an underlying malady—the dead weight of centuries. It was the bone-crushing exhaustion of being obligated to claim access to an unchanging Truth that was unbearable.

Now this unexpected reprieve.

The boy, this marvelous boy with his ersatz beliefs, had such a salutatory effect on Matsuki Makindo that His Holiness found himself willing to entertain whatever fanciful bonbons and bon mots fell from the boy's raspberry stained lips. It was refreshing just to be awake. Perhaps after ice cream they could play Frisbee on the lawn. He felt positively spry.

In any case, the mere fact that the Hierophant could make it all the way through a conversation without sudden nap syndrome punctuating the repartee at odd intervals was a most welcome blessing.

"Tell me more."

"There's someone you should know. Her name is Mother Mary Extraordinary. She's like you."

"Old?"

"Yes," Conrad grinned, "even older. But that's not it. She was the one who taught me how to make beliefs. Maybe if I could show you how to make one, you wouldn't be so sad. There's something I really, really want to tell you. And Skipper says I should just do it. He's the one who told me."

"The monkey?"

"Yes, the Gospel Monkey." Conrad licked his spoon and Skipper's tail twitched. "I know where your God is. The old one, from the Archaic Testament."

The Hierophant looked around. Even though they were in the safe room, sound proofed by the best technology and materials that money could buy, and money could buy some amazing stuff these days, Matsuki Makindo sensed that he was on dangerous ground. Not from without, but from within.

To be locked in a room with ice cream and such an enchanting boy was destabilizing the old saint. The only thing that Matsuki had was his faith. Yes, it was a despairing faith, a faith riddled with doubt, a worn out, ragged threadbare faith, but it was all he had left of the boy he once was. And he finally understood that the boy sitting across from him was about to take it away.

Makindo's finger hovered over the buzzer. He only had to press it and the Francine guards would enter and the conversation would be over.

"Tell me."

*Tell him,* the monkey urged.

"It's about Leonardo," Conrad began.

"What about Leonardo?" The Hierophant's heart pounded.

"Did you ever think that maybe Leonardo was an incarnation of your God?"

Certain rogue dots connected themselves in the Hierophant's mind. The Magus, Leonardo, the Creator. He immediately disconnected them.

This boy was dangerous.

How could this mere child have known the most carefully guarded secret hidden behind the old man's breastbone?

The young Matsuki Makindo had earned a Doctorate of Philosophy in Renaissance studies from the University of Turin. As a promising scholastic prodigy, he had written his dissertation on none other than Leonardo Da Vinci. He had poured over every document, every drawing, every available coded notebook of the Renaissance master, and had come to a conclusion that he had never shared with a single soul: that this astounding body of science and artistry could not have been the unassisted work of a mere mortal.

One particular letter in the archives had turned Matsuki's head. The letter was penned by a neophyte Leonardo on-the-make, the illegitimate child of a peasant girl, (the absence of patents of divinity on the part of the mother, just one among many parallels to the only biblically-certified incarnation). This bastard son of a Florentine gentleman, had little to recommend him to the world except his own self-esteem and his nice penmanship.

And yet.

And yet one fine day the ambitious youth tasked himself with the composition of a letter, a letter destined to secure the patronage of the Duke of Milan and launch a nobody to the stars, and as it turned out, a letter destined to reach through time and tempt the young doctoral candidate, Matsuki Makindo, to apostasy.

It was the most audacious, the most mind boggling, the most egocentric braggadocio ever penned. In an impeccable hand, the letter entailed an encyclopedia of aspirations—not accomplishments—but rather a rollcall of predictions, brash promises based on nothing but highly imaginative, if not whimsical, speculation.

Launching the list with promised designs for unheard-of war machines, weaving in a catalogue of artistic talents, the would-be paragon finished off with a breezy self-exaltation, proclaiming that he, Leonardo Da Vinci, could out-perform anyone, "Be he who he may!"

That long-ago afternoon in the library, holding the letter with protective white cotton gloves, Matsuki Makindo knew what the Duke of Milan could not possibly have known.

The brags were true.

Not yet, but Leonardo would make them true. In the course of one remarkable lifetime he would become the embodiment of the Renaissance man. And according to the historical record—a gay Renaissance man, a Florenzer in the parlance of the times, quite flamboyant in his dress and often employing his young lovers as his models for the angels who appeared in his paintings wearing exquisitely rendered bird wings. One drawing in the famous notebooks is of a hermaphrodite angel, with breasts and a penis.

The scholar wrestled mightily with that particular angel. Surely that angel was purely imaginative. Matsuki tried not to think why an angel should have any use for a penis, much less fulsome breasts. Eventually, praise the Lord, he stopped thinking about the disturbing drawing.

Nonetheless, the handprint of divinity was everywhere in evidence to the young scholar. On that fateful afternoon, when Matsuki looked with new eyes at the famous encircled drawing of the so-called Vitruvian man, he had the uncanny sensation that he was looking at the original blueprint, sketched from a primordial maker's memory.

And with that emergent thought—that Leonardo was an incarnation of the One True God—Matsuki Makindo felt the stain of an irremissible sin darken his soul.

There was no question in his mind that this line of thinking was blasphemy, a blasphemy that banged against his most passionate desire: to become a priest.

So Matsuki did what he must to rid himself of heresy. He took the anathema and compressed it into the tiniest ball of dark matter and hid it inside himself in a place where not even he could find it. Then he determined to call Leonardo what every other scholar called him down the ages: a genius.

Now, before that compressed ball of dark matter could unwind itself and swallow him whole, His Holiness turned to Conrad and said, "Leonardo Da Vinci was a genius."

"There's more to it," Conrad insisted, his voice full of wonder.

"No, there is not."

"Yes, there is! Your God is in my backyard."

The old man stood. His knees shook violently under his robe, but he managed to stumble to the glass cabinet where the hated mitre rested on its marble pedestal. He stood a moment in silence before he opened the glass door, lifted the weighty gold-beaked hat, and placed it on his head.

Then the Munificentissimus Divine Mallard of All Mysteries buzzed in the guards.

## Monkey Business

Something Was Not Right. His Holiness buzzed again, and the double doors opened on an unexpected scene. Conrad tightened his grip on Skipper. Two hooded figures in gas masks charged in. They scooped up the boy by the armpits and made their escape with Conrad kicking out furiously between them.

"This is an outrage!" The Hierophant picked up the silver platter, still dripping with ice cream, and hurled the disc through the open double doors.

His once passionate Frisbee practice paid off. The flying platter connected solidly at the back of the neck of one of the fleeing abductors, who crumbled to the ground. The other figure hoisted Conrad over his shoulder and ran down the hall unimpeded.

The Hierophant, in awkward pursuit, shouted for help. Where were his guards? The shocking answer lay just outside the doorway and all down the hall—to a man, his guards had fallen. No fool, His Holiness quickly surmised that the passageway had been gassed. He retreated back into the safe room, closed the doors, and reached into his pocket. For the first time in his life he was grateful for his cell phone.

Conrad Eppler's kicks slowed, then stopped. Just before the boy lost consciousness, Skipper managed jump from the boy's hand and fasten his Velcro paws around Conrad's neck.

The boy and monkey were dropped like rags into a waiting canvas laundry cart, the only colored objects in a sea of whites. The hooded abductor in the gas mask covered the boy with a bath towel, then disappeared down a stairwell. A man in a white jumpsuit stepped into a perfectly coordinated pass off and pushed the laundry cart onto a waiting elevator.

———

BROTHER UMBRUCO, AN UNTITLED but ranking member of the Hooded Crows, waited at a back entrance to the Quoborium. Aware that precision timing was critical, the monk checked his watch repeatedly. Umbruco, mastermind of the street-side kidnapping plot, was still smarting at being outwitted by the Hierophant's spies—damned Cooing Columbiformes. He peeled back the towel to confirm the recapture and gave the imposter laundry worker a thumbs-up. Umbruco was replacing the towel when he noticed the monkey. On a whim, he plucked up the toy. Then he signaled the laundry worker to load the cart into the back of an unmarked white panel truck.

"Hey, Stelvio," Umbruco called to the waiting driver who was leaning against the side of the truck. Swinging the stuffed animal over his head, Umbruco tossed it in the air and did a brief victory dance.

Brother Stelvio caught the flying monkey by the tail. Engine running, the two monks were waiting on Cardinal Delacroix, who came out at a rush and jumped into the shotgun seat just as Stelvio was winding up to send the monkey back to a running Umbruco. Instead, Skipper was sent sailing into the woods—pass incomplete.

Stelvio was behind the wheel and accelerating before Delacroix had time to buckle up. Umbruco leapt into the back of the truck where Conrad was stashed in the cart. The counterfeit laundry worker scrambled to shut the back doors on the already moving van.

There was only one road out.

As the truck circled around the Quoborium to the elaborately gated front entrance, Brother Stelvio caught sight of a hastily erected barricade and snorted, "Nice try, Mallard."

The electronic gates had been hacked by the Hooded Crows and were standing wide open. Breaking through the improvised barricade was going to be a lark. Stelvio gleefully pressed the gas pedal to the floor.

"Slow down," barked Delacroix reaching for his ferret. When he remembered he'd left Felix in the Sanctum with his personal Budgies, the Cardinal bit his own wrist.

"Leave the driving to me." Stelvio glanced over at the frightened Cardinal before slamming through the wooden barricade. When the wood shattered in a gratifying display of white and orange projectiles, Stelvio felt like an action hero in a movie chase scene.

"The switchback is tattooed on my brain. I could drive it with my eyes closed," Stelvio added with a chuckle.

"Keep them open," a flat-voiced Delacroix ordered.

"Yeah. Yeah."

Cardinal Delacroix allowed himself a moment's meditation on how distasteful he found working with thugs. The Hooded Crows were brilliant at subterfuge and worse, but the Cardinal's self-image precluded that he should know such men, much less employ them.

A more discomfiting thought slipped through his disgust, wedged like a splinter under the thin skin of his ego. He was not given to introspection. Plots were more his line. Still, he could not shake off the unwanted insight that he himself had become a thug. Clearly, he was no longer the widely-admired contender for the Hierophancy he had once been in the flush of his maturity.

Too much blood had been spilt on the road to his ascendance. Everything wrong in his life led back to the car-bombing that had taken his supposedly secret wife and son. The escalating payback and bloodbath of Cardinals that followed changed Delacroix.

Knowing it was a mistake, he let the memories come. They broke over him in waves. He had loved his illicit family, his wife, his little son. He never once suspected that the man he hired to avenge their deaths was the very man who had plotted those deaths. The loyalty of the Hooded Crows did not extend beyond their own brotherhood.

Just now, the death dealer was sitting in the back of the van with the unconscious Conrad Eppler. Brother Umbruco, also known as The Monk, was a master assassin, descended from a long line of master assassins. In practice, he was always the master of whoever employed him.

Cardinal Delacroix, once the golden boy rising in the elite circles of the Magistere, persecutor of nuns and protector of orthodoxies, failed to grasp what His Holiness saw so clearly. No one was safe in the house of spies. The Sanctum Avesticum Quoborium was a golden domed dynamo of interlocking plots, turning like the many circles of hell in Dante's *Inferno*.

Delacroix was speeding towards what would prove both his apex and his nadir. Although it had taken seven years of intrigue, one plan after another gone awry, Conrad Eppler was finally in the hands of the ambitious Cardinal. The Magus was gone, the Mallard teetering on extinction, and the boy captured. Cardinal Delacroix need only wait for the inevitable big sleep to overtake Matsuki Makindo and the Hierophancy was his.

Yet there it was—the splinter under his skin.

While the gold-beaked mitre was as good as won, the prick wedged in Cardinal Delacroix's conscience infected him with self-doubt, insinuated that he was no longer worthy of that crown, insisted that there was no difference between himself and the assassins in his employ.

One essential lie, repeated like a prayer, was eating at him. As acting Magistrate of the Magistere, he only meant to interrogate the boy—nothing more.

Nothing more.

That was the lie that damned him, the lie that paid rent on one of Dante's infamous circles. The unspeakable truth asserted itself like a pustule surrounding the infected splinter—boy killer. Cardinal Delacroix shuddered.

It was a crucible moment.

Now, when he was so close to triumph that he could smell the frankincense, feel the weight of the Mallard's cape on his shoulders, see himself walking the red carpet to the Hierophant's throne and receiving obeisance from the college of Cardinals, he wanted nothing so much as oblivion—to sail off the edge of Martyr Maker Point and into the sweet hereafter. He could not know that his wish was about to be granted.

The Monk in the back of the truck was suddenly alert. A death wish gives off a distinct odor.

"Roll down the window," Umbruco growled.

There was a rush of mountain air. The startling, high-volume crack of snapping branches drew the puzzled attention of the three conspirators in the van. Instinctively, Stelvio slowed down.

Something was happening in the woods. Tree tops thrashed, bent low and sprang back.

Something was sailing at lightning speed from redwood to redwood, increasing in size until the primal forest kings could no longer bear the weight of the noble beast.

Lord Hanuman jumped to the ground and the Earth trembled underfoot. Then the white monkey bowed his head to offer thanks—in the name of the bodhi tree, and the sun, and the holy grove.

*Vriksha namaskar.*

Praise to the heroic evergreens who bear his weight.

Praise to the forest kings who oxygenate the very air that breath by breath increase his power.

*Sri Hanuman namaskar.*

This white monkey leapt over an ocean in his day and battled an army of demon Rakshasas—one white truck was not going to be a problem. Gifted with two yogic siddhis, he could use these sun-struck powers to become as small as a subatomic particle or as large as the sky.

When Lord Hanuman stepped out on Martyr Maker Point he was twelve feet of pure calibrated muscle. The Hindu divinity paused to take in the dazzling beauty of Mother Mary on her rock. Locked in a trance of luminous prayer, her stunning yellow aura filled the sky and canyon, so much like his guru, Surya, the sun.

*Surya namaskar.*

His prayers said, the white monkey waited in the middle of the road.

Brother Stelvio was downshifting to take the switchback at Martyr Maker Point when the otherworldly glare from Mother Mary's effulgence glazed the windshield of the paneled truck.

Stelvio pumped the brakes, squinting to make out the almost imperceptible outlines of a white-furred giant standing in the road, backlit by Mary Extraordinary's golden glow.

The moment was dreamy, elongated, unreal.

Then it got real.

Really fast.

Hanuman began sprinting towards the vehicle and leapt like the flying that God he was. He landed with an Earth-jarring thud on the hood, a thud felt in the bowels of every man in that truck.

Staring through the windshield into Hanuman's savage anger, a mortified Delacroix smelled the acrid scent of his own fear. But it was the set of gleaming incisors that gave the Cardinal second thoughts about the sweetness of oblivion. Then with sublime agility, the monkey climbed over the roof of the truck.

"Do something!" shouted the Cardinal.

Stelvio accelerated, then slammed on the breaks. Delacroix hit the windshield, blood blurring his vision. Umbruco drew his Glock. The men winced at the ear-splitting screech of steel as Hanuman ripped off the back doors and scooped up Conrad.

Umbruco fired off one shot and blood blossomed on Conrad's shoulder, the bullet first passing through Hanuman's protective hand. The monkey screamed at The Monk, grabbed the gun and tossed it over the cliff.

Deftly and with utmost care, Hanuman carried the bleeding boy to the receiving arms of Mother Mary Extraordinary, who had been sitting like a sentinel on the rock. Keeping her wits about her, she quickly gathered a handful of moss and packed Conrad's wound. Then she cradled the injured child, warming him in her protective solar light.

It wasn't over, not by any means.

Enraged by the reckless gunplay, a supercharged Hanuman grew another five feet. Three bounds and the giant monkey caught up with the truck that was unsteadily backing up the hill.

Again, Hanuman gave a flying leap, somersaulting over the roof of the cab. Within a split second, he flipped himself inside the back end of the truck. A shaken Umbruco took aim with his spare.

Reflexes primed, the swift monkey lashed out with a bloodied paw and snapped Umbruco's wrist. Then the giant langur grabbed Umbruco by the throat and tossed him out of the truck.

Delacroix twisted around in his seat in time to see Brother Umbruco bounce on the pavement like a rag doll. Then the Cardinal sat staring into the eyes of unabated fury—and he knew he'd crossed an enemy like no other.

Hanuman reached forward and with surprising delicacy switched the gearshift into drive. One arm wrapped tightly around Stelvio's chest, the monkey pressed down on the petrified driver's right knee, forcing him to floor the accelerator and launch the truck over Martyr Maker Point. Stelvio passed out and Delacroix's scream filled the cab.

Then supple and swift, Hanuman somersaulted out the back of the truck and onto the roof.

———

A SPLIT SECOND LATER, Mother Mary and Conrad were wrenched from their restorative sun-trance by Lord Hanuman's unearthly wail.

As the curtain of yellow light parted, a terrified boy stared over the cliff in disbelief. An enormous Hanuman stood on the roof of a plummeting white truck as if he were riding the curl of a monster wave.

Conrad had never been so proud or so scared. Hanuman's descending howl rolled off the valley walls. Brave and loyal Hanuman—best of white monkeys—he had saved Conrad's life.

A deafening crunch of steel against steel ended the brief ride. A few falling rocks pinged against the metal carcass. Then silence.

Conrad paced along the cliff's edge searching the wreckage below for any sign of life. He yelled at the top of his lungs, "Hanuman! Lord Hanuman!"

The canyon mocked him with echoes.

The desperate boy sent out a series of mind signals. No answer. Blood was now flowing afresh from Conrad's wound.

Mother Mary took the boy by the hand, "Conrad, you must calm yourself."

The boy swallowed a deep breath and bowed his head. Then he wept—long painful sobs.

Mother Mary Extraordinary gathered up her wounded boy, and did her best to staunch the flow of blood and tears. With no sign of Lord Hanuman, a decision had to be made. They were so close to the summit. The Sanctum and possible help were within easy reach. But could they count on sanctuary? On the other hand, it was a very long walk down to the base of the

Mount Quoborium. Hitching a ride back to the convent, where she could heal Conrad's bullet wound in the quarry pool, was chancy at best.

"Up or down?" she asked out loud.

"Up," answered the desolate boy, "I have a friend up there. Unless—"

"Unless what?"

"Unless they killed him," a teary-eyed Conrad realized that his memory of what had happened after the ice cream was hopelessly blurred. "Why is the world so mean?"

Despair licked its icy fingers and looked for a place to burrow inside the boy. Suddenly chilled, Conrad told Mother Mary Extraordinary that he really did not know which way to go.

"Up. Down. I don't know. I don't care," the boy stared at his hands.

"You must care about something, Conrad. Caring is the thread we hang on, when we are hanging by a thread."

"I care about Skipper."

"I see," said the woman in the tent of white hair. "In that case, we must pray for Skipper."

Once more she folded herself into Padmasana and sat on the smooth rock at the edge of the precipice with Conrad nestled in the basket of her lap. Mother Mary sent out a very demanding sort of prayer. Conrad tuned in briefly and was shocked at how colorfully she prayed. Her ardent supplication bristled with swear words.

They both listened for an answer. At some point, they heard what sounded like a rockslide.

Someone standing on the far side of the canyon would have seen the most amazing sight—a large white monkey scaling the sheer side of a cliff, moving with quick grace and barely any effort at all.

Conrad bent his ear to the sound of falling rocks. With a flood of relief, he watched one startlingly large (but familiar) furry paw, then another—grasp the edge of the rock face.

Then—glory of glories! The great white monkey jumped back into the broken world.

Mother Mary Extraordinary raised a brow, "Skipper?"

The monkey bent close and inspected Conrad's wound. The boy and the nun were hardly allowed a moment's happiness, for the next thing they knew, Hanuman was bounding away into the woods.

"Where's he off to?" asked a rattled Mary Extraordinary. All that carefully cultivated Zen mindfulness, and she could be thrown off her game in a tick. It was infuriating.

"He said not to worry. He'd be right back. One of the bad guys got away."

Mother Mary's ineluctable frown was pulling at the corners of her mouth. "Super heroes," she said laying on a full measure of disapproval, "Call the monkey back. Now!"

Conrad sent a mind wave. Hanuman returned immediately, looking questions at Mother Mary Extraordinary.

"First the boy, then the heroics. I believe the Quoborium is renowned for its many pools and fountains. Drop us in the deepest one, so I can tend Conrad's wound. Yours as well, for that matter."

A chastened Hanuman complied, lifting Mother Mary and Conrad ever so gently. She wrapped one arm around the monkey's neck and one arm securely around Conrad's waist, tucking the weakened boy in close.

Then the wild creature flew from tree to tree, making himself just small enough not to be a burden to the forest kings, but large enough to easily carry his happy burden. Concerning his own wound, he messaged Conrad that it was only a minor injury. Then as requested, he dropped the Holy Mother and the boy into the deepest pool in the Avesticum gardens. Hanuman watched Conrad and Mother Mary sink into their familiar deep blue bliss.

———

LORD HANUMAN STRETCHED the muscles in his back and rolled his head, relishing the drumbeat of his own great heart. Apart from his brief engagement with the Magus, it'd been a while since he'd engaged in serious battle. Now he was refueled and full of unspent aggression. This was better. He could take his time. Make it count. Send a clear message to the enemies of light.

It was easy enough to find the bruised Brother Umbruco, who had managed to crawl to the camouflaged cabin in the woods where the Hooded Crows stashed their holographic projector and liquid nitrogen, and where they plotted untimely ends. Punching through a window, Hanuman reached in and grabbed the fevered Umbruco. The Monk squirmed helplessly, imprisoned in the monkey's steely grasp.

Now for the fun.

Conrad's protective daemon surged to an impressive eighteen feet, in homage the original RKO icon of the silver screen.

The gold-embossed Duomo that crowned the Sanctum Avesticum Quoborium glimmered in the distance. Hanuman accepted the summons.

With a new script in the works, the gigantic white langur took off at a run. As he gained speed the ground shook beneath his feet, and rock slides rumbled down the mountain.

The tremors were felt all the way up to the Sanctum. Cardinal Bunbury stared at the ice cubes rattling in his amber goblet. Oolumbo swore and held the sides of his tub. Delacroix's Budgies, Reynaldo and Pierre, soothed the frightened ferret, Felix. A weak-kneed Hierophant slipped a pair of binoculars from its case and wobbled to a window.

Abruptly Mount Quoborium stopped quaking. Hanuman had reached the foot of the postcard-perfect gothic cathedral, a replica of the original Florentine marvel, now with its landmark Renaissance dome awash in Humboldt sunlight. One handed, Hanuman began to mount the side of the granite church, Brother Umbruco held securely in his other hand.

Faintly at first, an unseen choir of insurgent angels began to voice an urgent cantata—*Carmina Burana, Fortuna Imperatrix Mundi*—growing ever louder as Lord Hanuman scaled the cathedral wall. The Gabrieline brass section gathered on a nearby cumulous for the big finish.

The window ledges made perfect footholds. The monkey moved with supple grace, careful not to break any of the lovely stained-glass window works. By the time he reached the upper ledge, skirting the foot of the curved basilica, and before he began his soon-to-be-legendary ascent, a hushed crowd of religious gathered in the courtyard beneath the Duomo— Budgerigars, Geococcyx, Cardinals, Francines, Red Kites, Goldfinches, Cooing Columbiformes, Sagittarius Secretaries, and Hooded Crows. The reclusive Ravens watched from a balcony.

A pair of Geococcyx began ringing the bells in the campanile. The angel choir swelled with answering bells.

Cell phones came out, held at arm's length to record the astonishing coup de grâce.

The Mallard of All Mysteries peered through his binoculars and focused them on the monkey's right hand. He was certain he recognized Brother Umbruco, his mouth stretched into a silent scream. Reaching the drum ledge, Lord Hanuman placed the severely shaken Umbruco in one of the circular clerestory windows set in a ring beneath the arc of the famous dome.

The celestial choir softened to a hum.

The monkey flew around the dome.

Once. Twice. Thrice.

A terrified Umbruco pulled up his dangling legs, and tucked himself into a fetal crouch. Pressing his back into the curve of the circular window, he cradled his broken wrist.

The Monk ignored a chant of "Umbruco, Umbruco" coming from the plaza, only daring to risk a hesitant wave of acknowledgement when it occurred to him that he might need to encourage a rescue party. The wave backfired; a large cheer went up as if the trembling monk were a part of a carnival stunt.

Then the monkey was back, pointing a huge boney finger at Umbruco's chest, looking as if he meant to rip out the assassin's beating heart. That's when The Monk wet himself.

His forefinger pressed against Umbruco's breastbone, Hanuman made a puzzling discovery—a computer chip. Curiosity aroused, the white monkey explored a virtual rat's nest of coded secrets, secrets embedded in secrets, threaded through thickets of secrets. It took some doing to sort the tangled clutch of information into two distinct strands.

The first strand consisted of a list of past assassinations, a long list—a columnar brag, like ribbons, bars, and stars marching in rows across the chest of a commander. Hanuman noted that Sister Merry Berry was the most recent entry on the lengthy list of departed.

The list of future assassinations was short, with Conrad's name holding pride of place at the top. When Hanuman saw the name of his beloved charge—a name inscribed in tiny letters on the monkey's every bone—his anger reached flashpoint. Jaws wide, the snarling monkey closed in on a trembling Umbruco. Hanuman let loose a bellow that rattled the clerestory window, and the tips of his gleaming incisors grazed The Monk's forehead, now awash in steaming monkey spit.

The Monk closed his eyes, his left hand clapped over his ear. Just before the kill, Hanuman stopped himself, and pulled the Monk's hand down. Apparently, there were more secrets to be gleaned from the miscreant Monk. Hanuman yanked Umbruco's left earlobe aside and ran his nail along a hidden tattoo, drawing blood.

Tamping down his instinct for vengeance, the conscientious monkey took his time decoding a third string of names, a priceless find. It was the membership roll of a secret society of assassins, a group so clandestine its name and insignia were virtually unknown. The insignia took the shape of two lowercase letters: vv, tattooed discretely behind the ear of each member. It was an old society, born in Italy, when Italy was just an association of city-states.

The name of the society—Vendetta Venezia.

The complete list of member names is known only to one man, a man with no title, simply called The Monk. Now that scurrilous Hooded Crow is hunched in a circular window too petrified to wipe the monkey spit off his face.

When Brother Umbruco's eyes begin to glaze over—and the master assassin knows in the pit of his stomach that he is as good as dead—Hanuman forestalls, swings out from the window and leaves The Monk to his private terrors.

The great white giant pauses on the drum ledge before he mounts the final arc of the Golden Duomo, a divine karmic plan forming in his beautiful monkey mind.

The angel choir swells. The boom box of creation thrums. An assault of celestial trumpets presses down on the throng below as Hanuman ascends to his moment of retributive genius.

Reincarnation Day is at hand!

All is bright noise in the Magellanic Cloud Casino. The heavenly throng crowds the roulette table. The celestial croupier is marking bets, fast business in the galactic pavilion. Vengeance is Lord Hanuman's for the taking. But will he take it?

At the top of the dome, gripping the spire in one hand, the divine monkey strikes the iconic pose and gives vent to a mighty roar—a roar that sunders the choiring air and shakes the surrounding woods.

The sonic reverberation reaches its intended targets. A murder of Hooded Crows and a few select Cardinals suddenly discover a wetness behind their left earlobes. Puzzling over the blood on their fingers tips, they soon realize that blood is dripping steadily from their double-v tattoos, and running in rivulets down their necks. They are marked men, each of them members of the secret society of assassins.

One cell of that secret society, led by Brother Redimus, is rushing up a long winding interior staircase. The brothers' faces are contorted with effort, their mission—to rescue The Monk from the clerestory window.

The Monk is the dark heart of their mystery. No one knows what will happen when that heart stops beating. In any case, someone must cut out the chip embedded in The Monk's breastbone. They don't know they are already too late.

Lord Hanuman has their number; their names and crimes are logged in his formidable mind. The rescuing party of Hooded Crows flying up the stairs halt in their tracks when they feel the blood running down their necks.

The Magellanic roulette wheel is set spinning, tuned to the atonal chords of creation. Om, the hum of chance and changes, rings down the annals of time.

"No more bets," the celestial croupier cries out.

Atop the Duomo, Hanuman suspends time and negotiates with his anger. He has touched pure evil, and it has changed him. He turns over the knowledge that the seven-year-old Conrad Eppler was meant to be the next kill. Once upon a sacred afternoon he made a promise to protect this boy, and he must keep that promise.

Lord Hanuman's keen intelligence, evolved over thousands of years, makes him acutely aware that this moment is tasked with high purpose. He is caught in a terrible bind. To kill or to grant mercy?

The resurgent angel choir breaks through the meditations of the monkey. Lord Hanuman is called forth to transcend the personal and mount the metaphysical wheel of infinite becoming. How will he answer?

O Sacred Wheel!

O Dharmachakra!

O Rota Fortunae!

So much is riding on the green zero. The mercurial ball clicks from pocket to pocket, then jumps the roulette wheel!

In a surprise move, Hanuman reaches into the heavens and steals the marble of chance.

The Angel Choir stops short of the cataclysmic finale.

The moment shivers and steps back, bells jingling at time's heels.

The cosmos waits while Lord Hanuman makes up his beautiful mind. So much depends on his next move. He studies the marble of chance and changes, and he decides to answer his ordained moment with artistry and wit. That is why he is currently host to an inner debate concerning monkey species; he deliberates between the langur hanumans (his genus) and the playful bonobos; but poetic justice seems to demand the capuchin monkey named after the Capuchin Monks.

The tonsured Capuchins are an offshoot of the Franciscans, the order founded by the beloved Francis of Assisi, Brother Moon, friend of all wild things. Yes, the white-headed, tonsured capuchin monkey with its lovely pink face is a spectacular beauty and will adapt wonderfully to these woods. Really, it's a gift to The Great Church, considered from a monkey point of view.

When Hanuman concludes his deliberations, time resumes its linear march, and a once-in-a-world video op arranges itself outside the cathedral. High up, along the clerestory edge, a string of assassins with bleeding necks, backs to the wall, holding hands like an accordion fold of paper cutout dolls, are cautiously inching towards their no-longer-fearless leader— The Monk.

Wait for it!

Brother Redimus reaches for The Monk, and he finds himself holding the small furry hand of a capuchin monkey. Then, like a string of firecrackers igniting in rapid sequence, the row of assassin monks becomes a crack-the-whip of chattering capuchins.

A cheer breaks loose from the amazed crowd on the plaza. Several Cardinals disappear into their red robes and crawl out the sateen sleeves of their former selves. Miraculously, their hats still fit! Handheld cell phones chase monkeys all around the cathedral.

Pop go the medievals!

A titillation of rumors rumbles the gathering of birdmen, chief among conjectures—the return of the Magus. Surely this display of theatrical trickery must be the work of Cardinal Cassowary.

From the lofty mind of His Holiness down to the lowliest Budgerigar, the collective Avesticum is clueless as to the true identity of the furred mischief maker. Lord Hanuman ranges so far outside the birdmen's cage of beliefs, the prankster monkey cannot be seen for the marvelous and ancient Hindu deity that he is.

Blame Kierkegaard. That renowned theologian imagined a blind leap into an existential abyss, not this quixotic monkey business. Alas, the redoubtable Lord Hanuman is a leap too far for both philosophers and faithful.

No matter. There will soon be plenty of vigorous spiritual leaping at the Sanctum Avesticum Quoborium.

While it is true that the poetics of innovative prayer will not cross the threshold of The Great Church for decades yet to come, canticle is not the only way the imagination leaps towards the ineffable.

In the days following Hanuman's legendary ascent, The Great Church was enlivened with a prayerful of monkeys.

Occasionally, a felicitous ferret joined the antics, amazed at the sudden abundance of furry playmates on the prayground.

Many of the frolicsome creatures inexplicably went about their monkey business in cute little Cardinal hats, others in hoodies. There was one chandelier in the basilica that became an instant favorite for monkeyshines; the fixture literally shook with prayer.

Avesticum Prayer rallies would never be the same.

Just when it seemed the show was winding down, and the celestial watchers were packing it in, two puzzled female capuchins pulled themselves from the wreckage of a white laundry truck at the base of Martyr Maker Point. They scratched their tonsured heads, examined their tails and their nether parts. Transformed and transgendered, the girls would prove very popular in days to come.

––––––

IN THE EMPYREAN HEIGHTS, Reincarnation Day was a blazing success and earned a coveted place on the heavenly Calendar of High Holy Days. A raucous celestial hullabaloo resounded throughout the plenum on that auspicious day when Hanuman played center ring and grabbed the marble of chance. Only later would the monkey realize that it was his very own marble, once lost now regained.

The disinclination of Lord Hanuman to assassinate assassins marked a happy evolution in his already expansive consciousness. The white monkey displayed an incomparable gift for sublime comedic vengeance. Here was superlative proof positive that evolution is an interactive sport, that deities evolve along with creation.

Hanuman put his days of badassery behind him, those gory glory days when he dispatched Ravana's demons by the dozens. The bear king, Jambavan, who had battled side by side with Hanuman when giants walked the Earth, let out a great roar, echoing from heavens to Himalayas.

"Good show!" chimed the Hindu pantheon of thousands. A blushing blue Krishna was showered with Gopi kisses.

"Good show!" chorused the angel hierarchy. The flock of Thrones, Powers and Dominions sent a confetti of diamonds glittering and butterflies fluttering through the galactic pavilion.

The great Wheels paused in their revolutions and emitted a heavenly om. Some say the lost chord was found on that day. Certainly, hope was given an unprecedented karmic booster.

At the close of his fifteen minutes of cosmic fame, Hanuman gave himself a moment to enjoy the exquisite view from the Duomo. A passing biplane, trailing a banner advertising Shimoda's Messiah Enterprises, narrowly missed hitting the dome. Hanuman plucked the biplane out of the air as if it were made of folded-paper and set it sailing on a new course.

The timpani built to a crescendo, the heavenly host unleashed its formidable brass section; then, into a dramatic silence, a carol of tubular bells tiptoed across the shivery air.

Asheilstarte lifted her bright wings in celebratory ecstasy and declared: "This is a great day in heaven!"

Wing I chimed in, "If Hanuman can make the great leap forward, then surely the Maker will follow."

"The Maker will follow the monkey," Wing II echoed prophetically.

Back at the convent, the cassowary remained blithely unaware, that in certain heavenly quarters, he was being discussed. Nor were the Wings aware that the bird's spiritual welfare was being seen to by the exceptionally competent Sister Mary Subordinary. She ran her fingers through the lush feathers of the flightless bird and fed him a daily holy communion of cinnamon toast and oranges. The good Sister would have been pleased to know that plans were afoot for his apotheosis.

It was an exceedingly busy, albeit leisurely, cosmos. The Wheels, like the mills of the Gods, grind slowly. The Maker would not meet his maker any time soon.

———

WITHIN HOURS, THE TALE of the giant white monkey went viral and remained a top search for weeks. An astonishing variety of commentaries exploded over the net, yielding a text both rich and strange—the capuchin monkeys had been loosed upon The Great Church by jealous Buddhists, subversive Jews, angry schoolboys, radical Muslims, Feminist spoilers.

Someone claimed to have seen a flying white monkey drop a white-haired witch into a pool. An exiled Wiki leaker countered that it was the ghost of Delacroix's mistress. The enterprising Wiki-man dumped a cache of the lovers' private emails onto the world wide web. Snopes' urban legend site was flooded with visits.

A war of Wikipedians changed the Hanuman page almost hourly, much to the annoyance of serious Hindu scholars who joined the Wikipedian war with pious intent to protect their holy texts. Like all high-minded religious, the priestly scholars vigilantly purged Hanuman's page of heresy and nonsense and news, most especially news.

All holy books like to lock themselves up tight and throw away the key, conveniently forgetting that the poets who penned the originals were themselves spiritual creatives evolving a many-authored story.

Outside the environs of The Great Church, consensus was growing among secularists that the white monkey climbing the Duomo was a holographic publicity stunt, staged to draw attention away from the more egregious offenses of the ecclesiastical birdmen. The talking heads groused that it was only the usual theological clowns up to their old tricks— creating endless distractions with cooked news. Online fanzines juxtaposed pictures of the iconic Kong on the Empire State Building and Hanuman on the Duomo, asking site visitors to vote for their favorite.

Within the Quoborium, it was widely accepted that the holy high jinks were the work of the missing Holy High Magus, who for unknown nefarious reasons had turned himself into a king-sized white monkey.

The crooked story never would be straightened out.

———

AFTER HANUMAN BREATHED in the sweet hosanna of heavenly praise, he disappeared down the back side of the dome, as graceful as you please. No one could explain how such a large creature could vanish in such a small forest. Only one small boy knew the answer, and he wasn't telling.

When Conrad emerged from the pool, his wound healed by Extraordinary's skillful ministrations, a boy-sized monkey ran from the woods and leapt into Conrad's welcoming arms. They hugged, rubbed noses, and made monkey noises at each other.

Scant moments later, when Mother Mary came swimming to the surface, Hanuman was Skipper once again. Conrad waited for her to make some telling remark. But she did not. It was as if everything had been sorted on the astral plane.

With such an overload of astonishing events, Conrad was barely surprised when Kilowatt pulled up in a sleek Mercedes. The relieved minion stepped out of the car, "Hey, Eppler!" And with a neat little bow, he opened the back door to the black Mercedes, acting for all the world like a hired chauffeur.

"Hey, Kilo!" Conrad hopped in the car.

"Sorry about the kerfuffle with the Cardinals, kid." Kilowatt was still deeply chagrinned that he had failed to protect Conrad.

"You know each other?" Mary Extraordinary gave Kilowatt a quick assessment, easily pegging his lowly rank among angels.

"Yes, we do. Kilo's a good guy. He'll get us home."

Mother Mary Extraordinary had other ideas. "Before we descend this hill that I refuse to call a mountain," she addressed their driver, "I would very much like to meet with Conrad's friend, the Munificentissimus Divine Mallard of All Mysteries, His Holiness, Hierophant of The Great Church. He has one of my paintings. It was unceremoniously ripped off my wall

462

during the persecution of the Sisterhoods. Believe you me, those men would not behave so abominably if they had to answer to women Cardinals."

———

KILOWATT CHAUFFEURED Mary Extraordinary and Conrad Eppler back to the Convent of Immaculate Conceptions after the historic meeting between the Mother Superior and the Hierophant. In the backseat, the boy and the prioress took up an argument that was to last, on and off, until the holy cows came home.

They never could agree if the Divine Duck were more saint or more sinner. Conrad might have guessed that the only reason Mother Mary had wished to speak to the Hierophant in the first place was so she could give him a huge piece of her extraordinary mind.

"The man needed a good scolding," she insisted to Conrad on the drive home.

"You could have been a little nicer, that's all. You didn't need to make fun of his mountain by calling it Crumpet."

"Dear one," Mother Extraordinary was eager to teach, "the Hierophant's incompetence had murderous consequences. That encyclical he wrote criticizing the female religious was the beginning of the purge. His disquisition set off a neo-inquisition that tamped down on spiritual innovation and sometimes tamped on the spirits of the innovators as well—tamped them right into the ground. I lay the devastation at the feet of the Divine Mallard."

"Are you saying he killed your friends?"

"I am saying he stirred up the sleeping Magistere," she meant to close the conversation.

But Conrad carried the argument into the convent.

"He was nice to me," Conrad said, thinking of the Baked Alaska, as he crawled into bed.

"Yes, he treated you well. He is a sweet man—all good intentions paving the way to you-know-where," she teased, tucking the boy in.

"That's not fair! What about his good deeds?"

"I concede his good deeds. How about this? I will write him a nice note in the morning to thank him for the tea and the splendid little peanut butter cookies."

"And the gold? He said you were welcome to keep the gold."

"Of course, we keep the gold. The Magistere gave it to us the day before you were delivered. Actually, the gold is yours."

"Mine?" Conrad sat up.

"Yes. It is being held in trust, by the trustworthy Sister Mary Subordinary. You'll inherit when you are fourteen, maybe fifteen. We'll see."

"Is it a lot of gold?"

"It's enough for a boy of imagination to get into a great deal of trouble. I'm sure the Divine Duck meant it as compensation. But I do not feel compensated. He absolutely refused to return my Botticelli. Denied its existence, even though we both know he's got it."

"But he gave you a present," Conrad said, encouraging her to ease up a bit on his friend. "That scroll."

"Oh, that," she tried to sound dismissive, but in truth she was keenly interested in the gift that had been offered almost as an afterthought, belated evidence that the old fellow regretted his trespasses.

"We might have a look at that drawing someday, you and me. It's a design for a vegetable garden. It has some remarkable innovations and an interesting provenance," Mother paused, looking thoughtful. "It bears the mark of the Magus."

Mary Extraordinary failed to mention a curious Sanskrit inscription camouflaged in a twist of jasmine vines in the bottom corner. *This is for the boy,* the dedication began.

"His Holiness apologized to you," said the relentless child.

"Yes, he did. As he ought. Still, he won't allow Genesis to come last. The perfect garden and the perfection of humankind is how the story ought to end. Anyone with a lick of sense can see that."

Mother Mary Extraordinary looked up. The cassowary poked his head in at the door, followed by a smiling Sister Subordinary carrying quilts. She had come by to kiss Conrad goodnight and make up a bed for the cassowary.

No one wanted to say what was most on their minds—how very much they missed Sister Merry Berry.

Despite the disheartening loss, each was glad that tonight they slept under the same roof. Even the lowly Angel Kilowatt, bivouacked in the wine cellar, was comforted by the proximate family. Besides, Kilowatt had some unfinished business with Conrad concerning a certain repeat-action squirt gun.

The cassowary slept on Merry Berry's quilts at the foot of Conrad's bed, dreaming of a golden egg. When the egg cracked open, a fat blue infant rolled out of the nest. The cassowary sighed in his sleep.

Had there ever been such a disparate collection of divinities mangered under one gabled roof?

O Holy Night!

BOOK THREE

# HER LIGHT MATERIALS

May You Find Your Worth
in The Waking World.

The Plain Doll,<br>Bloodborne

# Moonies

IN A TINY FOLD of the Milky Way, a singular Sister Moon experienced her first car crash, welcoming a drifting 1959 Cadillac Eldorado Biarritz onto her cratered surface. It was both a crash and a soft landing, cushioned by puffs of moon dust that lingered in the thin atmosphere like strands of cotton candy. The dazed passenger saw a bottle of pink chardonnay roll from beneath the passenger seat.

"Isn't that a piece of great good luck," Merry Berry perked up, believing she'd finally made it to a rest stop. "Now if only I could put my hands on a Twinkie." She rooted around in her satchel until, "Success! It's picnic time."

Distracted by the beauty of the star-strewn firmament, she'd been speeding along the celestial highway, loving the acceleration, clueless as to her destination, when she spotted what looked like a beckoning exit sign, winking its electric baby-blues at her. *Sister Moon.* The words were spelled out in one-foot-high translucent ropes of light. What a sign! What a skyway! *Veer right*, a light board blinked insistently. She veered. Why not?

Colonized by a spiritual collective of migrating cognate souls, Sister Moon was a destination spa in a highly-regarded reincarnation loop.

Most often, members of cognate soul systems break away from their group in the bardo corridor between lives, then spiral off, only to reconnect somewhat haphazardly in future reincarnations.

Sometimes, only after many lifetimes of indefinable longing and long Earth searches does a chance meeting occur. There is an aha moment, a deeply shared déjà vu, and the miracle happens—the lost soul mates recognize one another, if only fleetingly. Mother and child, mentor and acolyte, siblings, lovers, friends—the variations are infinite.

Sometimes, one brushes the sleeve of a passerby, adopts a puppy—all the blessed variety of miraculous et ceteras entailed in the big shuffle of karmic do-overs, the great spill and refill of successive lives—and one experiences, not necessarily a boom, but a frisson of recognition.

Rarely do permanent communities form on both sides of the great divide. The Joyous Mystery Sisters of Sister Moon are that rarity—a continuity loop that permits the group to travel together through successive Earth incarnations. Never all at once, a confluence of Sisters is always stationed moonside— some recently arrived, some ready for another Earth ride.

Albeit permanent, the community of Sister souls remains permeable: exits, entrances, and exchanges are known to happen. The population fluctuates at around two hundred, give or take the comers and goers. Although the loop itself is infinite, a member might exit the ride, drift sideways, search out other soul mates.

One slightly drunk nun had just made an unexpected early entrance and was about to rejoin her moonside sister soul group.

Merry Berry finished up her picnic of wine and Twinkies.

Something was awry. Instead of the anticipated high, a recent memory brought her low. She watched herself chasing after Conrad and flying off the cliff's edge at Martyr Maker Point.

"Oh no, I made a terrible wrong turn," she moaned and burst into tears.

An improvised greeting party, made up of a pair of Merry Berry's old besties on Earth, waited at a discreet distance. Observing their consoeur's distress, they did not wish to breach the privacy of her grief. Only when Merry Berry lifted her head from the steering wheel and began to wipe her tears did the Moonies come forward.

The bereft nun heard a light tapping on the driver-side window, looked up and saw two familiar smiling faces: the Vietnamese Sisters Mary Tuee.

Sister Merry Berry stepped out of her Eldorado Biarritz and into an ecstatic reunion. One hand firmly gripping her bottle of pink chardonnay, she received the tremulous hugs of her beloved friends. Covered in moon glow, her modified habit was being modified once again. Her quirky ensemble coruscated in successive shades of pink—from deeply saturated magenta to diaphanous bubblegum. Only her patent leather pumps remained their original apple-delicious red.

The conjoined Sisters Tuee gently reintroduced Sister Merry Berry to the protocols of Sister Moon. They reminded her that on the moon, all the joyous sorority took on Greek acronyms. The Sisters Tuee had become The Sisters Tau. Merry Berry frowned.

Explanations were necessary because memory did not usually extend to previous stop-offs on the moonside of the reincarnation loop. That was part of the existential thrill of electing a descent; one could lose one's way on Earth, become unsettled, rattled to the bone, unaware that one was on an eternally recurring journey back home. The Earthward trip and fall was traditionally called a descent, although there were no ups and downs in the great galactic swirl.

"Merry Berry, let us call you Sister Mu Beta."

"Moo? Like a cow?" Merry Berry, clearly unhappy with this call for re-appellation, let her old friends know that she would not like to be called Sister Mu Beta, and they'd better not.

Lucifer had given her a driver's license with a flattering photograph and some other name. What was it? Mary Jane Greystoke. The license was somewhere in her satchel. She rooted around, but something stopped her frantic search.

Another dreamy but vivid memory intruded. In that memory, she runs on the convent grounds towards a skinny black girl with an infant swaddled in a pink Barbie blanket. She stops and listens to her teenage mother cooing a name, in a voice lemony and southern, gone soft with sorrow. The name is redolent of rolling lemon grass, the Acacia tree, and the magical Baobab.

"You can call me Savannah. Savvy for short." Sister Merry Berry announced.

The Sisters Tau paused, uncertain how to affect the unusual name change request.

"Give us a day or so," the Tau Taus equivocated, "our daily bread has already been baked and buttered."

Dedicated professional celebrants, they were concerned that they were letting their beloved Sister Merry Berry down. However, just now they couldn't quite give the matter of her proposed name change the rapt attention it so richly deserved, distracted as they were by party preparations in play for another imminent moon-landing.

The Tau Taus tried to explain.

Sister Merry Berry tried to understand.

"There's going to be a party? Here? Now?" Merry Berry inquired, noticing the improving colors in her ensemble. "Am I invited?"

The twins, who were carrying sleeves of newly minted Mardi-Grace beads, began slipping the gleaming strands over Merry Berry's bountiful dreads.

"Oh dear, I've dropped the sparkling chardonnay." Merry Berry watched the pink elixir puddle at her feet and gave out a dispirited sigh.

It occurred to the merry-makers that it might be best to let their troubled friend remain inebriated for the next little while. To that end, they gifted Merry Berry with an eternal chalice. A beautifully wrought blown-glass affair with metallic wings; the chalice never spilled a single drop, and every sip was always the first sip.

Magical cup in hand, Sister Merry Berry was hustled along to a festively bedecked piazza that would presently serve as a landing pad.

A light show of fireflies encircled the stately marble columns set in a grand allée that led up to the crescent-shaped stadium. Carved in a hillside above the circular piazza, the stadium would soon fill with Joyous Sisters.

The Tau Taus and Merry Berry ducked under a swarm of choreographed butterflies that were being conducted by a Sister wearing a shimmering evening gown. The threesome made their way towards the stadium seating, on the lookout for the former Sister Josephus.

Lyres were being tuned, drum covers tightened, tambourines festooned with silk streamers. Pods of dancers stretched and preened. An unseen choir ran up and down the scales. Sister Moon, also known as The Colony, was a bustle of activity in anticipation of the arrival of an angel-in-transition, rumored to be a manifestation of the lost First Mother, Eve.

Among their varied endowments, the Joyous Sisters were threshold guardians of the highest order, mistresses of pomp for any circumstance, adepts in the creation of personalized sacraments, from initiations to deifications.

The Moonies loved to party.

The ultimate celestial welcoming committee, they practiced a wide embrace. Any lost lamb, dewy LuLu in rags, or vintage Lucy in the sky with diamonds could count on being hailed and aved with fanfare.

Come on down.

Or up.

Constantly dialing the universe, advertising their wares on celestial highways and byways, they loved nothing better than answering the calls they created. They were a self-sustaining, self-imagined loop of praise-makers. Their litany of blessed-bes rang down the halls of the plenum.

Holy, holy, holy bells and whistles.

The Moonies eagerly awaited the luminous blue rocket that was ferrying Aletheia. It was last spotted over Alpha Virginis, the stunning blue giant in Virgo, where the transport stopped briefly and picked up two gorgeous indigo angels, Thrones by denomination. One striking pale green stowaway slithered onboard unnoticed, taking advantage of the Virginis stopover.

The moon landing would be as soft as silk pillow tops and as noisy as sonic boom beats. Aletheia, cocooned in her rocket, hadn't the least idea what the fates had prepared for her.

Nor were the Sisters altogether prepared. Their spiritual artistry embraced spontaneous call and response. They habitually invented on the fly. They loved fringe and loose ends.

They adored do-overs.

Eve in any guise was a big deal.

The hum of harmonic oms built like oceanic rollers, wave on wave. The stadium thrummed with pink-robed enchanters. Dancers began to swirl around the circular landing pad, leaving the surface and touching down again like so many carousel ponies chasing Calliope orisons. The moment was upon them.

Incoming.

Incoming.

With an exhale of frothy blue steam, the rocket made its once-upon-a-fable landing, arriving on Sister Moon with it its own meticulously arranged atmosphere of hand-painted luminous clouds. This rocket came with personalized weather, raining the softest pour of miniscule crystals. Mild shaky thunders and yellow charm-bracelet lightning cracks punctuated the puffy blue clouds. The pointed spire of the rocket gleamed high above the array of cumulus floaters; and from deep within, a synthesized sequence of chords answered the steadily increasing dream-beats of the drumming nuns.

A set of double doors hummed open to reveal a triptych: Aletheia standing on a half globe of blue-green Earth in the center panel, her shapely bare foot resting on the head of a pale green snake. Rolls and flows of green angel hair rippled in

478

the light breeze. She was flanked by two attending blue angels, wearing star-emblazoned dhotis and red heart-shaped sunglasses.

The guardians took Aletheia by the hand as she descended to the bedecked platform. A welcoming fanfare filled the valley. As if cued to the trumpeted salute, the flanking angels beat their glorious indigo wings against the thin atmosphere and rose, stretching out horizontally to set a tiara of tiny stars in Aletheia's billowing ocean of green locks.

Every good Goddess deserves a Botticelli do now and again.

The two blue angels-in-waiting paused for the photogenic moment. Cameras flashed in the stadium. Then the all-attractive winged pair rolled out and ascended the dome of heaven. It was a collectible moment worthy of any five-star museum gift shop. Holy cards would be printed up and tucked in prayer books from here to eternity. A few of the more observant devotees in the stadium noticed how the green snake slithered off and curled under a moon rock.

Sister Rho Zeta brought the choir to a hush and addressed her consoeurs, "Sisters of the Joyous Mystery, come, gather round and see. Here is the prophecy."

Emboldened by the allure of mystery, some drew closer to the Magnificat. The blind Sister Omega Omicron held out her hand and felt the diamond rainfall slip like glittering sand between her fingers.

Then the rain stopped, and the excitable Sisters Tau rushed forward, greeting the refulgent Aletheia. "Welcome Sister. What gift do you bring?"

Startled and unhappy that she had no gift, Aletheia opened her empty palms. The chorus of Sisters let out a synchronous om of approval, precipitating a stadium wave. The iconic pose had been struck as if on accident. All accident, especially when déjà-viewed, drew admiring waves.

From the back of the crowd, a large woman in a float of gossamer layers parted the waters of the other smaller tides of devotees. She was reading the air like a psalm scored in Braille. The blind Oracle, Sister Omega Omicron, stopped just short of touching Aletheia, then she turned and addressed the gathering.

"I see her gift." A beneficent smile lit the face of Sister Omega Omicron. Then she turned back to Aletheia and announced in a carrying voice, "You are going to love being a mother."

A cry went up, "Annunciation! Annunciation!"

The crowd of Joyous Sisters dropped to their knees, their palms crossed over their hearts. A hum like the drone of honey bees filled the valley. Hands uncrossed, and palms opened in unison with arms outstretched like a great blooming chrysanthemum, Aletheia at its center. Pairs of hands turned like satellite dishes to catch the radiant energy of this limited-edition happenstance, with its vintage miracle tucked in Aletheia's womb.

The Sisters began a synchronous prayer, riffing on an old standard.

"Hail bright visitor, full of grace. What miracle comes with thee? Blessed be, blessed be the fruit of thy—."

"It's not a fruit," interrupted Sister Omega Omicron, asserting herself as was her nature—large and somewhat in charge of a group that resisted herding.

"Not altogether organic," Omega Omicron continued, placing the silver-plated listening disc of her stereo-audicon against the curve of Aletheia's womb.

The disc was about the size of a salad plate attached to a pair of earbuds by multiple translucent threads. This customized multi-use stethoscope was designed in such a way that any sound-waves Oracle picked up were instantaneously broadcast and amplified for all within the range of belief.

The enchanted Sisterhood listened attentively, expecting the familiar heartsong: boo-dah boo-dah boo-dah. Swaying in the moonlight, the stadium of Sisters waited out the silence.

There was no boo-dah.

A mounting susurrus of whispers swept through the amphitheater; cross currents of doubt and desire ebbed and flowed.

"Quiet, please. The Oracle is listening."

A faint heartbeat was finally picked up, soft as the chime of silver bells.

"What? What is it?" The collective blew questions, like air kisses.

Aletheia, wanting nothing so much as to arrest the developing mystery for a moment's reflection, ventured a tentative answer.

"It might be my destiny. Yes, it must be Conrad Eppler!" She saw puzzled looks everywhere.

"He's an Earth boy," the blessed mother added. "It must be a metaphorical conception, an inward sign of an outward—" Aletheia trailed off.

Omicron straightened up. "Wrong. Decidedly wrong. It is not a metaphor. Nor a fruit, as I said, not organic. It's some kind of physical-metaphysical mix."

The instrument picked up another sound—a soft thrum, like a shiver of newborn leaves, still wet and opening.

"What in the universe," exclaimed an enraptured Oracle, "I believe I heard a flutter. She has wings. Oh, my. Could it be an Earth Angel? Unheard of. Oh, blessed be. Whatever! It's unmistakably a girl."

"A girl?" whispered a stunned Aletheia.

A joy-suffused shout went up and the congregants fell to their knees once more, "Hail, Blessed Mother!"

"Thou art with Angel," finished the Oracle in her most orotund, oracular voice.

A weaving Sister Merry Berry tottered up the three steps to the elevated piazza. All eyes were instantly upon those pointy-toed red patent leather high heels.

"There she is! It's her fault. She," Sister Merry Berry pointed at Aletheia, "stole the boy!"

Sister Rho Zeta stepped in. Positive spin was an admired artform on Sister Moon. All were interested in how the mild-mannered Rho Zeta would negotiate this threshold. Prayer beads were being wagered in the stadium.

Joy was the watchword.

"Welcome home, Mu Beta." Rho Zeta greeted her soul sister.

"I am not Moo. I am Merry."

"Of course, you are. As in the more, the merrier," Rho Zeta lovingly repaired. "Remember me? Mary Rose."

"I almost do. Yes. You were in love with Mary Josephus. Forgive me. I accidently smash landed on your Moon. I mean crash landed."

"Then you are a party crasher. What a promising coincidence—we are having a party! And you've already met the descendent, our honoree. How auspicious is *that*?"

Beads rapidly exchanged hands as spiritual calculations were reconfigured.

"I'd say more suspicious than auspicious. In fact, I've met her twice. Two times at once. One of her had a pair of those things." At a loss, Merry Berry mimed flight.

"She's mistaken me for the social worker." Aletheia was distressed by this mix up, distressed by the memory of losing her wings, distressed by the excitable crowd, but most of all, dumbfounded by the announcement of a girl.

"No mistake," insisted Sister Merry Berry, "Twice. One was social, and one was nice. The nice one had green wings. The social one kidnapped Conrad. I've got on her Blahniks to prove it. Catch me if you can," Merry Berry laughed.

With that Merry Berry darted forward, tagged Aletheia and ran. She didn't get very far. She tripped on the piazza steps and immediately decided to stay put. She crossed her ankles beauty-pageant style and raised her cup to the stunned sorority as if she'd won a decisive victory in a game of Got You Last.

The excitable conjoined twins rushed forward, all blushing embarrassment. "Please excuse our Sister Merry Berry. She's only just arrived. Give us this day, our Merry Berry. Our most blessed inebriate." The Tau Taus begged pardons and understandings in one of their signature verbal duets.

"Taken by mischance," offered Tau One

"And mischief," Tau Too added. "She hit an ice slick."

"Crash landed," Tau One confided in conspiratorial hush, "driving an awesome 1959 Cadillac Eldorado Biarritz."

"Very pink, very ritzy," Tau Too concluded.

"Perhaps, I could give Merry Berry a lift. A designated driver seems to be in order." Sister Psi Lambda paused, worried that her mixed motives were showing.

"Mary Josephus, is that you? The keys are around here somewhere. But heaven knows where I parked the Biarritz."

In truth, the former Sister Josephus missed her old Ford Fairlane back on Earth. She was dying to get behind the wheel of the 1959 Cadillac Eldorado Biarritz, but more urgently and equally true she wanted to get behind what was troubling her old friend, Merry Berry. "I am sorry you fell into your cups, dear," added a flustered Sister Psi Lambda.

"I was not in my cups when I slicked. I mean slipped," Merry Berry faltered to her feet, inadvertently touching off another stadium wave. Merry Berry followed suit and sat at the end of the wave. "I mean when the Biarritz slipped," she raised her cup. A wild cheer went up.

Aletheia looked on in growing dismay, wishing she could plunk herself down on the steps with Merry Berry and share a tipple. Fortunately, the Oracle, Sister Omega Omicron, was monitoring Aletheia's distress.

Oracle addressed the stadium, "One voice."

"Yes, best we allow Oracle to speak for all of us." Sister Rho Zeta rallied in support, "I believe we're unnerving Eve, and that can't be good for the blessed cargo."

Oracle considered this new Eve, barely reborn to her recurring destiny. She wanted to put Eve in the big picture, an interesting challenge because the picture was still developing.

"There's been some trouble," Omega Omicron began her explanation to the baffled visitor. "Trouble on Earth. *Your planet*," she paused for emphasis. "Mother Mary Extraordinary is stranded there, minding the shop, not doing very well. Her faith has been blinking on and off. Hundreds of strands in her tracery of dendrites have shorted out. It is imperative that she come back to us, and yet we are afraid that the crossing over is too dangerous in her current state. She might break up into her constituent particles. With what net would we gather her up should she become star dust?" the Oracle gave Aletheia a moment to appreciate their difficulty.

"We could rewrite the story, but we are fond of the ending we've crafted for the story-in-progress. It is astonishing how one gets attached to a narrative of one's own invention. And there's the matter of the boy you mentioned—a kidnapping, a gunshot wound, and a failed adoption. Not to mention the necessity of drawing a veil over the boy's lineage. He has origin issues. Of the first rank. On both sides. One spiritual crisis after another," she summed up.

The Tau Taus nodded blissfully, "How we love chaos. We are devotees of chaos. We are devotees of change. We could change the story, amend the end."

The one voice was breaking up again into the many. Harmonic convergence hummed eternally on the brink of pandemonium. It was always an iffy proposition, conducting a visitor into the discordant music of the hive mind.

"These are the times of wonders, catastrophes and car crashes," enthused Psi Lambda. "How I loved my Ford Fairlane back in the bent world. My old bones still rest beneath that beauty. But why brood? The 1959 Cadillac Eldorado Biarritz is a smasher," she punned happily. "Sister Merry Berry, do you think we could go for a ride in the big pink?"

"Jah is the driva," Sister Merry Berry lifted her cup. She had no intention of leaving the party.

The Tau Taus gushed, "Gates between spiritual realities open and close. Open and close with increasing frequencies." They looked to Aletheia. "Have you noticed the changes in the weather? On *your* planet?"

Silence fell. There was a clear expectation in the amphitheater that Aletheia would answer this last question. She disappointed.

"No, I hadn't noticed the weather," she offered, losing all sense of proprioception in the tumult of talkback that seemed to advance by misdirection.

The weather on *her* planet? They kept calling Earth *her* planet. She didn't know where she was or who she was. She could not locate herself existentially, spiritually, or geographically. She wished this strange congregation would return to the topic most pressing on her conscience, but the Sisters' voices raced on and over each other in a cacophony of mismatched enthusiasms.

Now the Oracle was speaking again, "Your planet is depressed, dear. We are her Sister Moon, so we are tuned to her currents and her moods. This morning the tides wouldn't rise. We pulled, but the prevailing gravities would not give. First Mother Mary. Then the boy. Now this. Perhaps you could give us an assist."

The fluty voices of the Sisters Tau Tau topped off Oracle's doleful oboe, "Things have never been so amiss. Oh, what bliss!"

Aletheia's mind raced to keep up. Lucky for the tiara of miniature stars, set so charmingly in her curls; its constant twinkling sent reviving surges of positivity.

"Can you give a planet Prozac?" Oracle asked and then answered herself. "No, no. I don't think so. We need to invent new prayers for Earth. A salvation of poetry. We believe that prayer can alter destiny. But here's a question for you—can prayer change the weather? Perhaps you have an insight to share, yourself being the prophecy."

Again, there was the waiting silence. Aletheia felt the press of the amphitheater leaning into her, so much desire, hope and expectation nearly made her pass out.

"Please. Where am I?" she dared to ask.

"Why, you're on Sister Moon. Where did you mean to be?" Sister Rho Zeta inquired genially, mindful of Aletheia's rising and falling tides of distress.

"I was headed for The Colony. I was told The Colonists would prepare me for my journey, help me make the transition to the material plane on planet Earth. Perhaps it is my planet."

Sister Omega Omicron, the Oracle, smiled graciously and pointed up to something she could not see, but was vividly present to her inward eye.

And there it was, the wet blue jewel, swimming in the starry night. The hum of voices rose again.

"We are The Colony!"

"Professional celebrants."

"We do sacraments."

"What sacrament do you require?"

"Extra, extra, extreme Earthing?"

The calliope struck up its fairground melody. The whirling dancers started spinning again. Drums, tambourines, trumpets and fountains of rose petals excited the air. The whole show was back on. A recitative of possibilities thrilled through the stadium.

"I say, it's a naming ceremony."

"Yes! Yes! Yes!" a crowd of affirmatives were tossed up and got tangled with the rose petals.

"The angel cub has not arrived."

"It will arrive by tomorrow morn."

"Daughters of the etherics are quickly born."

"What if it's a litter? That will set the Gods atwitter."

"I say, Holy Matrimony, a wedding ceremony."

"Yes! Yes! Yes!" Another pandemonium of affirmations filled the stadium.

"But we haven't got a groom."

"You can never plan a wedding day too soon."

Laughter erupted. Applause. Then silence, and once again the Oracle led the service with an impromptu address.

"Blessed Magnificat, most honored guest, no one has ever arrived who required so much of what we do best. Bless us Mistress, how shall we serve thee?"

"Thank you," Aletheia began, "I hope you won't think it ungracious if I ask—?"

"Ask, ask, ask."

"Are you the one in charge here?" She looked to Oracle.

"Why, no. No one is in charge. We are a dis-order. We come to the moon to renew our vows, refresh and reinvent ourselves so that we may discover how and when and where we might best serve the Earth in the next forever again."

"We are The Colonists!"

"We colonize eternity."

"Forgive me, I've been rude. I am Sister Omega Omicron, the Oracle. This time. Last time on Earth, I was Sister Mary Mirabelle, a most memorable incarnation."

"And we are the Sisters Tau Tau, the spiritual twins, formerly Tuee."

"Cheers to you," Merry Berry lifted her eternal chalice in a wide gesture that would have flung a froth of champagne in Aletheia's face had the chalice not been skillfully designed to keep its contents.

Merry Berry took it upon herself to complete the introduction. "And this, my dear alphabetized Shisters," indicating with her chalice, "is Ms. Demeanor, the twit, as I now remember it. The other one had a set of those things."

"Wings." Sister Omicron supplied.

"Did I repeat myself? I don't want to repeat myself. This is not the life I was meant to be reliving. Please, someone help me off this moon," the blessed inebriate begged. "If I had never arrived, it would have been too soon."

Merry Berry tottered off to find her Cadillac, vaguely aware that there was some unfinished business she must attend. Then she turned back, "She's a trouble maker, that Margaret Demeanor."

"I am not Margaret. My name is Aletheia. I'm from the planet Grace. I did have wings once. But I relinquished them."

"That explains it," Oracle ventured.

"Explains what?" The Magnificat was letting her frustration show.

"How it is you carry an angel within."

"It explains nothing," Aletheia differed.

"Aletheia is an interesting name," began Rho Zeta, keeper of the books and namesake of the Rosetta stone. "It is Greek: Αλήθεια," Rho Zeta chalked the beautiful letters on a moon stone.

"The river Lethe is the river of forgetfulness. Alethe means unforgetting. When you are remembered to yourself, you will recognize your many links in the great chain of being. Remembering also calls forth the vast rolodex of past iconographic identities. Look at you—appearing to us as the green Venus." Rho Zeta smiled encouragingly. "All you need is a half-shell."

Aletheia fought for balance on the pink half shell that appeared beneath her feet. It rocked gently on the palest pink ocean that swiftly tumbled by. And just as swiftly, the ocean evaporated along with the shell.

"When you achieve self-knowledge," Rho Zeta continued, "your identities become a transparency, a one-in-the-many, a placemark in time. Each beloved Avatara remembered is a manifestation of a truth that draws from the past, sits in the present and holds the future. Thus in the Greek, Aletheia comes to mean Truth."

"May Truth prosper," the Sisters responded, "and multiply. Ah She."

"Put another way," Rho Zeta rounded off, "Aletheia in the act of remembering is the stepping stone to Eve."

A buzz of bliss ran through the amphitheater. Rho Zeta had struck a lost chord.

This time Aletheia let herself be soothed by the hive noise. The new Eve began to adapt to the constant commentaries and exultations. She realized that when she stopped separating the vocalizations into discrete words, the music of the hive became a hum. Then the volume decreased until it was an almost inaudible white noise.

Sound on Sister Moon was a tactile experience, brushed on the skin like ocean air. And like the salty waft of a sea breeze, the new Eve discovered the voice of the Moonies had a scent. When she tuned out, what she heard was love cresting in the scent of a sea. What she felt was a benevolence of curiosity, coming off the Sisters in waves of words that rolled on in a continuous caress.

"Who did you kiss?" asked the communal caress. "It must have been an astonishing kiss, thy sweet womb blessed, an angel sleeping in thy nest. Your hearts beating to the same rhyme, rhyme, rhyme. A rhythm synchronized at the beginning of time. Who did you kiss? Who did you touch, touch, touch? There's always an Adam about the mystery, we know that much."

She felt the collective mind of the soul-cognates enter hers and she answered by igniting the memory.

"I was an answering angel, caught in a little boy's prayer. He showed me a comic book. I brought him a time traveler. Roica's map of memories ran deeper than mine. One brief kiss, once upon a cloud. Then in a garden, deep inside the boy's vision, we stood on a promontory—and we kissed until the world turned over."

The cognate mind turned over and went with her to the promontory, watched the white caps curl on the beach below, heard the song of gulls. As Aletheia got closer to her origins, the breakers surged, and a wave of sorrow slammed her, knocking out her breath.

In a synchronous swerve, the hive mind located the original primordial kiss. And a betrayal.

Eve cried out and would have fallen to her knees in grief but for the translucent nets cast out by the Sisters, binding her in love. The community of prayer-makers held her up, allowed her to get dangerously close to herself and safely into her sorrow. The threshold guardians were doing what they did best.

Aletheia came up for breath. "Did I miss my chance?" She turned to the Oracle. "He's gone. And I have no idea where."

Sister Omega Omicron aimed her stethoscope at Aletheia's heart.

"There it is—the heartache, the almost heartbreak."

The community sighed but did not grieve. The wound in the heart of creation gave a chiaroscuro luster to this exceptional visitation by the Magnificat, she who magnifies the mysteries of love and procreation. A heartache was a sacred scar. It spoke of depths, secret chambers, tides and sea changes.

Broken cups.

Moon matters.

Oracle raised the audicon skywards. Her instrument found the matching beat, the matching ache, the almost break. The community listened to Roica fold space and speed away at a breakneck pace. His heartbeat was soon lost in the swallowing dark matter of space.

"He's chasing the Wheels," Aletheia told her community.

"Then we must turn our thoughts elsewhere. That chase is forever, and the birth of the Earth Angel presses near," observed Rho Zeta, who then asked Sister Delta Dawn and Sister Alpha Oceania to escort Aletheia to the Cat's Cradle on the moon's Southern cusp. "It is time for the laying in. Let us pray for a safe delivery."

The Moon Sisters began to rub their palms together in quick circular motions, creating a susurrus as soft as summer rainfall. Aletheia let herself be swept along in the currents of the sorority's calm and confidence. An unfamiliar percolation of joy overtook the mother expectant as Sister Delta Dawn and Sister Alpha Oceania gently guided her into the next mystery.

———

SO MUCH HAD TRANSPIRED at this conjunction of Moon and Earth. So much reveal. So much rapture. So much mystery remaindered. Rho Zeta, keeper of books, would be spending long hours recording the litany of sacraments performed during Aletheia's brief sojourn on Sister Moon—one transformative moment flowing seamlessly into another. When all was settled, a new holy day would be ordered up on the crowded calendar of moonside commemorations.

Omega Omicron, Psi Lambda, and Rho Zeta withdrew to a crystal cave at the back of the amphitheater to mull over the implications and fulfillments of the historic descent of the emerald angel from Grace to Moon to Earth.

"She has come at last to fulfill the prophecy. The First Mother is returning to her planet," thrilled Sister Omega Omicron, the Oracle. "A new age is upon us."

Sister Rho Zeta was flipping through the pages of an ancient beribboned book, pulled from the stacks and set on a podium. "The First Mother, yes. But the angel infant does not appear in The Book of Prophets. The next Avatar is supposed be a boy. There is no mention of a girl."

"There is a universal tendency to forget to mention the girls," Omicron looked thoughtful. "Right from the beget-go. Surely, Adam and Eve had daughters. I mean who did Seth marry? Did you ever wonder about that?"

"That's the problem limning prophecy from the Patriarchs' Testament. Besides, the text was already heavily redacted when it was passed on to us. The Godma was entirely bleeped as if She were the F word, which of course She is. Fecund." Lambda took a breath. "Let's face it. We need new prophets.

We need a testament with more variety. A book alive to all weathers and all genders."

"Until then, we have this," Rho Zeta asserted, finding the page she was looking for. "It says the First Father was to come down as well."

"You know men," conciliated Omicron, "you can never depend on them. Remember when Hermes impregnated that Earth girl and begot the goat boy, Pan? It was Hermes' fault entirely, disguising himself as a goat. What did he expect? Getting that poor girl got with goat. Then Hermes wings off in his cute gold booties and leaves the poor goat boy, Pan, eternally yearning for his father's lauds."

"Off topic."

"Not really. That poor little blue baby! What were those two deities thinking?"

"No thinking involved."

The three chuckled knowingly.

"Back to the matter at hand. How will Eve's descent fulfill the prophecy without Adam?" Oracle wanted to know.

"I'd be willing to wager that Roica is running as fast as he can, to get as far as he can from the despoiled garden," Psi Lambda looked over Rho Zeta's shoulder at the page under discussion. "Clearly, Adam is not an incarnation Roica wants to revisit."

"The kiss-and-run didn't buy in," Rho Zeta closed the book and gave Psi Lambda a knowing look. "So much for wedding plans. Well, I'm disappointed."

"Perhaps, we don't need a groom," Oracle mused, entirely missing the exchange between Rho Zeta and Psi Lambda.

Rho Zeta was suddenly inspired. "Really, it's all about the dress. And the liturgy. We can marry Aletheia to the moon or the sea. Pure poetry."

"I'm sorry Rho Zeta, I messed up last lifetime." Psi Lambda was not about to let that knowing look fly by unremarked. "Why refuse me now?"

"Darling Psi Lambda, eternity is a daunting prospect."

"Fine. Then marry me for one Earth life."

"Describe it." Rho Zeta challenged.

"I thought I'd have a go at pro surfing in my next incarnation. This unlived life keeps running in my mind. I'm behind the wheel of a restored VW van, tooling down scenic Highway 1. What if we meet on Ocean Beach in San Francisco? It's just a hop skip from the convent."

"Who am I in this vision?" Rho Zeta asked, wondering if they'd ever successfully share a vision.

"You could be a journalist. Let's say I'm a top contender in the Rip Curl Pro competition. I'm your Pulitzer Prize, looking oh-so-fine in my competition suit."

"I'd rather be your competition in the waves."

"You're on."

"Sisters! May I suggest you move your negotiations to the baths? On another day? We were considering the pressing matter of Eve and her sacred consort. I like Rho Zeta's suggestion. The sea is an enchanting possibility. We can marry Aletheia to the ocean."

"Or," Sister Psi Lambda countered, "we can find a proxy. A stand-in."

"There are historical precedents," Omicron conceded. "Remember the only begotten son? Where was the father then? Attending some off-world business, I suppose. What a reprobate, abandoning his beloved, his progeny, and his planet. No fathoming the mind of the Maker. I say yes to the proxy. We can find some good Joe to fill in the blank."

"Joseph? Not him. He was nice, but can't we find someone for Aletheia with a little more, I don't know—heat?" Psi Lambda winked.

"And fire and light?" Omicron teased.

"Not him!" Rho Zeta objected.

"Oh, yes." Lambda encouraged.

"Is there a redactor in the house?" Oracle was blazing with visions of radical revisions, "O happy erasures, emendations, and ejaculations!"

"Tradition better tighten its ass. It's going to get a tweaking," Lambda cracked wise.

"Practical matters, dears. When the emerald angel stepped off her pedestal, I saw a green snake slither off into the rock garden. She brought *him* with her." Rho Zeta folded her arms. "Someone's got to catch the snake," she added, implying that it wasn't going to be her.

"I'll do it, for Lord's sake," and the Oracle charged ahead.

# SECRET AGENTS

KILOWATT FOUND HIMSELF reflecting on the trajectory of his personal journey as Luce's minion—from the bright beginnings in the starry ether to the great tumble into the black hole, then back up to Grace, and now surprisingly ensconced in a musty wine cellar on Earth. Alone in the dark, he was contemplating the nature of loyalty, wondering if it was always a one-way street.

Kilo's thoughts ran back to his violent curbside confrontation with the Cardinals. Where was Luce in his hour of need? In the aftermath of the brawl, Kilo had sat dejected on a side street, his back against a brick wall, catching his breath and berating himself for the debacle.

Although he'd given better than he got, the bottom line was that the Cardinals had nabbed the kid. That was the low point— not knowing if he'd ever set eyes on the Earthworm again. He remembered looking up, and seeing a stencil spray-painted on the red brick wall across the street, somebody's idea of a despairing angel smoking a cigarette.

"Nothing like urban existencilism," he'd joked ruefully to the Banksy knock-off. It was a moment of truth for Kilowatt. He saw himself in that angel—caught between worlds, uncertain about being, much less being real.

"You and me both, brother," he addressed the art on the wall.

It struck Kilo that he got nearly as much satisfaction communing with the stenciled angel as he did with the Angel of Light. There was something cold about that light.

"You blew it," Luce scoffed, when the illuminato had finally come strolling around a corner and spotted Kilowatt sitting dejected against a wall.

Lucifer had taken his time deleting Conrad Eppler from the state system, unaware that the Hooded Crows in Cardinal Delacroix's employ had traced Conrad to the Protective Services building days ago. An abduction scheme was already in motion when Luce began scrolling through the files.

The delegation of Cardinals dispatched by Delacroix couldn't believe their luck when they spotted the boy on the loose, casually walking down the street with a stranger.

One cell phone call and their plans changed on the spot.

"It was a surprise attack, Luce. I'm guessing you didn't see it coming. Talk about your angels unawares."

"What are you implying?"

"I'm implying it woulda been nice if there'd been some back up," a flat-voiced Kilo had responded. "Twenty on one. The odds were a joke."

Unlike Luce, with all his ulterior motivations, Kilo cared about the kid. Truth be told, Kilo was so ripped up about the abduction, he'd barely been able to respond to Lucifer's insults. Lucifer had waxed on prophetic about the dire consequences of Kilowatt's incompetence, never suspecting that he was being measured by his minion. And coming up short.

"What's the plan, Boss?" Kilo had finally interrupted.

"The plan is for you to hightail it up Mount Quoborium and figure out what happened to the kid. In other words, get him back, Kilowatt."

"Consider it done. I take it finding the kid is a solo gig?"

"Very perceptive. I've got a promising rendezvous on my dance card. When a certain blue rocket passes through Alpha Virginis, I'm going to hitch a ride."

"Her Royal Luminosity ain't going to like it, you showing up on Sister Moon, messing with her various verdicts and proclamitories."

"She's not going to see me coming." He was just then deciding on the green snake ruse.

"That's it, then? No advice. No nothing." Kilo brushed off the seat of his pants and turned to go.

Luce had nearly forgotten the good advice he'd given a grateful Margaret Demeanor only moments earlier. With a quickly constructed afterthought, the illuminato had offered Kilowatt the benefit of his recently acquired insight, "When it all comes down to dust—angel dust, star dust, moon dust—what matters most is being ice."

"Ice, Luce?"

"Did I say ice? I meant nice."

Kilowatt didn't buy it, not coming from Luce, even though he could have used a little nice right about then. That's when the low-level angel witnessed one of the perennial wonders of cognition, a Zen koan for the clowns of creation—the sound of a brilliant mind slipping on the banana peel of its own ego.

"Human kindness," Luce mulled over the recently sampled virtue, "is kind of like kindling."

"You talking twigs, Luce?"

"Small combustibles. It's how you start a fire." In his beautiful mind, Luce was already racing off to the glowing blue giant in Virgo—Alpha Virginis. "Point is—I'm headed for a bigger show."

Later, Kilo would beg to differ. A humongous white monkey on the Golden Duomo above the Avesticum Cathedral was hard to top.

When Kilowatt finally took off for Mount Quoborium to track down Conrad and his abductors, the greatest show on Earth was well underway. On arrival Kilo had been immediately caught in the thrum of dazed observers who were crowding in the plaza below the Duomo.

Flocks of birdmen stood with one arm heiled in the ubiquitous strange-love salute of the cellphone-obsessed throng. Spotting the colossal white monkey on the Duomo, Kilowatt whipped out his cell. Almost of its own accord Kilo's arm rose in synch with the mesmerized churchmen, and the camera's eye caught the RKO-worthy spectacle.

Now he reviewed the recording and saw how he could put the video to good use.

The last one remaining awake in the Convent of Immaculate Conceptions, Kilowatt stretched out in his improvised lair in the dimly lit wine cellar. He let himself dwell on a dreamy scene of one-upmanship. He imagined showing off the video clip to Luce, certain that he'd caught the bigger show.

He saw the poster: Giant Blue Star in Virgo vs. Giant White Monkey on Duomo.

Monkey wins. Hands down. No contest.

The lowly angel was trolling for a smidgen of admiration from the Angel of Light, maybe even a dash of envy.

Kilowatt tried out several iterations of the projected scene, waiting for the payoff—a fist bump or thumbs up. But as it turned out, he found it was impossible to imagine any credible response from Lucifer that wasn't also a downer.

When Luce finally crashed Kilo's mind-party and snarked— "It looks like a fake," Kilo had to admit the remark sounded exactly like something Luce would say. The lowly angel was forced to concede that, no matter what he had to show, Luce would remain stubbornly unimpressed.

Kilowatt's projection was breaking up.

"Maybe you had to of been there," Kilo scoffed at the fantasy and let it go.

Flicking on his new laser-point wand, the angel drew a series of green, lazy eights on the cellar ceiling. As he mused on the past and gazed at the future, something shifted.

Kilowatt sat up. "Shift happens," he riffed on a bumper-sticker slogan he'd seen somewhere.

The lowly angel had finally arrived at the end of his long rumination concerning all things Luce, and he found what he was looking for—a green illumination, an exit sign.

It was over.

As far as he could remember, he'd always been a minion. And even though the decision to break free sort of crept up on him, when it finally arrived, it felt monumental.

He tried it out loud, "I am done being a minion." Then he laid back on his makeshift bed, waiting for blowback.

Nothing happened. Except a great big quiet. It was so quiet, Kilo thought he heard the sound of one hand clapping.

In the wee hours of the morning, Kilowatt's thoughts turned to Conrad, now tucked in safely in the yellow room upstairs. Kilo searched for a word to describe how he felt. He settled on *kindled*.

All things considered, it had been a productive all-nighter, possibly the most productive of his existence. Even before he began his long night's meditation, quite a lot had been accomplished in the practical world. He'd set up a Wi-Fi system in the cellar, edited his video clip, added a soundtrack, and was now looking forward to a morning spent hanging out with the kid.

Kilowatt jotted down a few notes. He was trying to locate the beginning of his new beginning. It could have started the very first day he wrote the name Conrad Eppler in his tablet. Or it might have been more recent. Maybe it started the day he drove Conrad and the old nun back to the convent—that odd interval when he surprised himself and accepted Mother Mary's invitation to stay over. His reply had been casual, a toss away.

"Sure. Why not?"

Then in no time flat, he had outfitted a nifty little spot for himself underground. He didn't know it yet, but he was happy.

Yesterday, he'd spent the day shopping. He had driven back to the city with the intention of returning the Mercedes he'd stolen in his haste to rescue Conrad. It turned out that the owner had three other highly-buffed Mercedes parked in an immaculately maintained garage.

"Thanks for sharing," Kilo said to the absent owner, and drove off in the Mercedes without a backward glance.

Now he came up the stairs bearing gifts: a cool new outfit with a trilby hat and shades for the Earthworm, a similar hat and shades for the monkey, plus a digital tablet for bargaining purposes. Kilowatt still had his heart set on Conrad's Mattel.

Before they got down to the brass tacks of bargaining, Kilowatt showed Conrad the video of the colossal white monkey on the Duomo and was rewarded with every enthusiastic response he would never get from Lucifer.

"Wow!" the boy cried out. "WOW! Unbelievable! Let's watch it again."

It was a love fest.

Next up, Kilo clicked on his doctored version—the one spliced with samples from various King Kong movies, but Conrad liked the original best. They watched it several times. The boy was green with envy.

"The good stuff always happens when I'm underwater," Conrad groused. "I missed the invasion of the Cardinals completely. At least I was there for the kidnapping," Conrad joked. "Tell that part again."

Kilowatt spun out a blow-by-blow recapitulation of the fight with the Cardinals, giving it the full comic book treatment. A rapt Conrad saw the swirl of red robes, saw every WHAM! BLAM! POW!, saw himself inside his own story, saw the infinite plays and replays—how a story could belong to the teller, the listener, the comic book maker, the readers, the world.

When Kilo came to the part of the story where Luce showed up, he flashed on the stenciled angel and made an edit. When he deleted his post-brawl encounter with Lucifer, he felt like he'd picked a burr off his sleeve. He paused, held the burr between his thumb and forefinger, then flicked dis and despair into the nowhere.

"What was that?" Conrad asked.

"Existentialism," replied the angel.

Kilo took up the story at the Mercedes, how he'd lucked onto a car with the keys sitting in the ignition like a "steal me advert." He bragged to Conrad how he had hauled ass up the mountain and caught the whole giant monkey act on his cell.

"Weird thing was," said Kilo, "I make it up to the Sanctum. I'm asking around about you. Nobody knows nothing. Then after the monkey business, I remembered how you said you and the old lady hid from the Cardinals in the quarry pool that time the bad hats invaded the convent. I put two and two together, and I start asking—where's the deepest pool? I drive around the Quoborium and boom. There's you and the spook and Skipper."

Just then, Conrad was wondering if Kilo would put another two together and come up with Skipper equals Lord Hanuman. The boy needn't have worried. The lowly angel never made that leap. Even so, Kilowatt became the giant monkey's biggest fanboy. In Kilo's mind, the monkey was the mystery that tagged him and got away.

Conrad wanted to shout out loud, "I know that white monkey! And he's right here in the room with us."

Skipper whispered an urgent *no*, in Conrad's mind.

*Why not?* Conrad shot back using the *Ransom Note* font he discovered just this morning on the digital tablet.

The boy had barely begun exploring Kilo's digital tablet when he'd come across a treasure trove of fonts. *Ransom Note* became an immediate favorite. The monkey refused to speak to Conrad in such an overdrawn, cartoonish font. Nor would Skipper speak in *Nueland Inline*, a script made famous in Jurassic Park posters and amateur musicals featuring Pumbaa and Timon. Even a stuffed monkey has points of dignity.

Kilo turned the conversation to the vintage Mattel, a repeat-action squirt gun that spoke to a childhood he never really had—possibly a childhood that no one ever really had. It was a childhood Kilowatt read about in Earth books and watched on TV clips posted on the world wide web.

Kilo was pretty sure the Mattel was his, that the digital tablet on offer would clinch the deal. But as much as Conrad wanted to own the technological marvel with its astonishing library of videos and texts, it did not precipitate the flurry of bargaining Kilowatt expected.

Conrad Eppler had a huge favor he was getting ready to ask of Kilowatt, and he couldn't afford to use up his one bargaining chip on electronics. The Earthworm didn't realize what the lowly angel was just discovering—Kilowatt was willing to jump over the moon for Conrad. And that was a good thing, considering the favor Conrad had in mind. When the two conspirators finally put together what Conrad wanted most with what Kilo was willing to try, they came up with a doozy.

———

THE NEXT EVENING Sister Mary Subordinary entered Conrad's room, her brow troubled, her body aching with exhaustion. Spotting Mother Mary Extraordinary in her wheelchair, she exhaled a long sigh of relief.

"There you are," Sister Subordinary addressed the ancient prioress, who sat in stony silence, staring out one of the windows facing the terrace.

Kilowatt immediately reconfigured his etheric lumens in such a way that he was both there and not there.

If Sister Subordinary had truly looked, she might have been able to see Kilo, but she preferred not to see. Subliminally aware of a shadow leaning against the yellow wall, Sister managed to dust the image from her mind without leaving a trace.

Sister Mary Subordinary had been on a frantic search this past half hour and wanted to bask for a moment in the sweet relief of finding Mother Mary Extraordinary.

It was not meant to be.

Since returning from the mountain, Mother Mary Extraordinary had gone into a rapid decline. The elderly prioress had used up her considerable reserves in her long ordeal: surviving the heart attack, climbing the mountain, healing the boy, and remonstrating with the Hierophant. Extraordinary had invested heavily in the fly-now-pay-later plan. Currently in the pay-later part of the cycle, she was wheelchair bound and having trouble keeping the laces of her Earth-boots tied.

"Somehow, your boots keep untying themselves," Subordinary observed with another sigh. "It seems I have become a veritable sea of sighs," she said to no one in particular.

Sister noticed a peculiar dampness in her thinking, as if she'd been tossed in the sea of her own of sighs.

Small disturbances were mounting.

When she knelt to retie Mother Mary's black boots, Subordinary became aware of a certain jitter in reality. The jitter always occurred when events happened in too quick a succession for Sister's mind to execute its habitual edits. Now the array of observables swelled, slipped by the censor, and gave her visual field an alarming frangibility. Her orderly world was shifting.

One particular visual refused to be whisked.

Extraordinary's habit seemed to grow, as if she were taking on layers and volumes of heavy black satin to balance out her increasing thinness. Her veil appeared fuller, lifted by folds and tiers of tulle.

Subordinary would have loved to question Mother Mary Extraordinary concerning these changes in her habit, but Extraordinary hadn't spoken a word since she'd tucked Conrad in after her return from the mountain. This morning Subordinary had lifted an extremely weak Extraordinary and set her carefully in a wheelchair. Upstairs.

Now here she sat. Obviously, she'd wheeled herself into Conrad's room. How had she managed that? And hadn't Sister Mary Subordinary tied double knots in Mother Mary's boots this very morning?

Subordinary stood. She was tired of puzzles. The order was near extinction, if one could call it an order at all. One ancient catatonic and one exhausted caretaker didn't amount to much. Conrad deserved better.

Too bad the adoption process had become a hopeless boggle. Apparently, Conrad no longer existed on the state rolls. So officially, there was no one for Alyssa and Rios Dante to adopt. Moreover, Grace's daughter, Alyssa, had proven to be disappointingly fickle. Alyssa Rosaria Dante was so much like her Grandmother Mirabelle—all changes, indecisions and moony visions. The adoption was on. The adoption was off.

Now Alyssa was pregnant and wasn't sure she could handle a newborn baby *and* a seven-year-old boy. She'd call back. Soon. Maybe tomorrow.

When Subordinary hung up the phone after last night's conversation with Alyssa, she looked up, startled to see Conrad framed in the doorway. He was looking at her intently with those mesmerizing blue eyes—the only remainder of his bright blue babyhood. He'd been listening. Had he heard both sides of the conversation? Before she could even attempt a salutary explanation, he told her not to worry; the green angel would be back.

Another sigh.

Now here was Mother Mary, seeming to shrink as her habit grew. This isn't happening, Subordinary agreed with herself.

"Oh, Mother Mary!" Sister Subordinary tried to make contact, "Mother Mary Extraordinary? Hello-oo. Can you hear me, dear?"

Conrad looked up from the telescope, poised on its tripod at an open window. He'd been observing the night sky for the last hour or so.

"There's no use knocking," Conrad said to Sister Subordinary, "No one's at home." The boy resumed his star gazing.

"You and Mother Mary make quite a team, each of you staring into your own infinities."

"I'm keeping the angel watch."

"Too much staring into space and the garden goes to seed." Mary Subordinary found herself plucking lackadaisically at the extraordinary burgeoning veil. "What an exemplary world it would be, if persons paid more attention to their vegetables."

Mary Extraordinary slapped away Sister's hand, almost bringing tears.

"Not you, of course, dear," Subordinary soothed. "You're clearly not a vegetable. I meant garden greens."

"Tough guys don't eat peas," Conrad interjected.

Subordinary noted Conrad's odd remark, but she did not respond. She was too busy puzzling over the slap. Was the slap an irritable response to Subordinary's fussing over the burgeoning veil? Or did Extraordinary think that she'd been called a vegetable?

Another sigh.

And what was this tough guy talk coming from Conrad? He seemed somehow to have acquired a new wardrobe, and along with it, an unfortunate new syntax. He was wearing an unfamiliar dark suit, and an unfamiliar matching hat was tossed on the bed. Skipper was also oddly appareled. The monkey had on a little trilby and a pair of sunglasses.

"Shades," Conrad corrected the puzzled nun. Then he flashed some sort of badge. And when questioned about the origins of the new wardrobe and badge, he'd said, "Sorry to clam up on you, Sister, but I ain't talkin."

What was that about? Ain't talkin? And that curious remark about tough guys and peas. It's not his fault, she concluded, he must be thoroughly traumatized by the kidnappings.

"I'll ring when supper is ready," Subordinary said, preparing to leave.

"Aw, Sister Subordinary, why do you have to be so—ordinary?"

"Indeed. Well, pardon me. I'll leave you and Mother Mary to your divine missions. Ground control is awfully busy these days. I believe I'll go man the pots and pans."

"Wait. I'm sorry I was mean."

"I'm sorry you're depressed."

"I'm not depressed. I'm just under a lot of pressure. Look at Mother Mary Spookiness. Now that's depressed."

"Conrad, I'm afraid we've done you a great, great wrong."

"What did you do?" Conrad was immediately on the alert, concerned that adoption papers had been signed behind his back.

"Why, we kept you. What right had we to keep a baby? But there you were on the convent steps. We took you in, and Mother Mary said we could keep you for the night and tomorrow we would give you up. And the tomorrows turned into weeks and the weeks piled up until there were years of you and here you are."

"You did the right thing."

"I'm afraid we did not. The dark wing of the Sorrowful Mystery had already descended upon us. It is a terrible thing when the angels no longer appear."

"Why does that happen?" asked the boy who desperately missed his particular angel.

"I don't know. But Conrad, you must not wait for the angels to come again." Her heart was breaking for him.

"Then you do believe I saw them?"

"I believe in the dandelions and the asparagus and the blue butterflies. I know the monkey blinked," she hadn't meant to say that.

513

"What?" Conrad perked up.

"Let me tell you something," she interrupted herself and stared down at Skipper, whom she thought looked ridiculous in sunglasses. When she resumed speaking, she addressed both boy and monkey. "You need only look as far as Mother Mary Extraordinary to see the devastation that comes from clinging to your yesterdays."

"I'm never going to be like her. She gave up, just when I need her the most."

"Oh, listen to you. I have never seen such brilliance as the light that beveled the air when Mother Mary knelt in prayer."

"I've seen her light," said the unhappy boy.

"I know you have. We have all seen her light. Bless her. Even as death walked among us and emptied our choir, Mother Mary continued to believe that the day would come when the Joyous Sisters would raise such a song that the angels would answer by ringing the celestial bells."

"What happened to her beliefs? I mean her old beliefs."

"I think you know. The angels, who kept her in her graces, rolled away in a gray cloud and left her. The garden went to seed. The convent emptied. The prayer books went blank. She said it was a test of faith. She did *not* give up. The angels abandoned *her*."

Subordinary sighed and carried on. "Remember how she called you her little Holy Ghost? Mother said, so long as you were among us, we still had a ghost of a prayer, a ghost of a chance. But you are right. She did, at last, give up. One night, she called us to her private chapel, and she told us it was time we found someone to adopt the little Holy Ghost. Then she wept. And when she stopped, she was just a remnant of what she once was."

"But I'm still here. That means there's still a chance. There's still a prayer."

"Prayer is out of date."

"No, it's not. You should have seen Mother Mary Extraordinary on the mountain."

"Prayer is ineffective, Conrad. I cannot pray you a dinner or pray you parents or pray Merry Berry back to us. It doesn't work that way. They say the new Sisters have their PhD's in sociology and such."

Sister Mary Subordinary was furious and near tears. "They wear pins on their lapels to designate their order. Very small pins, I might add. And high-heeled shoes."

"Like Ms. Demeanor?"

"No!"

She realized she had shouted, and then remembered Sister Merry Berry tottering about in those very shoes.

"Yes," she amended, "like Ms. Demeanor. They do useful things. Protecting children is a useful thing. Our only service was a song."

Although those were the words she spoke out loud, she remembered the garden in its salad days. She remembered all the lovely foundlings the Sisters had rescued and placed in loving homes. Such bright beginnings.

Do beginnings count? Or are we only as good as our endings? She filed the unanswered questions away for another day.

Mary Subordinary was struck with the irony that Conrad and Mary Extraordinary, the only two babies that were ever kept and raised at the convent, were also the last ones left. She had become so self-dismissive, she did not bother to count herself.

Conrad inadvertently compounded Sister Subordinary's worries when he assured her that he was "on a roll and everything was under control." Then he mentioned a plan, and when she inquired into the nature of his plan, she was told that the information was classified.

It was true.

Somehow Conrad had learned to classify his thoughts. Where Sister Mary Subordinary used to have easy access to his mind, now quite a few channels were closed off to her. She had never been a snoop, had always respected those drawers and doors that the boy marked private. She had never pried into his doings with Merry Berry. Didn't want to know what was under the bed, not really.

Now, she did want to know what in the world was going on. But when she turned the knob on one of the doors marked private, she discovered it was locked.

"It's that suit," she flustered, covering her attempted trespass. "It has the most unbecoming influence on your vocabulary."

"The doctor said I dressed like a shmuck. Would you mind calling me Agent Eppler?"

"Yes, I would. The doctor said that? A shmuck?"

"It means I dress too mumsie."

Yet another sigh escaped Mary Subordinary. She sat down on the edge of Conrad's bed and pictured her sighs hanging on a clothes line, one wooden clothes pin for each sigh. She watched the clothesline travel through a wide blue sky on a breezy sunlit day, watched the sighs laugh in the clear-day wind until an everyday miracle occurred. The picture itself refreshed her, restored her energy.

"Just out of curiosity, mind you, what do tough guys eat for dinner, Agent Eppler?"

"CACTUS!" Extraordinary interjected.

"She heard us!" Conrad cried out. He was beside himself. His secret plan absolutely depended on Extraordinary's return. "She's right. Cook us up some cactus, Sister Subordinary." Conrad gave Sister a handsome salute.

"Eating cactus just takes practice," Extraordinary teased.

Although both Conrad and Sister Subordinary were immensely relieved that Mother Mary Extraordinary was back on the scene, each privately wondered (and for very different reasons), which Extraordinary was returned to them. She didn't let them wait long.

This Mother Mary was a new variety: the irritable Mary Extraordinary magnified by a super-charged prescience. In other words, wildly unpredictable.

"We're dinosaurs, Subordinary. Creatures out of time. But children are fond of dinosaurs, aren't they Conrad?"

At the mention of dinosaurs, the unwary cassowary took his cue and poked his head in.

"Yes!" Conrad enthused, "Love those pterodactyls!"

"And flying monkeys!" Extraordinary added, with a wicked little grin.

The cassowary let out a mournful bleat and Conrad thought of the bird's flightless wings.

"And raptors with retractable toes!" Conrad beamed at the cassowary, wanting to appease the Hierophant's poor deity.

*It is him*, Conrad mind-talked to Skipper, not bothering to classify his thought. *You turned the Hierophant's God into a bird. Silly monkey.*

The boy and the monkey laughed raucously at their semi-private joke.

Sister Subordinary perked up.

It was the very same cascade of boy giggles Subordinary had once delighted in back when she and Conrad poured over tales from the Ramayana. Subordinary glanced at the writing on Conrad's mind wall and gazed into the eyes of the cassowary.

Could it be?

"Heaven help us!" Subordinary apostrophized, although she was understandably doubtful that any heaven-sent help was on its way.

Perhaps all the Gods had devolved, gone to feather and flower and seed. She was as rattled as she'd ever been and desperately wanted to get back to her kitchen.

"Would you care for tea with your cactus?" she turned to Mary Extraordinary.

"Mary Subordinary, I am concerned about you," the prioress replied. "I strongly recommend a stroll out of doors. You seem a bit damp."

"After tea and cactus, after I've served supper, and after the dishes are put up, I'll consider it," Sister Subordinary snipped.

"A little airing will do you good. You might want to pick your sighs off the clothesline. I believe they are dry." Mother Mary Extraordinary added mischievously.

Sister Subordinary almost said: *Mind you own mysteries.* Instead she turned away and headed for the kitchen. She hoped to find peace among the pots and pans. But no sooner had she stepped out of Conrad's room, than she heard a dismaying racket.

The kitchen was in pandemonium. A literal tower of baby Pan-gods were banging on the pots with silver spoons. It was an unmistakable brand of childish word play made virtual.

She'd heard the stories from the old nuns who raised the goat girl in the years when the toddler was covered in soft white down. With a rueful chuckle, she gathered the spoons, opened the window, and shooed out the errant Pan babies.

Whisk and away.

She noticed a small pile of neatly folded sighs on the kitchen counter top. Possibly an apology. She tucked them in her pocket.

*My mistress is certainly enjoying her second childhood,* Mary Subordinary mildly reproved.

Then she rolled up her sleeves; a nutritious meal and chamomile tea often put the world to rights and cleared the numinous jitter.

———

CONRAD WENT TO MOTHER Mary Extraordinary and took her hand. His great old friend was back, and Conrad could not believe his incredible luck. Mother Mary Extraordinary would know exactly how to sort the etherics on the moon.

"You're not a dinosaur," Conrad smiled at Extraordinary.

"You're no fun to play with," she frowned.

"I'm not playing games," he leveled his blue eyes at hers.

"Then I'm going away."

As good as her promise, she resumed her catatonic state. Then just as abruptly, her crystalline blue eyes blinked open.

"So, Agent Eppler, what's this plot you're cooking up?" She put the question to him matter-of-factly. She sounded preeminently sane.

"You were listening."

"I'm always listening, Conrad. You can count on that."

"I need you to go to the moon."

"Sister Moon?"

"Yes. That's the one! I didn't know about that one until just recently."

"Who have you been talking to? The monkey?"

Conrad glanced over at the Kilo, who was still making like a shadow, "I've got connections."

"Listen Conrad, I tried my very best to die. Twice. Not happening. I had every intention of sorting the Moonies for you. But I seem to be stuck here on Earth."

"You don't have to die. There's another way up."

Conrad explained to an intrigued Mother Extraordinary about his particular connection. She admired the child's ability to establish a loyal relationship with the low-level angel, Kilowatt. Conrad was proving to be an altogether impressive prodigy. There were so many signs that this small boy could make a difference in the world. Small differences mattered on the material plane.

"Kilowatt is your personal ticket out of here." Conrad smiled encouragingly.

"You mean that shadow leaning against the wall? The one I'm not supposed to see?"

"Yes, that's him. He's agreed to help."

"Do tell."

Extraordinary laughed delightedly when Conrad told her the high price he paid for insider favors: his Mattel submachine gun, a pair of vintage army flashlights, and three pristine archival comic books.

"Well, I certainly feel pricey. But I must warn you that my spiritual condition is—shall we say?—dicey."

"Dicey?"

"Depleted, Conrad. I've used up my reserves in near deaths and resurrections, not to mention healing your gunshot wound. Furthermore, this interval of lucidity is costing me. We need to get a move on."

"I couldn't agree more. Time to get ready," Conrad looked to Kilowatt, who picked up his cue and ducked out to put on his rented tux.

"There's going to be a party on the moon," Conrad began cautiously. "I'm not sure about the exact date. There's a wobble in it."

"Let me see the invitation."

"I don't have an invitation. I have visions. I can get to the Moon, but I can't get all the way in. I can see them, but they can't see me. That's why I need you. You'll be able to get inside. They'll be able to see you."

"You have visions?" Mother Mary Extraordinary questioned the boy closely about his visions and wasn't at all surprised to find out that Sister Merry Berry had given Conrad a bottle of prayer juice.

"I would advise you to stop spritzing. Save it up, Conrad. There isn't any more where that came from. Those are my distilled prayers, and I am pretty much prayed out. Eau d'Extraodinaire won't last forever."

"Close your eyes," said the boy, "I have a surprise for you."

"Nothing surprises me, Conrad."

Conrad did have something in store for her that she truly was not expecting. He and Kilowatt had gone down to the cellar and found her old pink habit from the Joyous Mystery days. She had created that gown when she was a young novice, in the first bloom of spiritual innovation, back when the order was still a branch of The Great Church. Her astonishing initiation habit was one of the first signs that she would lead the Sisters into a joyous heterodoxy.

"Don't peek."

Conrad spread the gown out on his bed. It was a stunning multi-fabric affair: a velvet bodice decked with chiffon rosettes, a diamond-patterned jacquard skirt with an uneven hemline, and a hand-painted silk duster. The sheer veil was covered in tiny silk florets.

It was her wedding dress. She wore it when she became a bride of The Great Church.

"Okay, open them," Conrad whispered.

Mary Extraordinary gasped and blinked away tears. The gown was her youth.

The boy begged her to put the dress on. He argued. He pouted. He flattered. He cajoled.

She refused.

Conrad believed, not without reason, that if she wore this lovely celebratory garment, he could count on her being of a benevolent mindset when she attended the coming celebration on Sister Moon. He had no earthly idea how angry she was. Her preternatural calm should have been a hint.

"I understand. You think it important that I be gracious. Conrad, let me assure you, a costume will not help. Bring it here."

He brought it to her. She ran her fingers over the rosettes, remembered how lovingly she'd painted the silk duster. It was still a beautiful garment. She held it to her face and inhaled the gorgeous memories of garden days and prayer parties gone by. And in no uncertain terms she let Conrad know that she could not wear the pink. End of conversation.

Conrad was not about to take no for an answer, and did his stalwart best to restart the conversation, "There's going to be a party for the Earth Angel, Aletheia's baby girl. A lot of your friends are going to be there."

"No."

"You'll want something nice to wear."

"No."

"Okay," he backed down. "But please say that you accept your assignment. You do accept it, don't you?"

"Yes, Agent Eppler. I will be your agent extraordinaire. You can count on that."

"And deliver my message? It's a simple message. *Don't forget Conrad.* That's it. That's all you have to remember."

"Don't worry about my memory."

He was worried. Conrad Eppler couldn't make out her rhyme or reason. He only knew that she was capable of sudden unpredictable shifts and surges.

Although Mary Extraordinary was spread wafer thin—communing in multiple metaphysical dimensions—the young Avatar could not guess that she was slowly reeling herself in, increment by increment, and that she meant to bring every last ounce of her powerful agency to the party. Too late the boy sensed he'd made a mistake; he'd set something in motion that he could not control.

Kilowatt's cheery, "Oh, knock, knock," interrupted Conrad's meditations.

The spiffed-up escort, in his beautifully tailored morning suit, was every inch the gentleman caller. He offered Mother Mary Extraordinary a gloved hand. She arose from her wheelchair and slipped her arm in his.

"I am charmed," she said.

For the first time, Conrad noticed that the wheels on her chair did not really touch the ground and were slowly spinning. In a mind flash, the wondering boy saw wheels within wheels turning in a great galactic whirligig. Then Mother Mary broke the hypnotic spell.

"Don't forget your Mattel," Extraordinary reminded Kilo with a wink at Conrad.

Conrad did not like that wink.

Then as if cued by an unseen celestial showrunner, one set of double mullioned doors opened on the starry starry night. When Extraordinary exited the room leaning on Kilowatt's arm, Conrad ran after them and watched another exit from the terrace.

The boy would never forget how her black habit continued to grow in billows and volumes as she and Kilowatt climbed the starry steps of the firmament. It seemed her veil still touched the lawn when they were halfway to the moon.

# EVANGELINE

THE CADILLAC ELDORADO BIARRITZ was the first automobile, in the annals of Sister Moon, to make the metaphysical leap from the material world to the ethereal one. And with its passenger intact, more or less.

Merry Berry slouched in her pink ride, wiping her eyes and rooting around in her satchel. It was the morning after, and once again the spiritual twins found their consoeur leaking fat tears. The Sisters Tau tapped lightly on the glass. A frazzled Sister Merry Berry glanced up and lowered the window. She looked exactly like she had slept in her car—because she had slept in her car. The Tau Taus were aware that they were witnessing an unprecedented failure to adapt.

"Here it is," Merry Berry shook a card at the Sisters, as if the card were an explanation to an unasked question. "I must find a phone. I've got to make a long-distance call," Merry Berry insisted. "To Earth," she added and looked up at them with puppy-dog eyes.

"Maybe Sister Psi Lambda can help," the Tau Taus replied with reassuring nods. "She is so fac! And totem! The ultimate factotum. A mechanico electronico whiz."

"Oh, right," Merry Berry pictured Sister Josephus bent under the hood of the old Fairlane. That picture gave her hope. "Hop in, then. Let's go find her. This can't wait."

The Sisters Tau climbed in the back seat and gave directions to Psi Lambda's domicile. Earthside, this foursome had made up a formidable muster of gardeners. Mary Josephus driving a plow chained to the back of the old Fairlane, the Mary Tuees sowing and weeding in their lovely garden hats, and Merry Berry tending the rain barrels and drip-lines—those were cherished days. The reunion ought to have been a joyous one. The Tau Taus let the mystery prosper. Time would tell.

Occasionally there were regrets, especially when a Sister left behind beloved friends unexpectedly; but almost immediately upon arrival moonside, there was a sense of ontological ease and spiritual refreshment.

The amazing Sister Loop, like a Ferris Wheel set free schoonering in the big blue, was a spiritual thrill ride nonpareil, winking multicolor lights and whooping calliope music. Riders on the loop shook off the past, as if their previous incarnation were a slightly weathered garment that had taken on a layer of star dust and needed a good rinsing. When it suited, the riders would begin to dream up future incarnations.

While the details of any future life entailed uncertainties— plot, character, and setting could change radically from one incarnation to the next—it was plain from the vantage point of Sister Moon that the loop of cognate souls was unbroken. Reunion was the through line. This purview gave off a lovely, comforting, clear-day effect that almost always dissolved all grievances.

Although Sister Merry Berry remained oddly inconsolable, driving the Biarritz shifted her mind into an easy alpha state, dendrites flashing in the cooler blue zone. The threesome rode on in an uncharacteristic silence, while the Sisters Tau waited for Merry Berry to venture off on one of her famous discursive rambles.

"I had a dream vision when I flew off the cliff," Sister Merry finally began. "I saw my birth mother, tucking me in a pink blanket. She called me Savannah. I want to be my mother's daughter and I don't know how. I want to be the repented give-a-away—the pentimento and the palimpsest. I want to be the page where the new story appears and the past that never had a chance emerges. I am split, like a banana, with at least four flavors of gelato. There's the fruity Merry Berry flavor. There's the creamy Savannah flavor. There's a nutty sprinkling of Mary Jane Greystoke, a jungle girl gone wild. And there's this caramel sea-salt," she tapped her chin, "the flavor of a kiss."

"And there's Sister Psi Lambda," the Tau Taus interrupted.

Merry Berry hit the brakes and the horn.

Sister Psi Lambda was balanced on a rock, mounting a whirligig on top of the crystal radio she was building in front of her cave. The former Sister Mary Josephus dropped her tools, hopped down from her rock, and jumped at the chance to go joy riding on Sister Moon in the fabulous Biarritz.

"First things first," Merry Berry insisted that her telephone call was the more urgent matter, a veritable three-alarm emergency that ought to take precedence over fun.

"Emergencies are forever. One quick spin. Oh, please," Psi Lambda importuned. "My lovely old bones are moldering under the Fairlane on Earth but there is a song in my soul of rides gone by. Once is never enough. I won't be denied."

As soon as Sister Psi Lambda was happily engaged behind the wheel, she peppered Sister Merry Berry with questions.

"What was it like to fly across the great divide in this divine set of wheels?"

"Compared to this bumpy ride," Sister Merry Berry grumped from the shotgun seat, "it was wondrously smooth."

Psi Lambda gunned it. Merry Berry gripped the armrest. The Tau Taus squeed delightedly from the back seat. It was a short but satisfying spin in Jah Bliss on the very rocky surface of Sister Moon.

Back at her tool bench, Sister Psi Lambda went to work with happy alacrity, doing what she did best—pushing against limitations. Nothing like a mission impossible. Within a couple hours of tinkering, she engineered a passable long distance calling device capable of tapping into Earth's cellular system. However, there was an unfortunate caveat; the person on the Earthside of the line would not be able to hear Merry Berry's voice. It would have to be a one-way call.

"Better than not hearing his voice at all, I suppose. If only he were a part of our reincarnation loop. Then at least, I'd be sure to see him again," she sniffled.

The Sisters Tau and Sister Psi Lambda nodded in sympathy. Of course, Sister Merry Berry would miss the orphan deity, Conrad Eppler. Occasionally, exceptionally strong attachments were formed with exceptional individuals. When the answering voice came over the makeshift speaker phone, the Sisters were taken aback.

"Tremont Montress, Jah Motors," announced a deep male voice with a Jamaican lilt. He repeated his name once more and asked, "Is anybody there?"

Tremont hung up, thinking about a beautiful woman with a bounce of Rasta curls, stepping down the car lot in red patent-leather stilettos. The image was high definition and heavenly scented, leaving Tremont dazed and puzzled because he could not remember her name. This strange lacuna may have been because his moonside caller was between names, a case of spooky action at a distance.

Later that afternoon, Tremont did not know why he pulled into the parking lot of the Italian Ices shop, or why he bought a pint of caramel sea-salt gelato. In the wee small hours of the morning, when Tremont stood in front of the fridge spooning gelato, he remembered the flavor of a kiss.

Tapping the dimple on her chin, Merry Berry wondered out loud why Roica's kiss mattered so much more than Tremont's kiss. It seemed to Merry Berry that she'd been so much less careless with hers.

"It isn't fair," Merry Berry took a sip from her cup.

"No, it isn't," Psi Lambda soothed, remembering that first illicit kiss between herself and Mary Rose. "Sometimes a kiss shared in one lifetime doesn't bloom until the next."

"I'm not jealous, if that's what you think," Merry Berry assured her consoeurs, "I would never begrudge the green Goddess her kiss, or you and Mary Rose your kiss, any more than I would dismiss Tremont's kiss—in the last life or the next. If there is a next. Mine was, after all, a near miss. An almost wasn't meant-to-be kiss. A stolen kiss, really. But I was assured that Jah would not miss it."

"Oh my," cried the Tau Taus, "what an ineluctable smooch."

"A kiss most worthy of spiritual reckoning," Lambda concurred. "Is that everything?"

"Not everything. Something else is bothering me." Merry Berry took a breath. "Last night, alone in my Cadillac, I realized I'd made a fool of myself at Aletheia's landing. It was not Ms. Demeanor who had arrived in the rocket. It was the green angel, bereft of wings; it was Eve. How could I have made such a colossal, theogenic mistake?"

With some hesitation, she confessed to her besties that she was unnerved by her Merry power or Mary power. The power was shorting out on her. She ought to have recognized the green angel, wings or no wings. Was it possible that she was winking out of existence along with her power? Was that why each of her names had lost their stickiness, slid off her like beads of mercury?

It is axiomatic among the inhabitants of Sister Moon, that the close examination of existential afflictions constitutes one of the primary pleasures of intimacy. Sister Merry Berry had landed on the moon with an affluence of anxieties and alarms. Her friends cooed and soothed and suggested a nice bathe in the hot springs.

The four women settled into a spring-fed pool, carved out from the indigenous marble. It featured a wide circular ledge, set a couple of feet below the waterline for lounging. It was one of many smart pools in the Moon Garden; sometimes years would come off the bathers. The omniscient water always understood exactly what restorative was most wanted.

The Sisters Tau and Sister Psi Lambda, settled in with happy anticipations, prepared for a long leisurely reminding and unwinding of their beloved Merry Berry. The troubled Sister soon gave herself up to the ameliorating springs, and her story began to flow like water over rock. It pooled, eddied and streamed—a possible love story interrupted, a boy abandoned, tippling with the Angel of Light.

Just when her consoeurs thought they'd heard it all, Merry Berry introduced the absorbing riddle of a cassowary she'd left on Earth.

"The cassowary was my singular devotee and I was his. It was mutual and deep. He gave me these red shoes and I gave him my best quilts. I don't mean to shock anyone, but I must own a particular soul connection with the bird," Merry Berry concluded, taking a sip from her eternal cup.

"You seem to have become exceedingly porous," Sister Psi Lambda offered. "That is a most admirable soul quality."

"Oh, Merry Berry," chirped the Tau Taus, "we are so jealous. A bird! Is he your personal daemon?"

"Not exactly. And I'm not sure that he is altogether a bird."

Encouraged by her enthusiastic listeners and the soothing froth of the bubbling waters, Merry Berry prepared herself to tell them about the mysterious smile. Actually, it was more of a smirk, when she thought back on it.

The day before she'd taken her ride into the sweet loop of hereafters, she was positive that she'd seen something— something in the cassowary that merited closer inspection, a shift, a sea-change. Unfortunately, her Merry power faltered at the perfectly wrong moment and the tantalizing glimpse into the nature of the bird flickered before she could register the imprint.

Still, she'd seen *something* on that telling afternoon, when she sat staring into the hypnotic, heavily-lashed windows to his soul. There was a time when all such window peeping paid off with instant identification. Now she doubted herself. It was too preposterous. She had the funniest sensation that the last time she peered into the black ovoid lens set in the cassowary's orange eye, Mona Lisa was looking back at her.

"He tilted his head and focused his gaze on me with one mesmerizing eye. I felt his impossible love. Then, the lens dilated and there she was—the Mona Lisa—smirking at me.

What do you make of *that*?" Merry Berry wanted to know. "And don't blame the wine. It never mattered a hoot, one way or the other. Or the Twinkies. Or the spritzer. So? What do you make of it?"

They mused in silence, trying their best to make something of it. They did not doubt her. If she said it was Mona Lisa, it must have been. They could not help but think of Leonardo. There is an ineffable connection between makers and their creations. A painting is like a scan of the mind of the painter.

This sleuthing was just the sort of theological half-bakery that these superluminaries loved best. Even if they couldn't immediately plumb the mysteries of Merry Berry's soul, they knew they were in for a good, long soak at the hot springs. More would be revealed in due time.

Of course, they wanted to try the spritzer and the Twinkies. Merry Berry obliged. They spritzed and twinkied and shared a few sips from her eternal cup. After all was mediated, meditated, and medicated, Sister Merry Berry tossed one more question into the existential pile up.

"What about the way my identity keeps flipping like a pancake on the griddle of the Godma? Any idea about who might be holding the spatula?"

"Why, you are holding the spatula, dear one," Psi Lambda thought that much was obvious.

"Flip flop," chimed the Tau Taus, "who are you?"

Merry Berry perked up. "Is it possible? Can I be Savannah?"

Sister Psi Lambda suggested they bring the matter before the congregation of Joyous Sisters. The Tau Taus reminded Psi

Lambda that the naming of Aletheia's miraculous bundle of stardust was on the menu for this evening. Almost nothing else was spoken of, thought of, prayed over, exclaimed over; barely two days old and the infant was already a spiritual sensation.

"We are gestating an idea," the twins announced.

"Sister Merry Berry ought to be given a naming ceremony," Tau One proposed.

"A sort of rebirthday, an immaculate reconception," Tau Too tweaked.

"Or maybe it's already happened, and this is her Bath-tism!" The Tau's kicked up a great splash, drenching Sister Merry Berry until at last they heard her much missed laughter.

Then they soaked in happy silence, contemplating the intriguing theological implications of becoming a Savannah.

———

THE GREEN SNAKE SLIPPED out of Oracle's grasp. "You might want to reconsider your appearance," she called after the disappearing Edenic icon.

A pale green snake was beyond cliché, a myth whose time had run its course. He knew that. Besides, this radically altered Eve was not going to fall for a snake, no matter how lustrous its scales, no matter how smooth its slither or appealing its patter. A new look must be devised, and new lines scripted.

A master at bespoke metamorphosis, one of his perennial pleasures was that of the dharma chameleon. This newly recycled Eve merited serious consideration, and Lucifer had means and designs. He meant to insinuate himself into the song of genesis in a heroic key. He would make her story his story—give it a fresh spin, give it a whirl, dance it to a new tune.

Studying the rich variety of Eve's past lives, Lucifer noted how she was drawn to earthly pleasures. A sensual being, she loved the human form. With that in mind, Lucifer doused some of his darker metallic lumens and shifted shape. Not particularly enamored of the male anatomy, he assumed a lean but muscular body—rock-star thin. Then, he refined the look with a lamina of androgyny.

Working up his presentation, Lucifer did a quick survey of vintage rock-and-roll reels. He was searching for that ineffable frisson that moved Earth girls to ecstatic response. He decided to go for a serious moonlight crooner suit, a lá David Bowie, circa 1980. Not the yellow one. The pale green. With matching pale green snakeskin loafers. He would be beautifully suited, if not an ideal suitor. Sentiment was not his custom.

Now that the elusive angel was restyled and retrofitted for a replay of the iconic seduction, he realized he could easily miss the mark if he failed to produce emotional authenticity. He needed a soundtrack.

Lucifer sampled hundreds of moon songs, mixing the score to the love scene he was staging in his mind. The Beethoven sonata for starters, and the Johnny Mathis rendition of *Moonlight Becomes You* for the finish, for the finesse. He tried on the Mathis voice, full of smoke and silk, then added a touch of reverb.

Almost ready, Luce lounged inconspicuously on a crescent-shaped sculpture in the Moonrock Garden. Humming softly to himself, he waited, massaging his strategies until one possible future morphed into a virtual fantasy. Then he tripped on his fantasy and did the unthinkable. He fell in love. Not with the emerald angel, or the new Eve, but with an idea of himself.

"Was ever a woman in this humor wooed?" Lucifer riffed on the old bardic standard. "Yes," he answered himself and laughed. From time immemorial, seductions have been tuned to the music of personal affliction. The object of his affectations was in crisis, an abandoned unwed mother pushing an angel babe in a pram, and headed absolutely nowhere.

Aletheia barely remembered how to be the plucky incandescent being who had plunged so fearlessly into a beckoning destiny, laughing off her littermates, leaving Periwinkle and Epiphany without a second thought. She missed them now. Missed the fun. Missed the show and showing off. The carelessness.

With hindsight, her audacity looked more thoughtless than fearless. Where she once believed she could steer her stars, she now saw herself as the gypsy bauble of a vagrant Earth—a throwaway, a once-upon-a-time, the accident that happens when the wind beneath your wings lifts you far and away from familiar markers, then drops you in a strange land without a map.

The Catechism of Angels was a hopelessly inadequate guide. Applying its principles, or evoking Nietzsche's aphorisms, only left her dazed when her promises to Conrad collided with Roica's kiss. She was doubly dazed when the kiss became a cooing bundle of glowing bliss. Her core identity rocked dangerously, going backwards in time and forwards into possible futures. Was she even an angel anymore? Her wings were gone. Was there a place for her and her angel babe? And if there were such a place, where in the worlds was it?

She had become a labyrinthine riddle. When this altered Aletheia came around a corner pushing the pram with its incandescent passenger, she was the perfect prey for the garden's hidden occupant.

As soon as he caught the scent of her self-doubt, the Angel of Light laced the air with the evocative lays of Beethoven's Moonlight Sonata. The starter was soothing and stately. Aletheia stepped on the mesmerizing notes and failed to notice the faint glow of a green shadow coming off one of the sculptures.

The garden itself couldn't have been more spell-binding. The travertine marble had been quarried by the Sisters and rubbed to a high sheen. The marble was pinkish in hue, with white and gold veins. All Moonies participated in polishing meditations, and recently they had been meditating triple time, their polishing rags deployed in happy anticipation of the arrival of the new Eve.

With its fantastical architecture, Sister Moon's rock garden was one of the aesthetic wonders of the galaxy. Long straight pathways cut through the monumental sculptures with smaller serpentine paths, making connections in and around the hot springs. Columns, balancing rocks, bridges, outsized frames, and cascading steps were among the signature features. Myriad unexpected vistas opened on sea-glass colored pools, spiraling fountains that shot upwards in intricate patterns, winding pathways that led to breathtaking descending staircases.

When Aletheia wheeled her pram onto the wide straightaway, the sound of Luce's silver smooth tenor was all at once everywhere—*Moonlight becomes you, becomes you.* The had arresting moment arrived. The Angel of Light stepped out, not looking much like an angel at all.

In his human aspect, Luce still managed to be a coruscating lightshow and definitely the most beautiful being Eve had ever encountered. Lucifer couldn't help himself; whether as Chief of Angel Police, Doctor D. Light, or this telegenic back-lit crooner, he was always the most beautiful creature in any room or on any moon.

A pale, gold apple appeared in his hand, "How about an apple, my lovely?" Another apple materialized in his other hand, "Or, would you rather have a pair?"

He stood there, wearing a dazzling fall-in-love-with-me smile. Then he offered an apple to the baby. The infant angel reached for the glimmering fruit with chubby fingers and the apple went poof. The baby girl giggled. Aletheia's heart smiled. She was his and he knew it.

Just at the strike of love, four naked women came running in a very merry berry chase right through the scene of the seduction, cleaving it in half. Savannah's spray of Rasta curls gave Lucifer's celebrity jaw a mighty slap when she whipped her head around to give Mr. Wonderful a twice over.

"Drop dead gorgeous," she stopped in front of him and wiped the spray of water dripping from his chin. Then she took off at a run.

"Love the green suit," the Tau Taus tweeted, skipping past.

"Love your green-haired girl," Psi Lambda tossed over her shoulder.

The startled couple—one laughing, one not—watched the streakers pile into a pristine Cadillac Eldorado Biarritz. It sped off, horn honking, colors flying.

"Lucifer, what are you doing here?" Aletheia asked, suppressing laughter, wishing she could join in the Sisters' fun.

"I followed a trail of rumors." Lucifer switched off the showy reverb that he had added to his singing voice and affected nonchalance, "I heard the Sisters are throwing a big bash for the angel cub."

"Isn't it incredible news?" Aletheia tried to sound upbeat. "I think she merits a gospel, don't you?"

"A gospel according to whom?"

"What about you? The Gospel According to Luce. You spread the news."

"Believe me, Aletheia, you already made the news. Front page. Headlines: *First Illegitimate Angel in the History of Grace.*"

"She's not illegitimate. She is a miraculous accident. I watched my sun cells divide and this little white tornado spinning inside; faster and faster and whoosh! She blew out my lights. When next I opened my eyes, I was holding a spinning ball of wind and fire and starlight. She's an Earth Angel, Luce, the first of her kind," Aletheia bent over the pram and brushed the cheek of her angel infant.

She was glad that her brave speech sounded so much like the feisty angel she once was. She could do this.

"You had no license to divide, no sanction to recreate."

She wanted to say that she didn't need a sanction, she had a destiny. But the destiny had picked up a wobble, and the sass wasn't there. Self-doubt had done its damages. Covering her wounds, she scrambled to pick a fight.

"Sanction?" she challenged, "Sanction means its exact opposite. Blessing and curse. Permission and penalty."

"Yes," Luce smiled, "it's a word that equivocates perfectly.

"My daughter is unequivocally beautiful. And what is beautiful is its own reason for being."

"You always had an attractive mind."

"Are you flirting with me?" She was angry.

"I can change your stars if you will give me your consideration," he punched up the reverb.

"Don't talk to me in riddles. And stop doing that funny thing with your voice."

"I'm trying to be nice," Luce said, dropping the game. "It's awkward. Surely, you are aware that the new angel must be placed in the hierarchy of wings."

"The Joyous Mystery Sisters are taking care of that."

"I want to help." There it was again. An uncomfortable lean into human kindness. "I know the rules."

"Your book of rules doesn't seem to apply on Sister Moon."

"Aletheia, I have two words for you—sacramental mate."

"Oh. That's being seen to," she pretended not to understand his proposal. "My wedding has already been planned."

"Who is the lucky groom?"

"The Sisters don't worry about details."

"The groom is a detail?"

"They're professionals, professional celebrants. They know what to do."

"Seriously? Don't tell me you believe that. The magical mystical bridegroom just miraculously appears. Is that how it works on Sister Moon?"

"I guess."

"In a nice green suit?" Luce brought out the all-star, A-list, celebrity smile.

"I don't know," Aletheia didn't mean to let her guard down, but there it was. Down. Dropped to the ground. Her confusion marching around in broad moonlight. Maybe it was just as well. The Angel of Light was, after all, a familiar. She missed planet Grace. Maybe Lucifer could point the way back again.

"What am I supposed to do? What does High Consul say?"

Lucifer scoffed, "She doesn't know. She's consulting with the Supernals, but you know the etherics—the higher up you go in the hierarchy—they're just not interested in individual destinies. Oh sure, they drop their little bodhisattvas and messiahs and prophets and Avatars, but you run into any kind of trouble—and where are they? They won't give you the time of day. Speaking of which, has dream-boots been around?"

"No." She knew exactly what Lucifer meant to imply. She'd been deserted. Plain and simple.

"Need I say more?"

"No! Don't say another word."

"You were the best of the nest."

"Don't do this, Luce."

"Why not?"

"Because I fall in love too easily."

Aletheia wasn't only thinking of Roica. She was thinking of Conrad. And this propensity she had to love what was in front of her. Be it apple or angel.

"How about this time, we make history and you take the fall with me?"

Aletheia was saved from answering by the entrance of Sister Omega Omicron, trailing a hallelujah chorus of Joyous Mystery Sisters, all bells and banners.

"What a blessed day! A naming ceremony for the angel initiate," Omega Omicron hailed the company.

"Not so fast, Sister. As highest-ranking angel present, I feel it is my duty to object."

"To what? We've not yet begun," the Oracle was studying him.

"Please, Luce. Give this day to Evangeline," Aletheia picked up her little bundle of light.

"Evangeline," Oracle resounded with pleasure. "What a lovely name you have chosen for the Earth Angel—something of the Earth and above the Earth."

"She is the leap over bounds," enthused Psi Lambda.

"Ring the bells!" cried the Tau Taus.

The Moonrock Garden filled with peals of celestial bells, and a chorus line of thirty cloggers skipped onto the travertine promenade. Then three nuns in pink plaid kilts began to blow holy ragas on the bag pipes.

"What kind of ceremony is this?" Luce hissed.

"It's a sacrament," Rho Zeta supplied, "the outward sign of an inward grace—plenary grace. From halos to hallelujahs, we make the signs that make beliefs."

"Make beliefs? You mean make-believe?" Too late, Luce tried to repress the outward signs of his disdain. He decided he needed to work his way back up to nice, so he defaulted to consideration and did his best to look thoughtful.

"We believe that a sacrament is a holy act of the imagination. Thus, it is our joyous practice to mix the make-believes into our festivities," Rho Zeta continued.

"Bagpipes? Cloggers?" Lucifer stopped himself. "Listen, the initiation of an angel cub is a matter of divine ordinance. I know there's a rule to cover this. Aletheia, help me out here."

A baffled Aletheia found herself reciting from the Angel Catechism, like some fledgling angelette: "Chapter 9. Rule 48. *The Book of Heresies.* 'No heterodox beliefs shall be entered in the Angel Litanies.' But Luce, that is so very Archaic Testament. This is a new, unclassified, unprecedented angel."

Rho Zeta appealed to Oracle. The divine diva was always happy to make a pronouncement.

"The making of beliefs is a Holy Office," Oracle declaimed. "It is the sacred calling—and the failure to answer that call is, by definition, profane."

A politesse of soft clapping fanned through the parade of celebrants. The cloggers answered with a muted double step, rock step.

"Well spoken, Oracle," the Sisters Tau beamed and then thought better of taking sides. They did not want to embarrass the impeccably groomed Angel of Light for the second time in one day. "Excuse us, our vanity is showing," the twins demurred.

Oracle carried on, "Thus it has always begun. In the beginning there was Act One of the Imagination. We all know where Act One takes place on planet Earth. Sisters, throw open the gate! Let us recreate the garden."

A monumental set of carved marble doors, skillfully camouflaged in a curved wall, slid open without a sound. And there it was—the fresh green breast of the new world, iconic, pristine. Exactly the way it never was, and thus the essence of a possible yet-to-be. It was the scene of a myth begging for another chance. If only the original cast would agree to a rewrite.

"Objection!" cried Luce. "The garden is not a spectacle worth re-staging."

"Why Luce," Oracle finessed, "We believe you made an incredibly handsome—you might say, striking—snake."

"We appreciate the part you played," the Tau Taus reflected.

A double step, rock step punctuated the moment. The chorus line of cloggers beckoned the hesitant mother to enter the garden.

Babe in arms, the new Eve stepped into the mythical Eden.

Oracle turned her unseeing eyes on Luce, "Had the serpent not entered the garden, the adventure would have never begun."

Double step, rock step.

"We think you are the universal darling," Merry Berry slipped her arm through his and ushered him through the gate.

The Sisters Tau held up two beautifully polished apples. "Take a bite. Take a bite," they prompted.

Double step, rock step.

"You give darn good advice," teased Omicron. This blind seer knew how to catch a snake.

"It's true, I know I do," Lucifer began to redefine himself. "Advice is my watchword. I've been known to be nice."

"Then, you shall be Evangeline's Godfather," Oracle dragged a finger through Luce's aura, saturating his violet lumens.

"Aletheia never mentioned there was a role for me," his green eyes gleamed.

"She couldn't possibly know. We make things up as we go," Omicron defended the green-haired Eve, thinking how lovely the primal mother looked in her garden.

"If it is an ever-changing story, what happens if dream-boots shows? Then, so long Godfather and you cast Roica as the hero?"

Sister Omega Omicron, the Oracle, kept rising to the occasion, impressing an appreciative Sisterhood with her oratorical acumen. She was every bit a match for the mistrustful Angel. She understood him.

All the Sisters were intimately familiar with what it feels like to be underestimated, underesteemed, and undermined. Their spiritual practice was to give away what they most wanted for themselves, and thereby to create more of what was necessary to boost the vitality of all souls in the plenum.

"Assume your role, Lucifer! And believe it!"

Double step, rock step, fan kick, fan kick. The fascinating rhythms ricocheted on the travertine, then stopped. An interlude of bagpipe flourishes died out.

Oracle began the formal orison.

"O Angel Most High, Divinity of Eternal Light, we honor your darker side. It is the hedge of protection against your limitless light, too bright for human eyes. Please honor us—at this event, this advent—and represent the element of fire and sunlight."

Happiness fell over him like a summer storm. Lucifer was an angel caught unawares without umbrella or galoshes. With a great flash of yellow noise he shook off the rain and reified his birthright—Star Maker. He held up a small nuclear-fired sun in the palm of his hand, and then hurled it into the firmament, "One for the angel cub."

Eve gasped. The star was set. Oracle opened her arms to receive Eve's daughter.

"I now present Evangeline." Oracle lifted the infant on high for the viewing.

"Come, let us adore her," the Sisterhood chorused.

"When we look closely at Evangeline," Oracle intoned, "we see the exquisite metaphysical mix. She is Angel, and yet if we truly look, we see the Earth and its makings. Ontogeny recapitulates cosmogony. Look deeply now and see— everything."

Luce stepped in and set a ringlet of tiny stars spinning above Evangeline's head. "In her heart there is fire, there is sun," Luce handed the infant to Aletheia.

With that gesture, the song of the Angel initiate was sprung, and verse followed on verse.

"In her soft skin, the folds of Earth begin," Eve sang, handing the babe to the Sisters Tau.

"In her eyes there is water, holy water," the Tau Taus praised and passed the star-swaddled infant to Rho Zeta.

"In the cusp of her feathered wings, there is wind, there is air. And in her throat, the sweet breath of prayer," Rho Zeta voiced in a lovely vibrato and placed Evangeline in the ritual nest, atop a carved pillar.

"Earth, Air, Water and Fire," Oracle chanted. "Now as the elements we mix. No separation lies between the celebrants and the initiate. Give it up, Sisters! A new God has fallen in among us; Her Holiness, the Evangeline. Welcome her with fanfare and bells."

Again, the bells pealed. The chorus line of cloggers clogged. The bagpipes blew. The Angel of Light tossed up a dazzling impromptu lightning display—cloud to ground, cloud to cloud, inner cloud, red sprites, green elf rings, blue jets, bolts and jitter.

Then something blew out all the lights.

# JUSTICE

MOTHER MARY EXTRAORDINARY'S voluminous black gown blotted out the light from every rude star that dared so much as a twinkle while she made her long dark ascent. She had promises to keep and no patience for the indifferent stars that collected children's wishes like birthday candles blown out and discarded with the paper plates and party hats.

On Sister Moon, the circle of chorusing celebrants stopped midsong; a tremble of notes caught in their throats. All eyes scanned the darkened skies.

Gradually, the vague outline of billowing black veils against an ink-black sky resolved into a discernible shape. It was so quiet the Sisters heard the toe of Mary Extraordinary's enormous black boot tap on the travertine landing some thirty feet above them. Then in quick incremental shutter clicks, Extraordinary reduced her size and stood with her escort at the top of the grand staircase, taking in the breathless company. She surveyed the scene, made her appraisals, and then charged down the opalescent steps—a bride in black, her train cascading on the decline, her voice thundering on high.

"IS THERE NO JUSTICE!?"

Her voice, her appearance, her question chilled the joy-makers.

"How is it that one babe's entrance is heralded with all this fanfare, thunder clapping, and festive trappings? And another is left on the porch steps in a cardboard box with a stuffed monkey?"

Recognizing their altered prioress and remembering themselves, the collective Joyous Sisters went gracefully to their knees, declaiming: "Mother Mary Extraordinary, blessed be."

One slightly drunk Sister Merry Berry stood alone, squinting at the dark silk specter, "Perhaps I can shed some confusion on the question. Perhaps there is a better question. Why does one kiss matter and not another?"

"They all matter, Merry Berry, but that is not the matter of the moment!" Extraordinary cut her off.

"My moment matters," Merry Berry was not prepared to yield ground.

Kilowatt, the almost-forgotten escort, stepped out from behind his extraordinary date. Perplexed by the unexpected confrontation, he causally aimed his Mattel at the blessed inebriate. An equally puzzled Merry Berry raised her arms, signaling surrender.

Then, certain that she recognized the Mattel, Merry Berry called out to the kneeling sorority, "Rise up, dears. Nothing to fear. I bought that gun at a yard sale."

She spoke too soon. The inspired Kilowatt, like a kid in a carnival shooting gallery with tickets to spare, was just warming up. When the confused community began to rise, Kilo pulled a three-hundred and sixty-degree sweep with his prized toy, blasting the ceremony with the rattling sound effects of a submachine gun. There was much ducking and dodging.

A brace of Sisters quickly encircled Aletheia, who huddled inside their protective cover with Evangeline snug in her arms.

Extraordinary, Kilo, and Lucifer remained standing.

"Kilowatt," Lucifer had the minion's full attention.

"Luce." Kilowatt at a loss for words, gave his former boss a conciliatory nod. The lowly angel hadn't worked out how to inform The Angel of Light about the change in their relationship status. Masking his unease, the retired minion tried for affability. "Imagine, running into you here. Looking sharp," he added, lowering his gun.

Kilowatt made a few quick calculations. A dedicated pragmatist, he always liked to be on the side of the most powerful person in any given room. Unsure, he glanced between Extraordinary and Lucifer.

"I am here to celebrate," Luce hissed. "This is a party, Kilo. What's with the gun?"

"Aw, Luce. It ain't nothing. It's just a toy," Kilo explained.

The celebrants, still shaken by Extraordinary's entrance, began to come out in hesitant twos and threes, from the various moonrock formations that had served as temporary cover.

"I thought it'd be fun. It's a repeat-action squirt gun." Kilowatt turned on the water feature and triggered successive bursts of water.

Again, the Sisters ducked for cover. A steely-eyed Mother Mary Extraordinary remained impassive.

"All in the Baptismal spirit," Kilo improvised, enjoying his own joke. "I come to celebrate this party too, just like you, Luce."

"Then why'd you bring the grim fairy with you?" Lucifer snarled.

"Grimm, is it?" Extraordinary looked bemused.

Lucifer made himself brighter and leveled a gaze at the implacable Mary Extraordinary. She pounced.

"You don't fool me Lucifer, dressed up in your fancy suit. You stay out of my wine cellar, you hear? Always uncorking the best years."

Merry Berry, feeling a guilty sympathy with the accused, let go a delicate hiccough, inadvertently drawing attention to herself.

"Ah, Sister Merry Berry. Nice shoes," Extraordinary smiled.

"And you, you're looking exceptionally well. The silk, the tulle. Who knew that such an old habit could be so beautifully revived? Black does become you. Cheers to you and black and funerals and unhappy endings everywhere," Sister Merry Berry raised her goblet.

"I see you are still in your cups. Thought you could run off to Sister Moon, did you? No more Mother Mary Extraordinary, to catch you out. But you're caught!"

"Completely by surprise, dear. You weren't on the guest list. How was I to know?"

Sister Merry Berry, suddenly certain she had taken a fatal misstep, stared down at her red shoes, hoping to puzzle it out before she took another. Not missing a beat, Mother Mary clued her in.

"Not on the guest list? Well then, this situation does have its Grimm precedents, doesn't it? If I know my Grimm, and I assure you I do, it is the responsibility of the uninvited guest to cast a spell."

A lovely Hazelwood wand appeared in Extraordinary's gloved hand.

"Oh, mercy," Sister Omicron cried out, "we don't need a witch."

"Every good narrative needs a witch," Extraordinary declared.

The company was appalled. Extraordinary was standing over the empty nest where the angel babe had been placed earlier in the ritual. The nest, built lovingly out of strands of gold and lined with down feathers, was set in a marble basin on a waist-high column. Mother Mary Extraordinary casually circled the empty nest with her wand.

"Kilowatt! Get her under control," Luce commanded.

"Mother Mary, Your Holy Mountain Majesty, blessed be. This is not what the kid had in mind. You're supposed to act nice. Remember? Sugar and spice. Like it says in the brief. Agent Eppler would not like this."

"Conrad is much too sweet. His strategies have not been leavened by defeat. I will fix the future for him, and wrap up my gift nice and neat."

"Holy Mother of Inventions, there's no mention of a spell. We're working for the kid. You gotta stick with the script," Kilo was doing his level best, but he was hopelessly outclassed.

"I have a right to improvise. Everyone loves a surprise," Mother Mary Extraordinary was enjoying herself. She turned toward the emerald angel, whose return Conrad had waited upon, hour after long hour. She saw all the lonely children, the long line of broken promises and unanswered prayers. A lesson was needed, and she was in the mood to teach.

Evangeline flew out of Aletheia's arms. The bright sylph hovered above the crowd; her wings like gold hammered to airy thinness beat rapidly against the pink air. Then Evangeline spiraled downwards and curled up in her ritual nest. A wee smile graced her lips before she closed her eyes and slept.

"Such a pretty spirit, she is," Extraordinary leaned over the nest.

A chorus of *YES* swept through the Sisters.

"Let's see. At the tender age of three, she will prick her finger on a CACTUS."

A chorus of *NO* bounced in the moonrock garden.

"Right. It's been done to death," Mother Mary paused, relishing the bated breath of her auditors. "I can come up with something more original. Like sin," she chuckled.

Aletheia stepped forward. There was something familiar about this uncanny being hovering uncomfortably close to her daughter. The new Eve put her hand on the black sleeve as if to stay the hand that held the wand, and she felt an electrical surge of connection.

It was a singular caprice, a charged holy credit card, a chance coupon ripped from time, a mystical moment worthy of a time out, a peek behind the scenes, a look up the Magician's sleeve. Eve could not have guessed that she was touching the very sleeve of her maker, her personal creatrix.

In the great mix-master of passages, evolved beings constantly brush sleeves with significant players from past lives. None more significant than the Godma, Asheilstarte.

It was She who created Eve as an improvement on the Maker's early, somewhat amateur efforts at creating a female. It was Asheilstarte who brought Eve back through the reification cycle as an angel. And it was Asheilstarte who took on an Earth incarnation as Mother Mary Extraordinary.

Just now Aletheia's hand is resting on her mother's sleeve. O, holy pause of pauses. How often in the rush of existence these brushes with immortal beings blow by unnoticed!

Hold. Hold.

Release.

"Please, Extraordinary Being, cast no spell that will harm Evangeline. She is innocent."

The extraordinary being turned on her, "I've been briefed on you. Mistress of appearances and disappearances, phasing out like the constantly disappearing moon. Cheap bag of angel tricks, breaking hearts just like match sticks."

"You don't understand," the ambitious illuminato charged in, prepared to make his bid.

That was the precisely the wrong thing to say to a cranky spirit who understood much.

"I have walked with angels of extraordinary power in my day, and I have also been abandoned by flights of angels in the course of my Earth stay. But I am ancient and wily. I have survived the absence of angels, my soul gone dry as dust. Incarnation is a harsh mistress—decades roll by, all ties to Supernals cut off. I watched gardens go to seed and dreams die. My heart was broken ten times ten-thousand times. This break after break will not be Conrad's fate. Give a visionary child a vision and then vanish—NO!"

Extraordinary allowed the silence to swallow hope.

"Listen carefully. This is the spell that is written in the stars. An angel of the highest kind shall raise Evangeline, in the State of Grace. She will be taken from you at the next quarter moon, at the tender age of much too soon. Thus, the interference has been removed. You may continue your journey up to the Earth, Eve. The planet Earth is overly orphaned. It was orphaned by its maker, orphaned by its patron parents. Orphans pile up at the borders of its nations. There it is beckoning you, the wet blue jewel, set in the crown of heaven. Look up. It is done."

A collective gasp let loose.

"Lieutenant Colonel Kilowatt, will you please escort me off this rock. On second thought, I'll find my own way out."

Her ascent back up the grand stairway happened so fast, it seemed she'd never been on Sister Moon at all. Evangeline slept. Aletheia was too stunned to weep. She lifted her eyes and addressed the widening empty sky.

"Is there nothing we can do?"

Luce picked up Evangeline. "The Angel of Light is here to serve you," he soothed, passing the sleeping bundle to Aletheia. Allow me to offer a solution both simple and aesthetically just. Aletheia, consider this, if you elect to marry me we could petition for the restoration of your wings. It's virtually an airtight case, practically a fate accompli. We take your Earth Angel back to Grace, and her destiny becomes our own. And if things go my way, and I believe this time they will, you and I will rule the angel forces together."

"And Conrad? What happens to him?"

"You will be his guardian angel, Angel."

"You do tempt me, Luce." She looked around, abashed by conflicting desires. "Oracle, please counsel me. What should my answer be?"

"Walk with me," Sister Omicron invited. "I believe we should take the pause that refreshes—a little pink lemonade and some prayer. Sometimes not knowing the answer is the most important part of the answer. You never want to skip past the doubt. O wondrous and revelatory doubt. Let us recall that omnipotence deadens the soul," Oracle pronounced. "Let us *not* know the answer and be refreshed. Think on this: if everything is known before it happens, then nothing happens. And we are all made dull. At this moment, it is unclear which way the waves will break. There may be cross currents and rip tides. Let's not go swimming just yet."

The oracular Sister Omicron was leading Aletheia to Moon Beach. The chorus line of cloggers followed suit and soon were clothed in swimwear, carrying bright beach bags. Like every-day Coney Islanders, they clattered down Sister Moon's boardwalk. Umbrellas and beach balls dotted the Felini-esque scene, and co-operating phonographs played Nino Rota oom-pah-pah circus riffs. The stranded Kilowatt stood on the decking, in a striped t-shirt, playing the accordion. It was literally seaside heaven on Sister Moon.

"You might want to hang back on the beach for the next little bit and study which way the waves break." Omicron continued, "I also recommend volley ball. The sand on Moon Beach is divine. Sisters! String up the nets."

The Angel of Light followed quick on the heels of his flighty intended, determined to push Aletheia to a conclusion, a conclusion that Oracle had purposefully placed in an elegant pair of brackets, beach brackets.

When troubled by the afflictions of contradictions, the Sisters liked to say, "Let's beach it." The Moonies practiced the three bees: bench it, beach it, or bathe it. It was considered impolitic to crash a beach party with the sole purpose of promoting a narrative that was being held in abeyance. This sort of importuning only served to create mental enjambment. Ideas need room to romp.

They need beaches.

And benches

And bathes.

Sister Alpha Oceania caught the high winds of Lucifer's force field, bristling with push and ambition. She and Sister Delta Dawn gracefully stepped in to arrest his momentum.

"Here push this," Alpha Oceania said, offering him the pram.

"If you plan on raising Evangeline, you might want to practice," Delta Dawn intoned.

Aletheia plunked Evangeline down into the pram and gave Luce an encouraging nod, "Go on, then."

Soon he was off and strolling down the boardwalk like any swank boulevardier with a pretty baby for passersby to admire.

The Sisters Tau zipped by on roller blades.

Rho Zeta and Psi Lambda simultaneously launched over a tremendous breaker on shortboards.

Aletheia tucked a volley ball under her arm and headed for the nets.

Just another day at the beach.

# COWBOYS AND ANGELS

CONRAD EPPLER WAS SUFFERING from a serious case of dream slippage.

First there was the nightmare of the irascible Mother Mary Extraordinary descending on Sister Moon like a banshee in a bad fairytale. He woke up in a cold sweat, concerned that the nasty spell she cast in the dream was a reality playing out in a parallel world.

And what was Luce doing on Sister Moon, hanging around Aletheia? Falling back into a dream-riddled sleep, Conrad found himself standing on a beach by a volley ball net watching Aletheia spike the ball to the cheers of her team. He tried to get into the game, but none of the other players could see or hear him.

He had become an invisible boy, a ghost boy standing on the sidelines of his own dreamscape, looking in but unable to break through the barrier join the players. Wandering down to the shore, he waded in ankle deep and noticed how his bare feet stayed curiously dry.

Conrad thought he heard Sister Merry Berry calling out to him. What had happened to Sister Merry Berry? No one seemed to know. At the convent, they were still waiting for her to come home. He turned to the sound of her voice.

A great red beach ball was tossed in the air and coming his way. He reached for it and the ball passed through him. Then he was back asleep in his bed.

The last dream of the morning was the real puzzler. He was solidly on the inside, but he was inside the wrong dream. The first thing that struck him was a tumbling tumbleweed. It literally struck him, blew through the window, tumbled onto his bed and ouch! He sat up and felt around for Skipper in the bedding. Then he heard the monkey's voice in his mind, saying, *Dude, look up.*

There was Skipper, wedged in the arms of a ghost-white Saguaro cactus. Cactus? A fragment of memory from a previous dream surfaced, then skittered away. Tumbleweeds and cactus tangled in the corners of his mind.

"Skipper, what are you doing on the cactus?" There it was— the memory blew back on a tailwind. The phrase, *prick her finger on a cactus,* echoed in Mother Mary Extraordinary's distinctive voice.

Conrad hopped out of bed and reached for his monkey, carefully running his fingers through Skipper's fur, checking for prickles. He was puzzling over Skipper's white cowboy hat and neckerchief, when he glanced down and noticed his own pair of white cowboy boots. And just when he was thinking—*Where's my white hat?*—a white Stetson appeared.

"Wow, Skip. Pretty weird, huh? I guess this is us in cowboy heaven."

Conrad buckled up a holster set with two nifty six-shooters and extra bullets in the belt. He spotted a Sheriff's badge and pinned it to his vest. Whatever world this was, he was happy to look into it. It had the scent of adventure.

"Looks like we're the good guys. At least, in comic books they mostly give the white hats to the good guys," he said to Skipper, starting to wonder why the dream makers had dipped his world in white.

His whole room was painted white: the walls, the furniture, the interior landscape of cacti and tumbleweeds. Where the mullioned windows used to be, a set of white saloon doors swung gently in a light breeze. And beyond the doors, piles of thick white clouds clotted the sky.

"I guess it's time to head on outta here, pardner. Sister Merry Berry's gone. Mother Mary's almost gone. It's down to Sister Subordinary, you, me and the cassowary. I've got to get me a set of parents, Skip. And we gotta go find us some blue sky."

Conrad was fastening Skipper's Velcro paws around his neck when he noticed a scruffy pair of brown boots on the other side of the swinging doors. He didn't have to look up. He knew those brown boots.

"Roica," Conrad said under his breath.

Better watch what I wish for, Conrad thought to himself, wondering how he should play out this panel with a guy who had basically walked out on him—the epic fail.

"Conrad Eppler," Roica entered.

"Kid Colt to you, Mister."

"How's it going?" the time traveler asked.

"I'm hanging in there." Conrad folded his arms. "What's on your mind?"

"I came to pick up you and Aletheia, son." Roica stepped up to the brass rail at the bar that had just materialized.

"I'm not your son," Conrad said, climbing onto a bar stool. "As I recollect it, you walked out on us."

"I'm really sorry about that. Maybe I can make it up to you."

"Maybe. Maybe not." Conrad stuck a tooth pick in his mouth. "I'm not saying nothing about whatever almost was."

Skipper's tail twitched. The monkey was getting a kick out of Conrad's poker-faced cowboy, a pitch-perfect classic, culled from many an evening spent deep in the thrills of vintage Marvel Westerns.

"So where's Aletheia? Got any ideas?" Roica downed a shot.

"Well, she ain't here, in case you haven't noticed. She never came back to Earth—like she promised."

"What are you trying to tell me, pardner?"

"I ain't your pardner. I'll say it one more time nice. It's Kid Colt to you, Mister."

"All right, Kid Colt. What's going on?"

"Well, I got some bad news and some sad news. Aletheia took a blue rocket to the moon. Sister Moon."

"She did, huh? What're we waiting for?"

"You better not be messing with me, Mister. How in tarnation are we going to get to the moon? I mean for real."

"I've got my trusty steed."

"Am I missing something? Does your horse have wings?"

"I've got a rocket named Steel parked outside." Roica let that sink in.

"I think I ought to give you fair warning. There's been some developments."

"Oh, yeah? Like what?"

"We've been replaced." Conrad had Roica's attention now.

"That's one flighty angel, pardner." Roica looked at him sideways. "What's the lowdown?"

"I'll brief you on the way up. We've got competition."

"Got to beat that competition," Roica flicked the brim of his hat. Conrad couldn't help but smile.

"Why did you come back?"

"Something someone said to me one time."

"What'd they say?"

"Earth is the best place for love." Roica stood up and headed out the swinging doors.

"Hey, I said that! Hey, wait for me and Skip."

———

MEANWHILE ON SISTER MOON, the competition for Aletheia's hand was set spinning in a great wheel of prayer. After their time-out on the beach, Oracle and the Joyous Sisters began their meditations in earnest, albeit with divided hearts and minds. A gorgeous proxy such as Lucifer was an undeniable prize, with his promise of an illuminated existence for Aletheia and Evangeline on planet Grace. And yet Sister Moon was a devotee of planet Earth.

As was their practice, the Sisters opened themselves to all possible outcomes—the wide embrace. And though the prayer benders mindfully cleansed themselves of prejudice, they couldn't help but indulge in pride and preference. Earth was their lodestone, perpetually magnetizing their collective will. Earth was where the action of grace propelled the evolution of consciousness. Earth was the glory of the material world. Earth was what mattered most to the Sisterhood.

The hive throbbed with the distress signals of their beloved planet. The shattered love of the primal parents was so vast, it reached everywhere. It was the quiver of arrows in the sacred heart of the Earth. It was the splintered wound in the soul of creation. When it all came down to moon dust, the Sisterhood was powerless to close that primal wound. The closure required nothing less than the reconciliation of the lovers.

To that end, the Sisters created powerful Gregorian enchantments. This is how they prayed.

"O most luminous Wheels, whose perfect bliss turns the universe," Oracle addressed the plenum, "We honor the wide array of resplendent stars and celestial beings."

"May you favor the Earth today," the Sisters petitioned, "Hold Eve in your wide embrace."

"O positrons of wisdom, quarks of grace," Oracle invoked the beloved particles.

"Guide Adam through the maze and amazement," the Joyous Sisters rejoined.

"Light the entrance."

"En Trance. En Trance. En Trance."

"Bring him home."

"Oracle, raise your audicon," Aletheia's hope sparked on the flint of her anger, "Match me."

The ultra-sensitive Oracle split Aletheia's response into its major and minor chords. *Light the match. Fire my soul. Amend my heart.*

Sister Omega Omicron tuned her cosmic stethoscope and registered Aletheia's heartbeat, its hidden sorrows, its irregular rhythm now quickened with anger and angst. Then the Oracle began to seek out the matching beat, the battered heart of the matter.

The blind seer scanned the skies in all six directions listening for the sound of an ancient wound, the mineral traces of the primal shattering that would lead her search from the long ago to the present crisis.

When she pressed the disc against the atmosphere, it appeared as if she were doctoring the sky. And she was.

The expectant Sisterhood leaned towards the circle of amplifiers. Ignited by the Sisters' prayers, Oracle powered her instrument higher and higher, scanning the farthest corners of the plenum. The hive mind was listening for the sound of Aletheia's eternal beloved.

"Something's wrong with this thing," Omicron gave the instrument a good shake. She tried again, testing each of the six directions. Then she bowed her head in defeat. "Please, accept my utter dismay and amazement. I have failed. I cannot get a lock on the runaway heart."

No sooner had she given up on herself and her instrument, than the hive sensed a shift in the ambient ether. Oracle turned around. The pink congregants watched her lift one hand. Then the blind seer began to read the particulate air with her sensitive finger tips. She rolled a stray electron between her thumb and forefinger.

"Lo and behold, I can feel an aha moment coming on," Oracle beamed. "O benighted world. O yesterday!"

The Sisterhood déjà-vued with the Oracle. The hive mind hummed with recurrents and recurrence.

Aletheia gave the oracular auditor a questioning look.

"Never mind my momentary slip into the abyss. I was aiming too high," Sister Omega Omicron admonished herself with a chuckle.

The Oracle corrected the angle of the cosmic stethoscope, lowering the disc to shoulder height. Immediately the deafening booms of a pair of heartbeats shook the amplifiers and announced the presence of two walk-ons.

There they were—in cowboy hats, no less—a man and a boy. Like their startled audience, the two travelers stood fixed in the stunned silence. Conrad recovered first and tipped his hat.

"We were not expecting cowboys," remarked Sister Rho Zeta, embarrassed by the collective failure to rejoice in their answered prayer.

"No one ever expects cowboys," Roica nodded and looked to Aletheia for a sign of welcome.

"Roica," was all Aletheia could manage.

The blind Oracle reached for the boy, and Conrad stepped into her embrace. She ran her telepathic fingers over his face and let out an involuntary whoop. That she alone among the sorority could discern his lineage, could read the patents of divinity, did not lessen the shock of awe that overtook her when she touched the face of the illegitimate God. *So like his greatest grandmother, Maa Bhavatarini. Surely, one day his divine blue effulgence will be restored. What a lineage!* She ruffled his hair to cover the upheaval in her heart. "You must be Conrad Eppler, the beneficiary of the spell."

"Sorry about that, Sister. Mother Mary got my messages mixed up. It's tough on a guy when he can't even make it into his own dream."

The Tau Tau's rushed forward to check out this much marveled-over boy, the source of such a stir of rumor and wish.

"Conrad, how would you like a super deluxe, personally guided walk-about-walk-about the moon," the spiritual twins chimed. "We can take you to Lookout Point in the moonrock garden. We've got our very own ocean."

Just then Sister Merry Berry gave out a shout, "Conrad!"

She ran as fast as her red stilettos would allow and scooped him up in her arms. "I saw you on the beach the other day. I so wanted to hug you, but you know how double visions are. Those

photinos! The way they jump about. I tossed you a red beach ball and it passed right through you. Nearly broke my heart."

"I tried to catch the ball," Conrad said, "I really tried."

"You're here! That's all that matters." Sister Merry Berry gave him another squeeze. "Conrad, you must take a ride with me in my Cadillac. Remember? I promised you a ride. Back when I was on the other side."

Conrad shook his head, no, and wriggled out of her arms.

Merry Berry bounced over Conrad's reticence. "Your special friend, Kilowatt, is here. Somewhere. Mother Mary left him in the lurch. Now he's motoring about the moon with Sister Psi Lambda who used to be Sister Josephus. She practically stole my Cadillac!" Merry Berry was aware she was babbling in her joy but couldn't stop herself. "Oh, look! See that trail of dust headed our way. That's them. That's my Cadillac!

"I can't go for a ride," Conrad stood firm. "This is high noon on Sister Moon. If I let the deciders decide things without me, I might get left out of my own story."

"Sorry, cowboy," Sister Omega Omicron intervened. "This is a love scene. The Sisters have been praying for its re-occurrence for eons. Everyone wants their happy endings, but we've got to get the beginnings right."

With perfect timing, Sister Psi Lambda pulled up in the Cadillac and gave the horn a succession of happy beeps.

"Hop in," the former owner of the Ford Fairlane signaled to Merry Berry and the boy. Psi Lambda looked as pleased as a bodhisattva, sitting in the cushy Biarritz. To each her own prayer wheel, she liked to say.

Kilowatt waved eagerly from the backseat of the convertible. "Earthworm," Kilo called out to Conrad, "what's with the cowboy duds?"

Then the lowly angel opened the back door of the Cadillac Eldorado Biarritz with a nifty flourish, and stood waiting. "Anytime, kid," he invited.

With a worried backward glance, Conrad climbed in. Kilo followed suit. Merry Berry plunked herself in the front passenger seat. Lambda gunned it and the four sped off, leaving the lovers in the moon dust.

The remaining Sisters politely folded themselves into a conveyance of fog. Sister Rho Zeta longed to turn back and catch the lovers' welcoming embrace. One for the holy books, she imagined. Had she turned back, she would have seen two figures keeping their distance, circling each other, careful as atomic clocks. The infinity hand stuck, measuring lost chances, rehearsals, betrayals, and despairs, against the perils of starting over.

"Is this a love scene, Roica?" Aletheia asked, her eyes hooded with doubt.

"You tell me."

"It seems like a sleepwalker's dream," she answered, "an enchantment that Conrad and the Joyous Sisters weave. Do you believe the story? That we were the first to walk in the Earth's garden?"

"You were a vision in the garden, and I was a fool."

The painful memory struck her full force. "You handed me a fig leaf! The first look. The one that matters most. A fig leaf!"

"Eve, settle down. I can't rehearse old arguments with you."

"As if I want them. I don't. They come crowding in, they block out the sun, hope, everything." She was suddenly caught in a powerful rip tide, pulling her back to Lucifer. "I want my wings back. I want Grace. I don't want these memories of the fall. I'm done with the old story and I won't have it. I've moved on."

"Eve."

"No."

"This is our chance," Roica was talking fast, aware that he was losing her. "When we look back at the yesterday of us and see ourselves in a burning garden, we know who we are. We are the ones who start over and come to this—this bend, this break in the story. If we change our stars today, the future will rewrite the past."

"Can it take away the pain?"

"Our mythos is ours to reconstruct—we are its originals." Roica had rehearsed this line that was meant to close the argument, but in the clutch of the moment it missed its mark. He didn't mean to shout, but she was turning away. "Everything starts now!"

She turned back.

He plunged on. "If we make today good, then every yesterday has been leading me back to you. The present can redeem the past, if you let it."

He let that lonely truth hang tough in the silence. He stepped towards her. She didn't back away. He gave her a rogue's grin, "Besides, you looked great in a fig leaf."

Mistake.

"Not funny." She railed at him, "You abandoned me! And you'll do it again." She was furious with him and with herself, drenching the moment with angry tears. "Under the gaze of the tripartite Goddess and the Angel of Light you left me without amen or farewell. And for what? To chase the Wheels. What will be different this time?"

"It's different every time."

That stopped her. He wasn't afraid of the memories. By the look in his eye, she could see that he always held the past close by. Was it possible to embrace the broken world? And the terrible beauty of the long emergence—all the stumbles, destructions, wrong turns, set-backs?

"I love you in all your aspects. I love the way you change in time," he wooed her.

"Not enough to stay with me when things don't go your way. What if the Wheels should call? Off you'd go. Chasing your adventure."

"Earth is my adventure."

"Easy to say. You never found the Wheels, did you?" She studied him. "I won't be your consolation prize."

"Never that," he took a breath. "Listen. The farther I fell away from you, the more deeply I felt the loss of you. I entered a black limitless night and battered my voice against the void. I want answers! Why the fall? Why is there death? Why must we pick our way among ruins and ashes?"

"Time after time," the lovers spoke as one.

"I want answers too," Aletheia rushed on, deeper into the heartbreak. "Where do dreams go when they die? Or the infants—the ones whose first breath on Earth is their last?" She did not know where that question came from. Was that Eve's eternal question? Did she mourn all her children?

"Hear me out," Roica lifted her chin. "When my breath was torn to rags, I turned my ship around, defeated down to my boots and headed homeward—and there was my answer. I saw how close the angels linger to the Earth. Look," he turned her around. "One tiny planet haloed in light. Even angels look to the Earth for love."

"Love takes us and time breaks us," her eyes brimmed with the sorrows of the world, her world, her poor abandoned world.

"As my ship plummeted to the Earth, I was pierced by so many arrows of longing. How I missed your look, and the miracle of how look after look becomes a life."

"And each life a fallen leaf—so brief a happiness, a misery."

"I stand before you, a fallen man. My heart on my sleeve. Rip it off."

"We made an angel child, you and I."

"I know. And Luce has been courting you. Don't tell me you are even tempted to go for the bliss and nirvana deal. That's not who we are."

He was right; they were the ones who tumbled time after time into the fray. The ones who got their boots muddy. They were the ones called to embrace the riven world. She knew that. But he had no idea how tempting the bliss and nirvana deal looked just then.

"You can't win back my wings. Only Lucifer can do that. I could soar over the vale of sorrows. I could be an angel, mothering an angel. I could keep Evangeline."

Sister Rho Zeta entered the scene, wheeling the angel neonate in her pram, "Have you seen the rapture? Have you seen the Evangeline?"

Rho Zeta lifted the baby up and Evangeline hovered in the sheltering sky, her delicately veined wings hammering the air, diaphanous and powerful.

She flew into her father's arms.

"No mention of her in *The Book of Prophets*, *The Book of Miracles*, or *The Book of Works and Days*," Rho Zeta mused.

"Look at you, Evangeline," Roica cooed, "A starbird. All filament and light." The infant angel softened at her father's voice and slept in his arms.

Oracle joined the family reunion, "There is Earth about her too. The exquisite metaphysical mix."

The Sisters Tau joined in, "She is the bridge, the rapture, the vehicle and the ride. Love always leaves a con trail. A way in and a way out."

"Yes, Evangeline is all of these inescapable mysteries," Aletheia said. "But Conrad? Who is he?"

"Don't you see?" Oracle asked, "He is the apple of his mother's eye—drawing you back into the wild green world that is always your destiny."

"He is the winter rose, a late bloomer in Earth's garden," rhapsodized Rho Zeta.

"Are you saying Conrad is the anointed one?"

"One?" Sister Omega Omicron was genuinely puzzled. "Why ever would the Wheels only send one? The Avatars are countless. And we've anointed some lovely muses and Avataras of late. Everyone is thrilled with the girls. But Conrad, he is our best western Avatar. We are so proud of him. Here he comes."

All eyes turned to the rapidly approaching Cadillac Eldorado Biarritz. It braked in the moon dust. Conrad slid out of the back seat and prepared to take a stand. Coached by Kilowatt, Conrad pulled out his six-shooters and fired caps in the air. A crowd was quickly forming on the plaza.

"Okay, everyone, this is a hold up. I've got something on my mind, pilgrims. And I've got to say it now or I'm going to bust."

"As you can see," Oracle interrupted, "there is still work to be done. Conrad dear, hand over the guns."

Conrad looked to Kilo who mouthed, "Your call."

The boy reluctantly handed over his Colt 45s. Sister Omega Omicron thanked him, adding, "All right, Conrad, the pilgrims are listening."

Disarmed, the boy stood his ground. "Here's the deal. On planet Earth, the sky fills up with prayers every single night. Out of all those millions of prayers, Aletheia answered mine. Now I've got something that she left behind."

"What did I leave behind, Conrad?"

"Your promise. I'm not going to hold you to it. I figure, if I give the promise back, you can't break it."

Sister Rho Zeta sat transcribing the historic interchange, definitely one for the holy books. She was so impressed by the boy's unexpected grace under pressure that she stood up to get a better view of the intrepid cowboy, inadvertently precipitating a ripple of applause. Conrad waited it out.

"I'm not done. See, tough guys, we don't get stuck in yesterday. I got a lot of tomorrows headed my way. But there's something you need to know about my planet," he turned to Aletheia.

"It needs help. And America needs lots of help. But it's still a pretty good place. We got purple mountain majesty. And the redwood forest. And we've got *two* oceans."

"Yes," said Aletheia.

Conrad did not hear his answering angel, and his words kept tumbling by. "At the very least, you've got to come visit us," he struggled to the end of his speech, "now and then."

When he stopped, her *yes* caught up to him. It hovered for a moment. It was a fetching yes, in a Ransom Note font.

"Is that yes meant for me?" Conrad turned to Aletheia, and her eyes brimmed.

"My heart is a puddle," she said. "You are as brave as the blue buttons on your white coat."

"Nice work, pardner," Roica touched the brim of his hat.

Roica looked up and was the first to notice Lucifer slip out from behind an obelisk. "Here comes the snake," he scoffed, not caring if Lucifer caught his rude remark.

"The light, Roica. Here comes the light." Lucifer was hot and openly relished the coming confrontation.

One glance at Aletheia and the Angel of Light saw that she was lost to him. Although Roica was much evolved from the monstrous Neolithic Adam, Lucifer still experienced a reflexive recoil at the sight this man.

"So, the quitter decided to show after all," Luce taunted. Still blaming me for the fall?"

"What in hell are you doing here?" Every cell in Roica's body was adrenalized for a fight.

"For the love of Evangeline," Aletheia called out, "please listen." She turned to her eternal beloved. "Remember your own words, Roica. We are changing our story. And in this new story, we have forged a new alliance. Hear me with an open heart. Lucifer is Godfather to our daughter, the Evangeline. If ever there was a time, this is the time for you and Lucifer to call a truce."

"I'd like to hear from Lucifer," Roica challenged. "Do you wish me well?"

Oracle glided into the prospering fare-thee-well. In her famous orotund voice, she announced, "This moment will not come again for ten-thousand times ten millenniums."

Everyone studied the Angel of Light.

"Please, allow me the dignity of a little animosity," Luce began. "When the Wheels decided to let one planet in the universe breed and be free, almost immediately they lost the courage of the very creation they commissioned from my brother. It's hard to live with the ambiguous, the incomplete, the flawed. To appease his critics, the Maker repackaged Earth and came up with a credible illusion of perfection, illusion being the operative word here. In an effort to sustain the mythical paradise, my brother began to bind Earth in rules and regulations. It was all so arbitrary. And a ruse. This apple, yes. That apple, no. You were no more than dumb happy animals. I broke the bounds of those limitations. I struck down the illusion; I tore away the veil and revealed a garden rich in danger and delight. An Eden embedded in reality, so called."

"Not *so called*," the bossy Oracle corrected. "The garden is always calling; it is a calling—a vocation, a devotion to an idea, an ideal. Logos to mythos, we amend, we evolve. Rebranding is the operative word here. And reality? It's a group maintenance project. We can all agree on that."

"Let me come to my point, Oracle. I was just about to the offer the olive branch, to make my personal amends," Luce averred. He folded his arms and leaned against a marble column. "Roica, I admire your willingness to bind your future to the Earth. My love for Aletheia has always been and will always be perfect and impersonal. That said, let the peace between us be a wedding gift to Aletheia. Accept my congratulations. Roica, what can I say?" Lucifer gave it up, "You got the best of the nest."

"You can't blame a guy for being lucky," Roica mirrored Lucifer's nonchalance.

Although Roica was not comfortable with or certain what Lucifer meant by impersonal love, he wanted to be a gracious winner. "I'll give you this, Luce, you put up a good fight. I'll never forget the day you fought your brother, the Maker, or Demiurge, or whatever he calls himself."

"Right, the deity with no name. In truth, my brother does have a name, but the artful dodger doesn't like his name spoken. In fact, he doesn't like his name, period. He's a deity in permanent identity crisis. Don't get me started." Lucifer's green eyes glittered. "I know that you and Eve watched the catastrophic brawl from your promontory in the garden." Lucifer paused. "Sorry about the collateral damage."

The collective Sisterhood held their breath. Would this offhand apology be accepted?

"What a fight that was," Roica came back, "the two of you crashing through the thunderheads, lashing out at each other with electric bolts." Roica's voice was full of unfettered admiration.

In sixes and sevens, the Sisters arranged themselves in circles. They sat on the ground and began to chant—oming lite, an almost imperceptible hum marking an enormous change.

From above, their scattered prayer circles appeared as if a careless Goddess had dropped pink peonies on the travertine concourse. The chanting peonies threw back their heads and opened their palms to the skies, emitting a powerful drone and heavenly scent.

"We all took a pounding," Lucifer acknowledged, exercising his newfound ability to empathize.

For an instant Luce wondered if he'd ever make peace with his brother, then he dismissed the patent unlikelihood. He turned back to Roica, "I was impressed when you stood up to High Consul. You winged her pretty good. The Supreme Being of mismanaged angelettes needed a little redress."

There was a precipitous drop in the etheric atmosphere. Then the hum of the hive mind went silent.

"What is this silence? Are you all struck mute by my charismatic rhetoric?"

The Joyous Sisters had been blissing out on the repartee and the rapprochement between the three iconic garden players. Now the Sisterhood arose in unison and stood shielding their eyes. It seemed that a giant wandering star was lighting up the firmament. The blind Oracle lifted her audicon; the beat of an unfamiliar tripartite heart was amplified.

Lucifer turned around.

Asheilstarte was descending the grand staircase, flanked by her two Wing Sergeants.

# ASHEILSTARTE

ASHEILSTARTE WAS NOT ONE to all beholders. The Godma shifted, continuously changing angles of pose and repose, purpose and repurpose. Apprising her altered the soul of the observer, in as much as She was altered by all that came within her purview. She thrived on change, the flux, the tumult, the daring errors, the gate openers, the game changers. The plenum was a constant creation that blinked in and out of enlightenments. Asheilstarte was the ultimate invitation to go on inventing the future.

Lucifer, aware that his patronizing remarks concerning High Consul's management style on Grace may have been overheard, advanced towards the tripartite deity with quick confidence. He meant to cover for any damages he might have done himself with some adroitly improvised courtly falderal.

Asheilstarte shot him a penetrating glance.

The Angel of Light experienced an unaccustomed reverence.

"High Consul, Chariot of Radiance," he acknowledged the ruler of Grace. This time when his eyes met hers, he was caught off guard by a shock of recognition. It was She. The Godma. The primordial She—the venerated womb of creation.

"To each his own mystery, my son, my sun," She sweetened the air with omnibenevolence.

The hush swelled with expectation.

All eyes were upon her.

Although inexorably drawn to the Godma, Lucifer averted his gaze. He did not dare look directly at She-From-Whom-All-Cometh, because the more deeply he looked into her, the more deeply She could see into him.

The Moon Sisters also hesitated, thrown off by the elegant pair of wings that graced the visiting Supernal. With the aid of Oracle's audicon, the Sisters were gradually able to make out the distinct and distant heart rhythms of Mother Mary Extraordinary, the titular leader of their order on Earth.

Although their prioress was again radically altered in appearance, her wounded heart song was a beloved familiar, carrying with it decades of struggle, interspersed with fleeting triumphs.

As the divine being opened her heart to them, the Joyous Sisters gloried in the deepening mystery of their soul cognate, Mary Extraordinary. This was not the troubled, Earthbound Extraordinary, billowing dark promises in black satin raiment, but a more subtle presence. She-Who-Is-Everywhere-At-Once was with them and within them.

Much like the phases of the moon, Asheilstarte appeared both alight and darkened, all shapes merged and emergent. The Sisters understood that they were audience to a beatific vision; the altogether rare moment when a supreme being reveals the multiple faces of her Avataras. They saw Aruru, Hathor, Astarte, Ishtar, Artemis, Amaterasu, Oddudua, Oshún, Ix Chel, Isis, Athena, Gaia, Nike, Sophia, Selene, Yemayá, Sita, Lakshmi, Mother Mary and so much more. Their beloved Holy Mother and Moon Sister was a Goddess ten-thousand times over.

"Mother Mary Extraordinary. I am blinded at your gate," Oracle knelt.

"Mother of Hours," Rho Zeta praised.

"Mother of Prayer," the Sisters Tau Tau offered.

Mother of Eve. Mother of Stars. Mother of Seas. Mother of Gods. Mother of All. Ah She.

The honorifics were amplified until salutes and praises filled the valley.

Aletheia was parsing the spectrum of salutations and coming to a new understanding of her relationship to this multifaceted, prismatic being. Picking up the thread of a lost storyline, the applecart of creation tipped over in her mind. The erstwhile Eve laughed at the image of spilled apples, and a cornucopia of red and gold fruit tumbled at her feet.

"Daughter, we are all about the Earth, her bounty, her gardens and her life-forms," She acknowledged Eve.

That Aletheia was overwhelmed was wildly understating her existential predicament. She was herself and not herself. She was remembering and forgetting a sweep of lives in rapid succession. Her eyes widened when she caught up with her current incarnation on Earth, a young woman named Alyssa Rosaria. Was it possible that her life with Roica had already begun to unfold on the material plane? It must be, because there they were—Alyssa Rosaria and Rios Dante, two young idealistic doctors out to heal the world.

A veil was peeled away, and Aletheia was allowed to see how the young couple had struggled to live out their high-minded, homemade dreams, how Alyssa and Rios briefly dwelt in a paradise on Earth, lived in a house that love built. She saw how all that changed when Alyssa lost a baby daughter. The miscarriage blacked out the light and blanketed the young couple in guilt and grief. Physicians, heal thy daughter. They could not.

Aletheia held Evangeline tighter. In a split second of clarity, she understood that Conrad was a gift for Alyssa. She almost passed out from the dizzying collision of coincident worlds. Oh, Mother of Sorrows, the world was so imbued with loss and the lost. Blessed Lethe, river of forgetfulness. Blessed Alethe, river of remembrance. The divine helix of memory and oblivion ribboned through her soul.

One could not live it all at once. And yet the Godma seemed to be everything at once. With a start, Aletheia saw how she herself made one facet of Asheilstarte possible on the material plane and how the inextricable mix of all existence leaned into the impossible geography of an individual soul.

Asheilstarte was watching Aletheia's epiphanies skip like stones on water, creating intricate cross-currents on the surface and rearranging the hidden patterns of the river rock beneath.

Queen of Heaven. Queen of Earth. Queen of Souls. Queen of Saints and Sinners. Queen of Angels and Angel Police. Queen of the highways, byways, roadside stands and attractions. Queen of the upturned applecart. Queen of gleaners.

Asheilstarte watched Kilowatt pluck an apple from the spill. He was standing just outside the circle of light, looking for entry, munching away with charming insouciance.

"Hello Kilo," She waited for whatever extemporized salutation he might devise. Beloved clown. Beloved gleaner.

"Holy Mother of Iconic Impressions. If you did voices, I could book you in Vegas. Just saying," Kilo laughed at his own joke. He held up the apple, "Not a bad apple."

"Not a bad apple in the bunch," she replied.

"Mother of," he sputtered to a stop, stymied by the mega-multiple-choice problem. Then he hit upon an answer: "Mother of—All Above and Below." A self-satisfied smile lit up his face.

She returned his smile. Kilo had his hand resting on Conrad's shoulder.

Asheilstarte streamed a swath of light around the young Avatar. "Beautiful boy," She called to him, her embedded diamond-studded monocle dilating as she spoke. "Conrad Eppler, you may approach me."

"Who? Me?"

Kilo gave Conrad an encouraging nudge and the boy made his way towards the Godma. He walked tall among the spiritual giants that day, his white Stetson catching the light, his boot heels clicking on the moonstone, Skipper slung carelessly about his neck. He watched Asheilstarte's bright wings fan the air. She said nothing. All was anticipation. He felt his moment arrive and stepped into it.

"Who are you? Do I belong to you?" Conrad ventured further onto more dangerous ground, "Have you come to take away the angel, Evangeline?"

"You are all questions, and I am watching your answers approach you." She looked into the distance. The monocle contracted.

Conrad risked a quick backward glance over his shoulder as if he might spot approaching answers. Instead he saw a sea of glowing Sisters.

"Look at me," Asheilstarte directed him. "Who do you see?"

"You look like the most beautiful angel in the whole wide world, but you remind me of someone else."

"Who might that be?"

Conrad didn't hesitate. "Mother Mary Extraordinary."

"Your guardians were appointed with extraordinary care. Imagine that she and I are two wheels propelling a single chariot. Or, imagine two stars guiding your apprentice-ship, one bright, one dark—it's nemesis and twin. Imagine that we divided to bring you to the heart of a mystery."

As She spoke, all the Joyous Sisters went with her into the heart of the Goddess Mystery.

"But which one really are you?" Conrad insisted.

"She is that, so I may be this."

"I don't get it."

"She is Earth, so I may be Sky. She is the Dark so I may be the Light. She has fallen that I may rise."

"Then she is the greater one because she made the greater sacrifice."

A burst of delicate, golf-green applause rippled through the Sisterhood.

"Well spoken, Avatar," Oracle called out, catching the eye of Asheilstarte.

"Yes, Sister Mary Mirabelle," the Godma nodded, "we are pleased with our young Avatar."

The Oracle, Sister Omega Omicron, was pleased as well. It was an exceptional honor to be recognized as the former Mary Mirabelle, a personal favorite among Oracle's long history of Earthside incarnations. If her sight were ever restored, she prayed one day she would open her eyes on Dagoberto Emilio Marquez, meet him once again footloose and afield on the good planet Earth. Sometimes an incarnation is carried off with such finesse that it becomes star struck in the celebrity walk of collective memory. Sometimes once is not enough. Mary Mirabelle. Would she ever be that lovely again? Setting that refulgent question aside, Oracle came back to the moment.

Asheilstarte was addressing the young Avatar. "Conrad, when you return to Earth, look deeply into Mother Mary's suffering so that you may see my beauty, just as now when you looked into my beauty, you saw her suffering. Now hear me, there is no greater and there is no lesser. We are one."

Many glistening eyes lifted.

Addressing Conrad, She addressed them all. *We are one*—the belle tidings tolled through the crowd.

Asheilstarte was peeling away layers of herself. Even so, the Godma remained unfathomable. Her essential self had no show, no mask, no persona. She was both a projection and a receiving medium. A creatrix constantly being created, she was illuminated by her devotees—her poets, artists, prayer-benders, and visionaries.

Now she illuminated the boy. A plenitude of identities coursed across her face. Like so many veils pulled aside, She morphed from Asheilstarte to High Consul, Queen of the Angels, Mediatrix of Grace. She paused ever-so briefly on Maa Bhavatarini, standing on the reclining Shiva. It was almost a wink. Then fleetingly, She appeared as the blue mother, Sita—an image fished from the boy's spiritual DNA. She lingered on her incarnation as Mother Mary Extraordinary. Then She quickly presented a rapid succession of her Mother aspects until she was certain that Conrad had glimpsed something of her mystery.

"Do you see me?" she asked.

"You are so many. And you are still my Mother Mary Extraordinary."

"Then we have served our purpose. For with your own eyes you have seen the matrix of matrices, the interlocked gears that turn the great Wheels of being. It is the pearl of our wisdom, the primary paradox of the plenum. Now it is yours to teach, Avatar."

Conrad's face fell. "Me? I can't. I sort of see what you mean, but I don't get it. Not really. I don't want to disappoint you.

Maybe, if you put it in a comic book? Then I could study how your powers work."

"It is simple math, dear. Two in one. Many in one. One in many. Although a comic book would be nice. Everyone loves a good story. We are all made of story, Conrad."

"There's just one thing I need to know—am I a good guy? Where did I come from? Who are my real parents? Am I your Avatar? Are you running me?"

She laughed delightedly, "That was five things. Lovely questions though, very deep. Your questions let me see who you are. Answers change over time. As do the questions. You exist in a field of fluid variations. Change, flux are bywords. Some promises will be kept. Some will be broken. You handled Aletheia's promise beautifully. You are most certainly a good guy."

"That's *mostly* all I want—to be a good guy," Conrad said, thinking about parents, letting go of that wish just a smidgen, just in case Roica and Aletheia didn't make it back to Earth. It made him sad, the letting go, but he didn't want to seem ungrateful in such illustrious company, so he covered beautifully and said; "I know you meant to give me something special. I wish I understood it better. That's all."

"Wisdoms are like water. Best to let the wisdoms of the Gods mount like a great wave and tumble you. Enjoy the swim. I'm going to give you a simple assignment, Agent Eppler."

"Okay," Conrad answered, visibly relieved. "Now you're talking. Agent Eppler, at your service. Or I could be Kid Colt."

"Be whomever you wish."

A startled Conrad watched the extraordinary being reach inside herself and remove a glowing heart. It was streaming a vibrant array of gold-dusted blue lumens, and it was beating lightly at its red center.

One of the Wing Sergeants produced a translucent box, made of molten sea glass. It appeared to be liquid, but was solid and cool to the touch. The other Wing Sergeant lifted the lid. The tripartite Godma placed her beating heart in the box and the Wings bent low, placing the box within reach of the boy.

"Take my heart and deliver it to Mother Mary. Her Earth time is running down, and she must have a change of heart for the crossing over. It's something of a spiritual emergency. I must gather her unto me. You must send her safely home, Conrad. Escorts, please."

Two Joyous Sisters came forward.

"I hope this is really happening," the boy looked longingly into the eyes of the extraordinary being.

"I am trusting you with my heart, Conrad. You do not have to believe it. Your call is to live it and so be it."

"So be it. So be it." the whispering Wings pressed the words on the boy's memory.

"You are the messenger and the message," Asheilstarte continued. "Deliver my heart. That is your charge."

"Just one more question. Please. I promise. This is my very last question," he paused. "Do you know about the cassowary?"

"Of course I know about the cassowary. Now step aside and let me sort this. Escorts, return Conrad to his planet."

Her heart in his hands, She watched him going and gone.

"Sister Merry Berry, you may approach me."

Merry Berry came forward in her red shoes—her dreadlocks bouncing, her eternal cup in one hand. She made a little curtsey and waited judgment with an ingenuous élan; her smile bright, the kiss twinkling in her dimple.

"Savannah James."

"James?" Merry Berry registered her surprise with a painful hiccough.

"Yes, Jamari James. That is your birth mother's name, the girl who left you at the foundling door. I thought you might want to know something of your Earth origins before you left the cognate soul group."

The gathering of Joyous Sisters gasped and let out a collective sigh. This was a rare event. A tear glistened down Savannah's cheek.

"I thought so. I thought maybe I—." Another fat tear slipped down her other cheek. She caught it with the tip of her tongue.

"I am going to roll back Earth time for you."

The sorority leaned in.

"For me?" Merry Berry snuffled. "I'm sure I thank you deeply, but I can't think what you mean, although I'm certain you mean well." Merry Berry curtsied.

"I found a place where I can slip you back in," the Godma smiled. "The Cadillac Eldorado Biarritz will run out of gas at the base of Mount Quoborium. You will never take that ride off Martyr Maker point. The Cadillac will stall. You will totter along the highway in your ridiculous shoes until you find a gas station. We both know who you will call from that station. At some point, there will be a love scene—and I wouldn't want you to miss it. I imagine that by the time you and Tremont show up at the convent, you will be Savannah Montress, née James. You will want to pick up your cassowary. Now click your heels, dear one. You are going home."

Now the fat tears fell in earnest. "Mother Mary Extraordinary will be appalled," was all that Savannah could manage between snuffles.

"Yes, of course she will be appalled. Here's a thought. Wouldn't the mansion on the convent grounds make a lovely bed and breakfast? It's just an idea to tinker with in the henceforth."

The Moonies immediately began to tinker in the now.

"All that is happening in this moment, Savannah James," the Godma continued, "is that you are being given one of the futures you were meant to have, and would have taken on, had you not been so afraid for Conrad and so afraid of Mother Mary Extraordinary. Go ahead and find out who you are when you are not afraid. All of us will enjoy watching you take that ride. Escorts, return Savannah to her vehicle."

Savannah brushed away her tears and gave her red heels a double click, by way of a salute and a so long. Then she hurried off to try out her new future.

"How beautifully each moment unfolds," Oracle was brimming with pride. No one could sort with as much exquisite dispatch as the bountiful Asheilstarte. And nothing could have prepared Oracle or the Joyous Sisters for what happened next.

"Lucifer, Archangel of Light, Pillar of Illuminations, you may approach me."

"High Consul," the angel stepped up. He was not ready to acknowledge her as *his* mother. It was infuriating to even have a mother. Her earlier salutation, "My son, my sun" was still ringing in his ears. Metaphor and homonym, mere poetry, he insisted to himself.

"Now you have seen how it is done."

"Seen how what is done?" Lucifer was uncharacteristically cautious, unsure of his footing.

"The early education of an Avatar, for one. The extension of a life into an unlived future, for another. Notice how beautifully I folded time. Those reprobates who murdered Sister Merry Berry are currently capuchin monkeys, so they have no memory of the ice slick and its aftermath. I must congratulate Lord Hanuman on that ingenious bit of karmic foolery."

"The monkeyshines? A nice day's work." Luce was still appraising her and not giving much. He figured that she would try to come at him sideways, so he redoubled his resistance. The calculating illuminato forged a barrier of fiery lumens to keep the tripartite being from reading him, thus he failed to get a good read on her.

"And the Eppler effect?" she asked the rebellious angel.

"Frankly, I don't see it. What's the big deal?"

"Love is the big deal, Lucifer. The essence of an Avatar is revealed in how that being occasions love. Surely you have noticed how this orphan created adopters. And mentors. And guardians. And scribes. And watchers, yourself among them. He has demonstrated considerable power. Effortlessly."

Sister Rho Zeta, keeper of the books, was penning away at a furious rate, dipping her pen in a jar of homemade ink, shaking out her numb fingers and looking longingly over at Kilowatt's laptop, his fingers tapping a rapid, happy dance on the keyboard. Her script was incomparable—she huffed to herself, as she made dainty scroll work of a capital E.

"Let us appreciate the Eppler effect," Asheilstarte continued, images flashing on the marble walls. "The boy's inauspicious arrival in a cardboard box, how Lord Hanuman protected the boy in the snow storm and rose to the occasion of his greatness on the golden Duomo, how Sister Subordinary's soul flew out from her body upon seeing the blue baby, how Merry Berry found her missing childhood. The boy created a cosmic ripple in the fabric of love. And here's a personal revelation for you, Lucifer—the Avatar attracted Elyon's notice," she paused and caught an unmistakable glint in Lucifer's gold-flecked green eyes.

"My brother? How casually you drop his name into the discourse."

"Yes. Imagine that."

"What has any of this to do with my brother?"

"Elyon. Let us take his name out of the closet and redress it for a long-overdue outing. Besides, Elyon has always been such a difficult paradox, perpetually tripping over his own proclamations. Don't take his name in vain. Don't speak his name out loud. He is jealous of all the others. There are no others. So rule-bound, it's a wonder he can move at all. And yet, he does move. He moves mountains and creates wonders.

Today we speak his misgiven name and record a pertinent piece of Elyon's story."

"My brother's story is riddled with improbables and embarrassments," The Angel of Light wanted his take on record.

"It is your story as well, Lucifer." She glanced at the two busy scribes. She appreciated the way mythos perpetually became logos at the tip of the pen, the touch of the keyboard.

Asheilstarte flexed her Wings. She was ready to redact.

"In brief, the cosmic midwife made her examination and declared that there was only one deity in the womb of creation on that holiest of holy nights. So it came to pass—that upon his first breath and great waking yowl, the infant was anointed: The One, El Yon. Not two seconds later, the midwife felt another stirring, a mere whisper in the womb of creation—*eosphoros*. And low, on that very same dark and teeming night, another boy was delivered. That infant was all effulgence, and so he was called The Light, Lucifer, bringer of light. One brother was illuminated, and one was not. One brother had wings, and one did not. One brother was beautiful. The first-born brother, less fortunate in appearance, was jealous. And he became a jealous God."

"You cannot fault me for his jealousy."

She continued building her story with a soft hammer. "Even in his youth, Elyon evidenced a genius for design. When the Wheels determined to let one planet breed life, Elyon was commissioned to draw up a plan. His misfortune was that he wanted nothing more than the admiration of his younger, more beautiful sibling. You know all of this, Lucifer. How he loved you. And how you mocked his every effort to engage you, to impress you. That infamous snicker."

"Where is my brother?"

She paused. "Elyon is enjoying a unique incarnation at the moment."

"He is an incarnation junkie of the first order. And a third-rate magician. He's a perpetual boy, always mucking about in the muddy Earth."

"Yes, he loves to tweak his creation. Remember the painter, Picasso? He was once caught amending one of his paintings in the Louvre. At first the guards mistook him for a vandal. Mastery is an illusion. One never arrives. There are only approaches. Excuse me, I am following too many lines of thought at once." Asheilstarte was perpetually bemused by the great chaotic crosshatch of creations and creators.

"Your point?" Luce was concentrating on keeping her out of his mind and on her own course.

"Yes. My point is Conrad Eppler. You will study his effects; how with no effort he changes those he touches. Kilowatt might attest to that," She paused to let Kilo snap a picture of her for his webpage, then carried on.

"Conrad is not the only Avatar, by any means. We explicitly command you not to privilege this notion of The One and Only. This command will become crucial should Conrad's origins ever be revealed."

Lucifer winced at the word command, but kept his own counsel.

"We throw a wide net," Asheilstarte went on, aware that Lucifer was momentarily snagged on a point of pride. "We search all the mythic configurations for potential Avatars. Lately we have detected some scrumptious candidates among the agnostics and the new atheists. There are so many promising genetic lines in development. It is the attraction of an unbound imagination that draws us in."

"And Conrad?" Lucifer studied her.

"So there was Conrad with the window thrown open wide. You were drawn in. Care to comment?"

"Personally, I resent your implication that I'm nothing but a figment in the kid's imagination."

"Did I imply that? Tell me this. When the garden comes to its full bloom and its gates are flung open wide and we see the heavenly city on Earth shining like a beacon in the midst of a flourishing garden—will the garden ask, who dreamed this? I would love to see that moment, all the dreamers, stepping up, taking their credits. Even so, what difference will it make, among Starfriends, who are the dreamers and who are the dreamed?"

"Then you tell me something, what difference will it make among all of us good Starfriends, if I refuse to let you take the Evangeline?"

In a daring move, Luce snatched up Her Holiness, the Evangeline, who had been sleeping in her ritual nest.

"I have the power," he announced.

"And the freedom," Asheilstarte added.

"Don't tempt me."

"I tempt you," the Godma blazed. "Wing Sergeants!"

The Wing Sergeants, each with one towering wing, disengaged themselves from Asheilstarte and positioned themselves on either side of Luce. He felt a current coursing between himself and the great Wings. Ancient memories arose, inflaming his beautiful mind. His suit caught fire, and as the fire ebbed, his human form reconfigured and was no more.

Lucifer was now a scintillation of shifting lights. The gunmetal sheen of moonstone grays coruscated in cross currents with platinum and sunny golds, revealing a majestic symmetry, fulgent with opposing forces.

In a swift and staggering jolt, Lucifer recognized the Wings as his own. He slowly turned from one Wing to the other. Then, fixed in silent reverie, Lucifer closed his eyes.

At first tentatively, then with gentle strokes, the Angel of Light began to fan the awakened air.

Asheilstarte addressed him, "You bear Evangeline in your arms that you may not bear arms. In matters of justice, err always on the side of mercy. Let the Wings be your counsel, High Consul. Today is a great day in heaven. It is Redemption Day! An angel once fallen has risen and is restored to Grace. Abide with us, Lucifer."

"As you will," he answered and felt a rumble of change move through the plenum. Steady on, her voice filled his mind.

"Mythos, logos, fabros," the Goddess refrained out loud.

"Fabros?" Kilo interrupted, his fingers on his keyboard.

"Fabros, from the Latin, fabrica or well made. Here is a moment well made, indeed. Strike a new medal Sisters, a charm for your rosary bracelets. A new icon is given unto us, The Archangel of Light bearing an infant deity in his arms. A girl."

"A girl," chorused the Moonies.

Applause rushed through the elation of Sisters. Witnesses to the elevation of the Evangeline, Roica and Aletheia felt unexpectedly reassured by Lucifer's ascent. In the arms of her elective Godfather, their daughter was safe and in her perfect place.

"Roica and Aletheia, you may approach me."

The archetypal couple came forward. A paparazzi of descending angels emblazoned the couple in flashing lights. Aletheia thought she caught a glimpse of Periwinkle and Epiphany twinkling among the heavenly host. Still wondering at the exchange of power between Luce and the Godma, the erstwhile Adam and Eve hardly knew what to expect.

Roica took Aletheia's hand.

Asheilstarte addressed the couple, "Mystical bride and groom, be astonished how this astral adventure has sanctified the holy bonds of your everlasting love. Even now as I speak, Alyssa and Rios are awakening in time, the evanescence of a dream still lingering in the morning light. Now I say, trip and fall back to your small planet. It is *everything*. Kiss the Earth. You are the lucky ones."

"High Consul, what will become of Evangeline?" Aletheia addressed the Godma.

"I am no longer High Consul. I was merely a bookmark in an unfinished story, a placeholder for The Archangel of Light," Asheilstarte redirected Aletheia's question.

A wondering Aletheia turned to the exalted Lucifer, who held the glowing Evangeline, "Give us hope, High Consul."

"I hold Evangeline hostage to the hope that Earth will one day be illuminated," Lucifer declared. "Thus, I shall bind myself to your fate and the fate of your planet. Let the Earth thrive. Let Evangeline abide as Earth's lost daughter, a rumor of a coming. Let Evangeline be your bookmark in a never-ending story."

After a moment's pause, The Archangel of Light turned to his Wings.

"Wing Sergeants," he said, "give us a prophecy."

The Wings answered in alternating echoes:

> The song of Earth will linger in her ear
> > like an echo clings
> > echo clings to a mountainside
> > and waits for the call
> > the call she was born to answer.
> So the time will come
> > will come when Evangeline
> > will hear her mother's distant call
> > distant call and she will fall
> > > into the masterpiece.

A song broke free from the multitude. The celestial bells rang with such heightened vibrancy that planet Earth heard the plangent promise and a certain cassowary began to preen.

Asheilstarte was gathering herself up and giving herself away.

"Joyous Sisters, I will not be among you in the forthcoming revival of the order on Earth. Let Oracle be Mother Mary in the next cycle."

Oracle wasn't sure and said so, "I was thinking it should be Mary Subordinary. She has a store of untapped gifts. And she is the necessary Mary at her present station."

"Hear, hear," Psi Lambda came forward. "The bed and breakfast venture is exactly Subordinary's cup of tea."

"May her cup runneth over," Rho Zeta put in.

"We want to drink from that cup too. We want to register at the Holy Holy Day Inn," the Tau Taus entered, brimming with enthusiasm for their next incarnation.

The Eden Hostelry and Eatery was moving rapidly from idea to storyboard. Sometimes, on Sister Moon, new ideas moved at the speed of delight. So many plans were already afoot. The Sisters were, after all, devotees of change, aficionados of chaos—the notional chaos that breaks loose on the verge of coming attractions.

Asheilstarte tuned to the hive and followed the swerve of the Sisterhood as it veered away from Oracle and settled on Sister Mary Subordinary to lead the Earthside colony in the next cycle.

"I see," the Godma concurred, "how Mary Subordinary might benefit from an extended stay on Earth. She will be a thread of continuity, as well as the perfect one to beget order from the coming chaos."

The blind Oracle bowed her head in assent, glad to be passed over, happy to stay put. Sister Omega Omicron was flourishing in her current residency on Sister Moon and still flirting with future variations on her previous incarnation as Mary Mirabelle.

"Oracle, abide with me. Let me finish the sorting, and then we'll walk the beach," Asheilstarte felt the surge of another Earth cycle. Did She really want to miss it? Maybe She'd do a drop-in as a surprise guest. Yes, She promised herself, one day She'd appear at the Holy Day Inn. Perhaps on a lampshade.

Kilowatt was approaching her. "Excuse me, your uh, her uh, Royal Used-To-Be."

"Kilowatt, yes. What is it?"

"What about me? Luce, he's got the Wings. Merry Berry's gonna get her beau and her cassowary. The rest of them's got your many blessings. And it looks to me like I'm outta work."

"Let me provide you with a grammar and a dictionary. You can write a testament, or a charming chronicle. A blog, perhaps? In any case, be sure and interview the monkey. Or you might consider the hostelry? I imagine you could find worthwhile employment at The Inn."

"You mean, go incarnate? Like on a semi-permanent basis?" Kilowatt smiled when he heard himself say, "Sure, why not? It might not be so bad."

"You'd make an adorable Major Domo. Major Domo!" the Tau Taus saluted. "We want to go too! We want to be Tuee again," the Vietnamese twins importuned the Godma, carefully pronouncing their oft mispronounced name; twee—to rhyme with tree.

"Look at yourselves," said Asheilstarte. "You're already on your way. Have you noticed how your colors are starting to fade?"

"Wait," the twins cried, "we haven't made up our minds. We're still arguing. We might separate. Possibly go identical but not conjoined. We could be Tuee One and Tuee Too."

"You'll figure it out."

"You lost me at Major Domo, if it please the court," Kilowatt appealed. "Where am I headed exactly? Are you going to slip me in at the convent?"

"No," the Godma smiled, "The municipal building in Quoborium City. Wait in the lobby."

The accustomed tumult was escalating in spontaneous, serial eruptions. The Sisterhood was creating a plethora of possible futures. Asheilstarte called for one-pointed diamond mind. The hive settled into silence. The Mother Goddess called forth Earth escorts for Aletheia and Roica. She watched questions mount in the minds of the lovers, as they prepared to transition.

"You have a question, Aletheia. Ask me." Asheilstarte invited.

"When we are Alyssa and Rios, will we remember any of this?" Aletheia was already mourning what would soon be lost to her.

"In time Alyssa and Rios will remember, but they won't necessarily believe what their memories suggest. Now and then, there will come a tapping on the mind's shoulder, something seen in an artwork, heard in a song, glimpsed by a stream, caught in a conversation. The muses are always at work, reminding us who we are.

"Omnia mutantur, nihil interit," the Oracle quoted Ovid, a beloved principle among Moonies: *Everything changes, nothing is lost.*

"Roica," Asheilstarte wandered into the mind of the first man, "I have a question for you. In all your travels, did you ever find the Wheels?"

"No. I'm no longer certain the Wheels exist. I'm okay with that. Uncertainty seems to be the price of Earth's freedoms."

"It is said that there are seven Wheels; but I have it on good authority that there are twelve Wheels turning within and without the plenum. Five of the wheels exist on the subatomic plane. It is impossible to locate those spinners. They are enormities, mostly made up of sacrosanct nothingness. I'm curious though, what makes you think that you've never seen one of the seven known Wheels? Wheels do sometimes careen onto visible planes."

She waited for Roica to make his surmises. He studied the transformative entity that stood bright before him.

"Watch this," She invited.

On that holy day of changes, Roica and Aletheia were permitted to see what no human, deity, or angel before them had ever glimpsed. First, Asheilstarte tossed a protective veil over the spellbound couple. Then she began to spin with the other eleven Wheels. The universe ripped open briefly on an unimaginable scene.

Lucifer saw the marvels reflected in the lovers' star-dazed eyes. Here was welcome affirmation that the rumored spinners turned in a surpassingly vast and incomprehensible realm that traversed and shot past the plenum. It was enough to know that much. It was a Horatio moment for the august angel. There were wonderments beyond his ken.

Then the vision faded from the lovers' eyes.

Heart spinning like a cosmic wheel, Roica turned to his eternal beloved, "Aletheia, don't let me forget this."

"Or this," she replied with a kiss.

And Lucifer saw that it was good.

At long last, he began to understand that brilliance was not enough. The universe needed lovers. The universe needed makers. And makers needed to make mistakes. Someday, he thought, I'll tell my brother that he did okay. There is much to be admired in creation.

"As my first Act of Grace, I return the lovers to their Earth," thus spoke the restored Angel of Light.

When the kiss and the couple dissolved, The Archangel of Light lifted his magnificent wings. Babe in arms, he began his ascent to planet Grace. As he soared on high, he wondered what other revolutions might be stirring in the plenum.

———

BACK ON THE BEACH there was much at play, so many bright balls in the air—prayer balls, beach balls, volley balls.

Asheilstarte walked with Sister Omega Omicron, the Oracle, the once and former incarnate—Sister Mary Mirabelle.

Omega Omicron still wore Mary Mirabelle's bracelet of sacred charms, with its dangle of miniature historical markers—a pair of gold weeping angels, (like the ones flanking the foundling door), a photo of Mary Extraordinary in a glass bead, a diadem of tiny roses, a tambourine, a yellow-enameled backhoe charm from Dagoberto, a platinum infant for her daughter Grace, a rosy-gold infant for granddaughter Alyssa Rosaria, and a ceramic Ishtar egg to remind her of the holiest of holy nights when she had served the primordial Godma as midwife at the birth the infamous fraternal twins.

"I cracked the egg," Omicron liked to joke, "and helped birth those two unruly hooligans, Elyon and Lucifer."

Oracle and Asheilstarte were the oldest of friends, dating back to the origins of the cosmocracy. The family tree was complicated. Godzillions of reincarnations made it a trackless wild. Still, these two kept a lookout on certain favored matrilineal threads in the ever-growing tapestry.

The line of begats currently under review was a ziggurat affair. It went something like this. In the most recent Earth cycle, Sister Mary Mirabelle was grandmother to Alyssa, the current incarnation of Eve on Earth. Aletheia, the exponentially distant great granddaughter of Asheilstarte, was the soul-sister to Alyssa. It was Alyssa who picked up the phone some seven years back when Mary Extraordinary needed advice about locating diapers and formula. More recently, it was Alyssa who had been grieving over the baby girl she had lost.

Evangeline was the way that two spiritually creative great grandmothers came to the rescue and made a miracle of what was miscarried. It was a supremely complicated metaphysical achievement, of which both grandmothers, in their varying degrees of greatness, were justifiably proud.

Although they had no earthly or heavenward idea how the story would play out in the cosmic halls of time, this day was a spectacular success. The two remarkable grandmothers allowed themselves a self-congratulatory run through the surf, kicking up their heels in the sparkling sand.

"Join us for a cup of moonshine," the Tau Taus invited Oracle and the Godma.

After refreshments were served on the beach, the Sisters of the Joyous Mystery began planning their next leaps in earnest. It was moon jump time and déjà vu all over again.

The idea of an Eden Hostelry and Eatery had caught hold of the collective mind. At some buzz point, the hive would arrive at a honey of a story.

Each Sister was busy redrafting her personal storyline. Some of the stories were co-authored. Some kept strictly private. Some cognate souls would incarnate. Some would stay moonside. A dare of foolhardy jumpers had gone Earthside before there had been any plans made at all.

Blessed be the unscripted!

Sister Moon was a happy scene of invention and re-invention. A small pledge of twenty Sisters, whose prayers had been eaten in the last Earth cycle, decided to become novelists in the next lifetime. They promised to create streams and reams of words. Holy logos—the prayer ball was rolling!

Sister Rho Zeta, keeper of books, thrilled to escritorial visions, possibly even a writers' colony. She would most certainly acquire a laptop. The Eden Writers Hostelry and Eatery, someone suggested. The sign above the prospective inn kept changing titles and neon colors until sun fall.

Psi Lambda, concerned that her proposal was getting lost in Rho Zeta's authorial enthusiasms, reminded her affianced of the two surfer girls who meet on Ocean Beach, one of them a writer, the other a mechanic.

"A rude mech?" Rho Zeta joked. "Ocean Beach—it's a bit redundant. Let's call it Sylvia Beach. It's more literary."

As ever, creative dissention fueled the progress of reinvention.

All agreed on one crucial Earth matter; there must be an organic garden on the grounds. Replenished by their stay on Sister Moon, many were eager to make another run at creating an Eden on Earth. Rumors of the existence of a secret plan for just such a garden bounced with the beach balls.

---

THE GODMA AND THE ORACLE saved a moment for themselves to reflect on the vicissitudes of motherhood. Elyon and his brother Lucifer had been difficult from the get-go. Now that Lucifer was sprung free from an unworkable storyline, they turned their thoughts to the other brother.

They settled themselves on a bench in a hidden cove and watched the sun turn the sands a dusky pink while they sipped thoughtfully from their cups of moonshine.

Like two GPS satellites, the mother and midwife searched the photogenic Earth and zoomed in on a certain cassowary who was strolling across the lawn beyond the convent. The Godma enjoyed a moment's amazement. This was a future She had never conceived for her infant deity when he had come squalling out of the womb and into the plenum, a riot of unfocused energy.

"Once again, we are beached on the shores of speculation." The Godma raised her cup, "Here's to the unknowables."

The midwife tipped her cup in silent agreement. Both were thankful that omniscience did not spoil the view. Predictable lives were infinity dull, and thus free agency was an aesthetic necessity. Nonetheless, knowing full well that they could not steer his stars, they were tempted to fiddle with those selfsame stars. At the very least, here was a welcome opportunity to turn over the dogged theological question: What to do about Elyon? And its correlative: How does one mother the self-emancipated?

Like his younger brother Lucifer, the very idea of a mother had always offended Elyon's overwrought sense of entitlement. Early on, Elyon had revised his origin story, insisting that he was his own parent, self-made, the uncaused cause, the unmoved mover—definitely and defiantly the un. Overly weaned, according to the Godma. Overweened according to the Greek formulation. Elyon was all that and more—the epitome of hubris.

Those ridiculous commandments, announcing there were no other Gods and that he was jealous of all the other Gods practically in one breath. Denying all that reeled so gloriously above and below him, he preferred his creatures not apprehend the vasty reaches of the plenum—the etheric realms of Wheels and Supernals.

On the other hand, the mothers agreed, Elyon got so many things right—flora, fauna and those absurdly fascinating dinosaurs. If the Godma had collected refrigerator art, her fridge would have been covered with layers of Elyon's boyhood drawings.

From adolescence on, the Maker was never seen without a plan scrolled up, tucked under his arm. He was quick to drum up enthusiasms for his projects. But he only made perfunctory appeals for permissions. Elyon was perfectly willing to carry on without anyone's say-so when approval was withheld. Why wait for the say-so when you've got the mojo? His motto.

Sometimes his plans worked well. There was his wildly successful incarnation as Leonardo, followed by the recent egregiously inept incarnation as the Magus, whose unbridled ambition had led to an embarrassment of folly and barbarity.

"I hate to mention those regrettable experiments he inflicted on himself," said Oracle, who went on to mention them. "Adding that extra set of eyes, as if he were some latter-day Dr. Jekyll. Concocting stimulants from purloined prayers, killing off our Sisters, albeit inadvertently, and all the while acting the ersatz drug lord from his jail cell in the Quoborium tower."

"His is a long list of crimes," She paused. "Shall we speak of the crimes that were mine? I consorted with riotous, violent enigmatic forces and brought forth this Caliban of a son. I won't give up on him," the Goddess sternly spoke. "He has never given up on his creation. At the same time Elyon was cooking up Humboldt Snow #7, he was drawing those lovely, lovely garden plans."

"Indeed, his work prospered under the considerable influence of Extraordinary's poetry. He literally breathed her in while he was cooking. The four-eyed beast nearly killed off your incarnation," Oracle huffed, doing her best to stir up some indignation.

"Don't miss the miracle, Oracle. Extraordinary's poems were baked in the transformational oven of the Maker's mind. What a Holy Communion! His plans are the risen loaf, so to speak—Mary Extraordinary has them now. Follow the metaphor to the magic. The Divine Mallard of All Mysteries passed the drawings along to my doughty incarnation when she visited the Quoborium with Conrad."

"Ah She! So that is the mothering playbook? A plan within a plan. A plan without a plan. The Godma moves in mysterious ways, her wonders to behold!" Oracle played fast with the traditional praises.

"Did you ever read Extraordinary's book of prayer poems?"

"I was distracted back in my Earth days," the former Mary Mirabelle could not hide her embarrassed blush. "The sight of Dagoberto Rosario Emilio Marquez on his yellow backhoe knocked the prayers right out of me. But he gave me Grace, Alyssa's mother," she added wistfully.

"Yes, I remember it well. You were pregnant when you left the convent. We should have let you stay. And invited Dagoberto to join us." She noted, not for the first time, how much easier it is to amend a life in retrospect.

"Your high and mighty incarnation disapproved of me, as I recall. I suppose I didn't pay as close attention as I might have to her poetry."

"You hurt her feelings. She loved you best."

"I know that," Oracle took the hand of her friend. "I loved the title of her book—your book—*What the Goat Girl Dreamed at the Holiday Inn*. Oh!" The former Mary Mirabelle was struck by a sudden insight. The epiphanies came in waves. "Mother Mary Extraordinary was the goat girl, wasn't she? I remember the stories now, the ones the older nuns told about a dandelion girl."

"She was such a beautiful white downy infant when I slid her through the foundling door in that lovely long ago," Asheilstarte reminisced about the girl She gave up.

"Who was the father?" Oracle caught a vision and stopped short. "Impossible. Tell me it isn't so."

"We all have our predilections, don't we? I have entangled sweet limbs with countless lovers. I have bedded trees and seas and stars. But Pan was, by far, the most extraordinary. Besides, how else conceive a goat girl?"

"Oh, brave and holy incarnations!" Oracle laughed. "Goat girls and blue boys, each one a star-packaged original. It is a pity that when infants take on the skeins of humanity, they eventually lose the traces of their divinity."

"The litany of infants is the text of the world writing itself," Asheilstarte smiled.

"What about Conrad?" Oracle wondered out loud. "Is the boy not to know anything of his origins? Ever?"

The two deities listened to the crash and roll of the surf.

The Godma was momentarily lost in a litany of *if onlys*.

If only Elyon hadn't been so desperate for admiration, so covetous of his brother's beauty, so careless of human life. Those floods and fires. If only She could trust him. It seemed his character defects were highlighted with florescent yellow markers all through his commandments. Not only did he covet his brother's goods and good looks, he coveted the neighboring deity's wife. Lord Sri Ram's beautiful blue consort, Devi Sita, was Elyon's fatal Hindu attraction.

And yet.

Without the covetous Elyon, there would have been no blue baby left on the convent steps.

"I will revisit the matter when Conrad comes of age," the Goddess meant to close the subject.

"Conrad is a bridge between two ancient and admirable divine lineages. Looked at from a certain perspective, he is the first blue Jew," laughed the former Mary Mirabelle.

"It is a delicate matter. Sita's divine consort, Sri Ram is much like Elyon—jealous and wrathful," the Godma cautioned.

"The miscegenation of the Gods," the Oracle deadpanned.

Asheilstarte had been alarmed when the Magus had gone abroad to India on his fateful spiritual junket. She knew he was looking for Sita—Elyon's everlasting, sapphire-blue obsession. Their conjunction was written before the stars were born. It was never an *if*; it had always been a *when*.

Elyon had arrived on Sita's shore decked out in the red regalia of his priestly incarnation as the Holy High Magus of The Great Church. He came upon the legendary Goddess at her ease, pinning jasmine and jali flowers in her hair, the great bull Nandin grazing at her feet. The Hindu deity was immediately mesmerized by Cardinal Cassowary's four eyes. Sita had only three.

"I'll be the first to admit that Devi Sita's story is begging for a do-over. However," Asheilstarte equivocated, "it is sometimes best to let the fabric of a story fray at the edges rather than take it on whole cloth and tear it into pieces."

Both Supernals were well aware that the redoubtable Devi Sita is always presented as a paragon of chastity in Hindu legends; although at one time, there had been a rash of rumors concerning an affair with a ten-headed brut named Ravanna.

Once upon a long ago, Devi Sita had been famously banished for life by her holy consort, Sri Ram, at the mere suggestion of impropriety. A messenger whispered in Ram's ear. And on that slight evidence, Sita was abandoned in a jungle with no food or water. She survived to give birth to Ram's twin sons. But Sri Ram never welcomed his divine consort home; only her sons made it back to the Kingdom. This affront had long burned in Sita's blue veins. It is no wonder the lonely Sita had been drawn to the mysterious four-eyed Cardinal.

"So, Conrad won't be told?" Oracle's eyebrows lifted, waiting for an answer.

"Let us praise the Divine Monkey," the Godma sidestepped Oracle's query, "clever and kind Lord Hanuman, who delivered the blue infant safely across the seas before Sita's misadventure was discovered and all holy heaven broke loose!"

The Godma flashed on the many faces of Sita, her eleven names, her eleven aspects until She found the thread she was looking for. "In one of the many folds of Sita's story, it is told that she was a foundling, discovered in a box in a plowed furrow. In this aspect she is Earth's daughter. Spit up from the clay itself."

"Lovely planetary pedigree for the boy. Will you tell Conrad or not?"

"Not I." There was a mischievous glint in her eye.

The Godma knew that Sita's anklet of silver bells was still tucked away in Mary Subordinary's dresser drawer. A cotton string with a cardstock tag was still attached to one of the silver links, and in faded letters the name, Conrad Eppler, was still legible in Sita's beautiful hand. His mother had meant to give him an American name. His last name was an accident of mispronunciation. When Sita sounded out the English word, 'apple,' her Hindi accent produced the phonetically charming mistake—Eppler.

"It's possible the boy will turn blue again when he reaches puberty," the former Mary Mirabelle conjectured. Unable to let the subject of Conrad's patents of divinity rest, she inadvertently flashed on a pastoral scene of two young lovers in a possible future. "O, blue heavens!" Oracle apostrophized. "The change could easily happen during love-making!"

The Godma reminded the farsighted Oracle that all of Conrad's tomorrows were speculative; he might not see twelve, much less twenty. It is a misconception that a life that doesn't include adulthood (and love-making) is somehow incomplete. The Godma knew to the contrary, that however many years he spent on Earth, Conrad Eppler's cup would run to full and over.

"Let us dwell on what is given, Oracle. Let us praise his resplendent blue infancy, and his variously-colored youth. Say what you will, these rogue deities do produce some stunning progeny. There's a study for someone; the history of divine erratica."

The Godma and the midwife agreed that it would be a gift to the good green Earth to let Elyon finish out this incarnation as a cassowary; being petted was having salutary effects. If only he could break free from the transgression and atonement cycle, the Wheels would breathe a great resonating om of gratitude. The evolution of the Gods scrolls slowly, the divine rotary press intricately interlocked with the word-works of the competing scribes and tribes on Earth.

"People should pay more attention to their poets," Asheilstarte took a little dig at the former Mary Mirabelle.

Before the two Supernal mothers parted, they paused to marvel at the infinitely various ways of being in the world and above the world. It had been a beautiful sorting, so many revelations and elevations. So much wild hope set in motion, so much great green good in the works.

"Until then, dear one."

"Whenever. Don't forget yourself. You've got one more sorting."

"Yes, my own beleaguered and ineffable incarnation. I suppose it was my turn to be last," remarked the first, before She blinked out and left her old friend, midwife and co-creatrix, Mary Mirabelle, Sister Omega Omicron, the Oracle, on the shore of Sister Moon Beach.

# INNS AND OUTS

CONRAD WAS SITTING on the floor of his room, carefully applying a thin layer of glitter to a cut-out construction paper heart. Colored pencils were scattered everywhere. The yellow was worn down to a stub, the result of a vigorously penciled under-drawing.

At one point, Conrad had torn the paper heart and now the repair was the best part, a jagged gold crinkle with blue flecks. He held up the heart to get a response from Skipper.

"*Not bad*," Skipper mindtalked.

"What? It's beautiful, and you know it."

Upon waking from the Kid-Colt-on-Sister-Moon dream, Conrad had been thrown into a panic. What had he done with the heart he'd been given? He searched everywhere, his dismay growing minute by minute, heartsick that he'd lost the gift meant for Mother Mary. After searching the wine cellar, he gave up, sat on the steps and bowed his head in despair. In the darkened quiet of the stairwell, the words of Asheilstarte's Wings began to hum in his mind, *so be it, so be it, so be it.*

She was with him and within him. *Forget the perfect glowing blue heart in dreamland, Conrad.*

*Who are you? Who are you?* The Wings refrained.

"I am the heart bringer," he said, and up the stairs he flew.

As soon as he got to work on the construction paper heart, Agent Eppler knew he had broken an essential encryption.

Seeker, finder, maker.

There was nothing he could put his hands on that looked anything like the sea-glass box the Wings had given him. He thought about putting the heart in the colored-pencil tin and dismissed that idea.

Crawling around under his bed, he came across an old cigar box from the Dominican Republic. It was almost perfect, with its gold ornamentation and old-fashioned painting of Romeo and Julieta on the cover. The box was filled with odd bits from childhood treasure hunts. Conrad set about gluing string, copper wire, and glass beads on the lid. Then he added a fan of colored gelato spoons and there it was—the magic box.

His anxiety quelled, he was living the dream, making it real. He knew it wasn't enough to deliver the heart. Somehow he must affix the heart to its rightful owner. For a moment the boy was stymied. Then he scooted back under his bed to look for a tin of safety pins.

Seeker, finder, maker.

———

AFTER HER TRIP to Sister Moon with Kilowatt, Mother Mary Extraordinary was once again confined to her wheelchair. The smallest effort left her short of breath. Still, she managed to wheel herself into Conrad's room. She only had to make it through the next few hours.

Sometimes her memory flickered on, but mostly it was off. She was spent. All delight had gone out from the world. She glanced out the window at the garden that had failed. Wasn't there a plan rolled up somewhere? She squinted, struggling to access recent memory. What she was doing in the yellow room? The answer came back to her with a pang; this was her moment to say goodbye to Conrad. She just wanted to get through it.

"Get out from under there, Conrad. You'll ruin your suit."

"I'm looking for something," came the muffled reply.

Moments later, a smiling Conrad crawled out from under the bed with the tin of safety pins.

Mother Mary Extraordinary knew that a hale sendoff was beyond her. Instead she mustered up and gave Conrad a good dusting. It seemed to go on forever—Mother Mary picking invisible lint off his jacket, out of his hair. Goodbye was stuck in her throat. She would not say it.

Conrad was wearing the adoption suit she'd sewn for him. Skipper was in a matching suit, also homemade. It wasn't her best work, but it didn't matter.

The old nun tried for a cheery note, "My, aren't we the handsome young pair? Just look at you two monkeys in suits." Mary Extraordinary was giving her work a critical assessment. The boy seemed unfinished somehow. "I haven't heard the magic words."

"Oh, right. Thanks. These suits are—well," Conrad didn't want to lie. "They are—amazing. Thank you so much," he beamed at her. "Now," he paused, "Mother Mary Extraordinary, this is a very, and I mean *very* important moment."

"Don't tell me. You are practically signed, sealed and delivered. Not to mention personally gift wrapped by yours truly. I signed a great pile of adoption papers this morning. Mr. and Mrs. Dante should be arriving any second. Come to think of it, they're both Doctors. I guess you could call them the Doctors Dante."

Conrad could see she was becoming flustered. "It's okay. I'll just call them Dad and Mom. Don't worry." He took a breath. "What I meant was—this is a very important moment for you."

"Yes, I suppose that's true."

"I have a present for you," Conrad said, handing her the box.

"For me? What could it be? A cigar box. Well. How generous of you. Imported, no less. I despise cigars."

"C'mon Mother Mary. Don't be grouchy."

"Only teasing. Let me see your box." She lifted the lid and puzzled over the contents. "What is it?"

"It's a heart."

He took it out of the box for her and safety-pinned it onto her habit, then stepped back to take a look. "It's your very own angel heart. How does it feel?"

"Well, it feels a little papery. A little thin."

To Conrad's horror she bent over, gasping for breath.

"Is something wrong? Should I get Sister Subordinary?"

"No. It's nothing. It's just—suddenly I feel profoundly sad."

He didn't know what he had expected, but certainly not this.

"Let's take it off," the boy cried.

"No, wait. Let me keep it," she put a protective hand over the glittery confection. "I would rather feel sad than nothing at all. It's been a long time since I've had a feeling. How could I have forgotten? I was once a child too. As beautiful and innocent as you. Did you hear that?"

He shook his head, no.

"I thought I heard the bells, the celestial Mary bells. When I was just a slip of a girl, I used to sit out on the steps, the ones that lead down to the quarry pool, and I'd listen to the angels play the bells. Yes, I can hear them."

Her eyes went soft, and she began to hum a little tune.

"Mother Mary Extraordinary, guess what? Now when I look at you, I can see who you truly are."

"Really? Who would that be?"

"You are the most beautiful angel in the whole wide world."

"Come here you little Holy Ghost. You do all the good, don't you?"

"When are you going to stop pretending?" Conrad asked.

"Pretending what?"

Conrad looked into her piercing blue eyes, held her gaze, and then whispered: "Pretending you're not God."

"We're all pretending we're not God. Keep pretending, Conrad."

He would frequently find himself puzzling over that remark in the days to come.

"Listen, I hope you are not expecting angels and miracles and comic book characters."

"Don't worry. These people who are adopting me? I'm going to treat them fair and square. But I know who my real parents are."

"Do you?"

At that moment the cassowary poked his head in, and Mary Extraordinary startled Conrad with a hearty laugh—something between a series of snorts and a coughing fit.

Sister Subordinary came running, "Is everything all right?"

"Yes, actually. For a person with one foot in the grave, I'm feeling almost chipper. Must be this new heart," she patted the yellow and blue valentine pinned to her habit. "What is that infernal honking?"

"It must be my new parents," Conrad jumped up and grabbed Skipper.

The cassowary bounded after Conrad. Sister Subordinary wheeled Mother Mary out, bringing up the rear.

Throwing open the front door that opened onto the porte cochere, they were just in time to see a shining yellow, 1970 Fleetwood Cadillac convertible—a gorgeous vehicle, the last of the great American land-yachts. It was flying down the road towards the convent, giving off the distinct odor of fast food french-fries. It would later be revealed that Tremont Montress made his own fuel from recycled french-fry grease.

The cassowary, recognizing his mistress at a long distance, took off at a dead run, heading straight for the Fleetwood.

Following the Fleetwood, the Cadillac Biarritz came into view. Kilowatt was driving the big pink. He had served as the official witness to the nuptials earlier that morning, when Savannah and Tremont arrived in the municipal building lobby exactly as the Godma guessed they might. Some futures do arrive in the nick time.

Tremont pumped the breaks to avoid a head-on collision with the rapidly approaching flightless bird who was emitting a series of urgent mating honks. The bird blocked the Fleetwood, and began pacing to and fro. Kilo got out his camera to record the shenanigans for his webpage.

Tremont honked.

The bird honked.

It was a standoff—cassowary vs. Fleetwood—until the bride jumped out to embrace her elegant fowl.

When the two devoted friends stopped cooing and clucking over each other, the bird circled the vehicle and eyed Montress. The cassowary slowly blinked his thick velvety eyelashes as if making up his mind. Apparently Tremont Montress was approved, because the long-legged Australian beauty took a few steps sideways, then stood by the back door to the Fleetwood, stomping one foot.

"Oh, Tremont, look," said Savannah, "the cassowary wants to join the bridal party."

"Open the door and let him in," Tremont grinned.

Savannah opened the door and the beautiful beast stepped inside the open-air Fleetwood. Then the satisfied bird sat down on the parade boot.

"Tremont, would you mind terribly much? I want to ride on the boot with Leonardo."

"Jah love," Tremont said.

"Oh, beloved beast," the bride petted her cassowary, "I hope you like your new name. Leonardo suits you." Savannah was remembering that not-so-long-ago moment when she'd looked into the cassowary's eyes and had seen the Mona Lisa looking back at her. She'd always meant to get back to that look, but other elations were currently in the way.

Savannah sat, parade style, with her arm around Leonardo. Tremont cranked up Bob Marley's *One Love* on the stereo, put the Fleetwood in neutral, and drove his bride in slow motion to her friends who waited on the porte cochere. She and Tremont called it idle driving.

"Is that Sister Merry Berry in a bridal gown, sitting next to our cassowary?" Mother Mary Extraordinary squinted and meant to frown. But her paper heart wouldn't let her, and so those habitually downturned corners of her mouth turned upwards in a dazzling smile.

Savannah Montress was the ultimate parade princess in her thrift store bridal gear—afloat in Tremont's yellow dreamboat, carrying off the queen's royal wave with patented finesse, her white-gloved hand gently stirring the air.

There was such a fuss over Savannah and her good-looking beau that no one noticed another less conspicuous car pulling up the long drive. It was a pragmatic, fuel-efficient gray sedan carrying the Doctors Dante towards their remarkable future.

Everyone had moved inside, and the party was on. The celebrants were sampling the small feast that had been prepared for the new adoptive parents. The tentative knocks of the Doctors Dante might have gone unheard but for Skipper, who whispered in Conrad's inner ear, "Your parents have arrived."

Conrad was off and running. He opened the door. "Aletheia?" he questioned.

"No, I'm Alyssa. Alyssa Rosaria Dante. And this is Rios Dante. You must be Conrad."

He nodded, "And this is Skipper. We're a team. You can't break us up. Me and Skip. Want to come in?"

Time stopped.

A veil was lifted. Conrad saw Periwinkle and Epiphany on a puffy pink cloud, a luminous conveyance that hovered over the expectant parents. The charmed Drs. Dante were temporarily encapsulated in a tunnel of pinkish light.

"We're back!" teased the two brightly colored angelettes, the very ones who had appeared with Aletheia that very first time.

One purple, one magenta, both wearing sunglasses—no one put on the glitz quite like Periwinkle and Epiphany. Conrad noted that the green angelette was conspicuously absent.

"What do you think? Of the parents?" Periwinkle and Epiphany wanted to know.

"They're great. They look almost exactly like themselves. A little smaller maybe." Then Conrad remembered the baby angel on Sister Moon and felt a twinge of guilt. These were her parents, after all. "Have you seen Evangeline?"

"Yes. She's all the buzz, the new queen bee in the rainbow pen. We left her playing kick the cloud with the Lucifer. Got to flash off and let time continue. Be good to your new parents."

"They're going to love my planet."

"Don't oversell it, Conrad," they tsked and blinked out.

"What was that?" Alyssa asked Rios, taking off her glasses and wiping them on his shirttail.

"*That*" answered Conrad, "was an angel flash. Welcome to my planet."

Rios realized he hadn't uttered a single word of the speech he had planned. He abruptly started in with, "Son, this is a very proud moment for your mother and me. I know it's going to take a while for you to get used to all this," he paused and took in the great blinking eye of the cassowary, who had casually walked in on the scene and was resting its crested head on Rios' shoulder. But Dr. Rios Dante had started his speech, and he meant to get through it, so he pressed on, "—take a while for you to get used to us. But I want you to know that you are a dream come true for your mother and me."

Conrad was close to giggles. It was Skipper's fault; the monkey was laughing uncontrollably in Conrad's mind. The boy held his breath until he was certain he could make a polite reply.

"Dad, it might not take as long as you think. Come on in."

Once inside, the adoptive parents found themselves standing in the divine concourse of change. Every now and then, Dr. Rios Dante would be able to finish one of his mindful speeches. But not today. This day was one surprise after the next.

Alyssa and Rios seemed to have arrived at a wedding reception. Introductions were made all around. Conrad introduced the cassowary. Leonardo bleated approvingly at Conrad's new parents. Rios Dante shot a questioning look at his wife. Kilowatt took videos and conducted interviews. All in all, it was a beautiful roar.

Mother Extraordinary invited the Doctors Dante to spend the night to smooth the transition for Conrad. The feted bride and groom, Tremont and Savannah, were offered Merry Berry's old room. And that is how the shift from convent to holiday inn began.

At dusk, the newly-weds went out and gathered great armfuls of wildflowers. They soon transformed Merry Berry's convent cell into a fragrant honeymoon suite. The cassowary slept, quite literally, on a bed of rose petals and lavender at the foot of the honeymoon bed.

After morning prayers on the good morrow, the makeshift party gathered outside on Conrad's terrace for breakfast. Sister Subordinary whipped up quiche and brewed mint tea. The Doctors Dante moved a dining table and several chairs outside. Kilowatt found linens and dinner napkins. Conrad set out the silverware. A sleepy-eyed Tremont appeared in the doorway holding hands with Savannah, looking fabulously disarranged— a halo of wild flowers twined in her dreads. The honeymooners arrived just as the piping hot quiches were being served.

At some point, Mother Mary Extraordinary wheeled herself out onto the terrace and demanded that everyone stop this instant and study a garden plan. Conrad helped her clear a place at the long dining table that had been hauled out of doors. Mary Extraordinary did not remember where the plan came from, but found herself tapping a finger on the logo—a bright, blue egg—inked in the bottom left-hand corner. She studied the Latin inscription, written backwards beneath the logo.

"*Bonum furcifer*," she muttered in Latin.

"Good scoundrel," Conrad translated, making his language instructor, Sister Subordinary, beam with pride.

No one noticed that there was a piece missing from the lower right-hand corner.

The plan precipitated a chorus of ohs and ahs. It was a remarkably detailed rendering, with cutaway sections and magnified illustrations of engineering marvels penciled in the perfect circles that lined the margins. When the drawing was unscrolled, it took up the entire table and then some.

The Doctors Dante admired the irrigation system, with its configuration of rain barrels. The templates for the multi-colored solar paving tiles were exclaimed over. Savannah looked out over the convent grounds, imagining a garden threaded throughout with light-up pathways. She pointed out the old Ford Fairlane chapel to an appreciative Tremont.

The garden plans included an astonishing energy-generating wind machine, cleverly disguised as a tree—a singing tree, it would turn out. When it was built later that year, it looked like a modernist mobile—as if the Magus had channeled Matisse and Mozart to design the colorful cut-out steel leaves that gathered energy and played enchanting wind songs when the leaves vibrated at certain speeds.

"Rios, look at this. It looks like a design for a self-replicating machine."

"Interesting—a machine with genes."

Studying the drawings, Conrad's adoptive parents were quickly caught up with the possibility of a sustainable community; it seemed only a motion away. That night, utopian visions would dance in the green dreams of the Doctors Dante.

"Where in the world did you get this drawing?" Rios Dante asked the old prioress.

Conrad reminded Mother Mary Extraordinary that the scroll was given to her by the Hierophant when they had tea with him at the Sanctum Avesticum Quoborium.

"Oh right, the Divine Duck served us peanut butter cookies. Crunchy," she smiled. Extraordinary was pleased that at least she remembered the cookies. "Look here," she paused, distractedly caressing the edge where a piece had gone missing in the decorative border along the right bottom corner. Then her fingers moved on. Pointing a long, tapered finger at another Latin inscription penned in a backward hand along the vertical margin of the scroll, she challenged the boy, "Conrad, can you read that?"

"This is the work of the Excellent Holy High Magus, Magistrate of the Magistere," Conrad translated the Latin. Easy Peasy.

"La di dah. A bonafide scoundrel, if there ever was one." Mary Extraordinary again found herself smiling and gave her paper heart a little pat.

Bit by bit, throughout the following weeks, Mother Mary Extraordinary would remember who she was and much more besides. The construction paper heart that the boy had crafted was a powerful talisman. Conrad Eppler's spiritual DNA was starting to show.

The cassowary bent over the garden plans and gave the drawing an exploratory peck. He looked as if he were getting ready to snatch it up.

"Leonardo," Sister Subordinary cautioned. The bird backed away.

The elegant fowl immediately perked up when he saw Kilowatt bearing an ornate silver platter, piled high with figs and plums. Conrad plucked two fat plums from the tray and ran off. The Cassowary gave chase.

Sister thought about the anklet of silver charms and bells that had graced Conrad's chubby foot when she first discovered the sky-blue infant in the cardboard box. She wondered if the charms were the breadcrumbs that would someday lead Conrad into the woods of his origins.

And then there was the curious inscription that Sister Subordinary had snipped from the bottom right-hand corner of the garden drawing. The tiny letters were entwined in a flourish of elegantly inked jasmine vines that bordered the entire scroll—artfully camouflaged, easy to miss. The Magus, for reasons of his own had, written this message in Sanskrit, possibly a sign that he was more of a romantic than anyone guessed. All those eons of coveting his neighbor's consort were, at the very least, a testament to a singular obsession.

Once Sister had detected the graceful strokes of the classic Devanagari script, the translation came as easy to her as it would to have to Conrad: *This is for the boy. Tell the boy his father is a God. And his mother is Daughter of the Earth, Devi Sita.*

It was Sister Subordinary who placed the missing piece in the silk envelope where she kept the anklet of charms with the original calling card still attached by a cotton string.

*Perhaps one day*, Sister mused silently. And the monkey silently agreed.

Around noon, the guests migrated down the steps to the quarry pool. Tremont and Savannah lounged poolside, sipping Château Latour. Kilowatt carried down the silver platter of fruit and encouraged the newly-weds to sample the figs and plums. Leonardo followed the silver platter down the steps and cozied up with the honeymoon couple. Mother Mary, observing from the terrace, forgot to be shocked by the elopement of Sister Merry Berry and found she was completely taken with Tremont. There was much to be said for Jah love.

"Here, hold Skipper for me," Conrad passed his monkey off to Sister Subordinary. She felt the same surge of love as the first time she beheld the monkey, as if the monkey's guru, Surya the sun, were rising in her heart. And she felt a familiar alarm; divine mischief was surely footloose and running far afield. She checked the drawer in her meticulously ordered mind where she kept the monkey's blink. It was still locked. As if that had ever mattered.

Conrad took a running leap. The Doctors Dante laughed and applauded when the boy cannon-balled into the pool. The old prioress noted with satisfaction how much Alyssa Rosaria Dante took after her grandmother, Mary Mirabelle, especially now that joy lit up the brown eyes of the young mother.

A week went by and no one was ready to say goodbye.

With a house full of hungry guests, Sister Mary Subordinary rolled up her sleeves and got down to the business of making miracles in the kitchen—to-die-for home-made loaves with cucumber salads on the side dressed in fresh mint leaves, melt-on-the-tongue crepes with raspberry glazes, stuffed mushrooms with chopped nuts, peppers and parsley. With Kilowatt's help doing laundry, keeping lists, and running errands, the household ran smooth as corn silk.

Cleaning up one day after a fine repast, Subordinary was just thinking how sweet it was to have the old place coming back to life again when she heard the ringing of an insistent bell.

"The foundling bell," cried out Subordinary. It had been so long, it took a minute to sink in. Sister started to beat a wooden spoon on a copper-bottom pan, rousing the household.

Oh, happy pandemonium!

There was a rush for the chapel. Everyone gathered around the swaddled and wailing infant, who'd been shuttled through the small wooden exterior door. The Doctors Dante immediately set about doing what they did best, giving the baby a thorough examination.

Savannah rang the answering bell to let the departing mother know that her baby was safe. And then she broke the rule. She stepped outside. She couldn't help herself.

"Come back," she called to the retreating girl. "Let us help you."

The girl turned around. Savannah dropped to her knees and kissed the Earth. Second chances. It was the first of many mother and child reunions.

So it began. A honeymoon couple, two nuns, an unwed mother, a baby, a set of adoptive parents, a boy and his monkey, a Savannah and a Tremont, and a Kilowatt and a cassowary.

Over time, the ragtag community was joined by other wayfarers, outliers, Gods gone AWOL, Marys coming home, a pair of renegade Budgies and their ferret, a couple of surfer girls in a restored VW van, a set of Vietnamese identical twins, reincarnates, first-timers—gardeners each and every one.

Their motto—One World, One Garden—became a popular bumper sticker in the Eden gift shop. Although it was Kilo's sticker—Shift Happens—that was the best seller.

———

A DAY CAME IN THE FALL of the first year, when Mother Mary Extraordinary put on her handmade pink gown with the velvet lace-up bodice, the jacquard skirt with its irregular hem, and the matching hand-painted silk duster. Conrad spotted her at day break standing alone out on the terrace.

Sister Mary Subordinary came into Conrad's room from the kitchen, wiping her hands on a tea towel. Conrad was pulling on a cardigan.

"Look," Conrad said.

"Oh," Sister Subordinary said to Conrad. "It's time."

Conrad ran outside, "Mother Mary Extraordinary, are you going to die today?"

"No, Conrad, today is the day I stop pretending I'm not God," she ruffled his hair, and he wrapped his arms around her skirt and wept.

"Here, Conrad, wipe your tears," she offered the edge of her duster. "I've got your paper heart. Pin it to my sleeve, dear boy."

Conrad went to work and Extraordinary gave Subordinary a long look.

"Mary Subordinary, the novices will come, just like I always said they would. Don't fail to recognize them—not all of them will be religious or female." Extraordinary paused. "Have you chosen a name for yourself?"

"No. I'm sorry. Each time I tried, I felt like I was erasing you."

"You, erase me? I hardly think so. Oh, surely in one of those many drawers of yours, you've got a name tucked away."

"No, I haven't."

"Fine. Then you will be MorningStar. Mother Mary MorningStar. Look up, Conrad, there's the morning star. Now, let go of me."

Mother Mary Extraordinary stepped up onto the balustrade without a wobble. She balanced on one bare foot and raised her arms. The morning star seemed to wink in her hair. A wind ruffled the edge of her duster. In quick increments, she became smaller and smaller until she was the size of a maple leaf.

Conrad ran to her and held her up in the palm of his hand— the white filaments of her hair quivering in the light breeze, just a dandelion of a girl, impossibly young.

"You're beautiful," was the last thing Conrad said to her.

A sudden gust picked up a twist of colorful fall leaves and the goat girl skated away in the whirlwind, one pink leaf turning among the reds and oranges and yellows.

THE NAME OF THE EDEN Hostelry and Eatery changed several times over the years. One day Kilowatt posted a picture of a pancake on the website. It went viral. The much-liked pancake displayed the iconic and unmistakable burnt image of the eternally smirking Mona Lisa.

And so it came to pass that the bed and breakfast, holiday resort, honeymoon motel, novitiate, writers' colony, organic garden, orphanage and unwed-mothers' sanctuary became the now famous, five-star, Mona Lisa's Holy Day Inn.

Order the griddle cakes.

ACKNOWLEDGMENTS

MY FIRST GRATITUDE goes to my original starfriend, ROD RUSSELL-IDES. I have been writing this story ever since he wrote me the love song that turned into a life song. (Although the secret seeds of this novel were probably planted by the Hollywood nuns who enchanted me when I attended a certain grammar school on Sunset Boulevard.)

In the daily mechanics of building this story, Rod was my steady. Often the paper was still hot from the printer when he read the frequently-revised chapters out loud. His readings were as careful and countless as the stars. He was also my generous National Endowment. I might have written a novel had I never fallen in love with Rod, but it would not have been this novel.

My next gratitude goes to my own Maxwell Perkins. Her name is ELOTA PATTON. She was my Breadloaf, my Yaddo, my Iowa Workshop. Encouraging and daunting, by turns, she always sweetened the editorial blows with kudos in the margins. After reviewing my second draft and sprinkling the document liberally with praises, she delivered the unwelcomed news that the manuscript was probably six or seven drafts away from completion. Elota made me work harder, run faster, reach further.

The gifted and dedicated SANDY SLOAN took on the formidable task (three times) of giving the manuscript a technical edit, as well as giving invaluable critiques in the tiniest, almost-invisible hand.

Thank you ALLAN IDES, my brother and patron, who has generously contributed to the publication of this work.

Thank you MARCO PERELLA for generously sharing a portion of your *Boyhood* residuals towards publication, and thank you to both DIANE AND MARCO PERELLA for your encouraging praises.

ACKNOWLEDGMENTS

I AM ALSO GRATEFUL to all my preview readers, especially those who waded through the wildly meandering first drafts. KIT WEBSTER reported that one early draft gave him whiplash, like a crazy carnival ride that constantly changed directions. My daughter, MICHELLE BISHOP, read several drafts. Like any cook, I was pleased to be asked for second and third helpings. And pleased again when my younger daughter, RACHAEL LEFEVRE, said she didn't want the story to end. GRANDSON DASCHEL COOPER read it once when he was sixteen, again when he was seventeen. GRANDSON EMERSON COOPER read it on a plane ride and chuckled all the way to Italy. Thank you JOY NYUGEN for your expressed wish to share this story with your daughter, and Don Hall for your bright enthusiasms. And as I approached the finish line, I received booster shots of enthusiasm from JEANINE SIH CHRISTIANSON and the critic, ALEXANDRA BONIFIELD.

Thank you DR. ALLISON GREEN for inspiring the vision of the bride at the ocean in flipflops. And decades earlier, for being the first angel-grandbaby in the House of Ides. Thank you BLAKE BISHOP who—at the age of four—shared with me his original idea about soul-clusters. Thank you JONAKAN O'STEEN for meditations on origin issues.

I would like to thank my friend, LINDSEY LANE, for steering me through the perils of writers' conferences. A shout out to TEX THOMPSON, of The Dallas Fort Worth Writer's Workshop, and BECKA OLIVER of the Texas Writer's League.

Many thanks to the amazing PAM MEYERS MORGAN for directing and championing the Echo Theatre production of *The Early Education of Conrad Eppler,* a previous incarnation of this work. Her production-photo of actor TAMITHA CURIEL graces Book II in the ebook edition. A special thank you to grandson ELLIOTT COOPER who attended every performance of the play, memorized every line, and who graces the cover of Book I in the ebook edition.

Who is this monkey Hanuman? Rama has set him loose in the world. He cannot be stopped.

Hanuman's rescue of brave Poets in any peril may be had for their asking, and that monkey will break the mask of evil kings.

Hanuman will take your sad tune and use it to make a happy dance. We have seen that white monkey. Especially take warning: never harm a free Poet!

The Son of the Wind, the warm dry night wind and all the trees swaying! I don't care for love or death or loneliness—here comes the High Wind, and what am I...?

Ramayana